THE EYES OF PROPHECY

THE EYES OF PROPHECY

RISE OF THE GRANDMASTER™ BOOK FOUR

BRADFORD BATES

MICHAEL ANDERLE

LMBPN Publishing
PMB 196, 2540 South Maryland Pkwy
Las Vegas, NV 89109

Version 1.00, August 2021
eBook ISBN: 978-1-68500-417-0
Print ISBN: 978-1-68500-418-7

THE EYES OF PROPHECY TEAM

Thanks to our beta readers
Kelly O'Donnell, John Ashmore, Larry Omans, Rachel Beckford

Thanks to the JIT Readers

Dorothy Lloyd
Veronica Stephan-Miller
Diane L. Smith
Jeff Goode
Allen Collins
Angel LaVey

If I've missed anyone, please let me know!

Editor
The Skyhunter Editing Team

LIST OF TIM'S CURRENT STATS AND SKILLS

"Tim" level eighteen Battlesworn
   Primary Stats
   Strength: 14
   Endurance: 21
   Dexterity: 22
   Intelligence: 46
   Wisdom: 53
   Perception: 6
   Vitality: 4
   Revitalization: 4
   Luck: 7

Notable Gear
   Weapons
   Simple Dagger of Dexterity, +1 (X2)
   Staff of Divine Retribution, +4 Intelligence +5 Wisdom
   Orb of Concentration, +5 Intelligence +4 Wisdom

Armor

Tarnished Circlet of Divine Wisdom, +1 Intelligence +3 Wisdom

Wilbur's Fur-lined Shoulder Guards, +1 to Perception, Vitality, Revitalization, and Luck

Battlesworn Robes of Justice, +4 Intelligence +6 Wisdom

Jerkin of Unmeasurable Delight, +1 to all base stats

Paul's Gloves of Mending, +7 Intelligence +4 Wisdom

Belt of Divine Inspiration, +1 Endurance +2 Intelligence +4 Wisdom

Hermit's Pants for Special Guests, +2 Endurance +2 Intelligence

Boots of Tranquility, +2 Endurance +2 Dexterity, increase mana regeneration by 2%

Jewelry and Accessories

Leather Wraps of Divergent Health, 10% chance for single target healing spell to jump targets and heal the secondary recipient for 50% of the value

Wristband of the Faithful, +1 Endurance, ten seconds of double mana regeneration

Ring of Luminosity, +1 Endurance +2 Intelligence +3 Wisdom,

Necklace of Unshakable Will, +1 Intelligence +3 Wisdom

Trinket of the Smiling Monkey, +1 to random stat

Skills

Appeal to the Goddess: Novice rank three

Infiltrator: Novice rank four

Quick Feet: Novice rank five

Disturbance: Novice rank six

Night Vision: Novice: rank six

Backstab: Apprentice rank one

Snare: Apprentice rank one

Throwing Knives: Apprentice rank two

Sneak: Apprentice rank five

Dodge: Apprentice rank seven
Flame Burst: Apprentice rank seven
Behold My Power: Apprentice rank eight
Small Blades: Apprentice rank eight
Weaken Undead: Apprentice rank eight
Healing Storm: Apprentice rank nine
Who Needs a Shield: Apprentice rank nine
Cleanse: Journeyman rank two
Curse of Giving: Journeyman rank two
Divine Light: Journeyman rank two
Healing Orb: Journeyman rank nine

Stances

Way of the River: Apprentice rank seven
Way of the Boulder: Journeyman rank one

Buffs

Armor of Eternia: Journeyman rank one
Attacks of the Faithful: Journeyman rank one

Open Quests

The Deserts of Naroosh
Breaking the Juggernaut
Take Her to the Theater
Tomb of Nemset

CHAPTER ONE

Eternia tucked the light blanket tighter around her shoulders and leaned back in the chair.

Tim kept his eyes on the goddess as he rested on one knee before her. She almost appeared frail. It was like seeing his grandma tucked into the chair by the fireplace at Christmas. Not a look he ever expected to see etched across Eternia's features. She was the goddess of light, an all-powerful symbol of all that was good inside *The Etheric Coast*.

Now she was as weak as a kitten.

"My sister has done the unthinkable and sacrificed the people of Naroosh to open a portal to her realm. Blocking her influence from spreading across the deserts like a disease takes all the power I have left. I need you to petition the king for the Stone of Immoratis."

Quest Received: The Stone of Immoratis

Recent events have consumed the Goddess Eternia's strength. Without the Stone of Immoratis, she won't be strong enough to stop her sister's eventual advance. All of *The Etheric Coast* is at risk. Do whatever it takes to secure an audience with

the king of Promethia and acquire the stone. You, brave adventurer, are the kingdom's only hope.

Reward: Twenty gold coins and a favor from the goddess.

Tim accepted the quest without hesitation.

Some things in this world were more important than gold or cool new weapons. If Vitaria took over *The Etheric Coast*, it would be devastating for everyone. He didn't want to live in a world of darkness and danger. It was nice to have something to come home to, a place where they could set up some roots as they continued adventuring.

If it came right down to it, Tim would've done the quest for free to protect his home. Instead, he was getting paid and being handed a favor directly from Eternia.

It was like Christmas and his birthday all rolled into one whatever the fuck he wanted.

The last time Eternia granted Tim a boon, it saved Cassie's life and kept their adventure going. Back then, a death would have set them back. Now it might only be a minor hiccup on their road to success. Still, because a death might not derail their entire adventure now didn't mean they could get lazy. So far, they'd managed to handle the fights without a major oopsie, but it wouldn't last forever.

Every encounter they faced was more challenging than the last.

Eternia gave Tim an exhausted smile as she took in his excitement for the prospective reward. "I fear it will be no easy task to gain an audience with the king, let alone convince him to part ways with the stone."

Cassie smashed a fist against her open palm. "Convincing people to do things they don't want to do is kind of our specialty."

Rising from where he had been kneeling, Tim looked at the tank. He loved her enthusiasm but was pretty sure they needed to handle this situation with a little less smashing and a little more diplomacy. "Let's try to avoid starting a war with the crown."

"That's weak sauce, and you know it." Cassie thrust her finger at Tim. "If Eternia needs the stone, we should take it."

Cassie started pacing back and forth as she warmed up to the idea. "Let's skip all the BS and get cracking skulls."

JaKobi wrapped an arm around her waist, pulling her tightly against himself. "Maybe we should consider a more Bond-like approach."

"Please, that guy was the worst spy ever. He was always getting caught and having to blast his way out of trouble with some crazy gadget." Cassie broke free of JaKobi's hug and turned, jabbing a finger hard into his chest. "I'm simply suggesting we save time by cutting out the spy stuff and get right to the fighting."

ShadowLily was twirling one of her daggers on the table like a game of spin the bottle. "Sneaking into the palace and stealing something from the treasury would be badass, but I'm with my boy toy on this one. We can't risk offending the royals. Not if we want to live here."

"Boy toy?" Tim lifted an eyebrow.

ShadowLily winked. "Just go with it."

Get me some oil and a bowtie.

Cassie groaned. "Ugh. I hate doing things the monotonous way. Grab me five of these. Kill four of those incoming." Cassie slumped into a chair, looking defeated about the quality of their upcoming quests.

"I hope when it comes to bartering for something as valuable as the Stone of Immoratis, the quests tasked to us will hopefully be a little more interesting than fetch this or kill that." Tim tapped a finger against his chin as he thought about their upcoming quest. "I don't know about you guys, but outside of the game offering a loot pinata or two, questing has brought me all of the best shinies."

Lorelei shrugged. "Might not be a bad thing if we had to knock out some easy stuff for a minute. We've been grinding hard and deserve a chance to catch our breath."

ShadowLily picked up her dagger and slid it home in the sheath on her thigh. "This is an epic quest. We'd better get used to the fact it's going to take a while. Let's take it slow until we find out the extent of what we're in for, then make an informed decision."

"It's like his voice." JaKobi pointed at Tim. "Came out of her mouth."

"Maybe it's a glitch in the matrix," they said in unison.

"Leave the poor kid alone." Cassie slapped his butt to snap him out of his daze. "You almost gave him a heart attack."

Lorelei shook her head and threw up her hands as though she was dealing with a bunch of kids. Her antics only made Tim's smile grow. At least one of them stayed grounded. He could've let that joke go on for another hour to see the fire mage sweat.

"Let's not forget how Eternia fits into our plans. If we brought her the stone this instant, she might not have recovered enough to use it. We need to make sure we bring it back right when she's ready to power up." Lorelei looked at the goddess for confirmation of her theory.

"Time is one of those things you never realize you need until you're out of it." Eternia sipped from her mug and pulled the blanket tighter around her shoulders. "As I sit before you, my fight against my sister's influence continues slowing my recovery."

Khalid looked like his world had been shaken to its very foundations, and yet when Eternia turned her eyes toward him, the warrior found a way to pull himself together. "What do you need from me, Goddess?"

"It is kind of you to ask, considering I failed you more than anyone else." Eternia's expression softened into one of regret, and a single tear trailed down her cheek. "I never thought Vitaria was capable of such madness or that a spell of such destruction was possible. Please forgive me."

Neema moved to stand next to Khalid and laid a comforting hand on his shoulder. Her eyes never left Eternia. "There is nothing to forgive. We know who's to blame."

"Then it is time for you to return to Nar'ha. The people there will be worried and looking for guidance." Eternia grimaced as if she was in pain. "We will need a base of operations for when I return."

Tim knew this situation was dire, but he grinned. He kind of felt like Jack Bauer, saving the world one hour at a time. This problem was fixable. All they had to do was play their part, and the pieces would fall into place. A quick trip to see the High Priest, and Neema and Khalid would be back in Nar'ha before breakfast was over. "We can use the portal at the temple."

"My magic powers the portals." Eternia looked exasperated with herself. "So they won't be of much use."

If the portals were out, they needed to find another way to get the two warriors back home. They would need to secure fast horses and someone who could get them an audience with Seraphina and passage under the mountain without the five of them tagging along. On the plus side, the two warriors wouldn't have to fight their way through the subterranean dungeon, making the trip much shorter.

Tim thought back to their trip to Tristholm and figured it would take them a day or two to get there and another to make it under the mountain and back to the desert. If he thought they could get their quest done and power Eternia up in less time, he would have told them to wait, but there was no guaranteeing how quickly they would finish the task the goddess laid out before them. Since they couldn't take the time to escort their friends from the desert themselves, it was his job to make sure they had the best guide for the journey possible.

Thankfully there was a person in the room who fit the bill.

Tim glanced over at Ernie. "Lucky for us, we happen to know someone who knows the back road into Tristholm like the back of his hand. He also happens to have enough pull to garner an audience with Seraphina."

ShadowLily smiled as she warmed up to the idea of sending the innkeeper on another journey. "My dad happens to be visiting with the ruler of Tristholm and should be able to smooth over any rough edges Ernie's last visit to the city could have caused."

Ernie was wringing his hands on a towel, cheeks turning slightly red. "Hey, that guy was trying to kill me. I couldn't possibly lead another expedition away from the inn so soon. I've only gotten settled back in."

"The inn can survive a little longer without you." Liz poured him a mug of beer. "Better get your traveling boots ready because you can't say no to Eternia."

Tim almost laughed, imagining the innkeeper trying to explain that he would rather stay inside his cozy little sanctuary than help the goddess. When it came right down to it, he knew Ernie was a pretty good person, even if he brewed poisons for a living and a den of assassins worked out of the basement of the inn. He waited to see what Ernie would do. If it was necessary, he had a few tricks up his sleeve to convince the man to go.

Plus, the werewolves were on their side now, so the entire back way to the city should be clear of trouble. There was really no way he could wriggle out of it.

Eternia nodded at the innkeeper's words. "If you cannot make the journey yourself, perhaps you can appoint another to take your place."

For the first time since they started talking, Tim noticed Gaston moving around the back of the room. The assassin stood next to the innkeeper and pulled him into a crushing side-hug. "Ernie and I would be delighted to escort our new friends back to the desert."

Ernie glared daggers at his burly friend but couldn't object without risking further harm to his person so he begrudgingly added. "I'd be simply delighted to help."

Trying not to laugh, Tim pulled up his user interface and looked at the time. It was almost two in the afternoon. If he knew anything about government bureaucracy, it was that they shut down at five, no exceptions. It might be better for the group to spend the afternoon putting all their ducks in a row for tomorrow. They all had excess loot to sell and things they needed to do in town that they'd been putting off. A good night's sleep in their rooms before heading back out would be what they needed to feel refreshed.

It would also give him time to develop a plan, and the goddess knew he loved a good plan.

Tim addressed his question to Ernie but kept his eyes locked on Gaston's. "Are you planning to leave now or in the morning?"

It took everything he had not to burst out laughing as Ernie's face puckered up like someone shoved a lemon in his mouth. He grew redder with each second Gaston squeezed him.

The burly assassin was grinning from ear to ear as though he'd never been so happy to escape the city for a while. "We can be ready within the hour."

"Fine, fine. I'll go to the stables and get things taken care of." Ernie stomped toward the door as he shouted, "Liz, get my traveling bag ready."

Neema watched Ernie as the innkeeper stomped out of the room. "What's his deal?"

"Oh, he helped save the city last time we went to Tristholm, but someone tried to kill him, and we all almost got eaten by werewolves." Tim shrugged. "Should be an easy trip this time around."

Khalid didn't look assured by the news. His eyes moved from Tim to Eternia. "Are you sure this is the right path?"

Eternia sipped from her mug. "I am always grateful for the assistance given."

"Then I'm ready to leave." Khalid moved toward the same door Ernie had exited. "I'm not sure I trust him to pick the best horses for our trip. I'll see to their selection myself."

Gaston jogged across the room to catch up. "I'll make sure he finds the stables and that Ernie doesn't gas him."

Lorelei took Neema by the hand and led her upstairs. "Looks like we have an hour to kill."

Liz shouted up the stairs, "Better make it two in case Ernie gasses Khalid before we get there."

Picturing Ernie and Khalid fighting over which horses would be better for the journey while Gaston was the calm one had laughter bursting from Tim's lips. The sound was right and full of love. This was his home now, and he loved every minute of being here. Part of him hoped he never had to go back to the real world.

Another part of him envied Lorelei's and Neema's alone time. He wouldn't be able to take his lady by the hand like that until he got a few more things out of the way. He had to come up with a plan of attack over the next couple of hours so he could free up his night to be attentive to his woman's desires. Which meant the next few hours were critical if he wanted to be back before she was asleep.

Tick, tick, tick.

Tim stopped thinking about what to do and jumped into action. "I'm going to send a few messages out and stop by to see the High Priest. If anyone can get us past the first few layers of bureaucracy, it will be him."

He turned slowly, looking at each of the remaining members. "This is your time to take care of any business you need to do in the city before we get to work." Tim grinned as he eased the serious note out of his voice. "In other words, the day is yours to do with what you will."

ShadowLily disappeared and popped back into existence right behind him to give him a gentle kiss on the cheek. "Just don't spend all your energy with that dwarf. I expect you in our room, with stamina to spare, by a reasonable hour."

She squashed his reply before he could get it out. "A reasonable hour." She headed toward the door.

"Bam, snap!" JaKobi put an arm around Cassie. "What do you say to a little Joe's before I hit the library?"

"Perfect. You hit the library. I'm going to the spa." Cassie pointed at Tim. "Thanks to good ole Moneybags' recent donation, I'm going to splurge a little."

"That's Mr. Moneybags to you," Tim shouted at the retreating couple.

Eternia still looked tired, but she watched their interactions with fascination. They probably should've behaved better around the goddess than they did, but what was the point? See all, hear all, felt like a pretty standard mojo for a god so why hide who they were?

Turning away from the doorway, Tim focused on Liz at the bar. He hadn't had many chances to check on her since hiring her away from the brothel. Still, Ernie hadn't killed her yet so she must be doing a great job. "How are things?"

"Better than expected. Ernie and I get along well, and I'm pretty sure he likes being able to spend more time in his poison cave than running the place anyway."

Tim felt good knowing that things had worked out well for her. It didn't take long for him to get around the bar and pull Liz into a hug. "Let me know if you need anything. I might not always be here, but normally I can get back for something serious."

"Go save the day so I can pour beers instead of fighting monsters." Liz turned and headed into the kitchen.

Tim stood behind the bar looking out at the almost empty room. It took him a moment to realize he was alone with the goddess. This was the perfect time to ask her about the portals, or maybe what she planned to do after Vitaria was defeated. He opened his mouth to speak as he rounded the bar, and an ear-splitting snore rattled through the room.

The Goddess Eternia was sleeping.

CHAPTER TWO

Eternia was still alive.

"That sneaky bitch!" Vitaria hissed under her breath as she poured the fourth glass of ambrosia.

How was it that her sister could thwart every one of her plans? The light-farting savior of the masses found a way to stop her strongest spell. Even when Vitaria risked everything—all her strength and almost every damn soul in the city—it wasn't enough to so much as knock the smiling debutante of glitter off her throne.

Not even for a second.

When did being evil fall out of vogue? There was a time when it paid to be a murderous, deceitful thug, and she missed those times greatly. The world needed more pirates, more rebellions, more tinpot dictators. If nothing else, there should be at least one cult worshiping the magnanimity of her evil.

Her brand of darkness was of the purest form.

The defeat at her sister's hands left a bitter taste in her mouth. It would be one thing if Eternia reveled in it and rubbed it in her face, but the good-for-nothing cream puff didn't seem to care.

She'd probably say something like, it wasn't about her. Innocent people didn't deserve to die.

What a crock of shit.

Right when she thought her sister had taken everything from her, Vitaria felt the pull of her realm below. Maybe she'd let her sister live by opening the door, or it could have been that she made the best out of a shitty situation, but either way, the nether realm was open.

The city and fields beyond were rife with corpses. She didn't have to call her children. They could smell the feast and knew what it meant.

Meat for the beast.

So her sister had finally made a mistake. In her haste to save her precious mortals, she gave away the key to victory. As her children ran out of sustenance, they would leave the city and spread through the world of *The Etheric Coast* like a plague. Nothing would be safe from them. The world was a field of wheat, and her children a swarm of locusts.

Soon the very fabric of this world would tremble.

Maybe then her sister would finally be knocked down a few pegs in the eyes of the worthless masses, and Vitaria would have the respect she deserved. She could feel it all right beyond her grasp. It was time for her to seize the moment.

And maybe the fifth glass of wine.

"Don't even get me started on those pesky adventurers," Vitaria huffed as she draped herself back into the throne. Half of her wine sloshed on the floor, and a good portion of the rest on her dress.

The goddess looked down at the bright red spot and giggled. It was the sound of a person in anguish, someone asking the simple question of what else could go wrong? She lifted a finger, and all the wine pulled out of the fabric of her dress and flowed back into the glass.

"Some people think magic isn't useful." Vitaria drained the glass and threw it across the room before standing to claim a new bottle and glass from a rack next to the throne.

She tried to let the bitterness go, but she couldn't do it. How had her sister turned those five idiotic adventurers into such a force so quickly? Sometimes it felt as if this entire world had been created to make her angry. Hopefully, those ridiculous adventurers would be dumb enough to show up without her sister's magic to shield them. Then it wouldn't take more than a flick of her wrist to slaughter them all.

If only things were that easy.

Now she was in a position where simply killing them wouldn't be enough. Vitaria knew she had to make an example out of them. To show the rest of the world that taking a swing at her only ended in one unequivocal result.

Permadeath.

She didn't know if it was possible to kill an adventurer, but she did know that she could make their life in *The Etheric Coast* so miserable that they gave up or rolled a new character to escape her notice. Safety was a myth the sheep told themselves so they could sleep at night. When the darkness came, there would be no stopping it. She would swallow this universe whole if that was what it took to control it.

Then she would shape it in her image.

Why her freeloading father gave Eternia the ability to create and build worlds and not her was beyond Vitaria. The light-sniffing whore hadn't used her gift to create a world. She was happy living in the one father had given them. It was a slap in the face. At the very least her sister could leave the people of this world to her and create her own.

Instead, she'd relegated Vitaria to a world of darkness.

The underworld had a certain kind of beauty to it. There was something to be said about waking up to the screams of a million souls. She delighted in their pain and anguish because it gave her power. There was no attempt at rehabilitation in her realm. The last thing Vitaria wanted was souls ascending into the light. Instead, she made the denizens of the dark hate their existence so much they forgot what it was like to be human.

Eternal damnation was the price sinners paid for her prosperity.

At some point, Vitaria assumed the people of the world above would've caught onto the trick. Don't do bad shit; bypass a trip to hell. Or, if she had her way, it would be more of a permanent staycation. It wasn't even the big things like murder that brought in the largest crops of souls. Now she mostly fed off the petty little deceits. The friend who always asked for them to buy lunch but never paid. It was the users and abusers, those who put themselves in front of others for material gain.

Vitaria reveled in their hatred, gloried in their wickedness. The fact that they couldn't stop being themselves for a minute, even in hell, was delightful. All of it fed her and added to her power.

Just like their souls.

Maybe it was time she used her power for something more ambitious than thwarting her sister. If she could only steal the means to make a new world, she would be happy leaving the remains of this one to Eternia to do whatever she wanted. She would finally be able to leave her sister behind and live the life she wanted without being judged. It was her turn to be the creator.

Vitaria wanted to return to the old ways where people didn't worship gods only with words. She wanted sacrifices and gifts. The people needed to understand she was in charge, that her word was law. Then and only then would they be grateful to receive the blessings she would bestow upon them.

Her plan for domination all turned to shit when Eternia refused to die.

Her sister lived, forcing Vitaria to start over once again. She told herself it was fine, but the amount of wine she was consuming said differently. Her original idea for taking her sister's gift or this world needed to be revised. Sometimes a goddess had to wipe the slate clean and start fresh. The best way to do it was to burn away the bad and replace it with something better.

Her children of the depths rose into this plane for the first time in this world's existence. Vitaria knew that no matter what happened next, she'd changed the face of *The Etheric Coast* forever. Rise or fall, the repercussions of their actions today would ring through the halls of fate—and they still hadn't seen anything yet.

The Goliath, the Juggernaut, they were babies compared to what was coming.

It wouldn't be long now before all her children emerged from the depths and began their exodus across the land. Nar'ha would fall to her, and her influence would spread like cancer across all the land she touched. Once she had this world under her thumb, then and only then would she strike against her sister. The goddess of light wouldn't be able to wriggle out of her clutches this time.

Vitaria watched her children feeding on the bodies of the fallen until a voice broke her concentration.

"Mistress, I have news from Nar'ha." The pharaoh knelt before her like a common messenger.

Vitaria grinned.

Breaking Phandar was easier than she ever imagined. The man was a gutless worm, only interested in what benefited him and nothing else. Normally, continuing a relationship with a human once their worth had ended was something she would never have considered, but seeing the pharaoh grovel before her brought Vitaria a certain amount of amusement.

She would let him live until he stopped being entertaining.

"Speak, I grow tired of waiting." Vitaria leaned back, enjoying another sip of wine as she waited for him to underwhelm her.

Phandar lowered his head. Fear rolled off him in waves. "It seems most of the resistance was protected inside the palace and have now gathered in Nar'ha. There is some confusion on the issue but Eternia, the desert rat, his brat, along with the five adventurers, appear to be absent."

"If they aren't in the city, what exactly are my spies confused about?" She sipped more wine, enjoying the look on his face as she reminded him that everything he once had was hers now.

Phandar risked glancing up, then quickly lowered his eyes. "The debate seems to be whether they lived or not, and what to do about it if they didn't."

"Send some of your men to sow the seeds of despair with lies about Khalid's and the goddess' untimely demise." Vitaria enjoyed this moment. It wouldn't be long until this realm was hers, or her sister gave her one of her own.

"Maybe we can get those idiots running Nar'ha to make a deal before they figure out the goddess is alive." Vitaria slammed her glass down on the edge of her throne, breaking the second one of the day.

"A deal?" Phandar sounded shocked as he looked up from where he knelt.

Vitaria tossed the remains of the glass onto the floor, and with a clap, summoned forward one of her favorite male consorts. "Of course there is a deal to be made. I'm not a monster." Her eyes glittered with nefarious intent. "They can join us or become food for the horde."

Phandar's head lowered so fast she thought he might have snapped his neck. "That is very generous of you, mistress."

"I thought so as well." Vitaria stood and motioned for her male companion to lose his pants and sit on the throne. "Come back if you have additional information."

Phandar backed away, keeping his head lowered until he was almost out of the room. Then he spun on his heels and exited the royal throne room with a straight back. Vitaria watched the pharaoh go, noting the small act of defiance, no matter how minuscule it was.

She reached out and ran a finger across her companion's chest. Vitaria let her skin get hot enough that her touch was uncomfortable but wouldn't burn him severely. There would be time for burning later if he failed to please her. "Get ready for a little divine inspiration."

Working with Vitaria wasn't exactly going the way Phandar planned.

Sure, for the last forty years he'd had everything he wanted and more. If the goddess hadn't shown up twenty years ago demanding he go to war with Nar'ha and claim the entire desert in Vitaria's name, he'd still be living the good life. Probably with more servants and an even larger palace. Sadly, when the goddess of destruction called in her chip, you either carried out her request or ceased to exist.

He didn't want to disappear.

Phandar kept his head low, making sure to sulk as he left the throne room. A niggling little suspicion was growing in the back of his mind that Vitaria was only keeping him around out of amusement. If he stopped looking disgruntled, he might turn into food like all the others. Some of those people had been his friends. Although it had been a long time since he'd truly had a friend, and if any of those people now lived, they'd be better off not mentioning it.

Seeing the city full of rotting corpses and the smile on Vitaria's face as the first of her children crawled from the underworld had been enough to convince Phandar he picked the wrong side. He'd been a little street shit with dreams of being pharaoh and sold his soul for power that was as useful as dust in the wind.

He was a puppet, and Vitaria pulled his strings.

It made him feel better to heap all the blame for the horrible things he'd done at Vitaria's feet, but the truth was he'd enjoyed many of those deeds. He took a certain amount of pride in seeing the fear in people's eyes when they met him. It felt much better than the looks of contempt and disgust when he begged for scraps in the market as a boy. In the end, his pride did him in.

Phandar was nothing to the dark goddess. Maybe he could use that to his advantage in the future. Until then, he would play the dutiful servant. Phandar would keep his head low, grumbling and bitching about feeling like a servant.

Hopefully, it kept her entertained while he looked for a way to screw the bitch over. Screwing over people who tried to fuck him was the one skill he brought with him from the street to the present, and he looked forward to seeing Vitaria's face when he brought her down.

Sometimes a man had to be real with himself.

It wasn't as if living his life after the fall was full of great hardships. Vitaria hadn't killed any of the staff or his wives. There was enough food to feed them for years in the storage rooms under the palace and enough wine to fill a river. Food, sex, and the luxuries of being a pharaoh were all still at his fingertips. All he had to do to keep them was look humbled until it was time to flip the script.

Phandar didn't play silly games, and he always came out on top.

When Vitaria was banished or destroyed, he would find a way to take control and crush the adventurers himself. He could use the enemy of his enemy to reestablish his kingdom. That was who he was, a snake in the grass waiting to strike.

Phandar was pulling on the strings of fate, and the world opened to him like a flower to the sun. It was the way things had always been, and there was no fucking way that was going to change now. He was too old to start over. This land was his now, and he would see it whole again, just to rub it in Vitaria's face.

Yes, he balanced on the thinnest of razors, but he'd stolen every breath for the last fifty years from the clutches of fate. He wouldn't stop fighting now. From the gutter to the palace and back again.

He was a fucking survivor.

Like the scars on his back, the lessons he learned in childhood would always be with him. Phandar gently rubbed the scarred flesh on his wrist and thought about how close he'd come to losing the hand. If the merchant's knife weren't as dull as a block of wood, he would've been rubbing a stump now instead.

The wheels of fate always kept spinning.

It was at that moment, cradling a broken wrist while huddled against a wall in an alley, starving and broken, that Vitaria had found him. He had been crying as he promised himself this would never happen again. He would never be weak again, never give in to another's demands, or be apologetic about the decisions he made. There were two types of people in the world, those with power and those without it.

Nothing had changed. He still wanted to be the one with the power.

CHAPTER THREE

Tim sent a message to Mr. Applebottom as he strolled toward the temple.

If the High Priest didn't have any way to help them, maybe Mr. Applebottom could. The savvy businessman certainly had connections inside the castle because he helped Tim acquire all his properties in the slums from the crown. Properties he was now paying a hefty amount of taxes on. He would've thought with the amount of gold they paid the crown monthly that he would at least be able to get an audience, but maybe he was a much smaller fish than he believed.

With the message finished and sent, Tim put the matter to rest and thought about what he wanted to say when asking the High Priest for help. Hey, I have a goddess in my room, didn't exactly seem appropriate. It was probably better to read the situation and ask for the help he needed directly, see what was possible and what it would cost.

It wasn't a big stretch of the imagination to assume the crown and the temple had some sort of relationship. The real question would be if their relationship was a healthy one or adversarial.

Tim needed to focus up. If the High Priest could help them in any way, it would be a blessing. Right now, he couldn't afford to waste Paul's time. With Eternia MIA and the portal network down, the temple was probably in a state of disarray.

At least he could ease Paul's mind as to what was going on with the goddess.

The scene outside the temple looked the same as it always did. The sick and needy made their way to the temple for help. There was a time not long ago when a faction in the temple would have turned the poorest families away, but they rescinded that policy when Cardinal Jepsom was torn apart by wraiths. Now everyone was helped at the temple regardless of whether they could afford to pay. Paul had also built a smaller building at the base of the temple steps to attend to those too sick to climb the stairs.

It was amazing to see such progress since the last time Tim had been home, and it reminded him that he needed to attend to the people in the slums before he left again. He couldn't let one of the priests do all the work for him, and he needed to check on Judy. It had been a while since he heard from her, and there was a good chance he was behaving like a crappy friend.

When he finally had a moment to catch his breath, Tim vowed to set that right.

This was how he always imagined a temple should run. It was a place of healing and light, not one for political backstabbing and ladder-climbers. All of the priests around him seemed happy to serve, and their dedication to helping others would only help Eternia regain her power faster.

At least he hoped so.

A few of the priests offered to help him as he ascended the steps, but Tim waved them away so they could help those who needed their attention more. One of the acolytes would be able to get him to the High Priest's chambers without an issue.

When Tim stepped inside the temple, he spotted one of the

younger acolytes standing off to the side. "Can you take me to the High Priest?"

The young girl ran off with a squeak and tugged on the robes of one of the priests. The man turned and looked where she was pointing with a frown. It faded as recognition dawned in his eyes. Clearly, Tim's status with the High Priest had garnered him enough reputation that some of the men working inside the temple recognized him on sight.

"You are Tim if I'm not mistaken?" The priest moved forward with his hand extended in greeting.

So maybe he wasn't that famous after all.

"That's me." He shook the priest's hand, trying not to look as embarrassed as he felt.

"I'm Brother Melvin, and this is my daughter Fiona." The priest introduced himself as the young girl poked her head out from behind his robes and flashed a shy smile as she curtsied.

Instead of bowing, Tim returned the curtsy while holding up his robes like a dress. "Pleased to meet you, Fiona."

The girl laughed as Tim turned his attention back to her father. "Can you take me to the High Priest's chambers?"

"Of course. Fiona will lead the way." Melvin bent and looked into the young girl's eyes. "To the chamber and back, no detours."

Fiona brushed off Melvin's hug. "Whatever, Dad."

That sounds more like it.

The one thing all pre-teens could agree on was that whatever their parents said was to be viewed with the greatest of skepticism and total apprehension. Naturally, they'd ignore any advice the parents gave at all costs, and every chore issued was an insurmountable task. Tim knew the feeling well because not too long ago, he was the same age. Pushing buttons to figure out the limits was what kids did naturally.

Luckily or unluckily for him, Tim's parents didn't play around when it came to him having any kind of control. You can be in charge when you start paying the bills, was a common utterance in their household.

"Before you go," Melvin continued, "I wondered if you might be able to handle a small problem on behalf of the temple."

Tim was still trying to shake off the image of his mother throwing his games out and saying there would be time for fun after college when the priest continued speaking. It took him a full two or three seconds to switch gears. His first instinct was to flat out refuse any quest Melvin would offer because they had enough going on. The last thing he needed was another quest added to the to-do list.

The next couple of days were going to be hectic, but if the quest was small enough, it might be something he could take on before returning to the inn. Eternia had done so much for him since he entered the game. Without her assistance, Tim wouldn't have been able to accomplish the work in the slums. He also knew without a doubt, the goddess would want him to help, even if it sent them on a small detour.

He knew the good guys didn't do good deeds only when the cameras were rolling, or it was convenient for them. Being a good person took a lot of work, and it often meant being humble and respectful to people who hadn't earned it. Tim wanted to be a good person, which meant sometimes he had to take on tasks even when at least half of his brain was screaming for him to brush Melvin off.

When in doubt, it never hurt to listen.

"It's a bit of a delicate matter." Melvin led the way to the side of the temple. Once they were alone in one of the hallways, he continued. "We have a small problem involving one of our priests not returning from a cleansing."

Oh shit. This was going to be good, maybe even his chance to play a little Constantine.

"Cleansing?" Tim was trying not to smile.

He was pretty sure that was a universal term for removing

something unholy from a person, place, or thing. Still, this was a new world, and the last thing he wanted to find out was that cleansing was a well-known term for fixing a noble's diarrhea problem.

Melvin reached down and covered Fiona's ears. "Of the narcotic kind."

Fiona smacked her dad's hands away and glared up at him before returning her gaze to Tim. "What he's trying to say is some rich guy got loaded and the priest he sent to fix it hasn't come back yet."

Keeping the smile from forming on his lips was damn near impossible so Tim let it happen. They were lucky he didn't burst out laughing. Fiona was so matter-of-fact about the problem, and Melvin was so stunned that it might as well have been a skit from a comedy on TV. Tim wasn't upset that he wouldn't get to battle demonic forces because the look on Melvin's face was worth the hassle of collecting a wayward priest.

Even if the job was a little below his pay grade.

"I can't offer you much." Melvin held out a small bag of silver coins. "It isn't like Jasper to be gone for so long."

Tim pressed Melvin's hand closed around the small bag of coins. "This one's on me."

Did he have the time to deal with this? Probably not, but that was the trouble with doing the right thing. Sometimes it wasn't very fucking convenient. When it came right down to it, Tim tried to focus on the details. Right now, those details were a missing priest named Jasper and his very concerned boss.

Melvin had come to the right guy.

If a priest was in need, Tim would help him. The temple and its people had been instrumental in creating his path through the game. The least he could do was grab a priest who maybe had a few too many drinks instead of doing his job. It wasn't exactly a hard quest, but it needed doing.

So Tim would haul Jasper back where he belonged.

Quest Received: Retrieve Jasper

Melvin sent a priest under his tutelage to cleanse a man thought to be suffering from some kind of intoxication. No one has seen Jasper in two days, and Melvin is worried for his safety. Find Jasper and bring him back to the temple.

Reward: You've offered to take on this quest free of charge.

Tim accepted the quest.

This felt like one of those times where a player ended up back in the starting village and thought they were getting new quests for some expansion. Instead, it was the stuff they missed rushing through the early game in the first place. If that was the case in this particular scenario, and based on the quest reward it very well might be, he could knock this out in a few minutes.

Team Eternia needed all the wins they could get right now, even the small ones.

"Thank you!" Melvin looked shocked that Tim accepted the quest.

Before Tim could respond, Fiona grabbed his hand and pulled him down the hallway. "Let's go already."

He gave Melvin a helpless wave as Fiona tugged him deeper into the temple. "I'll get Jasper back," Tim shouted before he turned a corner and the priest vanished.

Fiona tugged relentlessly on the sleeve of his robe, never giving Tim a moment of rest. She clearly wanted to be done with her assigned task as quickly as possible so she could get back to doing whatever it was young girls in the temple did. After two minutes of being tugged around like an unruly dog, they stopped outside the large golden doors.

Tim looked at the sealed doors, trying to catch his breath. Was it possible that the little girl was in better shape than him? If so, maybe it was time he started paying a little more attention to his secondary stats. He couldn't get winded faster than a teenage girl.

"See ya later." Fiona waved and disappeared into the maze of tunnels, leaving him alone in the entryway before he could respond.

Using the arm of his robe to wipe away a little sweat, Tim waited for the doors to open. He was about to pull up his quest log so he could start turning in his backlog when the doors opened. A gaggle of priests streamed out of the chamber like geese on the hunt for more popcorn at the park. The men and women were babbling at each other so loudly as they walked past, the image of the large mean birds stuck firmly in his mind. Two of the High Priest's guards appeared in the doorway at their rear.

Paul followed the guards into the antechamber, and a small smile creased his tired face when he saw Tim waiting there. "Things are a little busy at the moment, but I can squeeze you in before they all show back up in a few hours, looking for answers I don't have."

Tim followed the High Priest back into his inner sanctum, and the guards closed the giant doors behind them. This time all four men remained inside the chamber with them instead of two remaining outside. Tim's quick double-take revealed six more guards on each side of the room for a total of sixteen guardsmen in the chamber with them. That was a lot of ears for the sensitive information he was going to share.

"I hate to show up when I need help, but in this case, I might also be able to help you find the answers to a few of those questions." Tim stopped in front of where Paul was sitting and dropped to a knee.

The High Priest rose from his seat, stepped down, and lifted Tim. "Enough of the formalities. We know each other better than that. Tell me why you're here, and I will see if I can help you."

It was tempting to hold back some information to ensure he received the help he needed to finish his quest for Eternia, but if Tim couldn't trust the High Priest to be on their side, they had bigger problems than wrapping up their quest. "I know what happened to Eternia and where she is now."

Paul clapped his hands once, and a dome of silvery energy formed around the two of them instantly. When it reached the floor and sealed them inside, Paul motioned for Tim to continue speaking.

They were in a magical cone of silence. So Paul considered this information important enough to keep it from the prying ears of his guards. Tim realized he needed to be very careful about sharing Eternia's whereabouts in the future. It was dawning on him that if someone wanted to kill a goddess, while she was injured and alone would be a prime place to start.

Before Tim let his mind run away with the what-ifs, he told Paul everything. He spoke for ten straight minutes, detailing everything that happened since they left the city until they returned to Promethia that very afternoon.

"The good news is I can help you." Paul smiled. "The bad news is my help won't be of much use until you make it into the actual castle."

Tim shook his head. "I don't understand. If you hold sway in the castle, why can't you take us to the king?"

The High Priest gave him a knowing smile. "Let me tell you a little something about the royal grounds. They're twice as big as the rest of the city and consist of three rings. Each ring closer to the actual palace runs like its own kingdom."

Paul stopped for a moment, afraid he was losing Tim. "Imagine each of the outer rings as a city with its guards. One of the crown's closest confidants rules each one, and they use that advantage to enhance their wealth and stature."

Tim still wasn't sure what Paul could help with, but he knew he'd greatly underestimated the task ahead of them. He'd have to make three men who thought they were kings happy to get a shot at the real deal. Cassie was going to be so pissed. She hated side quests and working for the nobles.

"In short, if you can make it past the three outer rings and into the palace itself, our priest inside the castle can get you an audience with the king." The High Priest smiled as if he knew this was the most convoluted way to run a government ever, but that was how it was so he dealt with it like everyone else.

There was no point in looking a gift horse in the mouth. Without Paul's help, Tim had no doubt the final stage would be even worse for them than the three outer rings. "Thank you for the help."

"For Eternia, I would do anything." Paul snapped his fingers and the dome shattered and burst into wisps of smoke.

Five seconds later it was like the dome had never existed.

Tim reached out to shake the High Priest's hand. "I'll make sure to swing by once everything is back to normal."

"I'd like that." Paul motioned for the men to open the door.

For the first time since he woke up, Tim had a clear sense of what he needed to accomplish. If Mr. Applebottom couldn't provide them with any assistance, they'd have to earn their way through each ring so Paul's man on the inside could get them in front of the king. If anyone could find a way to dig through the political craziness, it was the Blue Dagger Society. If everything turned to shit, they could follow Cassie's plan instead.

Straight to the fighting.

CHAPTER FOUR

The fresh air felt good after being trapped in the twisting confines of the temple.

Even knowing that their quest might take longer than he expected, Tim felt a little lighter as he strolled down the steps. Maybe it was having a better idea of what they were facing. Nothing scared him as much as not having a plan, and right now he had a rudimentary one. They were three quests away from their meeting with the king. In the grand scheme of epic quests, it was all relatively straightforward until there was an unexpected twist.

Always expect a twist.

Tim wasn't the kind of guy who liked the sudden twist of fate at the end of a book or the late reveal of the best friend being the killer. He was the kind of man who liked never to find himself in those kinds of situations. He always had a plan, and most of the time, his plans had plans. If he weren't on the side of light, he would have been Palpatine.

What was life without having a few backup plans buried inside a contingency? He often asked himself the question when he found himself overplanning. Sometimes he had to get out of his own way, jump on a chair in an auditorium full of people, and sing. Spontaneity was hard for him. Sometimes he kind of envied people who could go with the flow.

Having that kind of freedom must have felt amazing.

It was the kind he was trying to have inside *The Etheric Coast*. Inside the game, Tim didn't have to worry about anything. His businesses were thriving, and his streaming contract took care of any fees associated with his time. The small stipend the contract paid was enough that he knew his family outside the game would be fine.

For the first time in his life, Tim was able to shrug off the burdens of expectation. He'd made it to a point where he could finally be him. All he had to do to maintain his dream was keep kicking ass.

Or, more importantly, healing the ones who got their asses kicked.

With the warm sun shining on his face, Tim took a moment to appreciate where he was. Yes, he had a lot to do, but would he rather be doing this or plotting charts for day traders in an office cubicle? The answer was never going to be inside Excel, not for a gamer like himself. Who would want to be trapped in a cube when they could be fighting the forces of evil?

Talk about an upgrade.

Tim pulled up his user interface and didn't see any new messages from the guild. Unlike him, they were all probably relaxing or shopping right now. Even his insider Mr. Applebottom was silent. The businessman must have been working his contacts because he usually responded almost instantly. With nothing new to occupy his attention, Tim closed his interface and looked back toward the Blue Dagger Inn with longing eyes.

As much as Tim wanted to get some rest, the trip to the temple hadn't taken nearly as long as he thought it would, and it gave him enough time to look into the quest Melvin had given him before the others would return. If it was as easy as he thought, he might be able to sneak in a little time at the forge before ShadowLily's demands took precedence.

Deep down, Tim already knew a reunion with Ironbeard would have to wait. As soon as he stepped inside the dwarf's shop, he'd be busy for hours and forget all about Jasper and ShadowLily. There was also a better than likely chance that if he blew off this opportunity to complete the quest, he would never return to it. Unlike other games where abandoning quests was no big deal, inside *The Etheric Coast* it felt like peoples' lives were on the line. Taking a quest and abandoning it could have long-term and unforeseen consequences.

Just like in the real world, when Tim gave his word, he honored it.

With his mind mostly made up what he would do next, Tim pulled up his user interface and flipped through the screens. He ignored the siren song of checking his messages and the backlog of quests he needed to turn in, knowing full well if he went down that rabbit hole he'd never get Melvin's quest done. It took a few seconds, but he found it and selected it.

While he waited for the information to load and plot a course on his map, Tim thought about what it would be like to hit level twenty. Tonight when he turned in his quests, he was pretty sure he'd hit level twenty and open up an entirely new world of possibilities for his class. Level twenty felt like when a class started to show its chops.

Whatever came next, Tim knew he'd find the right class to pick.

Pushing the thoughts of the future away, Tim pulled up his current quest and looked at the map. A small groan escaped his lips as he trotted down the remaining temple stairs to street level. "Why is everything always so far away?"

Then it dawned on him that he probably didn't have to walk anywhere. One of the benefits of having a little extra cash meant he could hire a carriage. *Walking was strictly for suckers.* Lifting his head to scan the street in front of the temple, Tim looked for a carriage he could hire. Not seeing any waiting, Tim lifted his hand as he reached the street corner like he was hailing a cab downtown. He'd never actually tried summoning a carriage before, but it wasn't like lifting a hand in the air and waiting was rocket science.

A few moments later, a sleek black carriage stopped in front of him, and the driver looked down at him from above. "Destination."

Tim read him the address and followed up with, "How much?"

"Fifteen silver coins and a tip." The driver gave Tim a look that said he'd better have enough in his change-purse to tip, or there was going to be hell to pay.

Fishing a gold coin out of his inventory, Tim flipped it to the driver. "I'll need you to wait for me and to bring one other person and me back to the temple."

The driver tipped up his hat, looking pleased, but then his look turned slightly sour. "Just know that a single gold coin doesn't buy my entire day." He pulled his cap back down in a no-nonsense manner.

Tim got the hint.

If he took a few hours to come out with Jasper, his ride would be gone, and getting another one where they were heading might not be as simple as it was in front of the temple. There was one way to ensure the carriage would be waiting for them. "I'll have another gold for you when I come out."

Tim met the driver's gaze and held it. "I don't want to be left hanging." He pulled another gold coin from his inventory to show the man he had his payment ready. "Be waiting when we exit and it's yours."

The driver hopped off the seat and opened the door for him.

"Name is Mr. Keppler, or Grant if you're feeling less formal. You ever need a ride; I'm your guy. None of these other bums can compare to old Ripley here and me." He stroked the horse's flank affectionately.

Tim stepped into the carriage. "Thank you, Grant." It seemed paying the driver a small fortune for a ride greatly improved his disposition.

The door closed and the conveyance trundled down the road. Unlike the carriages in the real world, the ride over the cobbles was completely smooth. It was like Tim was riding in a car with superior suspension. The guild needed to acquire a fleet of these carriages instead of riding horses. He'd be able to get so much done in these smooth, relaxing limos of the past.

He didn't have to worry about a mirrored window. If Grant wanted to see him, he had to stop the carriage and open the door. Tim could do whatever he wanted back there, although without ShadowLily he contented himself with pouring a glass of water from the decanter and drinking.

What felt like mere moments later, the carriage halted. Tim pulled back the curtain and looked at the mansion in front of him. It was hard for him to believe they'd come so far in so little time. The ride was so smooth they might as well have been flying. A few minutes longer and he might have fallen asleep.

How long had it been since he last slept? If getting zapped by Eternia's spell didn't count, it had been longer than he'd like to admit. Without sleep, people tended to get a little loopy. It was a known fact. He felt the crash coming and hoped for a small second wind to push him on until this quest was over.

The last time he stayed up this late, it was for his favorite MMO's latest expansion.

At least he would get a good night's sleep tonight. It was amazing what getting the proper rest and a little relaxation could do for the psyche. Sometimes he needed a recharge, like after finals or an eight-hour shift cooking burgers.

Tonight he was going to recharge like a Duracell.

The door to the carriage opened, and Grant popped his head inside. "We've reached your destination."

Climbing out of the carriage was a little more complicated than it should have been. Why was there such a small door and an even tinier step? Sometimes a guy needed a human-sized door to make a graceful exit. Instead, he hunched over as if he lived in a bell tower, trying to awkwardly slide one foot out the door in search of the step. Eventually, Tim gave up and hopped out.

"I'll pull the carriage around and be waiting for you there." Grant pointed to an area one house down on the right side of the road, pretending he hadn't seen the awkward dismount.

Tim smoothed out his robes, appreciating Grant's stoic expression. Although if he had to judge the man by the twinkle in his eye, he would have guessed Grant Keppler was enjoying this moment a great deal and might have made the door smaller to get a little extra merriment out of his day.

"Hopefully, this will be quick." Tim checked his map to make sure he was walking toward the right house and moved. He patted Ripley gently on the way past. The horse snorted and stomped its hooves as if it were angry.

"Don't mind Ripley. His arthritis makes him a little cranky." Grant fished a carrot out of his pocket. "He'd rather be out here than stuck in the stables at home, isn't that right, boy."

Ripley ate the carrot.

Tim had never tried using one of his spells on an animal before, and arthritis wasn't exactly a cut or a break, but it might work. Maybe Cleanse would help or a Healing Orb. It couldn't hurt to try. "Do you mind if I take a look?"

Mr. Keppler looked over at Tim with the same skeptical expression he had when they first met. "You some kind of horse doctor?"

"Not exactly."

Petting the horse gently, Grant whispered to the animal, "Try not to kick him."

Not the most reassuring thing Tim heard today, but it would have to do.

Thankfully for him, he could do most of his healing from far away. So if the horse kicked, there was a good chance it would only hurt the carriage. Still, he needed to make sure Ripley knew what he was about to do. Inside *The Etheric Coast,* the animals seemed more aware, so he would treat the horse like any of the patients he'd attended to at the healing shack.

Tim moved forward with his hand extended. Ripley lowered his head and let Tim caress the spot above his nose. "Hey, buddy. Sorry about earlier. I had no idea you were in such pain."

He continued rubbing Ripley's nose and murmuring sweet things as he cast Cleanse.

Stepping back, Tim started rubbing Ripley's neck. With each stroke, he sent a wave of healing energy through the animal. Then he focused on the horse's joints, hitting them with blast after blast of Healing Orb, and finally one last Cleanse.

Ripley reared, his hooves striking the air.

A hand clamped onto Tim's shoulder, pulling him roughly away from the animal. "What did you do to him, you bastard?" Grant's face was flushed with rage as he screamed.

Tim tried his best to remain calm. Blasting carriage drivers with Divine Light wasn't exactly a good guy move, even if the driver in question was about to throttle him. "I'm pretty sure I healed him."

Grant's hand twisted in Tim's robe, keeping him in place as the man turned to look at the horse.

Ripley pawed the ground, eyes looking happier than they had moments before. Grant slowly released his grip as he moved to inspect his friend. Satisfied that Ripley was not only okay but doing well, he returned and tried to smooth out the front of Tim's robes.

"Ah, sorry for the confusion, sir. It's just, I thought...I don't know what I thought."

This was one of those times where Tim didn't have any idea what to say. He understood the feeling well. If anyone had hurt someone he cared about, he would've fought to protect them with everything he had.

For him, healing the horse might have been a minimal gesture, but for Grant and Ripley, it was a pretty big deal. It went to show that what one person considered a small gesture might positively mean the world to the recipient.

The look of gratitude on Keppler's face was a little too much for him to take so Tim did what he always did in those types of situations.

He tried to get away.

Tim coughed into his hand. "I'll try to be quick."

Turning away from Grant and Ripley, Tim strode toward the mansion with purpose. It didn't take more than a once-over of the property for him to tell whoever owned this house had the kind of wealth that made Tim's look like small potatoes. The mansion was so large it made Lady Briarthorn's luxurious home look like a studio apartment. The place was probably twice the size of the inn, and that was saying something.

When Tim reached the gate, a man stepped out of a small guard hut and walked forward. "Lord Rictor isn't accepting petitioners," the guard stated boldly and stared at Tim with disdain.

"Then it's a lucky day for both of us, my friend. Melvin from the temple sent me to collect Jasper. If you can send him out, I'd be more than happy to be on my way without ever stepping inside the gates." Tim kept his eyes locked on the man, not backing down an inch from his icy stare.

The guard hesitated to look toward the house.

This was Tim's moment. The man was nervous. He could capitalize on his hesitation. "I could come back with a hundred of my brothers from the temple. We could camp out in the street and pray for the return of our brother."

Tim leaned forward and spoke almost at a whisper. "Or you could let me in, and we could handle things a little more discreetly."

The guard pulled a set of keys from his belt and unlocked the gate. "Frankly, I think you'd be better off with the army of priests at your back." He paused before opening the gate. "Don't go blaming me if you get hurt in there."

Tim paused at the entrance, thinking about what the guard told him. Maybe the situation was a little more complicated than Melvin knew. If Tim wanted backup, this was his last chance to summon the guild before going inside.

He looked at the mansion and back at the guard's worried face and decided to be reckless for once and chance it. The reward for the quest certainly didn't indicate he'd be facing a boss-level monster so it would probably be better if he handled the situation himself instead of calling his girlfriend for help.

"Thank you for your assistance." Tim nodded at the guard as he passed the man and made his way up the long walkway to the house itself.

Calling this building a house was kind of like calling the storage shed in their backyard a full-fledged art studio. Sure, a person could technically create art in there, but with the sheer amount of spiders, they'd probably be better off hoping they turned into Spiderman instead. Part of him was a little envious, but a bigger one screamed WTF.

The upkeep cost on a property this size had to be nuts—gardeners, guards, staff, serving, and cleaning. Running a mansion like this would take a small army. Tim couldn't even keep his room clean without help. That help came in the form of ShadowLily kicking him and telling him to pick up his damn mess.

He got it. She didn't want to clean either.

That was why living at the inn made so much sense for them.

Laundry, food, water, maintenance, and yard work were all taken care of so they could have fun. If it came down to cleaning his room or going out and doing something fun, Tim was always going to be on Team Fun. All he wanted from his home was enough room to lounge around, and since they didn't have vacuums, someone to sweep and mop for him. If he couldn't hear or see the neighbors, that would be a big bonus.

Lord Rictor had enough land never to see another living soul if he didn't want to.

The gardens leading up to his home were as phenomenal as they were large. Tim didn't even want to think what it cost to pay someone to sculpt and maintain topiaries when hiring the neighbor to mow the lawn cost a fortune. Still, he could appreciate the beauty and the skill it took to create a sculpture from a living plant. Living art was some pretty cool stuff.

As long as it wasn't in the shape of a maze, with a little kid screaming Redrum.

A man opened the front door as Tim approached and held it open for him. The interior was dark, minus rows of neatly lit candles. It was odd, considering how warm and bright Lady Briarthorn's home was that this house was so dark and foreboding. Nothing ran out and tried to kill him, but the doorman looked tense. He wasn't reading fear from the man though, so he felt safe stepping inside if he had to.

Tim stopped outside the mansion's threshold. "I'm here to collect Jasper. Can you point me in the right direction?" He spoke politely.

Taking a moment to inspect the doorman didn't reveal anything other than that the man's name was Percey.

"Of course, sir. Right this way." He moved down the wide central corridor at a slow walk.

Tim laughed, thinking about how in his house a hallway was something that moved you from one room to another. Here it was like walking through a museum. Art lined the walls. There were seating areas set at intervals as though the house was so large people might need to take a break as they strolled between rooms. Suits of armor and countless other items of war made quite the stunning display. They were about halfway down the corridor when something heavy hit the doors at the end of the space.

"Oh my." Percey ran toward the door.

The door burst open, and a man flew out and landed on his back in the hallway. The priest's robes gave him away. Tim had found Jasper, but the big problem was hovering in the open doorway behind him.

Naked from the waist up with blood dripping from his mouth like a hungry Labrador, the man in the doorway stared at them. Percey had frozen in place, and Tim had no intention of getting closer unless the man moved toward Jasper.

The priest moaned, breaking the complete silence that had frozen them all.

Mr. Bloody Fucking Smiles locked eyes with Tim. "Take your priest and get out." He stepped back into the shadows of the room and closed the door with a wave.

With the door closed, it felt like he could finally move again, and he didn't waste any time. Tim looked over and found Percey grabbing hold of Jasper's other arm so they could drag him away from the door. He wanted to get a look at the man's injuries but also didn't want to be inside one second longer than he had to be. With Jasper in hand, his quest was over.

Tim let Percey do most of the pulling while he fired Healing Orb after Healing Orb at Jasper. By the time they made it to the front door, some of the color had returned to the priest's face, but he wasn't fully conscious yet. Together they wedged him into a chair by the door and turned to face the final test.

Would the front door open so they could get Jasper back to the temple? In every paranormal movie he'd ever seen, this was the moment of truth. If they got out of the house, they were free and clear. If whatever threw Jasper at them kept the door closed, they were fucked.

Tim reached for the knob, his hand covered in sweat. He had to do this for Jasper. It was his job to get the man home. Despite the fact he couldn't seem to Cleanse the priest enough to bring him around, nothing had happened except a few parlor tricks. He needed to calm down and grab the damn thing.

With a flash of action, Tim darted forward, grabbed the knob, and yanked the door open so hard it flew into the wall with a *thud*.

Turning toward Percey, Tim commanded the man into action. "I need to get Jasper back to the temple. Have the guard summon my carriage."

"Right away, sir." Percey ran off.

Jasper tried to get up, mumbling, "I have to help Lord Rictor."

Slipping an arm under Jasper's shoulders, Tim steered the priest away from the interior and out the front door. "How about we make a deal." He tried to smile as he struggled to carry most of Jasper's weight. "You go back to the temple and rest up, and I'll help Lord Rictor. How does that sound?"

"I can live with that." Jasper sagged toward the ground.

Percey made it back from the gate puffing but didn't slow down until he had an arm wrapped around Jasper. The carriage pulled up moments later. Between the three men, they managed to get the priest inside the carriage. With the heavy work done, Grant hopped back onto the driver's seat, waiting to find out where they were going.

Tim reached inside his coin purse and pulled out two gold coins before plopping them into Grant's waiting palm. "Get this man to Melvin at the temple. If Melvin isn't available take him directly to the High Priest."

Keeping his eyes locked on the driver to make sure he knew the importance of the situation, Tim got out of the way so he could leave. "I'm still going to need a ride back to my inn when this is over." He left the implication out there that for all the gold he'd given Grant today, he expected a ride home.

"You got it." Grant leaned down and conspiratorially whispered so Percey couldn't hear them. "Need me to do anything else, maybe get in touch with some of your friends for backup?"

Tim couldn't help but smile as he responded. All it had taken to win Grant over as a friend was healing his horse Ripley. "I should be fine on my own, but if something happens, you can find my friends at the Blue Dagger Inn."

"Used to be a rough crowd over there. Now everyone calls it the place by the restaurant." Grant nodded his cap and pulled away, waving cheerily. "Let's hope I don't need to find your friends."

Tim called one last time over the clatter of hooves on the cobbled streets. "Get back here soon. If I don't need backup, I'll need a drink."

"A quick getaway and a good beer is something I understand all too well." Grant nudged Ripley a bit harder, and the old horse picked up speed like a much younger stallion.

The carriage took off at a gallop, and just like that, Jasper was safe. Technically, Tim had fulfilled the obligations of his quest and could call it a day, but he hadn't finished the job unless he wanted to break his word to Jasper. There was also the risk that leaving Lord Rictor unattended might have consequences he couldn't foresee. If more people got hurt it would be his fault, and Tim wasn't interested in carrying all the extra guilt.

Despite the quest Melvin had given him, Lord Rictor was acting like a man possessed.

Holy shit, could he be possessed?

Tim wasn't exactly sure how to handle possession. "Damn it, Jim. I'm a healer, not an exorcist."

Making *Star Trek* quips wasn't going to get him out of this mess. While inside the game Tim couldn't think of a better person to handle a possession case unless one of the pure healers showed up. Who knew? Maybe there was an exorcist class or a Paladin-type character built for smashing evil into tiny little bits. Oddly enough, they hadn't run into many other players, so Tim had no idea what the other healing classes were capable of.

Cleanse was going to be his only option besides just trying to kill Lord Rictor. Killing a lord probably wouldn't go over too well but would Cleanse work on him? It sure hadn't worked on Jasper. There was no way to know until he tried casting the spell, and not knowing left him without a viable plan.

He hated not having a plan.

Not knowing if possession was even a thing in this game, Lord Rictor could have simply lost his mind or be some kind of monster. Melvin hadn't sent him here to kill the man, and despite Jasper's injuries, he was willing to try to help Rictor. If killing wasn't on the table, running was the only thing Tim could do if things went south.

Quick Feet for the win.

As a gamer, it was good to know the limitations of the class you played. Tim knew he wasn't an offensive powerhouse and might not have the tools in his healing kit to remedy the situation. Not being able to fix a problem immediately didn't mean he should give up. It meant he needed to get creative or call for help. Paul would probably know what to do and Eternia most certainly would.

If she was awake.

Tim summoned his courage and chose to try handling the situation himself before asking for help. If Eternia could battle her sister and save all their lives, he could deal with one man in a mansion. Instead of trying to work up to it, he made his feet move. Once he started, he picked up momentum.

If there was something he loved, it was new problems to solve. Sure, he usually did his wizardry with numbers, but this was even better. Tim was going to learn by doing and not by laying out a step-by-step twenty-seven-point guide on how to achieve victory first. He was spontaneous again and rather enjoyed the feeling.

Percey was holding the front door open for him, but all the candles inside the mansion had extinguished, bathing the interior in shadows despite the afternoon sunlight. Looking into the estate was like when Brody turned and looked right into the soulless eyes of *Jaws*. Was he going to walk back inside willingly? Tim's feet kept moving forward so some part of him had decided the answer was yes.

He stopped in front of Percey, trying to figure out if the man would help or hinder going forward. He couldn't risk getting trapped in the room with Rictor and Percey both trying to bring him down. When the doorman didn't blink as he gazed at him, Tim knew the man was affected by whatever was happening more than he was.

Tim clapped loudly in front of Percey's face, hoping to snap him out of his daze. "Is there anyone else inside the house?"

"Just Lord Rictor and Sam." The man looked nervous to the point he might have a breakdown. It was scary to see the doorman falling apart because until now, Percey had been a rock. "Sam sent most of the staff home yesterday when Jasper didn't come back out of the room..."

Tim nodded as he followed the doorman's story. "The last time you saw Sam, he was in the room with Lord Rictor."

A small nod was all Tim received as Percey turned to look into the inky blackness of the interior.

"I want you to go down to the gate and wait with the guard. If I don't come out within the hour, go to the Blue Dagger Inn, and tell them I need help."

Percey completely ignored him and continued looking into the house as if something were calling to him from within.

There wasn't fucking time for this. He had a ton of shit to deal with, and Percey was slowing him down. Leaving the man behind was too big a risk. Whatever was happening inside the house was pulling Percey into its clutches. He needed to get the man out of here so he could wrap this up.

Not wasting time being delicate, Tim grabbed a handful of the doorman's jacket and dragged him out into the driveway. Percey tried to resist at first, even trying to run back and grab the door handle, but Tim was relentless in his effort to pull the man free from the house. Twenty feet from the door, Percey went limp in his arms, then stood and looked around in shock.

"I thought we were about to go back inside?" Percey looked at the door and back to Tim. "How did we… Why am I…"

Tim let go of Percey's jacket and straightened it. "I need you to pull yourself together and wait down at the gate for me, and if I'm—"

"If you're not out in an hour, go and get your friends," the doorman finished for him. "I heard you. It just seemed not to matter at the time."

Tim gripped Percey's shoulder and looked directly into his eyes. "It matters very much to me." He eased his grip just a bit. "I promise if there's any way to save your friend, I will."

Percey spat on the ground, looking furious. "Make sure you save him first. Lord Rictor brought this down on us. He can wait his bloody turn!" He turned away from the house and stomped furiously toward the gate.

It was good that he sent Percey away. The man was emotionally invested in this, which would make it impossible for him to make clear and rational decisions. If this was an actual possession, any kind of disharmony worked in the demon's favor. So while Percey might've been a help initially, an hour from now, he would probably be the reason Tim ended up in his caseworker's office.

He'd be better off handling the situation on his own.

Searching the entire mansion for survivors would've taken forever, but now that he knew the house was clear except for two people, it made his job easier. Take care of the Rictor problem, and the same problem solved itself. With his full group behind him, this quest probably would have taken ten seconds. As it stood, Tim was going to proceed the way he always did, slow and steady.

A hasty healer was a dead healer.

It always paid to take advice from the hobbits. Seriously, it was an entire race of people dedicated to good, clean, sustainable living, with lots of food. The napping and the food were what sounded particularly good to him right now, but sleep was out of the question until he wrapped this up. This was his Constantine moment. It was time to start enjoying it.

Tim stepped into the mansion, and the front door slammed shut, sealing him inside.

"Real creepy," Tim called, trying to sound as confident as possible. "I'm not going to fall for the old slam the door thing. That's amateur hour at best."

Despite Tim's boast, he felt a little shaky. Nothing said *Dead by Dawn* like being trapped in a building with at least one person who didn't mind having his face covered in blood. At least this wasn't an R.L. Stine book where the first person trying to help normally ended up dead. This was a game. All he had to do was be smart enough to win.

With all the candles snuffed out, the hallway might as well have turned into a haunted house. Every little noise, every flash of light from the windows off a suit of armor, anything that changed from one moment to the next was making him jump. It was time to reach down deep and find his cojones.

It was fine to be scared, but this was what he did. He was the wraith slayer, the defender of the light. One insignificant minion of darkness wasn't going to send him scurrying away.

"Evil is my bitch!" Tim stood a little taller.

Confidence rolled through him in waves. Tim took a step forward and then another. Soon he was practically running down the hallway, and that was when it all turned to shit. Something bounced off his shoulder. Hard. The impact sent him reeling into the wall, where he promptly bounced off and hit the floor with a *thud*.

"Nothing good ever comes from running," Tim grunted as he pushed himself back to his feet.

The eerie stillness of the mansion shattered.

Tim felt like he was storming the beach at Normandy as large pieces of furniture slammed into the walls and exploded into shrapnel. He covered his face with his robe and kept pushing forward, trying not to think about what would happen if a chair or suit of armor slammed into him in the maelstrom. It was all he could do to keep going with his head buried in the soft fabric of his robe to stop the flying debris.

Suddenly, the chaos stopped.

"Oh shit." Tim barely finished speaking before he was running full speed again.

The door was so close. He only had to get there. There was no way to tell what was happening behind him, but he knew it wasn't good. He imagined it was like one of those scenes in a horror movie where all the kitchen knives flew at someone because they challenged the spirit. He didn't want to get skewered, but there was no chance in hell he was looking over his shoulder.

Looking back would only slow him down.

When Tim's hand closed around the door handle, he let out a sigh of relief before he tried to turn it. Saved, was the word his brain kept screaming as he ripped the door open on the first try. His heart rate slowed until he turned and saw the wall of flying swords headed at him.

"Oh, come on." Tim slammed the door shut.

Maybe this was a horror movie.

Slamming a door closed while leaping backward was one of those things that seemed simple enough until he tried to do it. As Tim hit the floor hard on his ass, he imagined his mother watching him make the same move and shaking her head. He could picture her ranting about how dodging imaginary enemies as a kid didn't prepare you for the world the way calculus did. It was one of those lines parents tossed out there to try to keep their kids on track.

Tim had always been a dreamer.

His time spent fighting imaginary ninjas was certainly paying off now. Despite hitting the floor hard, he wasn't dead. Closing the door in a hurry had paid off as several swords had punched through the solid wooden frame. One particularly sharp blade almost made it through the center of the door. It still wobbled back and forth.

It was a turn of events. First, Lord Rictor had tried to keep him out of the mansion. Now he was luring him deeper inside. Tim had the very distinct feeling the fucker didn't want to let him leave.

He turned away from the door as something else crashed into it. Maybe the thing inside Lord Rictor wanted him to be scared. There was always the possibility that fear powered the evil.

Just like a boggart.

When the lights were out, and the thing you were fighting could move objects with their mind, it was hard not to be scared. There was always a good chance he'd bitten off a bit more than he could chew taking on this task alone. Fighting with a group was his preferred playstyle, but it wasn't like he could turn back now.

Tim had willingly waded up shit's creek. Now he needed to find a way to keep his head above water until he made it to the other side.

Forcing his eyes away from the sword blade sticking through the door, Tim turned to look at the room he was standing in. It didn't take long for him to realize the entire time he'd been staring at the door, he'd exposed his back to the entire room beyond.

The soft glow of the late afternoon sun filtered through the shredded curtains giving him just enough light to see. Compared to the hallway, this room was glowing, but every second he waited to act was a moment the light was fading outside. It was time to stop dicking around and end this. If Cleanse worked, awesome. If not, he'd blast him with Divine Light and hope the damage was enough to knock some sense back into the man instead of killing him. Knowing what he needed to do made it easier for Tim to act.

He was always a sucker for a plan, even if it was as half-baked as they came.

"Lord Rictor! I've come on behalf of the temple to help you sort out this little problem." *Little* was probably the understatement of the century, but there was no reason for Tim to rile the man up further.

"Life is the problem. Death is the solution." Rictor's voice whispered from the shadows.

There was a sound like someone running toward him coming quickly from his left, and the noise moved upward. *Upward?* Not only that, but it sounded like the man was running on his hands and feet. Things might've been worse than he thought.

Tim looked up at the ceiling and mouthed, "Please tell me he's not up there."

His eyes moved across the space, trying to zero in on the sounds as they shifted from one of the massive floor-to-ceiling bookcases to the other. It was clear that Lord Rictor enjoyed the tension he was building, and it wouldn't be much longer before the big reveal.

It took Tim a moment to realize what he saw as Lord Rictor bounded through the light. It was unnatural to see someone using their hands like another set of feet, not to mention his *Matrix*-like ability to run on the ceiling. It was one thing to know how they used special effects to create the shot in the movie, and another thing to see someone running on a surface he couldn't have jumped to touch with a ladder and a trampoline.

Every part of him wanted to blast the man and end this, but if the spell didn't kill him, the fall might. There was always the chance Lord Rictor was a victim in all of this. If that were true, Tim would kill an innocent man. He wouldn't be able to live with himself if that happened so he had to think of a new plan.

Maybe the light outside was brighter than he thought. The last time he'd looked the sky had been full of the hot afternoon sun. Opening the curtains would get rid of the shadows and Lord Rictor's ability to hide. Once they could face each other in the open, he might have a better chance of winning. The entire situation might be as simple as casting a few spells and walking out the front door like a hero.

Wouldn't that be a lovely change of pace?

Tim knew the asshole was feeding off his anxiety, but there wasn't much he could do to stop it. Seeing someone running on the ceiling and looking at you was bad enough, but sometimes Lord Rictor popped out of random shadows. It was like the worst game of Where's Waldo or Whack-A-Mole. The man wouldn't stay still long enough for Tim to blast him, and not knowing where he would be next left him paralyzed with indecision. He needed to summon the power of his two favorite exorcists.

Father Tomas and Marcus wouldn't take any shit from a demon and neither would he.

Those two prolific smiters of evil wouldn't stand around doing nothing because they expected someone to save them. They were fighters, which he needed to be now. Tim firmly believed that good would always triumph over evil. He was a warrior of the light, a servant of the goddess. A few shadows wouldn't cow him into submission.

He turned away from the bookshelves and ran.

"Ouch!" Tim spun and saw a book lying on the floor at his feet.

The son of a rat-sucking fart licker threw a book at him! The only time Tim liked to have the book thrown at him was when ShadowLily played a dirty cop or sassy librarian. There was something sexy about a girl with glasses or in a uniform. Hot, nerdy, and authoritative, that was his kind of shit. Having books thrown at him by a grown man hanging from the ceiling with dried blood all around his mouth, not so much.

The next book flew out of the darkness. Tim leapt to the side, hitting the floor as the book sailed over his head.

"If you can dodge a wrench, you can dodge a book," Tim spat through gritted teeth as he pushed himself up from the floor and ran.

Tomes flew at him from every angle. The disrespect to classic literature was palpable. It was one thing to toss a fifty-cent paperback across the room in disgust, but these books looked like leather-bound first editions. One thing became abundantly clear as he continued his mad dash toward the curtains.

It didn't matter who the author was. If Lord Rictor threw the book hard enough, it fucking hurt.

Tim's hand closed around the thick fabric of the curtain, and he tried to yank it open.

Lord Rictor wailed in anguish, and more hardbacks flew at Tim in waves. They tore through the holes in the curtains and broke through the glass windows. Shards of glass covered the floor, and Tim still couldn't get the damn things to open. He stopped trying to yank the curtain open and wrapped himself in it. The thick woven fabric was like being tucked inside the world's largest pillow.

Muffled *thumps* reached his ears as the books continued to find their mark, but Tim couldn't feel them anymore. The thick fabric of the curtain protected him and let light into the room as he continued to twist it around him. The only downside was he'd become entangled in the drape and couldn't think of an easy way out without undoing all his hard work. Not exactly the best plan he'd ever come up with, but it got him out of harm's way long enough to catch his breath. A Healing Orb dealt with the worst of his bruises.

Now he needed to climb free so he could fight.

Tim dropped to his knees and slithered out from under the massive curtain. Slithering almost made what he did sound graceful. In reality, it was mostly a lot of cursing, and he came out of it with his robe wrapped around his head like a turban that covered his eyes. A few moments of furious struggling later, he could see again and was surprised Lord Rictor hadn't throttled him while he fought with his robe. The fact he was still alive was a miracle.

Luck seemed to be on his side today.

The sunlight streaming into the room from the twenty-foot-tall windows lit up half of the library like someone discovered electricity. The other half of the space was covered in dense shadows, the bookcases still giving Lord Rictor plenty of places to hide. Books were still flying toward him, but the magic powering them faded as soon as the books hit the sunlight. The leather-bound tombs hit the floor harmlessly and skittered to a stop well before they made it to Tim.

With the sun providing Tim protection from Lord Rictor's tricks, he finally had time to look around the room. The pair of legs sticking out from under one of the reading tables had on pants and shoes that looked an awful lot like Percey's, probably making him Sam. There were two things he knew instantly from the discovery. Number one was that he didn't have to look for Sam anymore, and the second was that he knew where the blood on Rictor's mouth came from.

Getting zombied wasn't a pleasant way to go.

"Sam tried to stop me." Lord Rictor appeared at the edge of the sunlight with his mouth pulled into a grin of pure satisfaction. "So I decided to end his employment."

Part of Tim was completely fascinated by what was happening. Was this man possessed or was there something else at play? Lord Rictor's eyes looked frantic, but his words were calm and delivered with an even tone. He wondered if the man's consciousness was trapped in there, watching everything that happened but unable to stop it. The thought terrified him. As someone who lived and died by planning, not being in control was the ultimate nightmare.

Now with the protection of the sun on his side, Tim had to find a way to keep Rictor talking so he could get a better sense of what was going on. "Why don't you tell me about your vision for the future, and I'll decide if I'm interested in helping." Tim shrugged. "In other words, make me a better offer."

Lord Rictor's smile grew, and Tim wondered how many teeth the man had. It wasn't normal for someone's mouth to look like a great white shark's, right? Forcing himself to look away from Rictor's pointy teeth, he tried to focus on the eyes again. They were telling a different story than the rest of the man's body language. They looked sad and resigned to their fate.

It was a good thing for both of them that Tim had no intention of accepting whatever Rictor offered him. He was pretty sure the man was either possessed or cursed. If Lord Rictor made a deal with the devil, he was starting to figure out exactly what such a deal was worth.

Tim had seen firsthand the kind of lives Vitaria's best lived in the desert, and he would rather go back to living in the slums than be her pawn for a few worthless trinkets.

"I could offer you power." The possessed man paced as if he were thinking out loud. "Or wealth."

Lord Rictor stopped pacing, and his eyes blazed with triumph. "No, I don't think any of those things would do." A smirk oozed across his face, like the look of a pawnshop owner with a desperate customer. "What if I could give you the thing you most desire, the Stone of Immoratis. All you have to do is walk away."

It was tempting, and if Tim thought the thing in front of him could've delivered the stone, he would've at least considered the offer. Then he would've rejected it.

Everything worth having was worth working for. It was okay to move slowly and build things from the ground up. People still said, "Rome wasn't built in a day" for a reason. Tim would put in the work and do things the right way. When he beat Vitaria, he wanted to do it knowing he didn't have to cheat to win.

The way you win has to mean something.

So if a way to get the stone where he didn't have to waste days jumping through hoops presented itself, of course, he'd think about it. That didn't mean Tim was willing to sell his soul to get a few steps ahead. Still, the ruse wouldn't work if he didn't sell the act.

"Show me the stone!" Tim cried as if getting the stone was what he desired above all else, and he couldn't wait another second to have it in his hands.

He reached out and pulled his hand back, trying to look ashamed.

Part of him thought he might be laying it on too thick, and the other part said he deserved a fucking Oscar. The real question was, would Lord Rictor believe Tim desired the stone so desperately that he was willing to do anything to get it?

It didn't take more than a glance to tell that whatever was controlling Rictor was eating up his performance. The hungry grin on the man's face said it expected no other reaction and that Tim should step out of the light and make himself available for an early evening nibble.

"All you have to do is walk away." Lord Rictor's voice echoed as a whisper from nowhere and everywhere at once. "As you step out of the front door, the stone will appear in your pocket."

And I have a freezer full of ketchup popsicles.

Tim turned and headed toward the door. He picked up his pace to a panicked rush, then stopped dead in his tracks. Slowly, he turned and walked back toward Lord Rictor.

Tim tilted his head to the side and looked over the man as if he'd never seen him before. He let the skepticism hang heavy in his words as he spoke. "How do I know I can trust you?"

"Why would you doubt me when what you desire most is almost in your grasp?" Lord Rictor looked like a petulant child but tried to hide his dissatisfaction with another creepy smile.

Bending into a waist-high bow, Lord Rictor rose slowly with his eyes locked on Tim's. "All you have to do is believe."

Turning away to keep his smile from showing, Tim headed toward the door. He knew how quick the man was so hitting him with Cleanse from here was risky. There was a good chance he'd only get one shot to use his spell, and he couldn't risk misfiring from so far away. The sun would set in another hour or two, and the situation would be a lot worse. So what he had to do was find a way to get closer.

But how?

Tim stopped walking and faced Lord Rictor as if he had more significant doubts about their arrangement. "It might help if you gave me some kind of token, something that lets me know you have as much skin in the game as I do."

Lord Rictor appraised him for a moment. "Skin in the game, I rather like that." He snapped his fingers.

Tim tried not to panic as magic gently pulled him across the floor toward what might be a demon hiding inside a man. His feet stopped right at the edge of the light. Rictor looked disappointed, as if he expected his spell to pull Tim into the darkness.

When it became clear he couldn't yank Tim through the border, Lord Rictor grinned and licked a little of the blood from the corner of his mouth. "Can't blame a guy for trying."

"As for a symbol of my promise to deliver the stone, I can offer you this coin. This is the symbol of my once great house, and I won't need it any longer." Lord Rictor held out a flat golden coin the size of his fist.

There was no way to know if accepting the coin would seal the bargain he'd been using as a ploy. The last thing Tim wanted was to get hoodwinked while trying to pull one over on the possessed. This situation felt worse than making a deal with a fairy, and everyone knew the fairies always tried to screw you even though they only told the truth. This was a situation where the smallest wrong decision could make everything turn to shit.

Or the right one could end things in an instant.

Tim was only a few feet away from Lord Rictor now. He kept his eyes locked on the coin, hoping that the lord would interpret his anticipation of casting his spell as excitement over the treasure.

Slowly he reached for the disk of solid gold. Before his fingers closed on it, Tim cast Cleanse.

Lord Rictor stumbled away from him, clawing at his face. Not wanting to let him escape, Tim quickly cast Snare, then charged across the barrier of light and darkness. With a leap, he landed on the demon's back and blasted him with Cleanse.

Channeling his best Father Tomas, Tim screamed, "Back to hell, foul demon," as he continued casting Cleanse repeatedly.

The creature screamed like someone was dunking its head in a pot of boiling water. Steam rose from his flesh. The heat seared Tim's skin, but he held onto Lord Rictor with everything he had.

Someone was screaming, and Tim was surprised to find it was him.

A *crash* came from the doorway. Then it *thudded* again and again. Either someone was trying to break in, or Tim was about to learn what it felt like when a floating sword skewered him. The door splintered, but he didn't bother to look up. If a sword was coming to end him, the only thing he could do to stop it was completely cleanse Lord Rictor. The wood splintered more, and the door *crashed* open.

"I'm so close," Tim rasped as he put everything he had into his spellwork.

There was a wet *pop*.

The sound itself wasn't pleasant. It was almost like when the toilet finally unclogged, and everything got sucked back down where it belonged. A small black stone fell out of Lord Rictor's pants and landed on the floor next to them. Lord Rictor smashed an elbow into Tim's face as he tried to break free of his grasp and get farther away from the stone.

A quick Healing Orb took the sting of the blow away, but all he could think about was the little black rock, and the band of platinum wrapped so delicately around it. It was wrong of him to call the stone a simple rock. It was so much more than that. This was a jewel. Something to be worshipped. He had to have it. His hand reached out, and right before his fingers would have brushed the surface, something slammed into him.

"Sorry it took me so long to get back." Grant rolled off him. "Traffic."

Just like that, the stone's spell broke.

Tim climbed to his feet and brushed himself off. He looked at Lord Rictor, but the man huddled against the window, trying to keep himself as far from the shadows as possible. His eyes darted between the two men and back toward the stone. It didn't hold power over him as it had moments before, but he wanted nothing to do with it.

"Traffic?" Tim didn't remember ever seeing more than a couple of carriages in the same place before.

Grant blushed slightly. "Sounded better than I stopped to use the temple's facilities."

"Everybody poops." Tim pulled a spare shirt from his inventory and tossed it over the stone.

To make sure there was no chance he would touch it, he pulled out another shirt and tossed it over the first. Tim looked at the small lump nestled under his two shirts and back toward Grant. "If things get weird, don't try to help. Just go and get my friends."

Tim didn't wait for an answer. If he didn't make sure this was over now, he might not find the courage to do it again. So instead of running back to the safety of the inn, he reached for the shirts. The stone felt warm through them. Then it was in his inventory and out of sight.

What am I going to do with this? I can't give it to Melvin.

In a normal situation, next up on his list would be the High Priest. Now he had direct access to the divine. Maybe he should break the stone to recover some of her power. At the very least, Eternia would know how to get rid of the damn thing.

It was time to get the fuck out of here.

"Percey, it's okay to come in now," Tim called to the man as he loitered nervously in the doorway.

Percey ran into the room. He took one look at the dead body of his friend Sam and ran straight for Lord Rictor. Tim thought he might have to restrain the man, but instead, the servant helped the lord to his feet. "Let's get you cleaned up, sir. Then we can worry about the mess."

"Percey, I'm.." Lord Rictor's voice petered out.

Tim was starting to feel like he was intruding on a private moment. "If it helps at all, I think the stone cursed him." When both men gave him blank stares in return, he nodded. "I'll see myself out."

Lord Rictor pulled away from Percey and limped across the room toward the fallen coin. He picked up the heavy golden disk and shuffled back to Tim. "I want you to keep this. If you need anything from my family or me, all you have to do is ask. Turn in this coin and the favor is yours no matter the cost."

Tim looked into the man's eyes and didn't see a trace of the demon left. Before taking the coin he blasted Lord Rictor with Cleanse one more time, taking a certain amount of delight in seeing him sputter as he placed the coin in his inventory.

"Thank you." Tim cast Healing Orb on Rictor, hoping to take the edge off any lingering physical injuries.

Standing straighter but looking weary to the bone, Lord Rictor gave Tim a curt nod and made his way from the room. Percey trailed him.

"I trust you can find the door," the servant shouted as they left.

Tim looked at the body on the floor, wishing there was something he could do for Sam. He cast Cleanse on the corpse and would send a message to Melvin asking the priest to say some words.

It was the least they could do.

In the end, Tim still didn't know if it was a demon or a cursed object. All he knew was that the stone in his inventory was powerful and not in a good way. The sooner he could get the item to Eternia, the better.

"Let's get out of here." Tim motioned for Grant to follow him.

"Thought you'd never ask." The carriage driver moved to follow him. "Things might not have worked out well for Lord Rictor, but I think I might've made myself a good little business arrangement."

Tim couldn't help but smile as Grant continued to look for the upside in any situation. "If I ever need a ride, you have my promise I won't call anyone else."

They walked out the front door, most of the world none the wiser about what had happened within the mansion.

CHAPTER FIVE

T he Blue Dagger was a sight for sore eyes.

Tim climbed out of the carriage and stretched his back. Sleep was on his mind, but he also needed to eat and take a shower. The inventory trick did wonders for his clothes, but it didn't do anything to cover up his man-funk. Before he could think of accomplishing anything on his to-do list, he needed to get rid of the stone. Thankfully the one person who could help him with that was inside.

Turning toward Grant, Tim extended his hand. "Thank you for the help today. If you're hungry, I'd be happy to buy you dinner and a beer."

"As much as I'd love to stay, I've gotta get Ripley home. It's been a long day for both of us." Granted patted the horse affectionately.

Liz came out on the rebuilt front patio and held the door open. "Bring your friend inside already. I'll send one of the stable hands out to take care of his horse."

"Tell them to give him extra carrots. Ripley's a good boy." Tim patted the horse's neck and received a whinny in return.

Grant looked between the three of them and knew they'd outvoted him. "I'd love to join you for dinner."

"Good." Tim wrapped an arm around the man's shoulders. "Don't worry. This isn't a four-hour thing. I'm probably going to stuff my face and head to bed. We've been on the road for a bit, and I wasn't expecting quite so much excitement this afternoon."

Two lads came out of the barn and unharnessed Ripley from the carriage. A girl joined them, gently gathered the reins under his neck, and guided the horse around back to the barn. Grant watched them for a moment, ensuring they knew what they were doing, then headed inside.

Grant smiled at Liz. "Thank you for your kindness. I'd be a fool to turn down a free meal and the royal treatment for my horse."

"Don't tell any of these other worthless louts," Liz shouted through the doorway. "They aren't getting half the service you are."

A chorus of cheerful-sounding jeers rolled out the doorway.

"Fuck off, or it's no beer for the lot of ya." Liz winked at Tim and motioned for them to come in. "I'll make sure your big strong friend here gets a prime seat."

Grant stepped inside, looking enthusiastic about how his night had taken a turn for the better. Tim's smile faded as Liz stopped him inside the doorway.

"We thought your guest might like private accommodations so we have her stashed in the room next to yours." Liz passed him the room key. "She's waiting for you now."

Eternia must have sensed the stone like a disturbance in the Force.

"Make sure Grant gets whatever he wants. It's on me." Tim locked eyes with her. "Within reason, mind you."

Liz got out of the way and motioned for him to head upstairs as she slung her other arm through Grant's and dragged him deeper into the inn's common room. "Let's get you in a big comfy chair with an ice-cold beer. How does that sound?"

"Like I died and went to heaven," Grant breathlessly said as he let her pull him to the chair Eternia had been sitting in earlier.

Tim watched the two of them talk for a moment, wondering if his chance decision to call for a carriage might've sparked something interesting. There was also a good chance Liz was merely a boss at her job, taking care of Grant so Tim could handle something more important. Whichever it was, it was probably time Liz got another raise. She was practically running the whole damn inn now and deserved pay that matched her responsibilities.

Despite all his grumblings, Ernie liked doing less work just fine.

Walking up the cleaned and polished steps was different from the first night Tim stepped into the inn. Then the steps had been cracked and full of nails because they didn't want guests. Gaston and his crew of assassins worked out of a secret set of rooms in the basement and having several people above them wasn't exactly stealthy. Mentioning his reservation to Ernie almost got Tim killed, but when his name was in the book, the innkeeper couldn't turn him away.

His room at the inn wasn't any better than the slums outside his lone four-inch window. The sheet had been dusty, and his room didn't have a bathroom. Tim never appreciated toilets more than after he had to shit in a pot. It seemed like a weird custom to shit in a pot and put it out in the hallway for someone to grab, but when in Rome.

Now the Blue Dagger Inn was a thriving business. The bar was full, and Joe's next door was pumping out food like nobody's business. Mix in the good food with some drinking, all the new shops, and sometimes people even stayed for the weekend. The transformation from Day One was incredible. As much as he'd like to take credit for it, Tim knew he was incredibly lucky to have run into Liz. Without her, the Blue Dagger wouldn't be half of what it was now.

He even had a private bathroom.

A small part of him wanted to duck into his room first and take a moment to breathe. The more rational side of his brain knew that if he went into his room now, he wouldn't come out until the morning. It took more willpower than Tim would like to admit to pass his door and go to Eternia's room, but once he did, he felt like he'd conquered a monumental feat.

Tim stopped in front of her door, wondering if she knew he was there or if he should knock like he was going to visit a normal person. His knuckles hit the wooden door, and he felt like it was the right decision. Sometimes a goddess probably wanted to be treated like everyone else, as long as they still received the proper amount of respect.

It never paid to piss off someone who could destroy you with a thought.

When the door opened, he took a step back not wanting to be all up in the goddess' face. He needn't have worried. Eternia was sitting in a comfortable chair by the fireplace in her room. Again she reminded him of his grandma, and he felt a need to protect her. No one was going to screw with the goddess on his watch. Without her timely intervention, all of them would've been dead. The least he could do was return the favor.

"Do be a dear and shut the door behind you." Eternia gave him a look that said, why are you still standing in the doorway? All the warm air is getting out.

Tim stepped into the room and closed the door behind him. Despite his level of familiarity with the goddess, he also didn't want to waste her time. He was sure that despite her presence in front of him, she was waging a battle against her sister. All he needed to do was show her the stone and figure out what to do with it.

"When I went to the temple today, I accepted a quest to find a wayward priest. I've since returned him to the temple, but I also found this." Tim pulled the bundle of shirts from his inventory and held it out to Eternia.

Eternia frowned. "A bundle of rags?"

"Hey, those are my shirts." Tim stopped as he noticed the big shit-eating grin plastered on Eternia's face.

The goddess has jokes. Must've spent some time with Cassie while I was gone.

Tim pulled back the layers of shirts to reveal the stone. "What do you think?"

"I think my sister wouldn't want us to have this." She looked from the stone and back at Tim. "It couldn't just be simple luck, maybe a twist of the Fates?"

"The Fates?" Tim was lost.

Eternia plucked the stone free from the shirt and tossed the shirts into the fire.

Tim looked down and saw a gold coin in his hand where the shirts had been.

"For the clothes." Eternia focused on the stone. "It's better not to keep things touched by cursed objects."

He guessed her protection from such trivial concerns as cursed objects was absolute since Eternia held the stone in her hand while checking the platinum band wrapped around it. The stone didn't seem to harm her, and for the first time since he'd picked the damn thing up, he felt safe from its influence.

Crisis averted.

Eternia tossed the stone in the air, and it disappeared. "This might be the key to our victory. I may be able to use it to weaken my sister, perhaps even to close the portal she's opened between realms."

"I'll need my full powers back before I can know for sure, but you might have won a great victory for us today." Eternia rose from her chair and embraced him. "Thank you for standing by my side."

Tim didn't know what to do. He'd never been hugged by a goddess before. It was easy enough to return the hug with an embrace of his own. Then he tried not to think about it too much.

It was one of those experiences that happened, and if he told a million people, not a single one of them would believe him.

"The Blue Dagger Society is with you until the end." He meant every word.

Eternia moved back to her chair and tucked herself under the blanket. "Now go and get some rest. Tomorrow we continue the fight." She winked. "This time with a secret weapon."

A secret weapon. He liked the sound of that.

"I'll be down for breakfast in the morning. If I don't see you then, we'll be working to secure passage inside the castle for the rest of the day." Tim turned and headed for the door.

When his hand closed on the knob, Tim glanced back and saw that Eternia had already fallen asleep. He stepped into the hallway and closed the door as quietly as he could. Then he stuck the Do Not Disturb tag on it before ducking into his room.

Tim turned in Melvin's quest as he headed toward the promise of hot water.

Quest Complete: Retrieve Jasper

Isn't it funny how a simple request can turn complex? Luckily, you're handy with Cleanse, and despite the curtain incident, not entirely fumble-footed. You're also not afraid to be generous or take on solo side quests for the right reasons. Thanks to your adventures with Lord Rictor, you unlocked a hidden reward: the stone you acquired may help the Goddess Eternia win her battle against Vitaria and the forces of darkness.

Reward: You accepted this quest free of charge, but it paid off in other ways.

Congratulations, you've reached level nineteen.

It was time for him to hop in the shower and go over his stats and skills. By the time he finished, ShadowLily should be back, and they could get some food before crashing.

A small burst of energy shot through him at the thought of what was about to happen. He was going to hit level twenty and get to select the path to follow to his next class. Skipping his first class change was awesome at the time, but it left him with no point of reference for what would happen next. All he knew for sure was that when he ascended to his new class, everything would change. Better spells, more power, maybe even some cool new gear. Reaching the next leveling milestone always opened the door to new possibilities.

The unexpected was what kept him coming back for more.

CHAPTER SIX

Was there anything more relaxing than a warm shower?

Tim didn't think so, not for one second. The shower was where he did all his best thinking, other than going for a long walk. There was something about the warm water and the release of tension that made the ideas come to him in the shower. Need a plan? Take a shower. Stuck on a boss, anyone got a towel? It was a little weird, but it was also totally his thing.

If he never saw a bath again, it would be too soon.

Unless it was big enough for two.

This wasn't the time to be thinking about getting some action. ShadowLily would be back soon enough, and he had to have all of his quests updated before then so he could focus on her and not have her waiting on him like usual. No one liked it when someone was always late. It made a person feel like you didn't value their time.

There was nothing in this world he cared about more than her.

It was one of those things he knew instantly. It was like they were the perfect complement to each other. When he couldn't do something, she was great at it, and when she failed, he always had her back. There was a point in time where their relationship became easy. It was like they were the same person, always working together with one mind. Even when they fought, it was with love.

Unless it was over that last slice of Joe's famous carrot cake, then all bets were off.

The hot water took away the stress of the last couple of days as he made a cup with his arms and let it fall to the shower floor. Tim felt like they'd been going nonstop, and this was his moment to veg out and think. He might not be able to get his class change done until their business with Eternia was complete, but knowing he had the quest in his queue and he could knock it out before taking the fight to Vitaria was enough.

First, he had to hit level twenty.

Tim let the sound of the falling water take away the last of his thoughts about what was coming next and opened his user interface. Many things needed his attention, but first, it was time to claim some of the sweet rewards he'd been holding off on. Then he'd check out his skill updates.

Quest Complete: Breaking the Juggernaut

The Juggernaut ended up being a minotaur with a gastric problem. Those four stomach compartments must not have been enough to deal with all the bony humans he ate. You showed him a fart wouldn't stop you and saved a lot of Khalid's warriors in the process.

Quest Reward: Ten gold coins

Was it wrong that he felt like he spent most of the fights running for his life? Tim laughed at what it must look like for anyone tuning into his stream. Sure, they won a lot of battles, but they certainly didn't do it pretty. People back in the real world wouldn't be writing their strategies down for next time unless it was with notes on what not to do stenciled on the side. Some people probably even thought they got lucky.

His response would have been that luck is where preparation meets opportunity.

Tim was always known as the man with a plan. He worked on his skills and rotation to ensure he had a process for almost any healing eventuality. His stats were fairly balanced, and his group performed at a high level. So while their wins might look like luck to the casual observer, it was based on hours of fighting together honing their skills as a team.

Nothing quite so finicky as luck.

Turning in his first quest didn't get him to level twenty, but he was getting closer. A quick look at his experience bar and the three quests Tim had left to turn in, and he was sure it wouldn't even be close.

Level twenty is mine bitches!

Quest Complete: Take her to the Theater

I take it back, going to the theater was a bad idea for a date. Not only did you have to fight Goliath, but you also had to tangle with Jabari. What the two of you need is a quiet night in together, not another round of kicking ass.

Reward: Ten gold coins

Spend it on a vacation.

Damn, this game sounded like his mom after she pulled a double at work. The first thing she did when she got home was to tell everyone she needed a vacation and it was time to go to the beach. They never really went, but it was a nice idea and one that cooled them off a few warm nights when the AC was busted, and they didn't have money for the twenty-four-hour repairman.

A vacation would be nice, but in reality, his every day was a vacation. Tim could have ended up stuck in a cube. Instead, he was fighting evil, dating a total hottie, and if he continued living modestly, he was going to be kind of rich when it was all over.

This was his vacation, an escape from a life of tedium.

Fuck yeah!

Quest Completed: The Tomb of Nemset

You made it through the tomb winning several battles only to have Vitaria snatch victory away from you at the last moment. A loss like that has to sting more than a bit. In my experience, the best way to deal with someone trying to kill you is to kill them first. Are you strong enough to kill a goddess?

Tim hoped it wouldn't come to that. Eternia seemed to think they could lock her sister back in her realm. If that were possible, he would help the goddess accomplish it. There was no way the five of them could kill Vitaria on their own, and he didn't think Eternia had the will to do it. Normally, beacons of hope and light weren't known for slaughtering their family members. They would find a way to win the right way.

With Eternia on their side, how could they lose?

These were his favorite kind of quest rewards. The kind where he got to dive into a long list of items and pick the one he needed the most. Sometimes stats dictated his selection, replacing his oldest piece of gear first. Other times there was something that was a minor upgrade but too good to pass up.

Having a bunch of loot at his fingertips was so stimulating. Tim loved going through the options and figuring out the best possible choice. ShadowLily would have told him to pick something, but she should have been happy he wasn't as indecisive as Chidi Anagonye.

Tim zeroed in on the item he wanted rather quickly. It was time to ditch his shoulder guards. He never thought he'd find another pair of shoulder guards that increased his secondary stats. Secondary stats couldn't be purchased or upgraded and were still kind of a mystery to him, but now that there was a new piece of gear that also had them, it made the choice a no-brainer.

He was going to miss his furry shoulder guards. It was kind of cool looking like a Viking in the winter, but it didn't fit the esthetic of his robes very well. He needed to find some shoulder armor that had magical symbols on them or something. So what if his new shoulder guards didn't have the same rustic appeal? It wasn't only about looks. Sometimes it was about cold hard stats, even if Tim ended up looking like a unicorn taking an acid trip had dressed him.

He gave the list one last scan to confirm his choice and selected the item.

Item Received: Shoulder Guards of the Spotless Mind

Brian Dorchester was a healer of rather little renown. Instead of working in the big cities, he liked to ply his trade to the outlying villages and the hamlets. Brian was fond of saying to anyone who would listen, the people in the country needed healing as much as the nobles in the city. When the priests asked why he walked from one destination to another, Brian always replied that walking helped him organize his thoughts so he could arrive at his destination with an open mind and a welcoming heart.

+1 Intelligence +2 Wisdom +1 to Perception, Vitality, Revitalization, and Luck

Special ability: Clarity

Clarity removes any mind-altering effects instantly. Can be used once per day.

The stats on the new shoulders were sweet, and while he didn't know if the special ability would come in handy, it was nice to know it was there if he needed it. The only thing it was missing was a little endurance. No biggie. When it came right down to it, this was a flat-out upgrade. Additional stats and a cool special ability, not much else he could ask for.

Not to mention after they returned Eternia to full power, she'd have another epic quest for them. The big storylines always had the best loot so they would take on any challenge she offered. The future was starting to look bright for the Blue Dagger Society.

Tim equipped his new shoulder guards and looked over his stats. His intelligence was now at forty-seven and his wisdom at fifty-five. He'd made some real progress since his first day in the game. He also had a skill point to allocate, meaning he must have hit level twenty, and he still had one quest to turn in.

It was hard to focus on turning in his last quest knowing that somewhere below him was a notification about his ascension to level twenty and the start of his class change quest. Before he could peek at what was waiting behind door number three, Tim had a couple of things to do.

First, he dumped his extra skill point into Dexterity. It was the next thing he wanted to get above a milestone before he worked on his strength a bit. Tim knew he was never going to be as strong as a warrior, but having a decent baseline number would make his everyday life easier. Plus, asking ShadowLily and Cassie to carry heavy things for him still made him feel funny.

Tim chuckled as he thought about what others must think when they watched the women lead the pack carrying heavy things while their men followed behind in brightly colored robes.

Quest Complete: The Deserts of Naroosh

Eternia recognizes that you played your part in the desert well, but you didn't achieve the ultimate goal. Vitaria is still a threat, but you're already working to thwart her next attempt to take over *The Etheric Coast*. You didn't complete this quest in a traditional fashion, but it's complete nonetheless.

Reward: Eternia sacrificed much of herself to save your lives. Isn't that reward enough?

Tim didn't even have to think about the answer. If anyone deserved a break on dishing out the rewards, it was Eternia. Not to mention the fact she saved all their lives. Plus, turning in the quest still gave him a shit-ton of experience points. Tim was racking them up, and they'd already started another epic quest. One with guaranteed rewards.

Sure felt like everything was coming up Tim today.

You have a message.

Not the notification he was looking for.

Tim was half-tempted to swipe the message away so he could

get on with picking his next class, but he'd be able to concentrate better if he knew what it said. It was a short one from Mr. Applebottom simply stating he would meet them at the inn for breakfast in the morning.

Never misses a chance to mix food and business.

Tim's mind wanted to run off trying to figure out what Mr. Applebottom would share with them, but he was too damn excited about his next notification to give it more than a passing consideration. Then he swiped the message away and hoped the next alert was the one he'd been waiting for.

Congratulations, you've reached level twenty.

Tim skipped over the first couple of lines of text. He already knew he hit level twenty and it was a great accomplishment, yada, yada, yada. All he wanted to do was find out what he needed to start his class change. Was it a quest? Did he have to pick one? His eyes kept moving down the mountain of text until he found what he wanted.

Select the path of ascendance.

Below the text was a list of three classes and a breakdown of what it would be like to play them. The simple way to look at it was one leaned more toward doing damage to heal, one toward mitigating damage through shielding spells, and the last class was smack dab in the middle. He'd always prided himself on being a jack of all trades. Being able to heal by doing damage and stopping damage before it could happen seemed like a pretty awesome combination.

It didn't pay to be too hasty when making a big choice, but it only took a few more seconds to make up his mind. When it came right down to it, Tim already had a ton of utility. He wanted to get his healing numbers up, and if he could do it by doing damage, even better. He might never be a chart-topper, but he would be able to do things to help his group other healers couldn't do. The new class sounded perfect.

Tim clicked on the option and confirmed his selection.

A new screen popped up.

Quest Received: So you want to be a Hex Witch?

Wouldn't it be nice if you could just click a button and *whoosh*, you were exactly what you wanted to be? Of course it would, but that isn't what's going to happen. Before accepting your new class, you must understand it. The road to true knowledge begins with a single step. Your first step is to seek out Joaquin Thunderhawk and convince him to show you the way.

This was his last chance to bail out if he wanted to. Tim looked at the confirmation button and hit it. He was never one to doubt his choices when it came to gaming. He'd been playing for long enough that he knew what he liked. Not that he wasn't open to new things, but every gamer had a niche where they felt the most comfortable. His was healing.

Becoming a hex witch gave him the chance to do that and so much more.

He'd find Thunderhawk and learn the ways of the hex witch. He was looking forward to seeing what he could do with more curses at his fingertips. Being able to do more damage would make all their fights easier. So what if he wasn't a traditional healer? He brought the boom.

Once Tim learned the ins and outs of his new class, things were going to be awesome. Synergizing his new skills with the old wouldn't take too long, and he was sure that within a few fights he'd be extremely effective. All they needed to do was get Eternia back on her feet so they could start knocking out their class change quests.

It wouldn't be long now.

Level twenty with new classes normally meant a whole new zone was coming their way. It would be nice to have a change of pace. Not that he didn't like being back at the inn, but Tim was ready to put Vitaria in her place and take on some new challenges.

The best part about gaming was there was always something new to push a player to their limits.

Tim loved acing tests.

He pushed the class screen away and moved onto his last task.

Thankfully, the water would never get cold with magic heating it, but he wasn't immune from turning into a prune. If he stayed in the shower for much longer, Tim would look like he crawled out of the reverse of the fountain of youth. Unless ShadowLily suddenly found wrinkled wet skin a turn-on, it was time to think about drying off.

He could suds up one last time while he looked over his skills.

The thing about adventuring was he never knew when his next chance to get clean was going to come. After going a few days without something he thought of as a daily or twice-daily task he really started to miss it. Combine that with the fact most cities still only had baths, and his showers at the inn were a real treat.

Still, an hour was probably pushing it, even if it was all recycled rainwater.

Tim looked at the long list of his updated skills and noticed a small blinking light at the bottom of the panel. He mentally clicked on it, and a small pop-up came up.

We applied a small patch to skills. Some low-performing skills have received a moderate bump in viability, where over-performing skills have received a minor nerf. This is *The Etheric Coast*'s first balancing pass. Submit any feedback through the user interface.

Whoa, our first big patch.

Tim was even more excited to get in and peek at his skills. He'd wondered what changed since the last time he had a chance to go over them, and now he had to keep an eye out for information other than the minor upgrades he'd been receiving recently. Hopefully, none of his favorite skills got nerfed, and he picked up a few increases along the way.

Skill Increased: Appeal To the Goddess

Rank: Novice five

Seriously, you have a pipeline straight to the divine. Why aren't you using it more often? This skill continues to work as it always has. When you need a little divine inspiration, use this skill once a week to speak directly with the Goddess Eternia.

Tim knew he didn't use the spell enough. Shit, Eternia was right next door, and he still wasn't talking to her. Maybe he would feel better about harassing her for knowledge once she got the goddess groove back. There was so much she could teach him about magic. Even the smallest of her insights could be a huge advantage.

Skill Increased: Infiltrator

Rank: Novice six

Sneaky, sneaky. No one is going to see you crawling through an open window at night. Actually, they might if you don't level this skill more. Being able to hide in the dark is one thing. Using the shadows to your advantage is something else entirely. Keep breaking into places you shouldn't be and doing things you shouldn't be doing to level this skill.

The game made it sound more sinister than it was. Sure, now and again, he snuck onto a boat or into a house full of holy men and slaughtered them all. That was him handling his business. Even the benevolent healer had to strike down their foes when the situation called for it. Despite preferring to heal, he was kind of good at putting out some solid DPS when the situation called for it or his victims were sleeping.

Healer's gotta do what a healer's gotta do.

Skill Increased: Night Vision

Rank: Novice eight

You're almost to the point where stumbling around in the dark will be a thing of the past. Reach the apprentice ranks to see more clearly than you ever have before. This skill is now percentage-based. At novice eight you can see eight percent better than you could before, while the highest of Grandmas-

ters will receive a nearly seventy-five percent bonus. Night Vision also has several perks you can pick up along the way, so keep stumbling around in the dark. Eventually, you might see something important.

Tim wasn't sure how much the changes to this skill would affect him. He wasn't high enough in the skill to know if this change was a nerf or a buff. He did know that seeing in the dark was a handy feature to have, and he'd have to ask Gaston about ways he could do some specialized training to level the skill. He was always of the mind that it was better to see and not need to versus the other way around.

ShadowLily's skill was probably so much higher that he could use her skills to help them avoid any major pitfalls the others couldn't see. It'd be like having his very own safety net. Plus, if everything went to shit, she could always stab their way out of it while he fell back into healing. Truth be told, they made a pretty fearsome duo. Tim took one last look at the skill and moved to the next.

Skill Increased: Disturbance

Rank: Apprentice one

Disturbance has become two skills, Disturbance and Rectify. Disturbance will now focus as an interrupt. Certain fight mechanics can be interrupted, but some might take multiple interrupts cast in conjunction. There are also unavoidable mechanics. The only way to know which is which, is to watch the boss for clues and use this skill.

There wasn't too much he needed to think about here. He'd already spent some time trying to interrupt skills and had a pretty decent handle on it. Now they'd have to watch during fights for key mechanics. Normally in games, bosses would telegraph big attacks with a special move or saying a word. These were things they would all have to watch for now so they could stop whatever special ability was going to hit them next.

Skill Granted: Rectify

Rank: Apprentice one

Rectify removes one beneficial buff from the target. Not all buffs are removable.

Hell yeah.

If there was one thing Tim liked it was versatility. Being able to interrupt or remove a buff from an enemy at will was pretty damn awesome. His brain was already spinning through their previous battles, wondering what mechanics might have been interruptible. The fights going forward would be harder, but the game gave them a chance to mitigate some of that damage. He was excited to try out his new skills.

Skill Increased: Quick Feet

Rank: Apprentice one

Everywhere Tim went, he was running. Ok, so maybe it's not everywhere that you need to run, but when you need to get out of trouble quickly, this spell is your jam. Quick Feet now increases your movement speed by twenty-five percent for five seconds. Keep running away or toward things with great haste to level this skill.

Tier increases could include bonuses such as extended duration or increased dodge chance while running.

If Forrest could do it, so could Tim. Whenever he needed to get close for healing, he would have to remember Quick Feet wasn't only something he could use to get out of trouble. There was a better than even chance he could also use the spell to avoid getting cold when running back from the bathroom in the middle of the night. If he spent enough time trying to avoid cold feet, he might become the fastest healer alive.

Skill Increased: Backstab

Rank: Apprentice four

Isn't killing someone more fun when they can't see it coming? That feeling of elation that washes over a player when they execute the move just right is almost contagious. Keep

sneaking up on people and stabbing them in the back to increase this skill.

You must activate Backstab from behind the target. The attack will deal two hundred percent more damage, and at higher levels may apply a detrimental status effect to the target.

No wonder ShadowLily always took so long to get into position. If she was starting a fight by hitting the boss with a massive attack that also put a negative status effect on them, it was worth it. Increased damage or reducing the bosses' attacks always paid off in the long run. Anytime their group got stronger and the boss got weaker was a good time indeed.

Skill Increased: Throwing Knives

Rank: Apprentice four

As you well know, this skill increases the accuracy with which you can throw a knife. You might not know that it also affects how many you can throw, how fast you can pull an additional blade from your bandolier, and the overall damage.

At apprentice four, you will receive a ten percent bonus to accuracy, a five percent bonus to accuracy while throwing multiple knives simultaneously, and a five percent bonus to the damage inflicted.

Tim was pretty sure his overall damage took a small hit on this update, but the extra bonuses to accuracy and the speed at which he could throw additional knives made up for it. So far, the developers' first balancing pass on skills wasn't driving him nuts. He hadn't been slapped with a big nerf yet, but looking at the list of updates, he still had a long way to go before he'd feel safe saying he came out of this smelling like a rose.

Tim kept his user interface up as he turned off the water and searched for a towel. As much as he wanted to stay in the shower, he was starting to look like he was an extra in *Cocoon*. That was when he knew it was time to call it quits.

His towel was missing from the rack, but there was a bright pink one in its place. He didn't care what anyone said. Using a pink towel had to make you more of a man instead of less of one. He pulled the towel off the rack and dried off his shoulders as he looked over the next update.

Skill Increased: Sneak

Rank: Apprentice six

Sneak and Infiltrator have become one skill. Originally there was a need to keep the hiding in the shadows and the breaking into buildings bonuses separate, but it's easier to have them all in one place. Because Sneak is the higher of your two skills, the new skill is awarded to you at this level.

Skill Granted: Shadow Master

Rank: Apprentice six

Many can hide unseen in the shadows, but a true shadow master can find somewhere to hide even in the light. Your ability to hide in the shadows has been increased by sixteen percent while immobile and eight percent if moving no faster than a walk. There is a ten percent chance someone will completely ignore you if they see you for less than one second in any light conditions.

This ability also increases your chance to pick a lock by ten percent if you have the lock-picking skill.

To level this skill, keep hiding in the shadows and breaking into places you shouldn't be.

One thing Tim loved was when a game decided to cut down on the bloat. No one wanted to look at an action bar with forty to sixty buttons and ten macro combinations simply to walk down the street. At least he didn't have to click on stuff. Still, trying to remember all his skills and special abilities was a little overwhelming when they changed constantly. He liked it when things were simple, and he could focus on the fight.

Bosses didn't care if his metaphorical keybinds were fucked up. They just wanted to splatter him into itty bitty little bits.

Some of Tim's extra skills came from the fact he had two classes. One was lagging way behind the other in actual value, and yet in the right circumstances being able to use his daggers proved to be an incredibly worthwhile skill. He might not need to sneak around all the time, but when he did, it was nice to have some upgrades.

Skill Increased: Small Blades

Rank: Journeyman one

Welcome to the medium leagues, my friend. Seriously, you're almost halfway there. Of course, you got a boost from your sneaky little mentor, but we won't talk about that. Your damage with bladed weapons under eighteen inches in length is increased by fifteen percent and has a ten percent chance to deal half the damage of the original attack again as a bleeding effect over time.

It had been a long time since Gaston had helped Tim with this skill, and he was pretty damn sure he'd never referred to the man as a mentor. *A teacher, maybe.* When it came right down to it, there was no one better with a blade to learn from, and Tim was grateful for the opportunity.

Even when he had to dodge the murderball.

Skill Increased: Snare

Rank: Journeyman one

You've finally realized how important this skill is. When things are trying to kill you, stopping them from doing so should always be at the top of the priority list. Snare will now stop most targets for two seconds. When it's broken, the target will be slower by fifty percent for an additional six seconds.

Using Snare and Quick Feet together would be something he kept in his hip pocket for a quick get-the-hell out-of-Dodge moment. *If the boss decided to do something sketchy, he was so out of there.* Tim was of the firm belief that if he was going to run away, he wanted to do it as fast as possible.

Tim wiped down his legs, and in his Most Interesting Man in the World voice, intoned, "Tim doesn't always use Snare, but when he does, he uses the skill with amazing efficiency."

Laughing as he tossed the fluffy pink towel back on the rack, Tim equipped his clothes and headed to a seat by the fireplace in the main room. He could put his feet up and relax while finishing looking over the last of his skills. He wanted to finish before ShadowLily got back to the room. Hopefully, Liz was keeping Grant full of beer so he would forgive him for not coming back downstairs.

Big cozy chairs by the fire are a little too comfortable. No wonder Eternia loves them.

Skill Increased: Dodge

Rank: Journeyman two

Is he lucky? Does he know what he's doing? Those are the questions the system asks when it watches you try to dodge attacks. Fortunately for you, it's not all luck. You're surprisingly good at getting out of the way.

When this skill is activated, you have a twenty percent bonus to dodge for fifteen seconds. At all other times, you'll receive a one percent bonus to voiding damage.

Part of him wondered if it would be possible to hit a grandmaster of the dodge skill with really low dexterity. He imagined ShadowLily or Lorelei would be able to dodge raindrops if they wanted to at some point. This wasn't something he spent a lot of time grinding so the chances of him reaching that rank were small, but the thought of getting there and what it would be like was pretty damn cool.

Skill Moved: Weaken Undead is reclassified as a buff. All pertinent information for this spell is now under the buffs section of this tab.

Sweet!

He didn't have to blast the undead to make his Divine Light more effective. All he had to do now was have a buff up. At least he hoped that was how it would work. It was tempting to scroll past the rest of his skills and find out, but he was starting to get to the good stuff and wasn't ready to jump ahead yet.

Skill Increased: Behold My Power

Rank: Journeyman three

Admit it to yourself. Sometimes you like dishing out a little damage on your group. Let's hope no one dies because you were trying to show off. Behold My Power will take five percent off each party member's health per second for ten seconds. At the end of ten seconds, the missing health will be dealt as damage and give the target of the spell a Powershock debuff.

Powershock: Increase the damage the target takes from all sources by five percent for ten seconds.

Due to the powerful nature of this spell, you can only cast it once per encounter.

There it was—his first taste of the nerf bat. Tim thought about it for a moment. It wasn't so bad. As much as he liked casting the spell more than once in a fight, it was a lot of extra work keeping up with the additional healing late in the fight. Only being able to cast the spell once took some of the guesswork out of it. He simply had to make sure the Powershock debuff counted for all its worth.

When he pulled the trigger on this bad boy, the DPS needed to be ready to roll.

Skill Increased: Flame Burst

Rank: Journeyman three

The roof, the roof, the roof is on fire. Flame Burst has changed slightly in nature. It's now a coned ability. It will deal more damage closer to the caster and less when farther away. The added benefit of the spell's cone shape is that it can hit more targets at a greater distance.

Flame Burst has a ten percent chance to apply burns. Burns do fifty percent of the spell's original damage over five seconds as fire damage.

That was promising.

Tim mostly used Flame Burst to keep things away from him, almost like Snare. Knowing he could cast the spell and affect multiple targets now was interesting. He would have to try the spell so he could figure out how big the cone was. As much as he wanted to try it out right now, one look at the wooden walls and he decided to wait until he could step outside.

Ernie would never forgive him if he burned down the inn.

Skill Increased: Divine Light

Rank: Journeyman four

If sending out blasts of holy energy to smite your target is your kind of thing, you're in the right place. Divine Light hasn't changed, simply pick a target and let her rip. Twenty percent of the spell's initial damage is applied to the target as a DOT effect lasting five seconds. The DOT effect also has a twenty-five percent chance to jump to the two nearest targets.

Divine Light was his bread and butter when it came to doing damage without curses. The spell packed a punch, but it wasn't precisely cost-effective to use multiple times in a row. Joining the journeyman ranks certainly had its benefits. The DOT was great, but the chance that the damage could splash to additional targets was awesome. One of Divine Light's biggest drawbacks was that it was a single-target-only spell. While it might not do a lot of damage to additional targets, all his damage did a little healing.

This update made life a little easier.

Skill Increased: Healing Storm

Rank: Journeyman four

Healing rain that falls from the sky, what else could a healer ask for?

Healing Storm has changed slightly. The spell can heal a maximum of five people at a time. If there are more than five targets inside the spell's sphere of influence, it will automatically select the five most injured targets and heal them.

If you channel Healing Storm for an additional mana cost, the spell will select new targets inside the area of effect as long as three conditions are met. You must have enough mana to continue channeling the spell. A person the spell was healing

reaches one hundred percent health, and last, if someone leaves the area of effect.

As a journeyman, Healing Storm also provides ten percent of the original heal value to targets that reach full health as a HOT effect.

Tim read the last part a few times. It didn't make a whole lot of sense to him for a spell to put a HOT on someone that was already at full health. Then he thought about it more and realized it could be helpful. It would provide a small buffer against any kind of damage over time effect, and Cassie was always taking damage. It might not be perfect, but it would save him from sending out a round of Healing Orb as everyone ran back into position during a fight.

Not a big change, but again it made life a little easier if he was smart with his casts.

Skill Increased: Who Needs a Shield

Rank: Journeyman four

Who needs a shield, indeed. Well, sometimes you do, or that feisty little tank you're paired with. Frankly, having a shield seems like a good idea for everyone. We're kind of surprised they aren't more popular.

This spell now provides a flat damage reduction of ten percent to the target for ten seconds. When the spell wears off the initial target, each member of your party will receive a ten percent boost to their dodge chance for ten seconds.

At the master ranks and above, this spell may also provide buffs against additional status effects.

Part of him was a little upset by this one. He'd loved the idea that at some point, this skill might be able to decrease the bosses' damage on them by twenty-five or fifty percent for a small amount of time. While he knew that was extremely overpowered, it didn't stop him from being disappointed about not going into "god mode" once a fight.

Then there was the part of his brain stuck doing a happy dance.

Tim smiled as he thought about how the spell might work in the future. He imagined a grandmaster casting the spell when it not only gave them a ten percent boost to dodge but resistances to magic, bleeding, poisons, all kinds of detrimental effects. If something like that was still possible, the benefits to this spell remained significant. At higher levels, it would be even better than before.

He relaxed and drew a deep breath as he reminded himself, all updates weren't bad updates in *The Etheric Coast*.

What did he have to worry about?

Skill Increased: Curse of Giving

Rank: Journeyman five

Curse of Giving is now a damage-only spell.

Wait, what? How in the hell was he supposed to heal when the game was taking one of his biggest hitters out of the rotation?

Curse of Giving applies a damage over time effect to the target. Because you've reached the journeyman ranks, the spell also provides a one percent increase to damage done to the curse's target.

Wow. That felt like a kick right in the fruits.

Curse of Giving was his favorite skill. Tim always had it on an enemy, sometimes even multiple targets. The healing this skill provided in multi-target situations was invaluable. It let him focus on the fight and what they needed to do next instead of always worrying about who needed a heal. Even if Healing Orb reached the master ranks, he doubted it would make up for the loss of healing.

He would have to test this out in a fight, and if it didn't work out right, he might have to commit to being an all-out healer instead of going the hex witch route. Tim shook his head to clear it. This game was too big and had too many players for them to nerf a class into oblivion. He knew there was a catch somewhere. He had to wait for it to reveal itself.

Skill Increased: Cleanse

Rank: Journeyman seven

What do you do when you drink too much? Cleanse it out. Don't worry. We didn't take away your unintentional side benefit. As you get closer to the master ranks, Cleanse is only getting stronger.

Cleanse will automatically clear any debuff of the apprentice ranks or below. A journeyman spell has a seventy-five percent chance of being cleansed, where a master rank only has a twenty-five percent chance. If it's a grandmaster-level debuff or an unremovable boss debuff, the debuff will highlight in red, and you might as well not waste your time.

Keep working at this spell to obtain the master ranks and the ability to cleanse multiple targets at once.

This didn't make up for the loss of healing, but it sure made him feel good about his most trustworthy spell. Cleanse was the thing that pulled them out of the fire more often than not. His second favorite spell also came in handy when he cheated to beat JaKobi at beer pong.

That flame-y little punk was too damn good.

Tim cringed slightly at the thought of how badly he'd lost the last game they played together. He didn't know if the hangover debuff ever went past the apprentice levels, but it was nice to know that if it did, he'd reached a point where he could probably handle it.

Reading how Cleanse worked, Tim thought of a few times where he cast the spell and it didn't work. Maybe he'd been trying to remove something he had no shot at. At least now he would know before he cast it if Cleanse couldn't remove a debuff. That would save him time and improve efficiency during fights. If they ever returned and replayed some of the old dungeons, he wondered if he'd be able to Cleanse some of the things that were too tough in the past.

There might be time to tinker with re-runs after they saved the world.

Skill Increased: Healing Orb

Rank: Master one

Welcome to the master ranks. Yes, it's just one spell, while true masters have loads more, but you're on your way to greatness. Healing Orb has been modified from its original version.

Oh shit, here we go again.

The full power of Healing Orb's single target heal has reduced while the spell's mana cost remains unchanged. At the apprentice ranks, the spell also has a fifty percent chance of proccing the effect Rehydrate. Rehydrate places a healing over time effect on the spell's target for fifty percent of the initial value distributed over five seconds.

At the journeyman ranks, Rehydrate has a one hundred percent chance to apply to a single target and a fifty percent chance of proccing a secondary effect titled Splash. When triggered, Splash spreads Rehydrate to the two party members closest to the original target. Players that are not in your party will not be able to benefit from the effects of Splash.

At the master ranks, Rehydrate and Splash have a hundred percent chance to proc and have the additional benefit of removing an apprentice-level or lower detrimental effect.

So while the spell changed, it wasn't nearly as bad as he thought it would be. It reduced the initial heal value, but the spell now had a one hundred percent chance of casting Rehydrate and Splash, not to mention the fact it removed any minor ailments without him having to cast Cleanse. In short, his single target heal was now a small HOT on three people.

This was going to save him in a lot of situations. Every time he cast Healing Orb on ShadowLily or Cassie, it would proc the buff on the other and one additional person. Even with the small nerf, it felt like Healing Orb was his go-to healing spell for just about everything. If Curse of Giving didn't get a little healing back, it was his only real heal.

All he wanted to do now was get in a fight and test everything out. It might be prudent for them to go and pick off a few scrubby monsters to test things out before they got involved in a boss fight. Knowing their luck, they wouldn't have time.

So they would have to kick ass on the fly.

Stances

Your stances have been modified and are now simpler to manage. All damage done will be returned to the target or targets of your stances as healing. Damage done by curses will return as healing at one hundred and fifty percent of the damage done. Stances no longer have levels, but each of them has separate benefits.

This was going to be interesting.

Skill Increased: Way of the River

Rank: Stances no longer have ranks

Way of the River turns you into an AOE machine. All your healing caused by doing damage is split evenly between every member of your party up to a maximum of five. While in this stance, each member of your party will receive a one percent reduction in damage taken.

Basically the same as before, except Tim didn't have to worry about percentages or to figure out what kind of healing he would put out. Curses would provide more healing, and all his other damage-dealing abilities would give a moderate amount. This simple change made becoming a hex witch a no-brainer. Not only would he do more damage, but all that additional damage would do even more healing.

Healing by DPS. He loved this shit.

Skill Increased: Way of the Boulder

Rank: Stances no longer have ranks

Way of the Boulder turns you into a single-target monster. This stance requires you to select a single target. The target will receive a five percent reduction in damage taken, and heals from your curses will be returned at two hundred percent.

The changes weren't too hard to grasp. If everyone needed healing, Way of the River, if it was just Cassie or someone about to eat a huge cleave, Way of the Boulder was the way to go. Curse of Giving was going to be awesome, and if he got another curse that acted more like Healing Orb, he would be all set. So far, there were only a few minor tweaks he would have to make to his rotation.

Maybe we won't need a warm-up fight after all.

Buffs

Buffs always last eight hours unless specifically stated otherwise.

Skill Increased: Weaken Undead

Rank: Journeyman two

Weaken Undead is now a buff. Any members of your party, up to twenty, will receive a five percent bonus to damage against undead aligned creatures. At the journeyman ranks, all members of your party will also receive a five percent reduction in damage from the undead.

Simple and effective. Just the way he liked it. He'd probably cast this buff with the others on the off chance they ran into any kind of undead creatures.

Skill Increased: Armor of Eternia

Rank: Journeyman five

There comes a time when you have to admit you get hit by a lot of shit, and it hurts. Yes, the game's AI can swear. Pick your jaw off the floor. We try to address each player in a way that makes them feel comfortable.

Well, that explained a lot. If the game was reading him and responding in ways he deemed appropriate; it was snarky with him because he kind of liked it. Adaptive AI was getting to the point it was almost human.

Armor of Eternia provides a one percent reduction in damage. At the apprentice ranks, it adds a one percent dodge chance. At the journeyman ranks, it adds one percent magic resistance.

Tim looked at his user interface for a moment and read the description a few more times. He might have lost some damage reduction, but this was his first spell that specifically lowered magical damage. They were facing more spellcasters so increasing their resistance was important. Maybe at the master ranks, Armor of Eternia would gain additional physical resistance or something even more beneficial.

One thing he knew for sure was that the buff would only get better as it became more powerful.

Skill Increased: Attacks of the Faithful

Rank: Journeyman five

You know what helps in a fight? Doing more damage. There is no situation in which doing a metric fuck-ton of damage won't improve it. The good news is you have a spell that boosts damage to the entire group. All you have to do is use it.

Attacks of the Faithful provides a one percent increase in all damage done. At the apprentice ranks, the spell provides a one percent increase to attack speed. In the journeyman ranks, it increases the critical hit chance by one percent.

Tim grinned as he reached the end of the list and vowed to never again go this long without updating his skill and turning in quests.

Leaning back in his chair to take full advantage of the padded seat, Tim thought about what the developers were doing. He loved it when they started to streamline things. No one loved a game full of worthless bloat. Plus, some of the bonuses had been getting out of control for lower-level players. It wasn't exactly fun to play when everyone was walking around with a three hundred percent damage increase and a thousand percent decrease to damage taken.

Sure, they were only numbers, and the developers could always keep making them bigger, but why bother. Things started to lose meaning when a player hit enemies for a hundred thousand damage to remove a tenth of percent health. It didn't feel right.

He grunted as he shifted out of the chair and stood. If Shadow-Lily wasn't back soon, he'd have to go downstairs and get some grub. It was only now dawning on him that he was starving. It was also getting late, and if she weren't the kind of woman who could kill ten men with a look, Tim would've been slightly worried about her.

As things stood, she was usually the one who kept him safe.

The Fates must have read his mind because the door to their rooms opened moments later. Instead of ShadowLily entering their chambers, three men walked into the room. Tim would've been alarmed, but each of them had their arms so full of bags and boxes that they were clearly not a threat.

As each of the men set down their burden, ShadowLily gave them a coin and waved them away. "Thanks for the help, boys!"

"Shopping is so much work." ShadowLily sighed as she slumped against the closed door to their room. She looked up and saw Tim standing beside the chair. "It's amazing how helpful men can be with a dagger at their backs and a gold coin in their hands."

Tim looked at all the bags. "Or when you spend enough gold to make the queen jealous."

"Or that." ShadowLily winked. "I got you a few things as well, so you can't be upset."

Tim moved over to the loot and poked around in the bags. "Why would I be upset? Last time you came home with that librarian outfit."

"You should have seen the seamstress' face when I described what I wanted." ShadowLily moved toward the bags and ushered Tim away from them. "You'll get your presents when I'm ready to give them to you."

Tim thought about the woman's look when she described the super short skirt and abnormally tight button-up shirt. Now that he was thinking about ShadowLily all dressed up, it was hard for him to pull his mind out of the gutter. He looked at all the packages and wondered if she brought home another sexy surprise.

Wait, did she say she bought him presents?

Wonder who I'll be this time?

Sometimes when you found the right woman, you knew it way deep down. When your life was full of smiles, then everything felt right. Maybe it was time for him to bring a little joy into her life as well.

"There is something I'd like you to unwrap." Tim selected the bow from his inventory and deselected all his clothes. As he moved toward her, his robes disappeared, and there was a golden ribbon wrapped around his waist with a bow just big enough to cover his manhood.

The corner of her mouth quirked up. "As long as we can go to Joe's after. I'm starving."

Tim licked his lips. "I could eat."

"Then you have work to do." ShadowLily grabbed his hand and yanked him toward the bedroom.

God, he loved it when she took charge.

CHAPTER SEVEN

The robust smell of fresh dark coffee gently stirred Tim from slumber.

He lay there for a moment savoring the smell as he stretched his body into wakefulness like a cat. The one thing he loved about sleeping at the inn more than any other was waking up to fresh coffee. The worst thing was that he often woke up to an empty bed.

It wasn't a big surprise. ShadowLily was an early riser, and he'd be happier if he never had to get up. At least one of them liked to get shit done before anyone else woke up, but while he might be slow, Tim liked to think he always delivered in the end.

Getting out of bed, he headed past the delightful-smelling coffee toward the bathroom. When he finished with the morning business, Tim reversed course going straight for the coffee. With each step, he thanked Eternia for putting Liz in his path. That woman was heaven-sent.

One thing he could always count on was that Liz would antici-pate his needs and have them solved before there was a problem. In short, she was the best assistant in the world.

Was there anything better than perfectly brewed coffee?

After taking the first sip, Tim was pretty damn sure the answer was no. It paid to find joy in the simple things in life. For him, that started with coffee and ended with making ShadowLily happy. As long as he accomplished those two things, every day was a success.

For the first time, it felt like no one was banging on the door to get him to hurry up so he must not be as late to breakfast as he felt. After equipping his gear and topping off his cup, Tim headed for the door. Mr. Applebottom would be waiting for them downstairs, hopefully with some good news. Anything that could get them in front of the king faster would be a huge help.

The inn was quiet in the morning. Aside from a few folks lounging around the back tables, it might as well have been empty. Liz signaled him from the bar and pointed toward the door to Joe's. It didn't take a rocket scientist to figure out everyone was chowing down on the best breakfast food in the world. If he'd been up earlier, he would've been doing the same thing.

Joe was still in Tristholm. With the portal network down, that meant he wouldn't be back for at least a few days if he planned on coming back at all. His new love interest was the city's leader, and she couldn't exactly leave to follow around a chef. *Even one of Joe's caliber.* That meant Roberto was handling the kitchen. Tim didn't know how Joe found the man or if Roberto sought him out, but it was a match made in heaven. It had slightly elevated the food once thought of as perfection.

Not that he'd ever tell Joe.

"Straighten up, everyone. The boss is here." JaKobi gave Tim a jaunty wink and grabbed a chair from a nearby table for him.

Cassie snorted. "No one's the boss of me."

"Keep telling yourself that." Tim piled pancakes on his plate.

Lorelei's head swiveled between Cassie's withering glare and how Tim didn't look up as he continued loading his plate with food. "Girl, that man just said he owns you."

"Stop making trouble. It's too early for that." ShadowLily tried not to laugh as she looked up at Tim. "And you. You know better. Cassie isn't herself until at least noon, or she gets to hit something."

"We're about one smartass line away from me accomplishing the second part of that." Cassie stabbed a sausage with her fork and ripped the tip off before chewing it violently.

Tim sat and drowned his pancakes in syrup. "It's not my fault everyone agrees men should rule the world and are clearly better at everything." He shrugged. "It's just how it is."

"I'm going to assume that's sarcasm because I'm too tired to beat your ass." Cassie took another bite of her sausage.

Something slammed into his shin under the table, and Tim let out a little bark of pain.

Trying not to draw more attention by rubbing his leg, Tim cast Healing Orb under the table. He thought about doubling down on the sarcasm, but they were right. It was too early for that shit, and he wasn't nearly as witty as he thought.

Lorelei snickered, not missing Tim's cast under the table.

"Yes, it's total sarcasm. It kind of reminds me of a time when everyone told women to stay home and cook in the kitchen while also telling them they weren't good enough to cook in a restaurant." Tim put his fork to work, cutting up his pancakes. "People should be allowed to be whatever they want. It doesn't matter who they are as long as they're the best at the job."

JaKobi tapped his glass with his fork. "In evidence at this very table, a female tank, and two very badass DPS. Anyone that says girls don't kick ass can suck ass."

Cassie snickered, showing a smile for the first time. "Very poetic."

"Kinda thing that should go on a bumper sticker." Tim held up his hand and motioned like a car was driving by, and he was trying to watch it. "Get ready to suck some ass."

ShadowLily poured a glass of rumpleberry juice. "Sometimes

you gotta do what you gotta do." She puckered her lips like a vacuum and sucked in deeply.

He didn't remember spraying hot coffee through his nose, but that's what must have happened because it burned like liquid fire. Maybe the one time coffee didn't taste good was when he was spraying it through his nostrils and all over his pancakes. Nothing said fantastic morning like snot-covered pancakes and an empty coffee cup.

Their entire table was laughing so hard that Roberto came out of the kitchen to see what was happening.

Tim used a napkin to wipe the coffee off his face and arms, trying not to look as embarrassed as he felt. "I think we're going to need some new food."

"Ya think?" Cassie giggled. "You blew a schnozzle-rocket all over the table."

JaKobi stood. His robes flashed for a second and were totally clean. "It wasn't his fault. You can't start sucking ass like a Hoover when people are trying to drink."

ShadowLily sucked her cheeks in again and made a slurping sound, and it set them off on another round of laughter.

When Tim finally caught his breath, he looked up at an exasperated Roberto and knew he had to make it right. "I'm sorry, Roberto. Do you think you could set us up inside the inn, and if for some reason Mr. Applebottom shows up, will you direct him to the inn for me?"

"Of course I can, but next time try to keep the coffee in your mouth and off my food, capisce?" Roberto waved to one of the servers to take care of it and stormed back into the kitchen.

When the young woman showed up to deal with the mess, Tim pressed a gold coin into her hand. "Again, I'm sorry about this."

She looked at the gold in her hand for a moment in complete shock, then her training kicked in, and she pocketed the coin and started cleaning up the table.

The waitress called after them as they moved to the inn, "Any time you want to make a mess, make sure you're sitting in my section."

As he walked back through the doors, Liz appeared next to him. "Did you really shoot coffee out your nose?"

"Yes." There was no reason to lie.

It wasn't his fault his girlfriend turned into an ass vacuum. Man, he didn't know what it was about this morning, but he felt great. Maybe it was sleeping in his bed, but everything felt right today. Things were funnier. Life was the way it should've been.

Liz picked up on his good mood, and like always, found a way to lift it further. "Your guest has arrived."

Following her pointed finger, Tim's eyes settled on Mr. Applebottom's wide frame sitting at one of the tables. "Thanks, Liz."

"You save the day. I'll handle the small stuff." Liz turned and trotted back behind the bar.

The rest of the group had secured a big table for them, and new food was already making its way from Joe's to their new seats. Tim made sure his robes were free of any coffee stains, then headed to meet Mr. Applebottom and find out what he could do to help.

"Tim, it's good to see you." The burly businessman rose from the table and extended his hand. "I hope you're pleased with how things are going."

Tim shook his hand. "If I wasn't, you'd be the first to know." He winked to let Mr. Applebottom know he was kidding and motioned for him to sit. "So, you have something up your sleeve?"

"You could say that, but it'll cost you more than a parlor trick to pull this off." Mr. Applebottom leaned closer. "I have it on good authority that the watch commander's sister is being evicted from her shop this week. Failure to pay the rent."

Tim motioned to Liz for coffee. "Can't her brother pay the rent?"

A job as important as a watch commander would have significant pay, more than enough to bail out his struggling sister.

"Oh, he could have and probably tried." Mr. Applebottom

looked around to make sure no one was close enough to hear what he said next. "Someone was sending him a message."

That didn't sound promising.

Mr. Applebottom sipped his coffee and leaned back in his chair. "You never know with these royals and their games, but what they do is create opportunity for the little guys." He pointed between them. "His sister needs a new shop. You own some of the hottest real estate in town. I'm suggesting reduced rents for a year, maybe two, and a prime location."

"Do you think he'd go for it?" Tim couldn't believe it was that easy. He'd never actually bribed someone before, but it felt like there should be more to it.

Rising from his seat and polishing off his glass Mr. Applebottom smiled. "To keep the hassle of his nagging sister at bay, I'm sure the poor man would do almost anything." He reached inside his coat and produced three letters. "I've selected one of your properties and a reasonable price for it in the first one, the second and third have worse offers for you, but nothing that puts you in harm's way."

"Thank you for going through the extra trouble in case we have to negotiate." Tim looked at the letters in his hands and realized Mr. Applebottom's level of planning things out was on an entirely different level than his.

Mr. Applebottom extended his hand. "I have a few more errands to run this morning, but I'll be available should anything go awry."

Tim grinned at his business manager. "As always, the pleasure has been mine."

Replacing his hat, Mr. Applebottom stood. "Don't take too long to get there. Word of his sister's misfortune might spread. Then all the jackals will be looking to exploit the weakness."

Tim waited for the door to close behind his business manager, then rushed to his friends. "We gotta make this quick."

"Coffee in cup, snot in nose. Got it." Cassie smiled as she sipped her juice.

"Hey, if you don't mind spending a few hours doing pointless tasks you could've avoided…"

Cassie stood and bellowed, "Roberto, we need that to go."

Lorelei slapped her lightly on the shoulder. "Inside voice."

Not having to walk would certainly speed things up. He wondered if Grant had a big enough carriage for the five of them. He sent the driver a message and took another sip of coffee. The day was just getting started, and already it felt like they had things well in hand. With the jumpstart from Mr. Applebottom's work, they might be able to make it to the castle today.

Tim loved the start of a new epic quest.

CHAPTER EIGHT

Since spraying the table with nostril juice, Tim's morning had gotten considerably better.

Roberto sent them off with breakfast burritos. Tim didn't ask what everyone ordered because he was too busy inhaling his—corned beef hash with hash browns and eggs. The man even tossed in a little pico de gallo and cheese. If there was a saint of cooking, Roberto Joaquin Matherson was it. How the man blended Tim's favorite Hispanic dishes with his favorite breakfast dishes blew his mind.

With the canteen of coffee Liz gave him, he might as well have been sitting at a table at Joe's instead of trundling down the road in a carriage. Grant was Johnny-on-the-spot when Tim sent the request. He even had a carriage big enough for all of them to ride in comfort.

Three horses pulled their new ride instead of one, but Ripley was leading them. As before, the ride didn't take nearly as long as Tim expected. They stepped out of the carriage as soon as they finished their breakfast. Tim noted the anxious faces of the guards and thought he should look over Mr. Applebottom's instructions before approaching the gate.

Watch Commander Brennen is the one you're looking for. He's become a bit of a tyrant at the first gate, and his sister is a casualty of that arrogance. The man loves his sister and would do anything to help her, but no one will rent her a new shop or take rent money from him. So instead of relaxing at the gate, he's made things even more arduous by leaving her trapped in the middle.

Whatever you do, let him feel like he's winning. Start high and back down. The three envelopes I've given you are the same deal but in larger increments. All of them offer her a three-year lease with a flat rate. Red has the highest rate, which is half your normal fee. In the blue envelope is an agreement for twenty-five percent, and in green is a deal for enough to cover expected maintenance expenses and fees.

There are no strings attached to any of these offers. As long as she meets the rent and doesn't burn the place down, she won't face eviction for any reason. The documents reflect that in straightforward terms.

Tim looked up at his group and realized he should have forwarded them the message. Then he saw them all reading and nodding. Not knowing what was going on, Tim pulled up his user interface and saw the message's text added to the quest.

"It's gotta suck being a political pawn," Cassie grumbled. "It's like I wanna fly high, but not high enough everyone comes at me."

"The burdens of fame." Lorelei tossed her hair. "They aren't for everyone."

JaKobi's bark of laughter caught them all off-guard, and soon they were all laughing so hard it hurt. For the second time that morning, they all had tears streaming down their eyes. Grant watched them with a nervous smile as the guards took notice of the group.

Guy probably thinks we were hotboxing his carriage.

"Keep the carriage waiting, if you don't mind." Tim tipped an imaginary cap.

Grant nodded and tipped his actual cap. The look on his face said he had no idea what they were up to, but he was willing to drive them around to find out. "Same rate as yesterday?"

"That's highway robbery, good sir." Tim tried not to give away the fact ShadowLily was sneaking up behind him.

ShadowLily reached out and ran a finger across Grant's neck. "No one robs us." She walked in front of the man and winked out of existence.

"Come on, guys, that's not cool," JaKobi called as he watched their shenanigans. He turned his attention to Grant. "Don't worry. They did the same thing to me. Means you're part of the team now."

Cassie sprang onto JaKobi's back like a spider monkey and wrapped her legs around his waist. "Why'd you have to ruin it, you big idiot?" She smacked him on the head before jumping nimbly off his back.

"I swear it's like herding a bunch of wild cats." Lorelei fixed the collar of Grant's shirt and adjusted his cap a fraction of an inch. "There we go. Can't have you looking out of sorts if you're representing us, now can we."

The carriage driver looked bewildered, and Tim didn't blame him. He waved to get Grant's attention and produced three gold coins. "Same rate as yesterday is fine."

"This is going to be a bit more than I bargained for, isn't it?" Grant looked over the group.

Tim laughed as Cassie hit JaKobi again and tossed a Healing Orb in his direction before focusing on their newest recruit. "Who's to say, but I can promise it will be an adventure."

Grant pocketed the coins. "Then we're in." He nodded at the horse. "Ripley likes a bit of mystery, doesn't he?"

Ripley looked like going on an adventure was the furthest thing from his mind.

Tim leaned in closer to Grant. "I normally bribe them with carrots."

"What is all this commotion!" a shrill voice snapped.

Tim spun, taking in the stature of the man in front of him. Combined with the smug look on his face, this had to be the person they were looking for. "Watch Commander Brennen, I assume."

"You assume correctly." He looked over their carriage and back at Tim. "Certainly you're not here seeking an audience with Earl Dan Lilly. Not dressed like that."

All that matters is getting past the gate.

Tim tried to smile and found it lacking. He tucked the smile back where it belonged and let a frown crease the corners of his mouth. Being an alpha douche wasn't something he liked doing, but he could play the game when he had to. "I'm here to see you. I heard you've been having a little trouble with your sister."

"You little shit!" Brennan charged forward. "If you're the one behind this, I'll wring your scrawny neck."

Cassie stepped in front of Brennen, cutting off his charge and giving Tim enough time to see the armed guards moving to support their captain. At least they weren't dealing with an incident already. The fact she stopped before hitting him was a minor miracle. One he didn't plan on letting go to waste.

Turning to look at ShadowLily, Tim pointed at his neck, and she mouthed, "not the time?"

"You must have misunderstood my meaning, Watch Commander." Tim held out his arms wide in supplication as he faced the man staring daggers at him. "I'd like to help her out of the jam she's in."

Brennen's jaw was so tight it looked like it might snap from the tension at any moment. "What do you want for this help?" He spat the last word as if it tasted so vile he almost couldn't stomach saying it.

"Maybe there's somewhere we can talk that's a little more private," Tim suggested, eyeing the men behind the commander.

The Watch Commander spun on a heel and walked away. He stopped after a few steps, turned, and pointed at Tim. "You and nobody else."

Cassie started forward, and Tim put a hand on her shoulder. "It'll be fine. I'm trying to bribe him, not pick a fight."

The tank looked right past Tim like he wasn't there to address Brennen directly. "He comes back with a scratch on him; I'll rip this place apart."

"I could use a few more guards with your attitude. If you ever get tired of following around this band of riff-raff, I might have a job for you." Brennen turned away and walked toward a small eight-by-eight guardhouse.

The Watch Commander never looked back so Tim got his ass in gear. This was his chance to get past the first gate without having to go on an epic quest for the earl. If he had to rip up these contracts and give her reduced rent for life, he'd consider it as long as there was an understanding he could come and go as he pleased.

Inside, the guardhouse was even smaller than he'd imagined. The back three feet of the space was walled off. Based on the smell, Tim was pretty sure there was a bathroom in there. *Not a very clean one.* That left one tiny table and two chairs.

Tim made sure to let the Watch Commander sit first and took his seat a moment later. He noticed the man bristle when Tim didn't wait for the other man to offer. This was considerably more touchy than Tim expected. He would have to watch himself when they were negotiating.

This interaction had to go smoothly.

"So what is it you can do for my sister, and what do you want for it?" Brennen had a look on his face that was about one pound of pressure away from his eyes bulging straight out of his skull.

Drawing a deep breath to center himself, Tim thought of which tack to take and acted. "A friend of mine thought we could be of assistance to each other. I need to get past your gate without a lot of hassle, and he mentioned your sister needs a new shop."

"Just what would I be letting through this gate?" Brennen was watching him, obviously hoping for an opening that would let him kill him the deal without repercussions.

Tim smiled. If the heart of Brennan's problem was his duty to the earl, this would be easy. They weren't smugglers or trying to avoid taxes. They only needed to reach the king to make a deal.

He met the commander's gaze. "The five of us and our driver. You have my leave to search the carriage."

Some of the intensity left Brennan's expression, but he still watched Tim as if he thought he was a snake and might strike at any moment. "And for my sister?"

"I happen to own some very attractive real estate in the slums." Tim knew he screwed up almost instantly.

Brennen pushed his chair back. "You came here to mock me. Fuck you. Get out."

"I think you might've misunderstood." Tim rose, not wanting to provoke the commander further. "I own most of the revitalized section by Joe's and the Blue Dagger Inn." He slowly moved toward the door.

"Wait." Brennen spoke like he was issuing a command. "One of my guards has an idiot brother named Chris who works at the gate down there. Said it went from being the easiest job in the city to one of the hardest."

Tim stopped backing toward the door and returned to his chair. As he sat, he pulled the red rental agreement from inside his robes. "While I need to get through the gate today, your sister is free to look at the shop and reject it if she chooses. At that point,

I'd be happy to contribute some gold to help her find real estate more to her liking."

"So you're trying to get an audience with the king, huh?" Brennen had figured it out. "You know he hasn't seen a parishioner in years. I can't say I envy the task in front of you. Getting past the marquess and the duke isn't going to be this easy. As long as making no further progress doesn't upset the terms of our deal, I think we can work something out."

Tim unfolded the contract. "This is the current rate for the property and what we would charge your sister. These terms are set in stone for the next three years."

He hated doing this. It reminded him of being in sales.

"It's a better deal than I expected, but how do I know you'll honor it?" Brennen watched him for any signs of a lie. "Whoever is going after my sister is powerful, and they won't be happy with you for removing their leverage over me."

The implication being whoever it was might come after Tim. It was a good thing their inn was above the secret lair of the city's greatest assassin. He would have to tell Ernie and Liz, though, so they could increase security and keep an eye on any strangers.

"I'm willing to risk it if you are." Tim signed his part of the document. "No one will force her out on my watch. You have my word."

Brennen signed his half of the document. "Then I guess we'll see what it's worth."

Picking up the rental agreement, Tim placed it in his inventory. With a flick of his wrist, he opened the user interface and sent the attached document to Mr. Applebottom. He got a reply instantly that the storefront was open and his assistant would be there to hand over the keys if she wanted the property.

"The property manager has someone there now with the keys. Your sister is free to look over the store at any time." Tim extended his hand.

Brennen looked at the extended hand for a moment and finally clutched it. He gave precisely one hard shake before disengaging. "Let's get you through the gate. I want to see this property before you complete your business with the marquess."

The implication being if Tim screwed him over, he wasn't getting back out to the city without a fight or back in once he left.

"I'm sure she'll be delighted." Tim knew Mr. Applebottom wouldn't let him down. He hadn't done so yet. "If she isn't, you have my word that I'll help you find her something she likes better."

The Watch Commander moved toward the door and had his hand on the handle before he stopped and looked back at Tim. "Normally, I'd threaten you, but you seem like a decent sort, so I'll settle for giving you a little piece of advice. Whatever you're trying to do here with the crown, it's not worth it. If there's another way to accomplish your task, you should take it."

Tim shrugged. It would've been nice if their quest was straightforward. Go here, kill that, wham, bam, thank you ma'am, here's the Stone of Immoratis. If questing were that easy, it wouldn't end up being nearly as rewarding as it was.

They would get the stone by speaking to the king as Eternia asked them to.

"The king has something we need, and no one else can give it to us." Tim stepped toward the door. "Thank you for the advice, and send me a message as soon as you hear from your sister."

Brennen opened the door. "You can count on it." He stepped out into the courtyard shouting orders. "Open the gate, make way for that carriage."

Grant saw the Watch Commander pointing at him and jumped up into the driver's seat of the carriage, not wanting to miss their opportunity. He looked down from his perch at the others. "I think you should get inside."

Everyone piled into the carriage except ShadowLily, who waited for Tim. "How did it go?"

"Someone must be squeezing him hard because he didn't blink

at the terms." Tim hugged her, whispering in her ear, "Good chance we made a powerful enemy."

ShadowLily laughed as she pushed Tim away and toward the carriage. "Another one. You seem to collect powerful enemies like people collect Funkos."

There was no real denying it.

Grant leaned over. "Hate to break up the moment, but where are we going?"

"To the next gate, my good man, to the next gate." Tim didn't know why he liked pretending to be a bit posh when he rode in a carriage, but he did, and he was going to go with it.

The carriage rolled forward. Then they were through the gate and on their way to the next part of their adventure.

CHAPTER NINE

They were now about to travel through the earl's territory, hoping to gain access to the marquess' section of the city.

Mr. Applebottom had come through for them. Not having to do an entire quest chain for the earl would save them a ton of time. While Tim didn't have a rabbit he could pull out of his hat to get past gates two and three, getting past the first gate so quickly gave him hope that maybe this wouldn't be as arduous a journey as everyone was leading him to believe.

As they rode through the entrance, Tim kept his eyes on the buildings outside. There hadn't been much of a force on the city side, but inside were four large barracks and what must've been hundreds of soldiers. It was a stark reminder that should the kingdom fall under siege, this was one of the last three barriers before the king, and it was well-defended. While all these men worked for the earl, by default, their greater loyalty should be to the crown.

The next several blocks appeared to be housing for the soldiers' families and a small array of shops catering to their needs. The road widened as they left the guards and shops behind. Then they passed through a handcrafted stone archway, and everything changed.

The roads went from being simply cobbled to lined with multi-colored bricks. As their path changed, so did the shops. Three- and four-story shops that would've been considered small manors inside the city proper replaced the simple one-story buildings catering to the soldiers. If Tim was honest, most of the stores made Lady Briarthorn's mansion look like his first room in the slums.

It wasn't only the size of the buildings but the craftsmanship.

Each building was subtly different. It must've taken an army of artisans a thousand years to build these, and they weren't even the houses for the people who lived here, merely the shops they frequented daily.

The road turned again, doubling back on itself. The carriage passed through another large stone arch, and the land opened like countryside bordering the ocean. For the first time, he could see more of the castle than the distant towers and realized how big it must be. The castle might well be as big as the rest of Promethia combined.

The carriage trundled down the brick-lined streets at a slower pace than he would have liked, but he trusted that Grant knew what he was doing. The last thing they wanted to do now that they were firmly in the earl's territory was piss someone off and delay their adventure with a quest they should've been able to skip. It was the perfect time to fill everyone in on what happened so far.

Which didn't take nearly as long as he thought.

"So what you're saying is, it came down to probably doing some ridiculous quests or making a powerful enemy?" Cassie waited for Tim to nod before continuing. "Then you made the right choice. We get to skip the bullshit and might even get a showdown with a boss."

Spinning a knife in her palm, ShadowLily grinned. "All you have to do to get Cassie on board is mention danger."

"Tell me about it." JaKobi let out a dramatic sigh. "What's so tough about going to a place and fetching a few things when the other option is having to look over your shoulder all the time?"

Tim had to admit that since defeating the man with the orange sash and Cardinal Jepsom, sleeping through the night was a lot easier. It was nice not having to worry about when the next assassin might come calling. At the same time, they lived in one of the safest buildings in the city. Someone would have to be a fool to attack them there, and now that they had access to a carriage, it would be much tougher to ambush them in the street.

All of the best loot came from the biggest baddies. They might've opened a pathway to a new series of fights, but there was always a chance it could amount to nothing. Tim leaned back in his seat and thought about their new problem a little more.

Screwing with the watch commander's sister was a bold move. It would have to be someone with a lot of pull behind them to take such a big risk. This wasn't like a noble kicking over a beggar in the street. This was kicking a bee's nest at a hundred-pound pitbull and expecting a hug.

There wasn't a lot they could do about it now except keep their eyes and ears open. Until they had a clue, it was better to focus on the problem at hand.

"Let's worry about getting through the next gate." Tim had enough things on his mind. He didn't need it clouded with thoughts of an imaginary boogeyman.

Lorelei smirked. "Yeah, and how exactly are we going to do that? Got any more bribes up your sleeve?"

"I'd like to think of it as helping someone who ran into a spot of bad luck." Tim grinned like he stole a blueberry pie from the windowsill. "You know, instead of the whole bribery thing." Tim shrugged. His attempt at bribery was probably the most harmless one ever.

JaKobi smacked Tim on the shoulder. "Dude, you're gangster. Making deals, and taking names."

"Maybe a loan shark," Cassie quipped.

"Nah, my guy is a straight-up G." JaKobi dropped his voice and brushed the tops of his fingers against the underside of his chin before speaking. "I heard the man's sister had a problem, and I had the means to fix it. You can call that a bribe if you want. I call it being a good citizen."

The fire mage was really into it now. "That's some next-level crime boss speak, right there!" He held his hand up for a high five.

Tim followed the oldest and most sacred rule never to leave a friend hanging and slapped him five. "Damn, it feels good to be a gangster." He tossed his hands in the air. "What, what!"

"Just remember we don't have a printer for you to smash." ShadowLily slipped her knife back into her bandolier. "So maybe we should come up with a real plan."

Damn, just like that, he crashed back into Planet Earth.

As for a plan, Tim didn't really have one. He kind of assumed the game would provide them with a way to get through the gate. Then they would have to decide if they wanted to take the quest or try to find some way to sneak in. He didn't think it was worth the risk unless this turned into a shrubbery situation. Worst-case scenario, they could default to Cassie's plan and fight their way through and steal the stone.

Oh my God, they couldn't do that. What in the hell was he thinking?

"Let's play nice and see what happens." Tim tossed it out there to see how everyone felt about it.

Cassie growled. "Fine, but I need to start hitting things soon, or I'm going to go nuts."

"Hit me, baby, one more time," JaKobi sang in a squeaky falsetto.

Lorelei laughed. "Maybe after your balls drop."

It felt good that they were all back in sync despite the weird ending to their last quest. Maybe being home made things feel like they were getting back to normal. He liked laughing more than being stressed about what would come next so he let the doubts and fears he'd been harboring wash away. Whatever happened would happen, and he'd have his friends there to back him up as always.

The carriage stopped, and Tim realized he hadn't been paying attention to anything outside for quite some time. He looked out the windows and noticed neatly built barracks on both sides of this gate. While the gate was open, there weren't any other carts trying to go through. As Tim watched, a man strolled through the opening with casual arrogance. Two guardsmen trailed in his wake. The extra security marked him as the man in charge.

It was time to go.

"Cassie, best behavior," Tim chided.

The tank flipped him the bird but also gave Tim a fraction of a nod. That was all he needed to know that she got the message. Everything was ready. All they needed to do was complete whatever quest the official offered, and they were on to gate number three.

What was there to be worried about?

When Grant opened the door, Tim slipped out of the carriage and made room so ShadowLily and Cassie could quickly follow. In retrospect, he should've let the tank go first. Simply because he didn't *think* they would get attacked here didn't mean they wouldn't be.

Tim already felt himself slipping into paranoia. He nipped that shit in the bud real quick.

There was a job to do. Thinking about something that wouldn't help him obtain the Stone of Immoratis was unproductive. As far as he knew, there was nothing more important than getting back the stone. If they could shave some time by avoiding a few fights, he was all for it. If they ended up dying, it wasn't the end of the world. As adventurers, they didn't have to worry about starting over.

When death was only a distraction, Tim could afford to worry a little less.

"State your business." The leader spoke in a gruff voice.

Tim smiled and spread his arms humbly. "I'm on a mission from God."

Maybe he was feeling a little too loose.

A quick check of his user interface gave him the leader's name and title. He was now staring into the not-so-happy eyes of Gate Commander Kerr.

"Sir, if you'd like me to stab him and run the others off, all you have to do is say the word," the guard to Kerr's left said.

The man behind him on the right's face went red with embarrassment. "I'm sorry, Commander Kerr. I knew he wasn't ready for duty yet. I should've said something."

"See that he gets the proper re-education, and send someone more competent than yourself to take your place," the Commander replied coolly, never taking his eyes away from Tim.

The older man grabbed the younger guard with surprising strength and dragged him back toward the gate. "I told you a million times not to open your damn fool mouth! Now look at what you've done."

Tim pretended he hadn't noticed the exchange. "We have business with the king on behalf of the Goddess Eternia."

"There's a priest inside the castle. In fact, there's a whole damn flock of them." Kerr spat on the ground. "Why wouldn't she send one of them?"

"The goddess doesn't explain herself, but when she calls upon you to act, you do what you must." Tim kept his smile in place as the commander's new soldiers slipped into place behind him.

Kerr glanced at the two men and smiled, clearly impressed with the other man's choice of replacements. "With no paperwork, I'm afraid there isn't much I can do for you. You'll have to turn around and be on your way."

That was the one response Tim hadn't considered. He assumed they would offer them the quest right away.

"There has to be something we can do for the marquess to gain access to his lands?" Tim tried not to let the desperation creep into his voice, but he wasn't sure he succeeded.

Negotiating from a place of weakness was never a good starting point.

"By the looks of it, you can't handle much. He isn't in the habit of granting access to vagabonds." Kerr looked down his nose at them.

Cassie snarled. "Please tell me I can crack their heads together now."

JaKobi reacted before things could spiral out of control. With his arms wrapped around Cassie's waist, it was hard for her to lunge forward. Quicker than a fox, Lorelei was there to help him, while ShadowLily kept her eyes on the guards.

There wasn't much hope of them getting through the gate without an incident. Tim tried not to sigh as he thought about what Plan B might look like. There was a whole lot of open land out there, and if they waited until nightfall, there was a chance they could sneak through without being seen. All they needed to do was make it inside the castle grounds, and they'd be under the protection of the temple.

The earl, marquess, and duke wouldn't be able to make them do any more quests once they were inside the castle grounds. They had enough on their plate to deal with without adding the three most powerful nobles in the land and all their problems to it.

ShadowLily talked about making powerful enemies, and here he was thinking about making three more out of the most powerful men in the kingdom. Facing the unknown was one thing. Opening themselves up to this kind of trouble bordered on suicidal. There had to be a way to save this situation before things spiraled out of control.

Tim flashed Kerr an award-winning smile. "Can we take it from 'I'm on a mission from God' and go from there? Or maybe you have some injured men I can heal or milk a hundred cows.

There has to be something the marquess needs done that would grant us temporary access to his territory."

Kerr's sneer was growing to epic proportions. If it grew any larger, it might fly off his face and attack Tim by itself. One of the guards whispered into his ear, and the gate commander took on a more thoughtful expression.

"Is it true that you defeated the kobolds under the inn in the slums?" Kerr watched him, only occasionally glancing at Cassie to make sure she was under control.

To her credit, Cassie seemed to have calmed down, but her eyes were fixed on Kerr as if the next words out of his mouth better be spoken with kindness, or she was going to fuck up his day in a really bad way.

"Yes, we squashed them right out of existence." Cassie pointed at the bigger guard. "I'd be happy to give you a demonstration on him."

Kerr ignored Cassie and continued speaking to Tim directly. "I can't speak for the marquess directly, but I believe we can work something out. Get back in your carriage, and I'll lead you to his estate."

"Please, don't try to run. I'd hate to have to kill you at what might be the start of a promising relationship." Kerr still looked down on them, but his tone had a minuscule edge of respect to it now, instead of the total mocking disdain it carried earlier.

Tim bowed low. "I'll make sure to stay in the carriage. I'd hate for my death to mar an otherwise promising partnership."

He didn't wait to see Kerr's reaction. Instead, when he rose from his bow, Tim turned and walked straight back to the carriage. There was something deeply ingrained in his personality that wouldn't let him be anything but a smartass. Sure, he could contain it for a minute, maybe even a few hours, but eventually, it spilled out like verbal Ebola. People either loved it or hated it, and by extension felt the same way about him.

Sarcasm is a misunderstood art form.

Kicking himself about his smart mouth wouldn't make things better, and if Tim was truthful, he rather enjoyed the encounter. He got to drop in a line from *Blues Brothers*, and it wasn't easy to fit those into everyday conversation and have it be true. He was on a mission from the goddess, whether they wanted to believe it or not.

As soon as the carriage door closed, Cassie was on him. "What's the plan?"

"We're going to go to the marquess, and we're going to accomplish whatever task he sets for us." Tim leaned back in his seat and tried to relax.

"Within reason," ShadowLily quickly added as she looked over at her friend. "We need to make sure we get what we want, and the terms of the deal are clear. I don't want to get caught in a loop where this asshole keeps sending us on jobs until we give up."

He hadn't thought of the NPCs as devious, but thinking back on his encounters in the game, they clearly could be. The damn NPCs seemed to have the same motivations and many bad behaviors that people shared in the real world. Unless he was accepting a quest from the goddess, he would have to start paying more attention to fine details.

"It's not like we have a choice." JaKobi snapped his fingers, and a small flame sparked in the air. "There's no way we make it past all these men and another layer before they catch us."

Lorelei snickered. "Maybe for you."

"Don't even get me started," ShadowLily griped.

Tim tried not to smile. "I have some stealth too."

"I can light stuff on fire with my mind." JaKobi held his fingers to his temples and closed his eyes. "Ummmmmmm."

Cassie snorted. "Stop that shit. I can't stealth either. Plus, sneaking isn't my style. Problems need to be met head-on and smashed into submission with my staff of good intent."

"By calling it good intentions, she thinks it hurts less." JaKobi grimaced and rubbed his shoulder as if thinking of a time where her good intentions had hit him.

Cassie leaned in and kissed the fire mage. "I never said it hurt less, only that it was for your good." She leaned back and snapped her teeth shut.

"Warrior woman." JaKobi grinned. "Trust me. It's worth it."

Lorelei brushed some imaginary dirt from her shoulder. "I have a pretty good idea of how to take care of a warrior woman. Just ask Neema."

JaKobi's mouth dropped open as he thought about the two women together. Cassie gently reached over and pushed his chin up, causing all of them to laugh except the stunned mage. His cheeks burned bright red, and Tim was pretty sure steam wasn't far away from shooting out of his ears.

"Damn you lesbians. It's like you know it's super hot because we can't be involved." Tim tried to take some of the attention away from his friends.

Lorelei winked. "Yep, that's why we tease you with it but trust me, your man parts, not what we're into."

"Never even been tempted?" ShadowLily looked at one of her knives.

Lorelei looked at Tim and JaKobi. "Not once, girl! Some people are bi or bi-curious, not me. I like the ladies, and men are just big, smelly, and gross. Don't even get me started on those balls."

"Hey, balls are glorious. They even have their own song." JaKobi joined the conversation again, the tint of his cheeks slightly less red than a burning volcano.

Cassie snorted. "So one band out of all time wrote a good song about balls, and that's all you can ever refer back to."

"That and *Ow My Balls* on Idiocracy." Tim laughed. "Pure comedic brilliance."

Lorelei giggled. "I think we have a very different idea of what constitutes brilliance."

"It's got electrolytes." JaKobi's face was back to its normal shade.

Tim looked him dead in the eyes with a solemn expression. "We're certainly not going to feed our plants that stuff from the toilet."

ShadowLily smirked at him in the way that said his antics amused her, but it was time to wrap it up.

"So best behavior when we meet the marquess, and we'll take any quest he offers as long as it gets us past the gate and not stuck running errands for the rest of our days." Tim looked at Shadow-Lily for confirmation and received a nod.

Cassie grumbled, "If he tries to screw us, can I hit him?"

"Watch ShadowLily. She's your conscience." Tim looked at his girlfriend and hoped she understood that in no uncertain terms was she allowed to let Cassie bonk the marquess on the head with her staff.

ShadowLily moved to sit next to her friend and gave her a little hug. "I promise that if we do his quest and he still tries to screw us, you can rip his head off."

Not quite as gentle as a good bonking.

"Really?" Cassie smiled. "I've always wanted to hit a noble."

ShadowLily nodded. "But not until I give the all-clear."

"Don't worry, Cassie, if this guy tries to pull one over on us, I'm right there with you. Nothing I like better than putting a smug asshole in its place." Lorelei gave her a nod that said she'd crush that man into oblivion if he didn't honor the terms of the deal.

Tim cracked up almost uncontrollably. For some reason, he had a picture of a guy stepping up behind his lady and her butthole screaming, "This ass is way too fine for you."

He finally got himself under control and realized everyone was staring at him. "You don't even want to know."

"You're going to tell me later." ShadowLily put a hand on one of her throwing knives. "Or I'm going to get in a little target practice."

Tim gulped as the carriage stopped. "Looks like we're here." He didn't wait for Grant to open the door. He unlatched it and leapt out.

Hopefully, he could think of something better than his butthole joke when he spoke to ShadowLily later.

It didn't take long for Commander Kerr to appear. His sneer was less pronounced now, but he clearly didn't value them more than a spider he'd smash beneath his heel. "This way."

The marquess' estate was fantastic. It reminded Tim of the old castle grounds in England, or not a castle so much but maybe the prince's summer estate. Not that you could call the place small. It was a Tudor-style house mixed with a fortress. There were barracks inside the courtyard, with one more gate separating them from the marquess' actual estate.

The gate opened at their approach, and they followed Kerr as his heels *crunched* against the ground-coral walkway. Large topiaries dotted the fantastic lawn and garden. Tim could imagine hundreds of men and women dressed in bright, colorful garments milling around as they waited for their host's appearance. It was the kind of thing that would fit in any romance novel or historical war piece. The closer they got to royalty, the more he felt like one of the Three Musketeers.

Not that he carried a sword, and thankfully guns didn't exist in *The Etheric Coast.*

The guards at the front door opened them wide at their approach. One of them leaned in and whispered to Kerr, "The marquess is expecting you in the study."

The commander never broke stride or acknowledged that the guard had spoken as he continued inside.

They passed several armed guards as they walked through the house, as well as countless support staff. Tim wondered if it was worth having a big residence if it cost a fortune to pay for the upkeep. Cleaning their little fifteen-hundred-foot house was hard enough. A twenty-thousand-foot McMansion probably never stopped being cleaned, and by the size of the yard, he didn't expect a much different result for the maintenance outside.

All of that work so the person could use two or three rooms a day and maybe never use the yard for a single thing. It seemed like pure madness, but if there was a better display of wealth, he didn't know it. Everything inside the home reeked of expense. He liked some of the decor, but his overall feeling was that it was too much. He'd love to have a small house with a larger plot of land someday, but nothing like this.

Kerr opened a door for them and stood aside. "Marquess Dan Gunthar and his aide Uni are waiting for you."

Not wanting to miss a chance to make up for his behavior at the gate, Tim gave the commander a half-bow. "Thank you for seeing us this far, Commander Kerr."

"Of course." Kerr inclined his head a fraction of an inch. "I'll be waiting for you outside."

While he was speaking with Kerr, the others had filed past him into the study. Tim wound up standing in the hallway alone and quickly moved after them. The last thing he wanted was for Cassie to make their initial introduction.

Tim took in his surroundings as he walked at a brisk pace. They left him calling the library at his college a stack of books. A study to him was a room with a desk and a few bookshelves. This room would've made a museum jealous. The mountain of knowledge contained in these tomes probably had JaKobi salivating. For him, it was another sign of excess. If the marquess sat in this room for a hundred years, he couldn't possibly read a third of the books it contained.

They came out of the stacks into a wide room dominated by a fireplace against one wall and a row of windows along the other. Tim had a momentary flashback of his time inside Lord Rictor's estate and crushed it down so he could focus on his mission. He had the distinct impression that not giving the marquess his full attention would be a huge mistake.

"The Captain said you were an interesting looking bunch." A woman moved forward with her hand outstretched.

Cassie shook the proffered hand. "Uni?"

"My apologies." The woman bowed. "I'm so used to everyone knowing who I am that I forgot to introduce myself." She pointed at herself. "I am Uni, and this is the Marquess Dan Gunther."

The marquess grunted in acknowledgment of his title. "I understand you want to get through my gate." He let it hang there for a moment. "I have a task for you to complete to test your strength before I know how to make use of your services best. Then we can find something appropriate to secure your passage."

Quest Received: Super Slasher

There is a small group of monsters the marquess needs vanquished. Find and exterminate their leader.

Quest Reward: The chance for small talk and another quest.

Tim snorted as he dismissed the quest. He would rather die trying to sneak across the marquess lands than accept the quest on those terms. "I'm sorry we've wasted your time. I'll ask Commander Kerr to show us back to the gate."

Uni stepped forward and whispered something in the marquess' ear before stepping away.

"Oh, very well."

Quest Received: Super Slasher

Go to where I tell you, kill everything.

Quest Reward: Ten gold coins and access to another quest.

Tim was able to control his dissatisfaction this time but picked up the small shake of ShadowLily's head, reaffirming his decision not to accept this quest either. He rejected it. "It seems to me that a problem your guards can't handle would be worth a little more. If we Super Slash the Slasher, we want through the gate with unfettered future access. As a bonus, next time we travel through your lands, I'll heal any of your soldiers that have been wounded free of charge."

"You could if they weren't all dead," the marquess roared.

Uni stepped forward. "We don't know that for certain. Some of them could still be alive."

"Bah!" He waved her away. "I'm done playing games. This is my final offer."

Quest Received: Super Slasher

The marquess' grandson Nephram led a small contingent of guards to handle what appeared to be monster tracks in the marquess' territory. They tracked the creatures back to an entrance to the sewers. After sending a man back to report he was entering the sewers to pursue the creatures, Nephram was never heard from again.

Go into the sewers, kill whatever evil you find there, and return for your reward.

Quest Reward: Access to the marquess' lands.

Bonus: If Nephram is alive and safely returned to the marquess, he will let you select an item from his hoard.

Tim accepted the quest. "We'll leave immediately. I hope we can bring Nephram home unharmed."

"Just kill the damn things and be gone." The marquess sighed. "Get it done before my fool son runs off to try to do it himself."

"As you command." Tim turned and left, motioning the others to follow.

Uni moved into the middle of their group. "I'll escort you to the entrance and inform Commander Kerr of his new orders."

Tim let Uni take the lead as they followed her out of the mansion.

CHAPTER TEN

The entrance to the sewers wasn't what he expected at all.

They were standing at a small field bordering on some marshland. Tim had to admit, he kind of thought he'd be dropping down a utility hole cover and fighting in the tight confines of a small tunnel until they reached a boss. Instead, he faced a completely different scenario. His mind kept screaming, this isn't the sewer entrance from *It*, but he couldn't help but notice the similarities.

We all float down here.

The only thing missing from the entrance was a couple of red balloons. If he saw one of those pop up, he'd probably turn around and join Team Cassie. He'd rather fight a thousand soldiers than face off against a supernatural clown.

Commander Kerr was talking about the sewer system, but Tim completely tuned him out in his panic. All he could do was stare helplessly into the darkness behind the iron bars. He wondered if they'd put the bars in place to keep people out or something in.

"Beep, beep, Tim." JaKobi looked as creeped out as he felt.

Kerr realized they weren't paying attention to him and handed Cassie the key before storming off.

Cassie looked at the two robed men huddled together. "You guys are such pussies."

Planting her hands on her hips and staring them down, ShadowLily added, "We've been to a ton of places scarier than this. Get it together."

"Help me out here." ShadowLily pointed at Lorelei. "Tell them it's just a hole in the ground, and there's nothing to worry about."

Lorelei moved to stand with Tim and JaKobi. "I'm with the cowards on this one."

"Just for the record, my first time trapped underground, I almost got turned into wraith-food." Tim looked at the entrance and back at the two women. "As long as I have two tough, strong, independent women to lead the way, I'm good to go in."

Cassie snorted. "That kinda sounded like an insult, and yet I'm all of those things so it better not be." She spun her staff. "Let's do this."

"Did any of you hear what Kerr had to say?" Tim asked, wondering if he missed a piece of vital information while he was trying not to imagine the girl from *The Ring* crawling out to kill him.

Lorelei moved next to Tim as Cassie headed toward the gate. "Don't worry. You didn't miss much. You're probably going to die, don't fuck this up. I vouched for you. You know, the normal 'I don't care about you unless it affects me' type of stuff."

"So, no big help." Tim felt a wave of relief.

Cassie put the key in the lock and pulled the scratchy iron gate open. "Or maybe Kerr got tired of no one listening and left before he could tell us something important."

"It doesn't matter. We have something with us that none of Kerr's men had." Tim pointed at JaKobi. "Lights."

"And then there was light." He threw his hands into the air with a magician's flourish, and five brilliant orbs flew into the sky and hovered above them. "Each of you has a light for the duration of the buff."

Looking down, Tim saw a few small icons appear. Each of them appeared grayed out to a different extent, but he was pretty sure all buffs lasted eight hours now. So before going inside, it would be a good idea to recast theirs. Tim also set a timer to check his in seven hours. He hoped this part of the quest didn't take that long, but he didn't want to get caught in a battle without all their buffs.

"Buff check," Tim called as he cast Armor of Eternia.

With their buffs in place, Tim took the key from Cassie and locked the door behind them. If there were monsters outside that might try to get back in, the door might slow them down enough that the group didn't end up in a pickle. It was time to start moving forward so they could see just what kind of trouble the marquess had put them in.

Tim handed the key to ShadowLily. "If we all die and you manage to stealth out, I don't want you trapped in here until we get back."

The assassin wrapped her arms around him and kissed him. "True love is what brings us together today."

"That and the smell of shit." Cassie walked away. "Let's see what we've gotten ourselves into."

JaKobi clamped his nose with his fingers. "When she's right, she's right."

"I'll remember that next time you're bleeding out." Tim extended his hand and dropped it in mock exhaustion. "I couldn't make it in time."

"Seriously, man, take a big old whiff." The fire mage shook his head like he didn't really want him to do it.

Tim was pretty sure if he was going to smell something awful it would have already hit him, but JaKobi was in front of him so he inhaled deeply through his nose. JaKobi farted.

"Gross, man." Tim waved his hand in front of his nose. "I take it back, no more heals, not ever."

Cassie couldn't resist piling on. "Same goes for sex. Farters aren't sexy."

"I would've been on your side." Lorelei coughed. "But I'm back here too."

"No sex and no heals makes JaKobi a dull boy." Despite his cavalier words, the fire mage's shoulders took on a serious slump as he walked behind Cassie with his head down.

The tunnel they were in was about ten feet wide and twelve to fifteen feet high. There weren't any walkways or railings above them. Ankle-high marsh water flowed gently past them as they moved deeper into the sewer. At least, Tim hoped it was mostly marsh water and not the shit he'd been trying to smell when JaKobi ripped one in his face. His outfit wasn't exactly waterproof, and walking through actual shit was way outside his comfort zone.

If Tim had a safe word, he'd be screaming it now.

Slowly and surely they kept moving deeper into the darkened tunnels. The bricks were gradually phasing out for chunks of rough-hewn stone. The polished stone walls turned coarse, and soon what they stood in looked a lot more like a cave than a sewer system. The marquess might've pulled one over on them despite what Tim thought was some pretty solid negotiating.

It felt like the tunnel turned them in a full circle and was now heading downward. The water flowing past Tim's ankles was fast enough that his feet left little eddies as he splashed from one spot to the next. Part of him wanted to jump up and down and splash everyone, but they were making enough noise as it was, and anything could be waiting for them up ahead. Plus, if he sprayed poop on ShadowLily, he'd end up on the no-sex list like JaKobi.

No one wanted to be on the no-sex list, not ever.

Cassie stopped at the head of their group, holding up a single closed fist. No one ducked like in the old army movies, but they all gripped their weapons tighter as they moved into formation behind the tank preparing for an attack.

"Guys, you gotta check this out." She motioned for them to join her. "Babe, send one of your lights down there."

JaKobi stepped forward and stopped when Cassie's arm caught his chest. He sent his light out into the darkness. "That's the most badass thing I've ever seen."

"Makes that slide at Sooper Summers look like a Slip-n-Slide." Tim peered over the edge. "I mean, it has to be a slide, right?"

ShadowLily popped into existence right behind him. "Only one way to find out."

The hands on his back were firm and unrelenting as they shoved him forward, but Tim decided that when life threw a giant water slide at him, it was best to embrace the chaos.

Turning his awkward shove into a magnificent belly flop, Tim screamed at the top of his lungs. "Cowabunga!"

There was no way to know what was happening behind him now. Once he hit the slick wet stone shaped like a water slide, he was moving too fast to do anything but try to get his feet in front of him. Headfirst into a rock at this speed and he'd be right back in Barbara's office looking at a picture of his head exploding on a rock.

He let out a nervous laugh, then started to enjoy the ride. It was like they were going down a drain but in the most fun way possible. He had no idea how they'd ever climb back out, but the ride was worth it, even if they had to die to escape.

The angle of the slide shifted, and now Tim felt like he was almost flying.

It wasn't only the speed of his descent that had his attention but the roar of what sounded like a waterfall. *Slides didn't end in waterfalls, did they?* Tim flipped around on his belly so his feet were pointing down, and from there it was simple enough to flip onto his back.

His heart raced as he picked up momentum, but the ride was

awesome. The developers should've sold tickets instead of tucking the waterslide behind a boss fight. Tim tried to stay in the middle of the chute so he didn't flip over the side and hoped the ending was as pleasant as the trip down.

Everything flashed black for a moment, and when the light returned, the slide dipped to a sixty-degree angle.

"Is that a waterfall?" Tim screamed as he flew off the edge and out into the vast nothingness.

His legs wheeled through the air in shock for a moment. Then he pulled them in tight as he regained his composure. "I always wanted to be a Navy SEAL!" He crossed his arms and braced for impact in the giant pool of water below.

He didn't know much, but there was one universal truth when it came to badassery, and it was simply that Navy SEALs were a cut above the rest. He'd never been the kind of guy to do that thing in real life, but he was proud to know there were people out there willing to risk it all to protect his freedom. He wasn't a real hero. He only played one on the Internet.

Still, that was what video games were for. Nothing beat the feeling of victory or defeating evil, of being the hero of the story. Inside video games, they could do in hours what those men and women trained for years to accomplish. Hell, he was doing it now, and if he managed to save the marquess' grandson, Tim would have a moment of being the hero.

Water wasn't exactly soft when a person fell from high enough. Tim found that out with clarity as his legs snapped up and almost hit him in the face. Falling from a great height also sent him deeper into the pool than he expected, and it wasn't like he'd been holding his breath on the way down. He needed to get to the surface and pronto.

It might not have been the best idea, but swimming in his robes was tough, so as he pushed toward the surface, Tim unequipped his gear. He broke through the surface and took a giant gulp of air as another splash sounded to his right. Looking up, he saw three more bodies sailing through the air. JaKobi was flailing his arms madly as he rushed headfirst toward the surface. Lorelei pulled herself into a perfect dive, and ShadowLily matched the ranger's form almost to a "T."

He reflexively ducked as they splashed down around him. Not that ducking would've helped. If any of them had landed on him, there would've been two dead members of the Blue Dagger Society floating in the underground lake.

Cassie broke the surface next to him with a scandalized smirk on her face. "Are you naked?"

His cheeks blazed crimson as Tim realized the water down here was crystal clear, and with all their lights just above the surface, it was pretty easy to see. While he probably should've left his boxers on, it was easier to take everything off than one item at a time.

Right now, he was more worried about treading water. "My robes were heavy." He equipped his underwear but not before those coming up from below would have gotten a good look.

"I see some shoreline." Lorelei didn't care about his junk. She wanted to get dry. "Let's get out of the water and figure out where we have to go."

Tim followed her. "Let's go radio silent until we know if it's safe down here. I don't want to get into a fight without all my gear."

Silent as a drop of morning dew falling off a blade of grass, they swam forward, keeping their arms and legs below the surface and their heads barely above it. It wasn't the most efficient way to swim, but they were in enemy territory, so it paid to take precautions. As they made their way onto the dry ground, each of them unequipped and re-equipped their gear.

His clothes didn't seem to sop up the moisture very well, so he used his robe to dry off and re-equipped it as a perfectly clean and dry garment. Using the old inventory trick was almost as good as having a towel.

Cassie looked at him with a bemused expression. "Feel better now?"

"Not until we find you something to hit so you can get off my case." Tim pointed into the dark cavern. "Go smack something."

"It's about time. Let's Shake 'n Bake this shit." Cassie moved into the dimly lit space with her bō staff in hand.

It was dark down here even with JaKobi's lights. Like walking in the woods with a candle dark. The illumination was strong enough while they were all clustered together, but more than thirty feet outside their circle, the world might as well have stopped existing. Tim kind of wondered if this is what it would feel like for the first people to travel the far ranges of the galaxy.

It had to be scary wondering if there was anything else out there or just more black.

Something scuffed against the cavern floor in the dark. All of them froze instantly. Nothing was running straight for them, so the light wasn't attracting it. Behind them were little patches of fluorescent mushrooms. Their lights must have somehow activated them. The cavern was gradually coming to life all around them. Their energy was powering up the green fluorescent fungi.

JaKobi reached out to touch one. Cassie slapped his hand away. "Don't even think about it."

"Of course not." He backed away, but as soon as Cassie turned her back, he snipped one of the mushrooms off and slipped it into his inventory.

Tim didn't say anything. They'd been hanging out together for a long time, and the fire mage didn't strike him as the kind of guy to trip out on mushrooms, so why try to stop whatever quirky experiment he had planned?

"What made that sound?" Tim whispered. "Maybe Cassie should investigate."

The tank turned to look at him and glared. "Sometimes I feel like a sacrificial goat."

"Don't worry, when I have those kinds of jobs, I send your

boyfriend." Tim said it with a straight face. He was rather proud of himself.

Lorelei snorted but instantly stopped when something roared.

Tim pointed farther into the cavern. "Go do goat things."

Cassie was mere seconds away from knocking his teeth out, but the roar of the monster charging at the group stole her attention away. She ran toward the sound but stopped before an intersection of branching corridors. The tank leaned against the wall and waited for the threat to appear.

Nothing happened for so long that Tim was starting to think maybe she'd been Medusa'ed. Then she turned.

A message flashed across his user interface.

Be quiet and get up here.

All of them moved forward and huddled behind Cassie, but they didn't need to hide. The monster lurking around the corner was blind as a bat. Actually, the creature didn't look like it had eyes to begin with. So, maybe blind wasn't the right term to use. Tim watched the monster for a few more seconds, trying to find it in his internal lexicon, but he hadn't seen anything like it before.

If pressed to give an example, he would've said the thing could've been an orc or an ogre. It was a humanoid hybrid of some kind, with legs and head all where you'd expect them to be. The arms were a different story since there were two fully developed sets of them. Living in a cave miles underground might explain the lack of eyes. The thing also looked strong, as if it could bench a trio of NFL linemen with either set of massive arms.

A rat ran across the cavern floor. The creature whirled, zooming in on the sound. It ran across the cave on its legs and two of its arms, using the six limbs in unison until it snatched the rat from the ground. With a twist, the monster broke the rat's neck and ate it.

JaKobi moved his light a little farther down the passageway. They spotted broken bits of armor and blood strewn across the cavern floor.

There had been a great battle here, and recently.

If there was any chance of finding a survivor, they had to move quickly. "Cassie, do your thing."

The monster roared as it homed in on Tim's voice and galloped straight at the healer.

"Sooner would be better," Tim pleaded when the tank didn't jump in front of him right away.

Cassie smiled. "It's always nice to be appreciated." She charged toward the monster. "Come get a slice of this!"

The monster never knew what hit it. Fifteen seconds later it was dead. Cassie looked down at it. "Not much of a challenge."

"I'm guessing there are more of them." JaKobi looked around, but nothing jumped out at them.

While they had a moment, Tim inspected the creature. Now that he was closer to it, he could tell its skin wasn't black at all. The monster was purple, almost like a Drow. They'd faced something similar once before. If the underground parts of the marquess' territory didn't connect to the rest of the city somehow, it would mean there were things down here they hadn't seen yet.

At least the caverns were web-free. He'd had his fill of half-spider people.

The fact that they were running into trash mobs this early was a good sign that there was a boss of some kind up ahead. If these creatures were protecting the boss, it would be the kind of encounter that had the potential for epic loot. After their last quest was kind of a bust, he was ready to earn some new rewards.

A series of screams echoed through the cavern as more of the creatures charged into the intersection. Tim stood, taking one final look at the deceased form and noting it was called a Necro-Cog. Then they were fighting. Just like a single NecroCog, this next group of three didn't stand a chance. None of the creatures had weapons, and it was going to take way more than three of the fuckers to give them a hard time.

The risk here was getting too comfortable.

"Cassie, you're in charge. Lead us to the boss, but don't pull more groups than you can handle. DPS, please focus on killing whatever Cassie is hitting first." Tim tapped his staff on the ground with authority. "I'll keep you alive."

JaKobi nodded at the tank. "You heard the bossman. Let's get it done."

"Just try to keep up." Cassie ran into the next cavern full tilt.

ShadowLily sprinted past with a grin. "Oh, this is going to be fun."

"Always with the running." Tim huffed as he tried to keep pace with the others.

CHAPTER ELEVEN

"That's a big boy." ShadowLily let out a low whistle as she gazed upon the boss.

Tim was thankful that the boss couldn't hear them outside its zone. A thin film of shimmering light separated them from the boss. Once they entered, it would lock them inside until they were victorious or dead. For the first time in a while, it was nice to see what they were facing before they had to try fighting it.

A quick inspection showed the boss was called King Hundari. There wasn't any other information or race available. Tim still thought they'd evolved from a curse like the legendary Drow. These creatures might have once been orcs, but now they were something else. All of the trash they faced was sightless, but that didn't mean they had problems trying to find what was hitting them.

If the monsters had come at them in great enough numbers, they would've easily won the day without some quick thinking from their tank. Cassie set a pace where the group only had to face three or four of the monsters at a time. At one point there'd been six, and that was when they finally had to slow down. It was better to save their energy for the big dance.

The room King Hundari was sitting in must have been his throne room. This was indicated by the giant chair carved out of the cavern wall. The king's throne barely looked large enough to contain Hundari, but Tim was pretty sure if he sat on it his feet would dangle three feet off the ground.

Bigger baddies got bigger chairs.

Tim stifled his chuckle as he kept his eyes moving around the space to see everything he could without triggering the fight. The shimmering barrier separating them from the boss almost made him feel like he was looking through the cascade of a waterfall, so he couldn't make out nearly as much as he would've liked.

There was always the possibility of a servant's or guard's entrance at the back of the room. Tim also wouldn't have been shocked to find out there was a hidden surprise or two waiting for them. He didn't see any other structures or seats, so there was no way to be sure without going in. The throne room was mostly a wide-open space, not offering any hints of the mechanics to come.

It didn't look like any of the marquess' men were waiting inside. It seemed odd that after the initial signs of battle they hadn't seen another trace of the missing people. They had to be down here somewhere. Going back with the grandson in tow would get them an extra reward, so hopefully, they still had time to save him.

Time to get to work.

Tim turned toward Cassie. "It's your show. Lead the dance, and we'll follow. I'll call out changes as I see them coming."

Grinning from ear to ear like taking down a new boss was better than Christmas morning, Cassie stood her full height. "You heard the man, bitches, let's get down to funky town." She struck a pose like *Saturday Night Fever* and walked through the barrier.

Tim and the others entered right on Cassie's heels. The veil flashed for a moment and turned red. There was no backing out now. King Hundari was about to find out what it meant to be inside the circle of death with the Blue Dagger Society.

News flash, the king was about to get his ass kicked.

Once they were inside the shimmering barrier, Tim realized the glittery substance had disguised more than he thought. A large pool of water dominated one side of the room. The surface of the pond was still, but he heard water roaring somewhere in the distance. It was the same sound he'd heard approaching the waterfall but too far away to be a hindrance right now.

The king himself was another thing entirely.

He was at least twenty feet tall, and the shimmering wall that separated them from the boss had also hidden the third set of arms sprouting from above his shoulder blades. The extra pair was smaller than the other two. However, Tim's eyes were drawn instantly away from the arms and right to Hundari's crown.

The golden circlet held a single pearl, but instead of being set above the rim, the larger-than-normal pearl hung below it, almost making Hundari look like a cyclops. The king slowly rose from his seat. It didn't take a rocket scientist to see the swords strapped to his hips and the knives crisscrossing his chest.

"It is not so often my kingdom receives so many uninvited guests. The deep rejoices in your sacrifice." A bit of drool dripped from King Hundari's jaws. "One of you must stay. The rest must go below."

A low thrum of growls filled the edges of the room as hundreds of the four-armed creatures swarmed outside the faint red glow of the boss chamber. The NecroCogs beat against the barrier sending waves of sparkling energy crackling all around. Tim followed one arc of power with his eyes until he saw an armored leg sticking out from behind the throne. The boot was gone, and some of the toes were missing.

It was a rough reminder that in nature, everything is kill or be killed. As humans, they'd outsourced the killing part. They went to the store to pick up some meat, never having to think about the fact an animal died to put it there. He imagined a grizzly bear felt the same way when a line of hikers walked through the forest.

Prepackaged snacks.

Tim didn't want to be a snack.

To make sure he didn't end up as trail mix, Tim tried to be smarter than the average bear. In this case, his biggest fear was they would go into the fight expecting the king to be blind when he could see them. Lifting a hand high into the air, Tim waved to get the king's attention. If Hundari noticed him, they had their answer.

"We have a volunteer." King Hundari started forward.

Tim backed up a step, almost running into the barrier. "Uhh, I'm not volunteering for snack duty, only wondering if you could see me."

Hundari stopped moving forward. "Yes, with this gift from the Lady of the Depths, I can see. My kingdom is expanding daily. Soon we will take the fight to the surface dwellers. The meat sticks will pay for their treachery."

"I think he's referring to the full plate mail soldiers as push pops." JaKobi looked like he thought that was the funniest thing in the world. "I really hope if I have to visit my caseworker, it's before I get turned into a meat stick."

Tim ignored the fire mage and waved to get the king's attention again. "Are you sure we can't reach a deal?"

"The lady demands much for her gift. One of you will be mine. The rest must descend. Any who fight will be crushed for food until the rest relent. My minions are hungrier than usual after losing their last feast. I hope you fight well, so they can feed as I have."

The king inclined his head to the leg sticking out from behind the throne. "The last group of meat pops gave up one of their own willingly enough."

More drool leaked from the corner of the king's mouth.

They'd come looking for a fight, and they were going to get

one. Tim certainly didn't want to end up as an after-dinner snack so he looked at Cassie and gave her the code phrase. "The wolfman has nards."

"You guys and your balls. I thought we discussed this already." Cassie gritted her teeth as she looked up at the self-proclaimed king. "Listen here, Pearl Vision, we're not fucking meat pops!"

Cassie ran forward, and Tim started casting.

The first thing he did was make sure Curse of Giving was active and that he was in his Way of the Boulder stance. Then he blasted Cassie with a Healing Orb, all before she clashed with the king. ShadowLily had disappeared, and JaKobi and Lorelei were waiting to ensure the tank secured the boss before joining the fight.

With Who Needs a Shield becoming more of a cleave buster, Tim didn't have much else to do until the damage started pouring in. He might as well get his big hitter out of the way while things were going well so he cast Behold My Power. Then he checked to see if the boss had any beneficial buffs for Rectify to remove. Not seeing any listed, he settled for casting a round of Healing Orb as the damage feedback from his curse took effect.

King Hundari had his two swords out and worked to keep Cassie and ShadowLily at bay while two of his other arms used the knives to deflect Lorelei's arrows. JaKobi's spells, on the other hand, were incredibly effective, but the two arms sprouting over the king's shoulders were starting to twitch.

Tim wasn't sure what was about to happen, but it sure looked like the start of a boss mechanic. He wondered if this was one he should interrupt or if he should let it go and see what happened. Behold My Power was about to hit, and he didn't want anything to screw up his chance at a big DPS burst. He went with his gut.

"Disturbance!" Tim pointed at the king, and his arms stopped twitching.

Hundari flashed bright red and shoved Cassie aside, charging straight for Tim. A look of murderous rage rippled across his features as he ignored everything in pursuit of the healer. Whatever attack he stopped with his interrupt must've been important enough to trigger a rage mechanic.

Next time he'd have to let Cassie take the first interrupt to avoid running for his life.

Tim waited until he saw the king commit to a swing, activated Quick Feet, and sprang away to safety. He ran in a wide circle avoiding the others until Cassie was between him and the king again.

Lorelei noticed the change in mechanics and followed Tim in his mad dash across the room, but JaKobi was so focused on his DPS that he missed the fact Cassie didn't completely control the boss. With everyone else tucked safely behind Cassie, the king did what any boss worth fighting would do. He turned his attention on the person doing the most damage and prepared to ruin their day.

JaKobi realized the boss was running toward him after he clapped his hands above his head, sending the burning Phoenix screaming toward the king. Hundari used his swords to block the attack, but the heat washing over his arms left blisters. That made the king scream even louder as he rushed to end the fire mage's life.

"Guys!" JaKobi called. "This isn't going to end well."

Tim cast Who Needs a Shield and switched the target of his stance from Cassie to JaKobi. Then he splashed the fire mage with a Healing Orb as Hundari broke through the hastily built wall of fire Tim's friend tried to erect. Their chances of coming out of this alive were getting slimmer by the moment.

The king's swords came down in a violent arc. Tim wasn't sure if he was going to be able to handle all the damage. Going back to the marquess with their hat in hand wouldn't yield the results they needed. Before they got another shot at this fight, they might get stuck doing ten fetch quests.

This might also be their only chance to save Nephram and gain the unlimited access they needed.

Something wrapped around JaKobi's waist and yanked him to the side as the swords crashed into the stone where he'd been standing. Cassie had the chain she kept around her waist out, and she'd used it to pull her man to safety. The fire mage was bleeding heavily from a cut on his arm, but it was nothing a Cleanse and Healing Orb wouldn't fix. As soon as their fiery friend was stable, Tim switched his stance back to Cassie.

King Hundari looked at the spot where JaKobi had stood and the notch the rock created in his sword blade. His body shook with anger as the boss ignored all the damage they were doing to him. There was no way to know what would happen next, but Tim had the feeling something big was coming.

"Stop kissing your girlfriend, and start lighting things on fire." Tim cast a bolt of Divine Light to emphasize his point.

Cassie ran back toward the king with her staff held high. "You're jealous because you've never kissed during a fight."

"Need tank. Hit by boss bad." Tim grunted a few times to make himself sound like a caveman.

Lorelei let an arrow go that split into six different arrowheads right before impact. "What's in the fuck is the boss even doing? It's like he glitched out or something."

Tim followed Lorelei's gaze back to the king. Hundari broke from his daze and rushed to the edge of the pond. When he reached the water's edge, all the damage they were doing stopped hitting the boss. This was the start of a new mechanic and one they couldn't stop.

There wasn't anything Tim could do so he checked the boss' stats. At some point, Behold My Power had gone off. He was becoming so accustomed to the additional damage he didn't even realize when it stopped coming in. He wasn't sure if it was his spell or Lorelei's, but Hundari was sitting at an even seventy-five percent health. The dip in health must have triggered a boss mechanic.

"Stay behind the little lady and try not to die." Tim looked around nervously as he watched the water's surface.

Cassie stopped twenty feet from the boss and stared at him as he smashed the flats of his swords against the surface of the water. "What in the hell is he doing? It's like watching a five-year-old throw a tantrum."

The swords continued slamming into the water. Tim noticed that with each strike, some of the blood from Hundari's wounds dripped onto the surface. Each hit spread it farther into the pond where the current would pick it up.

The wounds on the boss' arms started to close, but his health didn't go back up. As the last of the slashes in his skin sealed, Hundari started chanting.

The bastard was summoning something.

"Something's coming out of the water." JaKobi sent one of his orbs deeper into the surface of the pool of dark water. They all saw the bubbles as they frothed against the surface.

Cassie took a couple of steps back, creating space so she could react to whatever was coming next.

"Servant of the Depths!" King Hundari called as he ran back to his throne, pulled the armored leg from under it, and tossed it toward the bubbles. "I need your strength."

Tentacles moved across the water, and nestled in their grip was the largest ax Tim had ever seen. The weapon was custom-made to be swung by four arms. He'd never seen anything like it. The metal was black, but a vibrant blue lined the blade's edge.

He instinctively knew it was either poison or sharpened with magic.

Dropping his swords at the edge of the water, King Hundari bent down to take the ax from the tentacles. He lifted the weapon high above his head and whispered in awe, "You honor me, great one."

Hundari turned to face the group and shook the massive weapon above his head. The ax blade was so large it almost looked like a scythe. When he *swooshed* the blade through the air, it had the same effect. Tim was happy Cassie was the one who had to step in front of the weapon. If he tried to block the attack, Tim was pretty sure the blade would cut right through his staff and send him back to Barbara faster than he could scream, *oh shit.*

Their tank was as fearless as ever.

"You know what they say, the bigger the weapon, the smaller the…" She brought her staff down with a vicious twist, turning the attack at the last second so it came in under the ax and right at Hundari's knees.

There was a *snap*, and the king fell, clutching his leg. "You never really have to finish that sentence. Once the secret is out there, you can't contain it."

The ax pulsed in the king's hands as he climbed back to his feet. The smile he'd worn when they first entered the chamber was gone. In its place, the NecroCog wore a mask of utter loathing. Tim imagined the boss probably felt like he would have if the shrimp in his cocktail started talking back to him.

There was nothing left to say. This was a battle for life or death. The king came at them with everything he had.

They were better.

Tim had worried that their next encounter might blow their socks off, but the fight was going great. The monster in the pond was lingering at the back of his mind. He didn't know if the creature would be a further part of this fight or next up on the chopping block when they finished.

The damage King Hundari was taking seemed to have dwindled since he picked up the ax. If they wanted to come out of the encounter on the winning side, they needed to find a way to pick up the pace. The new weapon pulsed every so often. It must've been healing the boss with each flash. It felt like the ax restored three percent of the boss' health for every five they chipped off.

Slow and steady would've been fine, but the new weapon's higher damage was eating into Tim's mana reserves. He couldn't afford to fall behind this early in the fight. They needed to change the narrative or flip the script to come out on top.

Tim's user interface didn't show a buff he could remove, and he already used his interrupt. They would have to keep grinding. Slowly they moved around the room in a deadly dance. As the boss' health dipped closer to fifty percent, Hundari retreated toward the dark water.

ShadowLily took the king's retreat as a personal affront and did her best to make him pay for every inch as he tried to reach the pond. The last thing any of them wanted was the monster in the water to use some kind of magic to summon a suit of magical armor to go along with the ax.

King Hundari roared with rage and the small arms sprouting from his shoulder blades started to twitch again.

"Interrupts!" Tim called to the group.

Maybe they'd already used theirs, or maybe no one else had an interrupt, but the king's hands finished their twitching motions and whatever spell he'd cast threw all of them off their feet. As they stood back up, Tim realized a DOT had hit all of them.

A quick look at his interface showed JaKobi's health was the lowest so he started by casting a Healing Orb on him. The master-rank healing spell didn't remove the DOT, so he cast Cleanse.

Cleanse stopped the spell from ticking so Tim focused on Cleansing everyone before he sent out more healing. With the bulk of the incoming damage halted, he turned to find out what the boss was doing.

King Hundari strode into the waters of the pond, offering himself to the creature and begging for help. The boss wasn't taking damage again, and while Tim needed to recharge as much mana as possible during this phase, he couldn't waste the down-time by not getting everyone back to one hundred percent health.

Healing rain fell from the ceiling as Tim cast Healing Storm on the group. The spell did its job taking care of the rest of their wounds in a matter of moments.

The sound of Hundari slapping the water with his arms as he cried out to the creature brought all their attention back to the fight. Lorelei fired an arrow, but it winked out of existence at the water's edge.

The tentacles of the beast had been caressing the king, coaxing him gently forward, but now they tightened around him. The shock on Hundari's face would have been priceless if he wasn't so damn terrified. The king fought against the creature's grip and tried to make his way back toward the shore, but the monster had him firmly in its clutches. There was no escape.

"No!" King Hundari cried as the tentacles swept him under the surface.

Tim watched as the boss' hands flailed, splashing great swaths of water around as he was dragged under the surface inch by painstaking inch. It must have been his imagination, but he swore he could still hear the king screaming although his head was underwater. One by one the king's fingers disappeared from the surface, and the water went deadly still.

Whatever was happening under the surface wasn't going to be good for them, but there was nothing they could do to stop it. "Cassie, be ready for anything."

"Like I'm ever not ready." The tank had her feet spread in a wide defensive posture as she watched the surface for any sign of where the boss would come from. "I can't wait to introduce the business end of Mrs. Norris to this fucker."

Lorelei was smirking as she moved into position. "Mrs. Norris?"

"Like the cat." JaKobi had a twinkle in his eye that said, see I'm rubbing off on her. "That's fantastic."

ShadowLily looked kinda mad. "Why that cat? Mrs. Norris is the kinda girl who would ruin all our fun."

Cassie spun her staff in a giant swirling circle. "Because Mrs. Norris doesn't take shit from anyone."

Bubbles erupted from the center of the pond. It made what

they saw before when the creature brought the ax look like someone opened a can of soda versus Niagara Falls. The bubbles fell silent almost as fast as they started. Then there was a small burst and another closer to them. Something gradually rose to the surface.

At first, Tim couldn't tell what it was, but then he realized it was King Hundari emerging step by awful step. He wouldn't have had any clue it was the same man except for the fact the pearl on his crown still hung in the center of his forehead.

Barnacles covered the sides and top of the king's head. Coral patches coated sections of his body like armor. The stubby little arms sprouting from Hundari's shoulders were replaced with twelve-foot-long tentacles. Tim couldn't even begin to explain the change that came over the NecroCog. He only knew that when magic was an option, things didn't have to make sense to be happening.

Cassie roared and smashed her staff on the ground. "If I wanted calamari, I would've ordered take-out."

Laughter bubbled out of Tim like it was the funniest thing in the world. He doubted the king even knew what take-out was so Cassie's boast meant nothing to the boss. One look at the boss' coral armor and big-ass tentacles was enough to wipe the smile from his face. When he reached down and picked up the ax out of the shallows, it sobered his mood completely.

Tim double-checked to make sure his Way of the Boulder stance was on Cassie and sat back waiting to see what would happen next. Their best bet for damage was still JaKobi, but Lorelei had switched to using more of her stylized attacks and was catching up nicely. The new armor could put a dent in things, though. They needed to find a way to stop the ax from healing the boss as they tried to end this. That or knock his bloody crown off.

Holy shit.

Could they knock off his crown and make the king blind again? Tim had the feeling the king had grown so accustomed to his magical sight that if they removed it, he might not be able to recover before they took him down. If they were really lucky, it might even break the magical link between Hundari and the ax.

Tim didn't believe in miracles. He believed in the grind.

The battle was raging at full speed, and Cassie was taking a considerable amount of damage compared to what she had taken before Hundari's transformation. Tim quickly reapplied Curse of Giving and blasted Hundari with Divine Light to give Cassie a small health boost and him some satisfaction.

ShadowLily was having a rough go of it.

Trying to stay as damage-free as possible had the assassin spending as much time avoiding the tentacles as she did DPSing. Her damage was helping, but the tentacles hindered her more than either of them would have liked.

Playing a melee character wasn't for the faint of heart.

There was nothing he could do to boost her damage unless his plan to dislodge the crown worked. "It's time to cancel Pearl Vison. I want that shit broken or off his head, now!" Tim barked out the order like a drill sergeant on his recruits' first day of boot camp.

He always loved it when he took charge, even if it was for only a second.

Cassie's next hit smashed King Hundari right in the face. His crown lifted for a moment but slid firmly back into place. If they were going to make this happen, they were going to have to coordinate their attacks. Tim scanned the room, looking for something that would give them an advantage.

Where was ShadowLily?

The assassin appeared as she launched herself off Cassie's shoulders and straight toward the boss. The king brought the ax up to block her, but somehow she twisted, avoiding the blade by a fraction of an inch. She hit the king with a *crunch*, wrapped one arm around his neck, and grabbed the crown with the other.

Two seconds later, she was flying across the room with the crown in hand and a huge portion of her health missing.

"MY EYE!" King Hundari screamed as he fell to the cavern floor and wildly patted the ground around him, searching for the crown.

The boss had totally forgotten about them as he wailed.

"Attack!" Tim blasted the king with Divine Light.

The rest of the group descended on the king like he was the last size eight at a bridal blowout sale. Hundari couldn't do anything to defend himself against their relentless assault, and without the ax to boost his health, it was plummeting quickly. It didn't take long for the boss to hit twenty-five percent.

Almost to the instant that the king's health passed the threshold, the coral covering the king exploded like a shrapnel bomb and blew the entire group backward. Hundari moaned in pain as the parts of his flesh destroyed by the attack knit themselves back together. The boss' health dropped to fifteen percent, then ten. Tim stopped watching and focused on his job. The coral hadn't been kind to any of his group's health.

Not seeing any status effects that needed cleansing, Tim cast Healing Storm. It was a bit flashy and certainly not cost-effective, but the fight was almost over. Plus, it was the fastest way to get all of them back to one hundred percent health. Finishing his cast, he looked up feeling satisfied with himself and realized how much trouble they were in.

The creature from the pond was slowly becoming visible. Two eyes on giant stalks rose above the large oval-shaped head. Tim didn't see a nose, but there was no missing the ten-foot-wide mouth with enough razor-sharp teeth to make Jaws jealous. The monster had two long tentacles and about six others about half of the length above the surface. Tim clearly saw hundreds of smaller tentacles churning in the water.

Fucking thing could probably crawl right out of the lake.

The longest of the creature's tentacles closed around Hundari's leg and dragged the king into its feeding pool. The boss screamed and struggled against it, but with his health so low and his vision missing, there wasn't anything he could do to fight off the tentacle monster. His hand closed on the ax, but when he swung it at the beast, it winked out of existence as if it had never been there in the first place.

A voice filled the chamber. "You have failed me for the last time, Hundari. Back to the darkness."

The king gave a final scream as the monster sucked him under. The creature sank until only its eyes rested and uppermost tentacles rested above the surface. Then the first horrible *crunch* reached their ears, quickly followed by another. As blood spread through the water, it was clear to all of them King Hundari was no more.

"You have defeated one of my minions and thus deserve a small token of respect. Leave now, and I shall spare you. Continue into the darkness, and only death awaits you."

Tim felt weird speaking to the air. He was pretty damn sure whatever the voice was it wasn't coming from the hungry tentacle beast. "What of the men we came looking for?"

"They have been given to the deep and are of no consequence." There might have been a hint of annoyance to the voice now.

He looked around at his team and knew instantly they were all resolved to see this through. He looked out over the pond, not sure of what to focus on besides the monster. "Then I guess we'll see you soon."

A scream of incoherent rage filled the room. Rocks fell from the top of the cavern but nothing big enough to send them to their caseworkers. The water bubbled again, and the creature that had remained hidden for most of the fight started to emerge. One thing continually screamed through Tim's mind as he prepared himself for a battle.

Don't let it pull you into the water.

"Don't get dunked!" Tim shouted to the tank.

Cassie glared at him as she prepared to tangle with the boss. "Super helpful as usual."

"It's also clearly magical so watch your ass." Tim hoped the tank remembered how the boss helped Hundari with the ax and the armor.

Cassie looked at her man while waiting until the creature reached the edge of the water. "Ugly ass thing looks like a Kraken had a baby with a Beholder."

"I've never been prouder," JaKobi called after her as she ran toward the boss.

Tim got to work hitting Cassie with a Healing Orb as she crashed into the boss. Then it was time for Curse of Giving. A quick check of his status bar confirmed that Behold My Power hadn't reset when the bosses changed and wouldn't be up for a while. So far, only ShadowLily and Cassie were taking damage so he might be able to start contributing more DPS.

The guardian's eye stalks twitched like Hundari's upper arms, and Tim wished he had another interrupt. "Can anyone stop the attack?" He heard the desperation in his voice and wasn't ashamed of it.

A beam of pure white fire blasted from JaKobi's hand, but the spell didn't reach the boss in time. A wave of green energy pulsed out from the guardian, and they all started taking periodic damage. Tim cast Cleanse on himself and the tank before he realized it had no effect.

There didn't seem to be a timer on the debuff so it would keep ticking until they died or won. Normally this would be the point where he used Healing Storm, but it was the perfect chance to test out the benefits of hitting the master ranks with Healing Orb.

Tim cast Healing Orb on ShadowLily, then on himself. He watched as the Rehydrate buff applied, and the Splash effect spread it to two other people. In this case, two casts spread Rehydrate to everyone in the party. The HOT wasn't enough to erase all the damage, but it did minimize the effect of the boss' attack.

While the rest of the group was busy doing damage Tim continued casting Healing Orb where appropriate, constantly rotating the large single target part of the heal to whoever needed it most. He was casting the spell so often that all of them would keep the Rehydrate buff indefinitely. Part of him thought about switching to his Way of the River stance, but for the moment, he had everything well in hand.

The eyestalks started twitching again.

"Who's got an interrupt?" Tim hoped everyone hadn't already blown theirs. For the next fight, they were going to have to come up with a rotation.

"Mine's down," Cassie and JaKobi said simultaneously.

ShadowLily shook her head.

"I must be a level behind you guys because I don't have one yet." Lorelei looked pretty pissed about the fact she was missing such an important skill.

The second wave of green crashed into them and the debuff they were suffering from now hit twice as hard. The guardian of the dark was at thirty percent health, but the race was officially on. They didn't have the interrupts to stop the guardian from continuing to stack the buff, so they had to kill it before Tim ran out of mana to heal.

Tim flipped into Way of the River, spreading the healing from his damage-dealing spells and curses to the entire party instead of just Cassie. Quickly reapplying Curse of Giving, Tim scanned the field to see who needed the most help. Cassie was getting hit harder without the extra defensive buffs, so he started there. In a few more casts, it became apparent the tank was the only one he needed to keep an eye on until the third wave came.

When the boss hit fifteen percent, it sent out a double wave of green energy. All of them were now suffering from four stacks of the debuff, and things were getting out of control. Just tossing Healing Orb around wasn't cutting it anymore. They were all losing health at a rate Tim couldn't keep up with. Even if he squandered all his mana, the damage coming out was too much for him to handle alone.

The guardian of the deep hit ten percent, and another double pulse of energy hit them.

With six stacks of the debuff, they were all getting hammered. Tim cast a round of Healing Orb, followed by Curse of Giving before throwing up his arms and channeling Healing Storm with everything he had. Either they were going to die now, or this would be enough to see them through.

"Come on, Barnacle Bob, fucking die already!" Tim closed his eyes and pushed every ounce of himself into keeping the spell channeled.

He was so focused on what he was doing that he didn't realize the fight ended until a flash of golden light forced his eyes open. The beautiful motes of light swirled gently through the air as he fell to the ground in exhaustion.

King Hundari and the guardian were dead. The way below was open.

CHAPTER TWELVE

"That chest has all kinds of shine to it," Cassie said as she wiped some tentacle slime off her shoulder.

Tim looked at the glowing golden chest and felt a wave of relief wash over him. Not only had they won, but there was loot. Big, fat, shiny loot. Entering the sewers was so vital to their quest that loot almost seemed like an absurd bonus.

One he was more than willing to partake in.

"Then you better open that mother up before someone else gets there first." Tim pretended to run for the chest.

Cassie liked to go first. It was kind of her thing. With all the loot being individual, it didn't matter what order they went in, but sometimes he liked to mess with her.

In actuality, he liked watching the others get loot as much as he enjoyed getting his. When his friends' faces lit up with joy as they got an epic drop, it kinda made him all tingly. Every piece of gear the group received as an upgrade made his job as a healer easier. A little extra armor and health never hurt anyone's chance of staying alive.

Cassie walked toward the chest. "What is up with this weird-ass dungeon? We faced a one-eyed king and a tentacle monster."

"Sounds like a rock band," ShadowLily said as she popped back into existence right next to the tank.

Lorelei laughed and put a sultry expression on her face. "Or a cheap porno movie."

"I don't know what kind of porn you watch, but mine doesn't have tentacle monsters." Tim's cheeks reddened as he realized what he said.

"Mind on the loot people," Cassie gruffed. "And off my tentacle porn."

Still snickering, the tank placed her hand against the chest and let out a sigh of ecstasy. Cassie turned to look at them and smashed her new bracers together like a gladiator. "Bracers of the Endless Night. Crazy high magical resistances and a small bonus to my deflection skill."

"Damn girl, you look like a warrior princess." JaKobi looked like he was imagining doing the horizontal limbo with Cassie and Xena at the same time.

The fire mage laid his hand on the chest and looked back at the guild. "Belt of the Lucid Dreamer. Magic resistance and converts a small amount of my damage into health."

JaKobi tied the belt around his waist. "At first, I was afraid I wouldn't be satisfied, but with this belt around my waist, there is no reason to hide. No, no. I will survive. The more gear I get, the more I want to carry on. Hey, hey."

Everyone froze in place.

Yes, they were all singing *I Will Survive* in their heads as he sang, but none of them expected what happened and they were all stunned.

JaKobi looked confused as he glanced up from examining his belt. "What?"

"Why don't we let Ms. Gaynor sing the song, and you can go

back to working on those bitching dance moves." Cassie poked him in the ribs to emphasize her point.

"I thought you banned me from dancing."

Cassie looked right into his eyes with all the love she could muster. "If this is the alternative, you can dance your little heart out."

ShadowLily did the JaKobi shuffle as she moved toward the chest. "Plus, I always liked your dancing."

Tim laughed. "Of course you do. It looks a lot like mine."

"I don't know how both of you ended up with men with no rhythm, but it's impressive exactly how little they have." Lorelei smirked like all men were missing the kind of rhythm she desired.

ShadowLily waited as Lorelei moved to take her turn at the chest. "At least they aren't as bad as Elaine on *Seinfeld.*"

"That's like saying, worked out better than it did for the dinosaurs, every time an asteroid hits." Lorelei settled her hand on the chest. "Leather Jerkin of the Twilight Dancer."

The ranger equipped the black leather armor. "Boost to accuracy and damage from a distance greater than seven yards."

Tim wasn't quite ready to let things go, especially when he had a brilliant idea. "JaKobi, when we get back to the inn, let's work on a dance for our next chest opening. It'll be epic."

"I want to stop him because he's my man, but I also want to see what happens." Cassie was trying not to snicker at the thought of their synchronized dance moves.

ShadowLily took her turn opening the chest. "Girl, sometimes you have to sit back and let it happen. That's what wine is for."

"Headdress of the Silent Night. Boosts my stealth and damage from behind." ShadowLily equipped the gear. It looked like King Hundari's crown, but instead of gold it was black metal, and where there was a pearl, the assassin's new circlet had an onyx stone cut in the shape of a diamond.

It was Tim's turn to have a date with the loot fairy, so he moved toward it with reckless anticipation. Everyone else received a pretty good piece of gear or something useful to their class so he wondered what the game had in store for him. There was always a chance he could get a bad roll, but there was also the chance it could be epic.

Tim rested his hand on the chest.

Item Received: Greater Staff of Yin, +3 Endurance +7 Intelligence +7 Wisdom

The Great Deceiver Yin spent his days walking the earth claiming to be a healer, but where he went, only suffering followed. You see, for Yin to heal, he must take the life from someone else. After an incident that left a member of minor nobility scarred, they burned Yin at the stake as a warlock. One of his apprentices managed to save his staff, and now the Staff of Yin lives on with you.

Special Effect: From light to darkness

For ten seconds, all healing caused by doing damage will receive a ten percent boost. Can be used once per encounter.

Tim looked at the dark wooden staff and couldn't do anything but grin like an idiot. This item was more than he expected from the fight. He was thinking gloves or maybe boots, but to get a main hand weapon was always a cause for celebration. Plus, it looked fucking awesome. The wood separated at the top almost like tree branches, and hovering in the center, not touching any of the branches, was an onyx orb.

The globe hummed with power.

Tim looked up and realized everyone was looking at him, waiting to hear something about his new staff. "Greater Staff of Yin. Boosted stats, and a special ability for more healing in a time of need." He tapped the butt end on the ground with authority. "It's pretty badass."

"I can hear my new weapon calling." Cassie lifted a hand to her ear and leaned out as though she was listening hard. "Go kill whatever is down below and it will be yours." She turned and looked at Tim. "Let's go already."

"Was that a *Field of Dreams* moment, or do I need to check you for dark influences?" Tim reached toward her.

Cassie smiled, but it was the kind that promised pain if he didn't back off. "How fast do you want to lose that hand?"

"And she's back." Tim clapped his hands to get everyone's attention and pointed at the pond. "As for who's going in the water first, not it."

"Not it," JaKobi snapped almost instantly.

Lorelei looked like she couldn't believe she was being this childish but didn't want to be first in the drink. "Not it."

ShadowLily and Cassie almost said it simultaneously, but Cassie lost out by a fraction.

"Like it wasn't going to be me going first anyway. It's kind of my job," Cassie grumbled as she dipped a boot into the water.

A few uncertain steps into the pond, Cassie disappeared. Seconds later, she came to the surface spluttering. "Watch that third step. It's a doozy."

"Cannonball!" JaKobi shrieked as he ran for the edge.

The fire mage's robes disappeared mid-leap, and he grabbed his knees. The splash was big enough it sent Cassie back under the surface. Tim waited for a few moments, making sure they weren't going to be slaughtered by another tentacle monster and ran for the water. He jumped out as far as he could and tried to dive, but it ended up being half a belly flop.

"It's kind of warm." Tim spat out a mouthful of surprisingly clean-tasting water.

ShadowLily and Lorelei shared a glance, and both of them instantly switched from their gear into bikinis.

"After our trip to the desert, it seemed smart to pick up some swimwear." ShadowLily dove into the pool much more gracefully than he managed to.

Lorelei walked into the water, searching for the false edge with her toes. "Cassie has one too."

"What?" JaKobi's head spun so fast he missed Lorelei plugging her nose with one hand and jumping in the water with the other above her head.

Cassie already had her suit in place. "To be fair, when I jumped in I thought there might still be monsters."

"That's fine, baby. Later we can ditch these losers and come down here for a swim." The fire mage made flames dance across the surface of the water.

"Save that sexy stuff for later. We still have a boss to kill." Cassie kissed JaKobi.

"And some people to save." He kissed her back.

ShadowLily and Tim put their hands on the shoulders of the kissing couple and dunked them underwater.

When the two of them came up looking mad, Tim pointed into the darkness. "Let's try to focus. If King Hundari and the guardian were the warm-ups, whatever is waiting for us down there is going to be fierce."

Lorelei swam deeper into the pond. "I hope there's another slide."

"This time, I want to go first." Cassie dove under the surface and took off like a dolphin.

Tim swam behind them at a more leisurely pace, thankful that he wasn't going to get thrown headfirst onto the slide this time. *If there was a slide.* The pond led to a large crack in the back cavern wall.

Not a lot of room in there.

There was roughly two and a half feet of space between the water's surface and the top of the passage. Not the kind of thing he'd swim into in real life. Not without a big-ass rope tied around his waist and some scuba gear handy. It took some effort, but he talked himself out of being scared by repeating that it would be stupid for the game to bring them here only to drown them now.

"Tell me it's not under there." ShadowLily looked worried.

Lorelei pulled a flower from inside her leather vest and let it go on top of the water. The flower flowed under the crack. "Looks like."

"This slide better be the shit." ShadowLily drew a big breath even though she still had plenty of room to breathe and ducked into the crack.

Tim swam up beside her and gave her hand a brief squeeze. "Is the current getting stronger?"

Not the reassuring thing he meant to say, but right after he squeezed her hand, he felt a tug at his feet like the water below him was picking up speed.

JaKobi flew past them with a huge grin on his face. "Maybe it isn't a slide. Maybe it's something better."

"I love his endless fucking optimism." Lorelei swam past, trying to keep up with the fire mage.

Cassie passed them next. "Come on, can't do much without our best DPS and healer."

Tim looked over, pulled ShadowLily close, and kissed her. The others were too far away to stop them, but he heard JaKobi call "Hypocrite." He kept kissing her as the water turned into a torrent. They held each other as they went over the edge of the waterfall.

CHAPTER THIRTEEN

"Shouldn't they be attacking us?" Cassie looked down the hallway lined on both sides by thousands of NecroCogs.

Tim knew how she felt. Seeing so many enemies not attacking them or trying to stop them from advancing toward the boss was off-putting. There also was a sense of finality as the creatures closed in behind them, cutting off their only means of escape. It was enough to make anyone feel a little jumpy.

"I never imagined there would be so many of them." JaKobi didn't sound scared at all. It was more like he wanted a chance to study the creatures closer. "Them letting a meal walk past means whatever is waiting for us ahead is going to be awesome."

We have very different ideas about what's awesome.

Still, the fire mage was right. There was something abnormal going on here. As they approached, all the NecroCogs dropped to their knees and lowered their heads to the floor. The creatures didn't rise again until the ones already trailing behind them passed.

"Let's hope when we kill the boss it doesn't set these things free." Lorelei didn't have her bow drawn.

There was no point in having their weapons out. If these creatures swarmed them now, they were dead. It was like when a swarm of zombies picked off the slowest human. That didn't stop Tim from pulling out his new staff. If he was going to go down, he was taking one of these things with him. What he really wanted now was to get to the boss and get all these eyes and teeth off his back.

It felt just like the first time he stayed up all night playing Resident Evil 3: Nemesis.

In the game, the player would be going along, taking down zombies with headshots and searching for clues, and suddenly Nemesis would show up, and they were fucked. All a player could do was run and try to get somewhere safe until the showdown. It wouldn't be long until the Blue Dagger Society reached their showdown. It was too bad Mila Jovovich wasn't going to be there to see him throw down.

Maybe he could find a seamstress to make ShadowLily that red dress from the first movie. He didn't know what it was about badass women that got his attention, but they sure did. From Lara Croft to Katniss Everdeen, he was completely smitten.

Every single time.

Tim pulled his mind away from fantasy-isle long enough to see that their journey was quickly ending. The long corridor they were traveling down ended in a large dome-like room. It was almost like walking into an arched cathedral a mile underground. The NecroCogs stopped at the room's entrance and waited. The thin film of shimmery light that separated the boss fight from the rest of the world descended from the dome, sealing them inside the room. Normally that would have freaked Tim out, but in this case, it made him feel at ease. At least they didn't have to worry about the army of NecroCogs anymore.

In the very center of the space with the only light beside theirs shining on it was a solid black lectern with a purple leather-bound book sitting on top of it.

"Books, my nemesis," Cassie grunted as she shoved JaKobi forward.

Tim laughed and finally started to feel like himself again. The tank had been brushing up on nerd culture but mostly through the brilliance of cinema. Books weren't for everyone, and that was fine because everyone who's anyone knew the book was always better than the movie. So when she was ready, JaKobi would pull her to the dark side.

Sure, there were a few exceptions to the rule, but not many.

"What's in the book!" Tim cried in his best Brad Pitt *Seven* imitation. "Seriously, guys, I'm not sure we should touch it." He stopped far enough away that there was no chance he'd brush against it.

Lorelei pointed off to the right, and in the distance, Tim barely discerned some cages, with a few men still moving around. Hopefully, one of them was Nephram, but if it wasn't, they would still take the survivors with them back to the marquess.

No one deserved to be a NecroCog snack.

"If we can't touch the book, how do we start the fight?" JaKobi's fingers twitched.

Tim knew it was only a matter of time before the fire mage reached out to grab the book regardless of what he said. "Maybe we can kick it over."

With his best Bruce Lee imitation, Tim flexed and kicked the lectern. His foot crunched into the black rock and almost snapped. He fell to the ground clutching the limb in agony.

"No one else try kicking," Tim hissed as he cast Healing Orb on himself.

Cassie nudged the book with her staff, sending it clattering to the ground. "You know you had a big stick in your hand, right?" She turned to look at ShadowLily. "And he's supposed to be the smart one."

The book flew from the ground and back into place. It rested there for a moment, then the cover flipped open, and pages started turning at an inhuman rate. Everything went calm as though they were in the eye of a tornado, then wind rushed through the room again until the book settled on a page with a single word written on it.

Croatoan.

All he could think about was Roanoke Island where every single man, woman, and child disappeared off the face of the earth. Sure there could've been simple explanations for why the only people on an island would disappear in the middle of winter from a fortified fortress that showed no damage, but he couldn't think of one. When Tim thought about the lost colony, there was always a more sinister twist, maybe even something demonic. If the real world still held such mysteries, what would they find in the game?

The book called to him. It screamed for him to read the word.

"He's not going to do what I think he's going to do, is he?" ShadowLily tried to pull Tim away, but he held his ground.

Cassie motioned for everyone else to get behind her. "Get ready."

There was something he should have been doing, but what was it? The book on the lectern looked interesting. There was a certain beautiful glow about it he never noticed before. That word on the page looked like it would roll eloquently off his tongue. All he had to do was say it.

"Croatoan," Tim whispered.

The room snapped back into focus, and Tim realized he was standing by the book alone. Where was everyone else? How had he not noticed what was going on? He didn't like to brag, but his situational awareness was normally spot on.

He turned and saw the rest of the group huddled behind Cassie. They all looked scared and were motioning for him to join them as if something big stood right behind him. If they were looking at him like that, it could only mean one thing. The boss had spawned behind him.

Without a second thought, Tim activated Quick Feet and ran toward safety.

Only he didn't move.

His mind turned back toward the only important thing in the room. The book on the lectern called to him, and he didn't know why everyone else was so scared. The boss wasn't here, only a well-loved storybook.

Tim rushed toward it and reached out. Pain lanced through his shoulder, making his arm numb. He tried to ignore the pain as he reached for the book with his other hand. Its pages would protect him. The book would save him from himself.

What harm could come from reading a book? As soon as his fingers were flipping through the pages, everything would be fine.

"Son of a biscuit-eating donkey," Tim yelped as the pain radiated through both of his shoulders and dropped him to his knees.

His mind cleared enough to reach a conclusion, and he activated the special ability on his new shoulder guards. Clarity washed over him in an instant, and Tim scrambled away from the book as if it were a puddle of blood containing the Ebola virus.

When he was safely behind the rest of the group and breathing easier, he pointed at the book. "What in the fuck was that?"

"You're asking us? I almost shit." JaKobi slapped him on the back with relief.

A voice thundered from the top of the dome. "This could've been easy for you."

The book snapped closed.

JaKobi looked around and cast lights all around the room. "I don't like the sound of that."

"Instead, you will die in a way that I find entertaining before I call in the horde to clean your bones from my floor." The voice came at them from every direction.

Cassie smashed her staff onto the ground, making the room shake for a moment. "Big words, coming from something too scared to show themselves."

"If you give us the prisoners and your word not to venture to the surface in the future, we might let you live." ShadowLily stood boldly, daring the boss to make an appearance.

It was then that Tim realized how much he loved her. She'd seen what the boss had almost done to him with the book. Now she was goading the boss into action because she wanted some payback. Those were the kind of feels you couldn't buy for money, and he knew for sure that what they had was the Real Deal Holyfield.

"If you want my snacks, you'll have to go through me." A leviathan of mist rushed out from the back of the cavern.

The dragon stopped twenty feet away. As the mist dissipated, a woman strode forth to meet them. Her skin was white as ivory, and her hair and clothes were blacker than midnight. In her hands, the Witch of the Depths held a staff much like Tim's. The hungry look in her eyes promised that they would suffer before they died.

"She's probably wondering why he didn't finish reading the book," Cassie grunted.

Lorelei snickered as she pulled her bow free. "It's a real problem. It's like kids forgot all that shit they Google is called reading, and you can also do it for fun."

"Kids, how old are you?" JaKobi held up four fingers and a closed fist.

The ranger flipped him the bird. "I'm going to find the biggest bag of dicks and beat you to death. Fuck off with that forty nonsense."

"Thirty-nine," ShadowLily mouthed from behind.

JaKobi mimed zipping his lips as the boss spoke again. Tim was thankful the fire mage had the good sense to drop it. Not everyone liked reminders about how many trips they'd made around the sun.

"Even now you mock me. Let me show you the error of your ways." The room flashed red as the witch cast her first spell.

They had been having too much fun on the swim over to set an interrupt order, and Tim really wished he remembered to bring it up as he saw Cassie and JaKobi both blow theirs at the same time.

"Everyone else, save your interrupts." Tim looked at Lorelei. "You have one now, right?"

The ranger grinned as she nocked an arrow. "You just say the word, big boy."

"Hey!" Tim patted his belly. "Unless you mean the other thing." He lowered his hands as though he was cupping two big balls.

"Don't you even sing that fucking song." Lorelei fired an arrow that flew suspiciously close to his head.

Tim turned away from the ranger and made sure Way of the Boulder was on Cassie, and got ready to cast Curse of Giving once she had control of the boss.

A scream of rage washed over them, freezing their entire group in place for three seconds while they took periodic damage. When the spell she cast on them broke, the Witch of the Depths pointed her staff at Cassie and blasted her with a spray of black mist.

Dodging to the side saved Cassie from most of the damage. It was a good thing, too, because taking that full blast might've eaten half of the tank's health. They couldn't afford to fall behind the curve this early in the fight. If that was the witch's opening salvo, this encounter was going to be a metric shit-ton harder than the last one.

What had they been thinking, pissing off a witch that lived in a cave surrounded by some kind of orcish troglodytes?

There wasn't time to worry about how they ended up here. The fact was it didn't matter what they faced. This was their only choice if they wanted to complete Eternia's quest, so they had to do it. At least they were only taking on her and not her entire army of NecroCogs. The boss alone was no slouch. Shit hit like a freight train.

They were going to have to up their game.

"Stay loose but focus the fuck up!" Tim called as he cast Curse of Giving and Healing Orb.

He scanned the field. Then something hit him from behind. Standing back up, Tim cast Healing Orb on himself and saw JaKobi and ShadowLily were also recovering from a blow from behind. The next time the attack came, he saw it clear as day and still couldn't get out of the way. Some attacks you couldn't dodge, but usually, they didn't come accompanied by a knockdown.

Then there was the damage.

This attack was eating up his health as fast as a school of piranha took down a cow. Cassie was doing the best when it came to damage mitigation, but Tim topped off her health with Healing Orb.

The two other women used their high dexterity to avoid a large portion of the damage, but JaKobi wasn't so lucky. The poor mage was getting hit repeatedly like the Punisher had a concrete wall that needed to come down and some anger issues to work out.

It would have been the perfect time to cast Who Needs a Shield, but Tim wanted to save it for later. The fire mage's health was still above fifty percent, and with a Healing Orb and Rehydrate on him, JaKobi's health was ticking upward nicely. A small burst of Healing Storm and everything was back on track.

Their DPS was a little behind with JaKobi's fire magic hampered by the witch's water magic. When he did score a hit, it looked like it did amazing damage, but the boss blocked more strikes than got through while blasting three of them at a time with each wave of her staff.

A wave of water rose, pushing them all to the back of the room.

The group wasn't taking any damage as it carried them. Tim guessed that this was a setup for a more devastating mechanic. The witch was only at eighty-five percent health so it was a bit early for a large-scale attack unless they were a solid ten percent behind on their damage.

It was time for them to turn up the heat.

The witch laughed as they were set back down on their feet. Her hands crackled with dark energy, and ice shards flew from the sides of the room. The spikes hit the sides of the circular space and rebounded back across the room. It took Tim a few moments of watching the shards fly, but then he picked up the pattern of whirling death they needed to get through to reach the boss.

At least he thought he did.

"Tick, tick, boom!" The witch crackled again, and a wave of dark energy washed over them.

Tim looked at his status effects and saw a debuff with the initials TTB. It had a timer of ninety seconds, and it was ticking down. He'd only played a few games that had mechanics like this, but his best guess was they had to run to the boss and interrupt her before the timer expired. If they didn't, things would get real bad—trip to Barbara bad.

"We need to move." Tim prodded Cassie. "Everyone stay on her ass. We move as one."

Cassie moved toward the swirling wall of ice, waiting for the opening. "Just for the record, my ass isn't big enough for all of you to ride on."

"Don't forget the boom part," Tim chided as he nudged Cassie into the gap.

He couldn't hear Cassie's shouted reply in the chaos of the swirling ice storm, but he was sure that he would pay for his remarks about her ass later. If they made it out of this, Tim would gladly pay for whatever the perceived insult was with a chunk of his health.

All they had to do was win.

Once they were inside the storm, the pattern became easy to master as they pushed forward. It seemed as though moving a little clockwise gave them enough edge to avoid the ice blades. Tim looked at his debuff and realized they were running out of time.

There were only thirty seconds left, and they'd only crossed half of the space to the boss.

"Run faster," Tim shouted over the maelstrom.

Cassie didn't hesitate. She knew their situation must be bad if Tim told her to run. "Just keep up."

"First person there has to hit her or use an interrupt. No repeats!" Tim huffed as he kept his feet moving.

Cassie slammed her staff into the witch. Nothing happened. Lorelei went through the gap behind her and fired an arrow that pulsed with red light as it sailed through the air. When it hit the boss, the storm stopped, and she turned to face the group with a frustrated expression.

"Impressive for mortals, but I tire of the game." The witch fell back into her routine of normal attacks.

Tim started healing as he let out a sigh of relief. They made it through the first major boss mechanic relatively unscathed. It wasn't a huge accomplishment with so much of the fight left, but their early success boded well for their long-term chances. All they had to do was find a way to up their DPS, and they would come out of this smelling like roses.

The witch's health continued to drop slowly.

Looking at his status bar told Tim that while her attacks hit hard, his mana could keep up with the challenge. He'd be able to keep this going all day, which meant there was another trick just around the corner.

When the witch hit seventy-five percent health, she sucked them toward her as she powered an attack. The boss turned, focusing her attention on ShadowLily as a beam of dark energy built between her hands.

"Get the fuck out of there!" Tim screamed, hoping the assassin would find a way to stay ahead of the catastrophic damage.

ShadowLily sprinted as the beam of dark energy lanced out. The witch turned, struggling to contain the power as she chased

ShadowLily with her deadly magic. The rest of their group rotated, staying behind the boss and well away from the attack.

After completing their second circle, the witch let out a cry of disgust and the attack stopped. "Wretched humans, why won't you just die."

A blast shot them away from the boss, and the cycle started again.

The attacks weren't hitting harder or more frequently, but the continued assault started eating into his mana pool. Tim was a little less generous with the heals since it looked like the fight had turned into an all-out grind fest. All they could do now was keep plugging away and hope they figured out whatever new mechanic was coming up before it wrecked them.

The witch looked a little crazed as her health hit the fifty percent mark. It was dawning on her that this might be a fight she couldn't win.

Tim wanted to be happy at the thought, but he knew cornered animals always fought the hardest.

With a wave, the witch sent them all back to the front of the room. This time jagged ice arrows shot across the space between them. Tim knew this interrupt was probably on him to execute so he got ready to run as the blast of dark energy crashed into them. This time Tick Tick Boom had a sixty-second timer, and they were taking small amounts of periodic damage.

"Yippee-ki-yah-yay." Tim rushed forward, doing his best to miss the flying ice as he raced headlong toward the boss.

Based on their last few rounds, Tim knew it didn't matter if they all went together. As long as he reached the witch and interrupted her, the attack would stop and give them all time to group up and do their thing.

So Tim ran like their lives depended on it. Now and again, he tossed a Healing Orb behind him, but he focused on his end goal. He had to reach the witch. Nothing else mattered. This was an all-

or-nothing kind of moment. Was he going to hit the shot to win the championship or miss and take a trip to Barbara's?

In his haste to make it, the last of the sharpened ice crystals hit his leg hard enough to shatter the bones. Tim hit the ground screaming in pain but fired his interrupt before healing his leg. Healing the bones hurt as much as when he broke them, but the pain only lasted for a second. Then he was back up and moving into position.

Tim's interrupt did the job, and the storm and shards of flying death disappeared from the room. The witch's hands came together as she powered up her beam attack. He looked around furiously, trying to figure out who she was pointing at but then he realized it was him. The witch's eyes crinkled in triumph as the beam of pure death shot from her hands.

Really?

"Guess that interrupt pissed her off more than I thought," Tim muttered as he began his least favorite task in the world, running.

When the beam of dark energy started to catch up with him, Tim activated Quick Feet and sprinted. The spell made him fast enough to create a decent gap between himself and the beam. Who knew running away would be such an integral part of kicking ass?

Tim huffed as he hoofed it around the room. At least everyone else should be safe for the moment. He dodged the final bit of energy, and the witch roared in frustration.

"You have vexed me for the last time. Behold my true power!" The Witch of the Depths rose into the air, and tentacles replaced her legs as she hovered above the ground.

The cavern floor beneath their feet shook. Soon, large chunks of it fell into deep pools of water hidden beneath. When there was magic at play anything was possible, so making the floor fall away shouldn't have surprised him. The deadly monsters he saw swimming around the small islands told him that going for a swim would be a horrible idea.

The room stopped shaking, leaving them standing on a

perfect little island. Small outcroppings of the floor remained scattered around the room. There had to be twenty or thirty of them in total. Each slice of safety was big enough for their group to stand on, but it didn't give them a lot of wiggle room to maneuver.

From the looks of it this fight was going to involve a lot more running, and the fact there were so many islands didn't fill him with confidence.

What is given can easily be taken away.

The voice that spoke inside his head wasn't his. He didn't know if he remembered a quote from a movie or if Eternia had given him a little nudge, but he instantly knew the voice was right. These islands were a gift, but they could also be the death of them if they didn't manage the situation right.

"I can't wait to introduce you to my babies. The poor things never get as much fresh meat as they deserve." The witch's laughter filled the room as tentacles rose from the water and latched onto their little bit of safety.

The entire island shook.

"Cassie, pick the next island. Everyone, stay on that ass." Tim knew he was going to pay for that later, but it was so worth it.

The tank ran and jumped to the next island. "Starting to give me a complex, like I have SlimFast on speed dial."

She landed on the other side. JaKobi shouted, "Don't worry, baby, your ass still fits in those skinny jeans."

ShadowLily nudged her shoulder into Tim. "He knows how to sweet-talk a girl." Then she ran toward the gap.

Everyone should have been running, including him. Why was he still standing there? Tim put his foot to the metaphorical pedal and sprinted forward as he shouted new instructions. "Remember to try to use all of the islands. We don't want to run out. Swimming isn't an option."

Tim looked down at the churning water full of hungry sea creatures as he leapt across the gap. The old island continued to shake as he launched a blast of Divine Light right at the boss, who took damage.

When did that start?

"Fire in the hole!" he screamed. "Burn her like we don't have a tomorrow."

The entire group opened up with all of the DPS they had as the witch's spell sucked the first island under the surface. From there, it was a race to see if they could do enough damage to kill the witch before they ran out of islands. Would they end up in the water before the boss died, or did they have the stuff to see this through?

Time to kick it into overdrive.

Tim put his healing into conservation mode, making sure he'd have enough to pull them out of the shit if there was one last big surprise waiting for them. So far, this part of the fight was going surprisingly well. Most of their success had to do with Cassie being a pure genius as she led them from one island to another. It was easy for him to tell what she was doing as he watched their surroundings between heals.

The islands were the trickiest part of this fight. If she led them in the wrong direction and they couldn't leap to the next one, the fight was over. If there were an MVP award, he'd pin it on her right now. The DPS was excelling as they moved around the room. With only five islands down, the witch was sitting at twenty-five percent health.

That was when the island next to them also started to shake.

"Double hop this time," Tim called as they all ran.

The first island dropped into the depths as they crossed to the second. They all made it to the third, but the additional time they spent running was eating into their opportunity to DPS. It felt like they were only on the new island for a moment before it started shaking as well. At this pace, they would lose all the islands well before the boss hit zero percent, but all they could do was keep grinding at her health.

With the group not taking an obscene amount of damage during this phase of the encounter, Tim cast Behold My Power. There wouldn't be a better time for it, and they needed all the help they could get DPS-wise. Running and gunning weren't as easy in an MMO as they were in a first-person shooter.

For the next ten seconds, it felt like they were in a constant state of movement, but the witch's health continued to go down. Before Behold My Power hit, Tim flipped his stance to Way of the River, spreading the healing over the entire party instead of wasting it on only Cassie. The witch's health hit ten percent with the powerful attack, but they were on their last island, and it was already shaking.

"The darkness will protect me. I call on you now, Vitaria. Lend me your strength." The witch lifted her hands toward the heavens, but nothing happened.

Screaming in rage, she wove her staff through the air. "Then I forsake you as false and will crush worthless intruders on my own."

The floor around them started to solidify, and the witch was dumped back onto the ground on two legs. "This can't be. My power, it's fading."

"Man. Vitaria is one cold-ass bitch." JaKobi almost sounded like he was in awe. "Just like that." He snapped his fingers. "We're back on an even playing field."

Cassie ran forward with her staff raised high above her head. "Nothing is even until she's dead."

The witch shattered the orb in her staff and drenched herself in the liquid that ran out. As it moved down her body, it turned into a mist. When she emerged, the witch had doubled in size, and icicles shot from her body in waves. Each pulse of magic sent five shards out from her body that wiped out an entire quarter of the room. Then she started to rotate.

"DPS on the move!" Tim ran as he cast Curse of Giving, followed by Divine Light.

He flipped his stance back to Way of the Boulder as Cassie made contact.

The witch was down to nine percent health as the tank picked her up again. However, the witch seemed to be doing her own thing and ignored the tiny warrior completely.

A pulse of energy shot out from the boss, staggering them as they ran. JaKobi took an icicle to the leg and fell. The rest of them couldn't slow down. Tim could only hope that his heal came fast enough to get the fire mage's health up enough that when they circled back, he'd still be alive.

"Shitballs," Tim cursed as he looked at his status bar.

The pulse of energy put a DOT effect on the entire party. The easiest thing to do would have been casting Healing Storm, but he couldn't channel it on the move so that was out. So he basically had to cast Healing Orb on repeat and Curse of Giving when it fell off the boss.

As they came back around to the fire mage he was already standing up doing a shit ton of DPS. He joined them in their rotation as if nothing was amiss and they continued to destroy the boss as they rotated in a slow circle.

At one percent health a beam of pure white light came down from the top of the cavern, and the witch fell to her knees encased in its protective glow. All of their damage stopped registering. Tim motioned for the group to stop casting. Something was going on here, but it didn't feel sinister.

Eternia appeared next to the boss as she shrank back into a young woman. "Can you let go of your hatred and allow yourself to walk in the light?"

"What they did to me, it wasn't right. I can never forgive them for it." The witch started weeping, and her name in Tim's status screen changed to Nancy.

The goddess reached down and lifted Nancy into her arms. "You were right to seek justice, child. I only ask that you inflict the punishment on those who did the crime and no one else."

Tears streamed down Nancy's cheeks. "I'm so sorry."

"Come. Let me introduce you to the light again." Eternia rose into the air, and when the light winked out, they were gone.

Beautiful golden motes swirled down from the spot where the two disappeared and landed on an exquisite golden chest.

The battle of the deeps was over, and the Blue Dagger Society was victorious once again.

CHAPTER FOURTEEN

"Should we help them first?" Lorelei pointed at the cages.

Cassie looked at the cells and back at the exquisite golden chest. "My guess is once they get out of jail, they aren't going to want to stick around while we get our loot."

Tim didn't like the thought of leaving them in a cage, but he knew she was right. If he were trapped in a cell by underground monsters and kept as food, he would've been out of there the second he was released.

Fuck the loot. I'm gone.

However, Tim wasn't trapped in the cells, and they earned their loot. "Let's try to make it quick then." Tim pointed at the chest. "Someone care to get things started?"

Lorelei ran full speed and dodged between Tim and Shadow-Lily before flipping over Cassie to land in front of the chest. She turned, stuck her tongue out at the tank, and winked. "If you wanna beat the best…"

"You gotta be able to beat the guy everyone forgets about." JaKobi laid his hand on the chest.

The fire mage grinned, and his robes changed from their

normal fiery red to a deep crimson lined with black. "Robe of the Fiery Depths. Has the special ability to cover the robes in dark flames absorbing all damage for three seconds."

"It's about to come in useful." Lorelei feinted a punch but instead placed her hand on the chest.

"Hunting Knife of the Silent Killer." The ranger smiled as she pulled the blade free and held it up to the light. "It might be my off-hand weapon, but it sure is nice. Bonuses to ranged attacks while immobile and to knife attacks while moving. Not always helpful, but it could make a huge difference in the right fight or with perfect positioning."

Cassie looked kind of amused by all the trouble they went through to beat her to the chest as she rested her hand on it. "Circlet of the Hammerhead. Gives a bonus to aggression on the first hit and increases my armor by a flat one percent."

It sounded like an amazing item for tanks. Almost every tank Tim ever played with loved something that put them at the top of the aggro table and kept them there for the whole fight. Tanks mostly had to worry about the boss slipping away from them when they were pugging, or the fight was so close they needed to eke out every last second of DPS. It was a fine line between starting the DPS too early and losing the battle.

Everyone seemed to be getting awesome items, but it always paid to be courteous. "After you, babe."

ShadowLily set her hand on the chest, then broke out in the dance fondly known as the JaKobi shuffle. "Leather Pants of the Unseen. Boosts to stealth, damage from behind, and Silent Feet."

"No wonder I never hear you get up to go to the bathroom." Tim wanted to ask her if the skill was teachable or class-related.

Cassie nudged JaKobi in the ribs. "It's too bad they don't have a Silent Noise spell for this one."

"Hey, it's only if I sleep on one side." The fire mage looked gravely offended by having his snoring brought into the public light.

Tim ignored them as they continued to bicker and laid his hand on the chest.

Item Received: Necklace of Hydration

The greatest healer the temple has ever known was Jezel the Magnificent. This necklace didn't belong to him. Instead, it belonged to one of his assistants, Marcus the Blunderer. Jezel would never cast one of his apprentices away and admit failure. Instead, he found a way to help them become successful with the limited skills they had.

+1 Endurance +2 Intelligence +5 Wisdom

Special Ability: Enhanced Hydration

When you apply Hydration from Healing Orb to the target, it now has a fifty percent chance of applying Enhanced Hydration. Enhanced Hydration adds a secondary HOT at fifty percent of the strength of Hydration.

Item Upgraded: Tarnished Circlet of Divine Wisdom

Item Received: Circlet of Divine Wisdom

+1 Endurance +3 Intelligence +5 Wisdom

Like Luthar the Great, you have a penchant for healing, and it's undeniable. Heal the people of Eternia for a combined one hundred thousand health to upgrade the circlet to Polished.

Hell, fucking, yeah!

Not only did he get his reward, but his circlet also upgraded. It was like winning the lottery on Christmas. If everything went to plan when they returned to the marquess, they would receive another reward, maybe something equally valuable.

Tim broke out into his version of the JaKobi shuffle and added his moves to the mix. "Sometimes I just wanna dance like a sex maniac."

"You know, my managers noticed you've been over here for a long time." ShadowLily did her best Ramona impersonation.

Yet another reason Tim knew he picked the right girl to ask out at graduation. Things worked out better for them than he'd ever imagined. Not only were they a good team on the battlefield, but they were also good together everywhere. She understood him on a level no one else even came close to.

Tim gave his girlfriend a giant kiss. As they broke apart, it dawned on him that he still hadn't told anyone what loot he received. "I scored an upgrade necklace, and my circlet got its first upgrade."

Not wanting to be the center of attention any longer, Tim pointed at the cages. "Let's go help those guys out of there before they have a breakdown."

The group walked toward the cages. As they drew closer, a man sighed with relief. "Thank the goddess. I thought you couldn't hear us."

Lorelei and ShadowLily cut the hemp rope ties holding the cages closed, and soon all the men were free.

Now that they were out of the cages, the men stood a little straighter. One of them moved to the head of the group. "We've been down here for days. Did my grandfather send you?"

"I've never seen anyone fight like that," one of the soldiers said with awe.

Tim felt pretty good about himself. They saved more men than he expected. Now they only had one more quest to accomplish before they met the High Priest's envoy inside the castle.

If they could find their way out of here.

"Your grandfather requested our assistance." Tim started healing the wounded men. "Help us find a way out of here." He pointed back the way they had come from. "There are thousands of those things back there, and I don't like our chances after we killed their leader."

Nephram looked astonished. "You also defeated King Hundari? This is a banner day. We'll return as heroes."

Cassie kicked the cavern floor. "Some of us, more than others."

"Hey, I found a way out," Lorelei called from a crack in the wall behind the cages.

The captain looked up. "Surely, you can't be serious. We've been through quite the ordeal."

Tim looked past the man toward one of the more grizzled-looking guardsmen. "If we take the lead, can you make sure he keeps up?"

The guard's face perked up. "I'd be more than happy to, sir."

"Listen here. You can't ignore me. Umph." Nephram stopped speaking as the guardsman's fist slammed into his belly.

The guard looked at Tim as he shoved his captain forward. "We'll be right along."

Once they were inside the crack, the passage was wide enough that it was comfortable to walk in single file without feeling like it was crushing them. They walked in silence until a faint blue glow became visible. The men behind them started to mutter.

Walking around the corner revealed a vortex of swirling water, only this one went up.

"Wicked." JaKobi walked forward. "Let's hope it doesn't feel as bad as the way into the game." Without waiting, he jumped into the water. It sucked him up like a tube on *Star Trek*.

Cassie took off. "I'll make sure he doesn't get in trouble."

"I'll watch them." Lorelei let out a sigh only a stressed-out mother could make.

Tim looked back and motioned to the guards. "Why don't you guys go next?"

"I'm not stepping in there. We don't even know where it goes," the captain whined.

Not one to waste an opportunity for a little retribution, the guardsman Tim assigned to watch over Nephram grabbed him by the back of his pants and jacket. A quick twist tossed him into the portal like a bouncer tosses a drunk into the street. "Thank you for your help, sir."

The rest of the guards followed him out, muttering their thanks as they passed.

Tim looked over at ShadowLily. "We're almost to the king."

"After completing this quest, I can't begin to imagine what he has in store for us." She winked at him. "Not that I couldn't use more loot."

She jumped through the portal before Tim could reply. He'd almost forgotten that after they made it through the third gate, they still had to negotiate with the king for the stone. Not to mention he'd need a little time to squeeze in his class change quest before they took on Vitaria. Tim stepped into the vortex, excited about the work ahead.

CHAPTER FIFTEEN

"I almost can't believe it, adventurer." The marquess clapped Tim heavily on the back. "My grandson Nephram returned nearly unharmed."

The guard standing behind Nephram coughed.

"Yes, I've returned not only victorious but completely uninjured. While these adventurers have contributed in a meaningful way, I do believe all of the honor belongs to us."

The guard shot Tim a look that said, now that we're back, there's nothing I can do to keep the little shit in line.

Brimming with pride, the marquess pulled Nephram into a hug. "Of course it is, my boy. I'm sure we'll be able to find some token of our appreciation for the men and the families of those who didn't make it back."

Nephram deflated at the thought of the guards who didn't make it back, and his color paled. "Of course, you're right, my lord. I'll pen and deliver the letters to the families and have the head of the guard see to the others in the meantime."

"Very well." The marquess looked relieved as he turned away

from Nephram. "See that it happens. The adventurers and I have business to attend to."

Nephram gave a stiff bow and left the room with the rest of the guards following.

"Maybe there's still hope for the glory hound." The marquess sagged into his ornate chair. "I love the kid to death, but how about actually accomplishing something instead of just taking credit for it."

The marquess sipped his wine and looked like a great burden had been lifted from his shoulders. "Adventurers, you've exceeded my expectations in every way. As long as I'm the marquess, you'll have access to my lands. Now I believe I owe you some gold and a reward."

You have received ten gold.

A small screen appeared in front of Tim with a list of items on it. He scrolled through the list a few times and finally settled on something he liked. He highlighted the one he wanted and hit select, and the familiar prompt appeared.

Item Received: Jerkin of Fortuitous Solitude

+1 to all base stats

Not every healer likes to get right up in their enemy's business. Just like Sammy the Snake, you can heal from afar while your group takes the hits. When wearing the jerkin and standing at least twenty feet away from every member in your party, you'll receive a ten percent bonus to healing done.

On the surface, the item wasn't super sexy. Its stats weren't an upgrade, and the special ability also wasn't perfect for their style of play. Tim spent a lot of time right in the thick of things so he could get to everyone easier, but there was no reason not to take it.

Under the right circumstances, an extra ten percent healing could be the difference between life and death. Even though being that far away would make him feel like he was sitting at the kiddie table trying to hang with the grownups.

The marquess rose from his chair and moved to shake all their hands. "I better make sure Nephram isn't making a mess of those letters." He strode from the room and mumbled, "Or keeping any of the gold for himself."

The marquess' attendant motioned for them to follow him. "I'll see you back to your carriage now."

Cassie grumbled louder than the marquess. "Not even an offer to use the bathroom."

"Maybe there'll be one between here and the duke's." Tim shrugged. He could have Grant pull the carriage over and pee just about anywhere.

"Remember this moment when you're paying that carriage driver extra to clean the seats." Cassie picked up the pace.

The trip through the marquess' estates took about twice as long as it had for them to go through the earl's lands.

Stopping in his land also gave them a chance to stretch their legs and use nature's facilities. With the thrill of victory rapidly fading, all the adventurers were getting tired. Tim started to doze while thinking about what it might take to get through the next gate. Almost as if his thoughts made it a reality, the duke's gate appeared on the horizon.

"Ready for round two?" Tim looked out the window. "I don't have any tricks for this one either so let's try to do as little work as possible to get to the throne."

Lorelei snorted. "Do not pass go, do not collect two hundred dollars."

"Come on, guys. It could be easy." JaKobi put his book down. "I'm just saying this could be our lucky day."

The fire mage could find the bright side of just about anything.

"Who even cares about saving the world? I want to know how Joe is coming along with those pizza ovens." Cassie mimicked eating a slice. "I'd kill a couple of bosses for a slice of some New York pepperoni."

Tim could always be drawn into a discussion about pizza. "Please, I'm a Chicago-style deep dish. It's not pizza unless the sauce is on top."

ShadowLily leaned into him. "That's my man. Fame and riches? Oh, no. He'd rather have pizza."

"If you have simple goals, you'll never be disappointed." Tim watched through the window as Grant dismounted and waited for him to open the door before exiting.

Grant nodded. "Third time's the charm, eh sir."

"Let's hope so." Tim looked up at the sky and realized they'd already lost an entire day.

This gate was also open but without a single carriage lined up to go through. Tim wondered how the people who lived here got food. Maybe there was an underground passage for servants to use.

He didn't like the thought of anyone treating others like a second-class citizen, but the nobility wasn't always known for their kind treatment of the peasant folk. Tim liked to believe it didn't matter whether a person mopped the bathroom or designed it. Everyone who worked hard at their job deserved respect.

It was equally likely the servants went from shop to shop in carriages he couldn't see. With all the players in the game, the streets should've been lined from one side of the city to the other with worse traffic than Los Angeles. Yet, he only ever saw a few carriages.

The game designers must've figured out traffic was boring and worked around it. Tim didn't need to know how it worked. He only had to stay in the back of his ride and be comfortable until they reached their destination.

It's like a limo with a horse.

The guards on the marquess' side of the fence milled around. On the duke's side, they were training in a large square, running drills in the distance, and there appeared to be a pretty orderly line around the chow building.

Three men stood a couple of feet back from the dividing line between the two lands. One man on each side of the gate carried a large halberd. The man standing in the middle had a fancier uniform with a couple of medals pinned to the front to go along with his sword.

Clearly, the man with the medals was who they wanted to speak with.

Making sure to stop on the marquess' side of the gate to avoid being disrespectful, Tim started to introduce himself. The man abruptly cut him off.

"Do you have an appointment with the duke? If not, the duchy isn't accepting unapproved visitors." Captain Rictor looked down his nose at them as if they weren't worth more than the dust on his boots.

Tim bowed low as he took in the name on his interface. It sounded very familiar as if he'd met a Rictor before. He was about to put the pieces together when he realized he had to say something or risk the captain mistaking him as simple. "We've been sent on behalf of the temple to speak with the priests inside the royal compound."

"Then word should have been sent ahead from the castle. Let me take a look at the sheet for guests and see if they added your name to it." Rictor snapped his fingers with a cruel crinkle at the corner of his eyes.

A man ran out of a small guard hut off to the side and handed him a clipboard with a sheet of paper on it. Rictor looked at the clipboard and turned it around so they could all see the blank page. "I don't have anything on the books."

"Maybe there's a service you could provide the duchy." Rictor waited for them to reply with a smug look on his face.

Tim had seen that look before, but it wasn't the same face. Not exactly. The similarities were there, though, enough that they might've been family. It was worth taking a shot. If the man didn't recognize the crest, they wouldn't have anything to discuss. If he did, it was their free pass to the castle.

He reached into his inventory and pulled out the seal Lord Rictor had given him.

"Where did you get that?" the captain hissed and reached out to snatch it away.

Tim pulled the seal back, trying not to look at the guards who dropped their halberds into fighting position. He felt Cassie and ShadowLily move into position on either side of him, and it gave him the courage to stand tall.

Whenever he moved the seal, the captain's eyes followed. "I did something to help your brother, something I'd rather not talk about out in the open."

"That was you?" The captain looked as though he didn't believe it, but his eyes kept darting to the seal.

Tim nodded and slipped the seal back into his robes. "I believe you're honor-bound to assist me."

Rictor motioned for his men to stand down. The guards snapped into position in an instant. "While it seems as though I have no choice in the matter, with a thousand men at my back, I doubt there is anything you five could do to stop me."

For the first time, the look on his face softened. "For the man who saved my brother, I would help him without the seal."

"Tell me, adventurer, what do you require of me?" It was easy to see that saying the words pained the man, but he was willing to swallow his pride for honor.

Tim thought about it for a moment and went with his gut. "We need access to the castle, and we might need it again depending on what the king requires of us."

Rictor gave a little bow. "Then I swear on the blood of my family to see you safely through the duke's lands to the castle for as long as I hold my position as watch commander."

Turning away from the group, the commander called, "My

horse." Without looking to see if a guard followed the order, he returned his gaze to Tim. "I'll escort you to the castle myself. If the castle turns you away, I'll see you back to marquess' lands as well."

"Thank you." Tim inclined his head in respect. He turned to his party, held his arms out wide, and made a shooing gesture. "You heard the man, back in the carriage."

As soon as they were all inside and the carriage door was closed, Tim filled the group in on how he spent his afternoon off.

"He really can't be trusted to go anywhere alone." ShadowLily laughed.

Cassie looked relieved. "Sure saved our ass with that Rictor guy though, I could tell he was going to be a total dick. Go here collect me a bazillion mushrooms. Now I'll take you to the duke so he can make you collect two billion more."

"It's going to be nice skipping some of the fluff and getting right to the heart of things for once. Even if it means fighting." JaKobi was bouncing a small ball of fire between his hands.

Tim didn't know if they would make it through the royal gate unless the High Priest's man inside was there to meet them. He sent a quick message to Paul, letting him know they were on their way and needed all the assistance possible to ensure their entrance to the castle was smooth. All he wanted to do was make it to the king and plead his case for Eternia.

From there the chips would fall as they may.

If they could believe the watch commander, everything was not right in the castle. Tim wasn't sure what that meant or why the king wouldn't see anyone, but he would see them. Even if they had to jump through a million hoops, Tim wouldn't fail in his quest. Whatever challenge appeared before them, they would deal with it in due turn.

Their carriage stopped.

"You know it's pretty sexist that a game in this day and age can't have one female leader?" Lorelei groused. "They're all men."

JaKobi pointed up. "You know, except all the gods are women. And Seraphina."

"They're sisters. By definition, that means they have a father." Lorelei winked at him. "Just saying this game could do with a little more pizazz."

ShadowLily snorted. "Someone should introduce her to Lady Briarthorn. She has all the pizzaz in the world."

Tim could have kicked himself for not thinking about Lady Briarthorn. It wasn't like the woman relied on Paul. Their relationship worked the other way around.

Lucy would have contacts and might've shortened their journey by a great deal. When they got a chance, he would have to stop by her house and tell her what a great bumbling mess he made of things by not going to see her first.

She'd love that.

"No one has the balls to tell Lucy she isn't in charge, that's for sure." The carriage door opened, and Tim stepped out into the torchlight.

Lord Rictor was there to greet him. "I present to you the boundary to the castle grounds." He held out his hand.

"As soon as we get inside." Tim brushed past the lord, unsure if he was up to something, and moved toward the gate.

Waiting for them at the gate was a plump little man that made Brother Colton look like a track star. His blue and white robes left no question that he was a priest. His ebony skin looked awesome with the robes and set off the electric blue of his very tall hat quite nicely.

Why was it important men always had bigger hats?

Tim almost giggled as he thought about Cassie snorting and saying something about small dicks. He was pretty sure the hats had to do more with men's egos than their dicks, but sometimes a person had to wear a hat because it came with the job.

Like that summer he worked at Burger World.

"Brother Khalil, I'm Tim, and this is the Blue Dagger Society."

He motioned toward the other members of his group. "It's a pleasure to meet you." He extended his hand to shake.

The priest waved the hand away and pulled Tim into a warm embrace. "It's good that you're here. Paul said you might be able to help me."

"Funny, he didn't mention anything to me." Tim watched the man, looking for any sign of deceit.

Brother Khalil looked into Tim's eyes, searching for the truth of the matter. "It seems there may have been some confusion. I'll provide whatever assistance Paul promised. If all goes well, I hope you'll consider returning the favor."

Tim wanted to say no, but he remembered how this adventure started. All he did was take on a little side quest, which saved them a ton of time. Was this another one of those opportunities or maybe the chance to make a friend in a position of influence? Either way, helping the man seemed like a good idea.

As long as he wasn't asking for the moon.

"After we meet with the king, I would be happy to help." Tim hoped it would be worthwhile.

Looking over the group, the priest made a decision. "Then you best get on this side of the gate and move your carriage." He turned and motioned to the guards. "They're with me."

The men gave a little bow of respect, and Grant pulled the carriage across the threshold. No sooner had they all crossed to the king's side of the gate than a small army of horses crested a hill in the distance of the duke's lands, charging straight for the gate.

There was a woman at the head of the group, with long autumn brown hair flowing behind her as she rode. Tim watched her, unable to take his eyes away. The woman racing toward them was as beautiful as the goddess herself, even covered head to toe in full plate armor. It reminded him of the first time they saw Seraphina fight.

The woman reached them and dismounted, storming over to

the gate. At her approach, Lord Rictor dropped to one knee. "Duke Ravenstorm."

"Why were these people escorted across my land without my permission?" She glared at the man.

One of Duke Ravenstorm's soldiers moved to stand beside the lord with his hand on the hilt of his sword. It was clear he was only waiting for the command to cut him down before acting.

Tim whispered to Cassie, "Don't let him die, but don't move unless it comes to it."

More of the duke's men from the gate gathered around, forming a semi-circle around their half of the gate. The castle guards took notice of the ruckus and moved to do the same. They were surrounded now, in what was quickly becoming a cage match. Things were going to boil out of control if Tim didn't do something to stop them.

Rictor kept his head bowed, never looking up at the duke. "I'm sorry to have failed you."

The soldier pulled the sword from his sheath, and Lord Rictor lowered his head, ready to accept his fate.

There was no way Tim could stay silent anymore. The man was about to die because his honor made him too stubborn to tell her the truth. If Tim learned anything watching *Hamilton*, it was don't point your gun in the sky during a duel.

That shit never worked out.

The soldier's blade went high into the air, and Tim screamed, "Stop!"

The soldier's blade descended without hesitation.

Cassie blocked the attack with her staff. The weapon was long enough she didn't have to leave the safety of the king's protection.

The duke was frothing at the mouth in anger, but she turned her deadly gaze away from Lord Rictor to Tim. "Explain yourself, or so help me. I'll storm the castle grounds to kill you myself."

"Happy we didn't end up working for her," Lorelei chided from behind. "Maybe I was wrong about the woman thing. A couple of goddesses, Neema, Seraphina, and the good Lady Briarthorn, maybe that's enough."

"Don't let this bitch ruin your mojo." Cassie locked eyes with the duke. "Girl fucking power."

Tim felt the weight of the situation resting heavily on his shoulders, but this was a situation they could still get out of without causing an incident. Pulling Lord Rictor's family seal free from his robes, Tim held it aloft so everyone could see it. "He was honor-bound to help me, Duke Ravenstorm."

Crossing the line knowing that the duke could have ordered him killed at any second, Tim lifted Rictor back to his feet and pressed the seal to his chest. "Don't forget the rest of our deal."

Turning toward the duke, Tim dropped to one knee and addressed her directly. "I'm sorry if we've given offense, but we're on a mission for the Goddess Eternia and had to make it to the castle as quickly as possible."

Surprisingly, the duke smiled. "If you've given no offense, then none will be taken, but you owe me one, stranger."

Rising to his feet, Tim met her eyes. "I'm not sure that I do." He slowly retreated until he was standing on the king's side of the fence again. "If you have a quest and the proper payment, we'd be more than happy to consider your offer."

"It seems we may be at odds then. I will not be denied what is owed to me." She leapt onto her horse and looked down at her watch commander. "And you, return to your duty. I'll deal with you later."

Lord Rictor ran to his horse. "As you command."

The duke gave their party one last icy glare as if she were burning all their faces into her memory for later retribution, then lifted her chin to look down at them before turning her horse and spurring it into motion. As soon as she left, life around the gates returned to its normal slow pace, and the guards moved back to their duties.

"Why do they call her duke?" ShadowLily watched as their horses retreated. "Isn't she a duchess?"

Brother Khalil turned and headed toward their carriage. "The Lady Ravenstorm didn't want to be seen as inferior to any man by claiming a weaker title. As you can see, no one has opposed the switch."

"If she wasn't such a bitch, I might like the balls on her." Lorelei sounded shocked by the thought.

Brother Khalil climbed into their carriage and pulled a little cake from inside his robes. "Just like these cakes have an endless amount of flavors, Eternia's light shines differently upon us all. The duke hasn't had an easy life. Even now, she claws desperately to hold onto what is hers."

Tim felt like that was a setup for a questline they didn't have time for right now. "How about you tell us about the king and what it will take to get him to help us?"

Brother Khalil brushed some crumbs from his robe and spoke in a soft tone. "It seems our two problems are aligned. You see, before you can see the king, you'll also have to cure him."

The carriage trundled down the road, and Tim sat in stunned silence. They were right here, so close to everything they fought for, only to find out the real quest was just beginning.

List of Tim's Current Stats and Skills

"Tim" level twenty Hex Witch
    Primary Stats
    Strength: 14
    Endurance: 26
    Dexterity: 23
    Intelligence: 53
    Wisdom: 61
    Perception: 6

Vitality: 4
Revitalization: 4
Luck: 7

Notable Gear

Weapons

Simple Dagger of Dexterity, +1 (X2)

Greater Staff of Yin, +3 Endurance +7 Intelligence +7 Wisdom

Orb of Concentration, +5 Intelligence +4 Wisdom

Armor

Circlet of Divine Wisdom, +1 Endurance +3 Intelligence +5 Wisdom

Shoulder Guards of the Spotless Mind, +1 Intelligence +2 Wisdom +1 to Perception, Vitality, Revitalization, and Luck

Battlesworn Robes of Justice, +4 Intelligence +6 Wisdom

Jerkin of Fortuitous Solitude, +1 to all base stats, and bonus to healing when standing twenty feet away

Paul's Gloves of Mending, +7 Intelligence +4 Wisdom

Belt of Divine Inspiration, +1 Endurance +2 Intelligence +4 Wisdom

Hermit's Pants for Special Guests, +2 Endurance +2 Intelligence

Boots of Tranquility, +2 Endurance +2 Dexterity, increase mana regeneration by 2%

Jewelry and Accessories

Leather Wraps of Divergent Health, 10% chance for single

target healing spell to jump targets and heal the secondary recipient for 50% of the value

Wristband of the Faithful, +1 Endurance, ten seconds of double mana regeneration

Ring of Luminosity, +1 Endurance +2 Intelligence +3 Wisdom

Necklace of Hydration, +1 Endurance +2 Intelligence +5 Wisdom

Trinket of the Smiling Monkey, +1 to random stat

Skills

Appeal to the Goddess: Novice rank five

Night Vision: Novice: rank eight

Disturbance: Apprentice rank one

Quick Feet: Apprentice rank one

Rectify: Apprentice rank one

Backstab: Apprentice rank four

Throwing Knives: Apprentice rank four

Sneak: Apprentice rank six

Shadow Master: Apprentice rank six

Small Blades: Journeyman rank one

Snare: Journeyman rank one

Dodge: Journeyman rank two

Behold My Power: Journeyman rank three

Flame Burst: Journeyman rank three

Divine Light: Journeyman rank four

Healing Storm: Journeyman rank four

Who Needs a Shield: Journeyman rank four

Curse of Giving: Journeyman rank five

Cleanse: Journeyman rank seven

Healing Orb: Master rank one

Stances

Way of the River
Way of the Boulder

Buffs
Weaken Undead: Journeyman rank two
Armor of Eternia: Journeyman rank five
Attacks of the Faithful: Journeyman rank five

Open Quests
The Stone of Immoratis
So you want to be a Hex Witch?

CHAPTER SIXTEEN

"Mother, it's clear we need to give in to their demands," the crown prince and acting king of Promethia implored.

The queen sipped her tea. "We will not give in to the demands of these treasonous bastards."

"Even if he dies?" There it was. He said it out loud.

Prince Desmond didn't want to believe such a thing could be possible. His dad was the strongest man he knew. The man was a hero; his life was easily worth a hundred thousand others. If he were sick or falling victim to the ravages of age, Desmond would've been able to handle the king's death. Knowing someone out there could stop it in an instant made him feel like following his mother's orders was as good as killing the man himself.

Oh, Desmond already knew what the common folk thought of him. The power-hungry princeling, ready to take the crown before his father passed away. When the truth was, he'd burn the entire kingdom to the ground to save him. Politics made fools out of everyone, and even now, the bonds of duty tied his hands. It might become his job to let his father die for the pride of the kingdom.

"Then he dies." The queen stifled a sob. "We cannot let Isadora and her band of thugs ransom the kingdom. If keeping the kingdom secure means your father's death, then we *do our duty*."

Duty and honor were finicky concepts at best. The last thing he wanted was to live his life by a code so rigid that he couldn't help the people he loved and the citizens that counted on him. They needed to deal with Isadora, but he couldn't send any more of his men. The prince needed to find an outsider strong enough to handle the task.

But who would he find to answer the call?

"I see that look on your face," Queen Charlene chided. "Don't even think about it."

Setting aside her tea, she got up and moved to her son. "I know you want to save him, but we've lost our three best knights, and the battalion spent a month looking for the entrance to the lands she claimed and couldn't find it."

It was true.

The battalion of soldiers returned home after a month-long expedition. They'd faced bouts of sickness and delirium. After losing several scouting parties and the defeat of their three finest warriors, the battalion returned home.

Honor and glory were fine things when one had the comforts of home all around them, but once Isadora started picking them off at will, the concepts faded quickly enough. The prince knew the rigors of battle and what it could do to a man.

He'd fought in four pitched battles and nineteen raids. Desmond wasn't a coward. If anything, he was too driven. How else could he live when everyone expected him to follow the greatest monarch the kingdom had seen in a hundred generations? Mastering every study, every weapon, every task assigned to him was all he'd focused on for the last twenty years.

His pursuit of greatness left many ripples in its wake. Now that he might have to assume the crown under a cloud of uncertainty, those ripples could turn into tidal waves.

Still, being a quick study also meant he had dirt on all his rivals.

Desmond didn't want to be the kind of king who ruled through intimidation, but he wouldn't stand to have his deeds questioned by those power-hungry bureaucrats. It was enough he had to listen to them squabble over whose lands were more prosperous as if who taxed their peasants the most was something to be proud of. His only true chance of avoiding a plot for rebellion was to keep his father alive.

Isadora had eyes and ears everywhere.

Desmond didn't know how she did it, but the woman had found a way to get her spies inside the castle. Even here in the king's chamber, it was possible their conversation was being listened to. Isadora knew what they were going to do before the orders even left his lips. It was infuriating, and it cut them off from taking further action against her.

Finding their champion was going to be the key to the kingdom's survival.

His mother moved away from him and returned to her place by the king's bedside. She picked up the book she'd been reading to the king earlier and watched her son with tired eyes. "Just know that he loves you and that your father would gladly give his life to keep Promethia safe."

"Of course, mother. You're right as usual." He gave her a small bow and retreated from the room.

Desmond knew he had to do something, but he'd never be able to think trapped in there with his mother. What he needed to do was to find somewhere quiet that he could get away from all the madness of the castle and have a few moments to plan, unmolested by the demands of others. There was only one sanctuary that could afford him the freedom to think in peace, and he was heading there now.

At this time of night, the temple would be empty.

His two guards stopped at the temple doors, and the crown prince entered on his own. Walking past the rows of empty seats, he looked at one of the beautiful woven tapestries hanging between the windows and wondered if Eternia liked them. Had anyone ever sat and asked the goddess what she wanted in her temples?

He let his mind continue wandering. Sometimes Desmond did his best thinking when he let his mind work around what was bugging him. So logically, he needed to think about anything but his father to get closer to the solution. What art the goddess might be into was as good a topic as any.

Desmond looked toward the statue of the goddess and felt something stirring inside him.

His vision twisted and blurred before clearing into a crisp picture of the city proper leading to the castle. Out of the city ventured a band of five adventurers. These were the men and women he needed to find to take on Isadora. Their faces remained hidden to him, but Desmond knew that they would be coming soon. When the brave adventurers arrived in his path, all he needed was the courage to act.

A noise sounded from behind him and Desmond whirled, startled that anyone made it past his guards. No one should have been in here with him without being announced. His guards would have seen to that, but instead of an empty room, he found himself looking into the bright yellow eyes of a woman.

The leather clothes she wore were camouflage for the forest, and she bore Isadora's mark around her neck. As if the yellow eyes and the dark green hair weren't already enough to distinguish her as one of the witch's disciples. Even now, his pride demanded that he dismiss her as inconsequential, but anyone who could sneak past his men with such ease was someone he might have to fight.

He reached for where his sword should be and realized he'd left it at the door with his guards.

"There is no need for a weapon, Desmond. I've only received instructions to remind you that your father's time is running out."

She gave him a mocking bow. "The Lady Isadora demands the titles to the land she's claimed and warns that the next soldiers you send won't merely return home with a case of the shits."

The bitch had some balls making threats while his father lay dying from one of her spells. If he had his sword in hand, he would gut this little tree hugger and send her body back as a reply to her offer to heal the king. Without his weapon, it gave him time to think of a more rational reply. As much as it sickened him to do it, for now, he had to eat her shit and smile like it was the best meal he ever tasted.

"We still haven't decided on your offer." Desmond managed to keep his voice calm even though his heart was racing. "We beg for Isadora to give me more time."

The witch laughed, and to his ears, it sounded like broken glass.

"Time is something we all run short of eventually. Tick, tock, the clock never stops, but the king's heart won't last much longer." She sliced her hand down in a violent motion.

Desmond flinched and let out a cry for help, fearing some attack. Instead, he mostly felt foolish as his guards burst into the room to see a small cloud of smoke and nothing else. He straightened his coat and looked around, satisfied he wasn't going to take a dagger in the back.

Despite being determined to find a way to help his father, Desmond knew his mother was right. They could never give in to Isadora's demands. It would start with the land. Then there would be something else the witch wanted. Whose head would be next on the chopping block, his mother's, his own?

NO!

The goddess had shown him the way to end this. When the adventurers showed up, he would recruit them into the crown's service, whatever the cost. He could save his father and defeat the threat Isadora presented in one fell swoop.

All praise Eternia.

Brother Khalil walked into the room eating one of his little cakes. The man had a thing for the tiny pastries, and it showed in his waistline. The prince always had a fond spot in his heart for the man, despite the fact there was never any cake left for him.

No one on the castle grounds was more grounded in good, solid sense than the family priest. Secretly, Desmond was also kind of jealous of how well the man's dark skin went with the white robes.

Half of fashion seemed to be finding the right colors to wear.

Desmond thought about the time his mother spent an entire month finding the right shades to match her skin for her new wardrobe. A small part of him was thankful someone else managed that part of his life for him. He got up and dressed in whatever preselected outfit was ready for the day, never giving a thought to how he looked. Who would have the balls to tell him he looked ridiculous?

Brother Khalil motioned for the guards to retreat. They did after an acknowledging nod from the prince.

The priest sat and motioned for the prince to join him as he nibbled on his little cake. "You seem troubled, Desmond. Is your father getting worse?"

"His condition hasn't changed." He looked down at the floor. "That won't last forever."

Pulling another treat from inside his robes, Brother Khalil sat in silence for a moment. "I've reached out to the High Priest. He assures me they have someone who can help, but their price is steep."

The prince sat there in shocked silence as Brother Khalil tore into his next cake like he hadn't already finished three since walking into the room. If the priest had a way to end this, was any price too high?

"What do they seek in compensation?" Desmond was almost afraid to ask.

Brother Khalil's eyes took on a sterner quality, letting the prince know he wasn't kidding around. "The Stone of Immoratis."

"Unthinkable. The stone has been in my family for twenty generations." Desmond stood, feeling like the priest and the adventurers were shaking him down in his temple.

Brushing some crumbs from his robes, Brother Khalil made to leave. "The real question you have to ask yourself—is keeping the stone in your family's coffers worth your father's life?" He gave the prince a sad smile. "If they fail, it costs you nothing that's not already at risk."

Desmond had said he would do anything, give anything, and the stone was merely another powerful object littering a treasury full of such things. His father would probably be furious, but he wouldn't be able to refuse the adventurers their boon if Desmond promised it to them. The offer, along with his vision, made the choice a no-brainer. Still, before he decided anything, he wanted to meet this group of people so he could decide their worth for himself.

"I will think on your offer." The prince let a bit of coolness tinge his tone.

Brother Khalil bowed his head in respect. "Please do not mistake my words for a bargain. I have no such right to make one. I only wanted you to prepare for what they're asking so your shock at the request doesn't ruin your judgment.

"Please use the temple as long as you'd like." Brother Khalil bowed again and left the room.

Desmond found he had no desire to pray, and now he had more to think about than when he came. Maybe these adventurers would be what was needed to save his father. Was the stone really too great a price to pay for the life of a loved one?

What he needed now was a drink and maybe a fuck. Tomorrow the sun would rise, and there would be a decision to make. Until then, he wanted to try to forget the world existed for a few hours. He sent a message to his favorite consort and headed for the door.

As he stepped out into the cool night air, Desmond decided. If the adventurers saved his father, he would give them the stone. The resolution left him feeling lighter than he had in ages. Despite his doubts moments ago, he finally felt at peace with the situation. They might find their way out of this yet.

CHAPTER SEVENTEEN

Tim was still trying to wrap his head around what Brother Khalil told them.

It was like they climbed in the carriage, and the entire scope of the quest changed. Getting past the earl, marquess, and duke was supposed to be the mountain. This leg was the slow descent into the valley. Yes, he knew they would have to do a quest for the king, but a quest to get a quest?

This was starting to get ridiculous.

Then there was the fact that he couldn't cure the king himself. If the High Priest couldn't handle it, there was no way Tim stood a chance. If he wasn't here as a healer, that meant there really would be a quest before they got the stone. Unless they could find a way to tie the two rewards together.

Whatever happened next, Tim knew they had one priority—to secure the stone as quickly as possible. They couldn't spend days searching for ingredients for some cure without knowing the stone was theirs, win or fail. He needed to channel his inner ShadowLily when it came to negotiating and be bold.

"I told you there would be more pointless crap," Cassie huffed as though Khalil wasn't sitting right across from her in the carriage.

Sure, Cassie was blunt sometimes, but it was nice to know exactly where you stood with someone. Now they had to get her to keep the sharing inside the group, and everything would be perfect. Considering he'd been lamenting the very same thoughts, he was willing to let it go.

It was time to get to work winning over the brother.

Smiling like he was standing in the checkout line and his little brother ripped a huge fart, Tim tried to steer the conversation back on track by playing dumb. "Is there something wrong with the king?"

"Why, of course not. He's as robust as ever." Khalil was shaking his head as if he was trying to tell them no. "Once we reach my chambers, I'll fill you in on your new duties." The priest gave him an exaggerated slow wink as though he was trying to get them on board with some scheme.

Who knew priests could be so crafty?

It was a good thing Tim was pretty quick on the uptake and had seen the High Priest use the cone of silence trick before. He had a good idea of why Khalil wanted to be back in his chambers before speaking freely. Even here in their carriage, it seemed Khalil was worried someone might overhear them. Tim guessed anything was possible with enough magic, even spying from a distance.

"Of course, and I'm sure there will be somewhere our driver can attend to his animals as we learn what you have in store for us?" Tim tried to sound like everything was normal, but his heart was racing.

If Brother Khalil was going through all this trouble, it meant they had an enemy in the castle, someone who had a vested interest in the king not getting healthy. In any normal situation, it would've been safer to turn around and call it a lost cause, but with the fate of the world on the line, they had to be willing to walk into what could be an inescapable trap.

"The temple on the grounds has a stable and extra housing should the need arise." Khalil produced another little cake from inside his robes and took a bite. "Oh, butterscotch."

ShadowLily nudged Tim to get his attention. Her look was clearly asking if he thought Brother Khalil was all there.

There was no way to know, but Tim doubted Paul would put someone not at the top of their game inside the castle. Which left them with three realistic options on the table. Khalil was fucking nutso. Like *Twelve Monkeys*, Brad Pitt-style crazy. Two, that the priest was putting on a show in case anyone was listening. It always paid to appear less than a person was and doubly so when being devious. Three, that option two was correct, and Khalil really loved those little cakes.

"Is there anything you can tell us about the castle or the temple on the way?" Tim tried to leave his question very open-ended to give Khalil as many ways to answer it as possible in case someone was listening.

As the carriage made its way through the castle's estates, Brother Khalil told them about the history of the temple and the priests that served there. By extension, they learned about the royal family and some of the history between the two. In Promethia, there was a very clear division of power. The crown had it, and the Temple didn't interfere. It was their job to guide people to the light, not to force it upon them.

Traditionally one of the seats on the closed council belonged to a temple priest, but in recent years as the prince took on more responsibility, those invites had been coming less frequently. The prince was setting a clear precedent that he would make the important decisions when his father passed and wouldn't require the help of as many advisors.

It all seemed like pretty standard stuff until Tim remembered that the king was sick. Was this some kind of regicide happening, or was there something else at play? They needed to get the stone for Eternia, and it seemed like negotiating with the prince was going to be a bad idea. There was no way to form a plan until they had more information.

He sat back and listened to Brother Khalil as he droned on about the history of the land. Before he knew it, the carriage stopped. A few moments later, the door opened, and Grant stuck his head in. "We're here."

Brother Khalil was the first to get up, and he barely fit through the carriage door on his way out. "If you'll all follow me into the temple, I can give you the tour."

Cassie was about to grumble something, but instead of saying what was on her mind, her eyes moved around the walls and the armed guards wearing the crown's livery instead of the temple's.

JaKobi looked thrilled about being here. His mind was probably already focused on scouring the temple's library. "Maybe there's a place we can refresh ourselves and get something to eat?"

Tim nodded and continued. "It's almost evening now, and we've been going non-stop since this morning. Maybe a spot of rest, and we could meet you for dinner."

Brother Khalil held his arms wide in supplication. "Of course, that would be fine. I only ask that you stay inside your quarters until I join you for dinner."

It almost sounded like a threat, but Tim couldn't see any malice in the priest's eyes. If it wasn't a threat, it was a warning. Things inside the castle were worse than they thought. The entire time they were here they needed to tread carefully. As the rest of the group entered their chambers, Tim stopped and extended his hand.

"Thank you for your help." Tim tried to convey with his eyes that he'd picked up on a little of what was going on but needed some help to get the rest of the way there.

Brother Khalil slapped the hand away and pulled him into a hug. "Just stay put until I return," he whispered.

They broke apart with Khalil laughing warmly. "It's good to see you again, old friend. I will join you as soon as the food is ready."

Maybe ShadowLily was right, and the priest wasn't all there. "Of course." Tim bowed low. "Don't let us keep you from your duties any longer." He turned and headed into their rooms, not liking the sound of the door locking behind him when it closed.

"What in the hell was that?" Lorelei glared at the door. "I thought this was supposed to be the easy part."

Tim didn't know where to start. "All I know is that there's something wrong with the king, and we'll find out more when Brother Khalil comes back."

"Ugh. Now we have to do a quest before we can do a quest," Cassie groused. "Just send me to the big-ass thing so I can bop it on the head already."

"Bop it on the head, really?" ShadowLily giggled. "It might be more complicated than that."

Cassie gave her a knowing smile. "Tell me, when was the last time we solved a problem without violence?"

"We didn't fight the duke." JaKobi held up his hand so he wouldn't get smacked. "But she has a point."

Tim thought about it for a moment.

Yes, it normally came down to them winning a fight to move forward, but how they got to that fight mattered. They couldn't blast their way toward the king's chambers and expect a warm welcome. They needed to find out more about what was going on and how to handle it. If Brother Khalil thought there were ears on them all the time, there was no easy way for them to know how much of what he told them on the journey over was true.

"I'm tired of waiting to do my class change quest. I wanna level up so I can dish out some more hurt." Cassie smashed her fist into her palm so everyone was clear on the situation.

He'd been feeling that way as well, but the last thing Tim wanted to do was abandon their main quest while they were still winning the fights. If they could keep taking down the bosses, they could do their class changes after getting Eternia the stone.

Wasn't saving the world more important than self-gratification?

Despite the answer being yes, the siren song of new skills called to him. "How about this, we lose a battle, and we'll take a break to focus on our class changes. Until then, I say we buckle down and get Eternia the stone. Neema and Khalid are counting on us."

Tim looked over the group. "This isn't a dictatorship. What do you want to do when we get the next leg of the quest?"

"You know my vote." Cassie sat. "That's even if we have to do the marquess run again or a quest for the duke."

JaKobi looked stunned. "If she wants it so bad, she's willing to do side quests to get it?" He shrugged helplessly. "I'm with her."

Lorelei jumped in next. "I don't want to be the swing vote, but I'm with Tim."

ShadowLily looked between her best friend and her boyfriend, faced with a tough decision. Her face clouded with doubt, and she looked like she would rather be anywhere but there. Tim felt his heart go out to her and was about to tell her everything would be fine when there was a knock at the door.

The lock turned without waiting for their response. Tim didn't have to say anything to Cassie. She stood in front of all of them with her staff out, ready to take on whatever might be coming their way.

Two men in full armor pushed their way into the room and drew their swords.

Tim had no idea what was happening. They were supposed to be safe inside the temple. If Vitaria's corruption had reached this far, their quest was in great jeopardy. He'd feel bad about having to slay some of the king's guards, but he wasn't going to let them kill him. He dropped into his Way of the Boulder stance and prepared for battle.

A man dressed in a simple tunic with tight but flexible leather pants strode into the room. His haircut was a no-nonsense military style, and he wore a crown. It wasn't the type of thing a king would wear so this might've been the prince.

Why would the prince be here?

Tim's mind was spinning in circles as the man looked at them, turned to his guards, and calmly stated, "Swords down, and get out."

"But sir, they're armed." the guard retorted, clearly worried about what would happen to him if any harm befell the crown prince.

"I gave you an order." The prince didn't snap or lash out. He uttered the words in the same calm tone he'd been speaking in.

This was the kind of man they couldn't risk taking lightly. He had power, commanded it with calm assertiveness that left no question about who was in charge, and did it without sounding like he was talking down to them. It was a real skill, and one Tim wouldn't mind having someday.

"We'll be right outside." The guard sheathed his weapon and nudged his partner to do the same.

When the door was closed, Crown Prince Desmond of Promethia turned to address them. "Now that the circus is out of town, do you mind if I sit?"

Tim double-checked the NPC's nameplate and double-checked again to make sure it was who he thought he was. "Of course," Tim mumbled and pointed toward the table.

"I'm surprised the High Priest sent such untrained adventurers to handle our problem." Desmond sat. "I don't see how the five of you could succeed when some of our bravest knights ended up slaughtered."

Cassie bristled. "We have that kind of juice."

ShadowLily tapped her foot against Tim's leg under the table and mouthed "negotiation."

Tim blinked a couple of times. It was odd how the prince phrased what he said. The High Priest hadn't sent them to help the crown. They were coming because they needed something. Either it was a bold tactic to throw them off guard, or the wires had gotten crossed somewhere. He was betting that his girlfriend was right.

"Maybe you've come to the wrong chambers. The High Priest hasn't sent us to handle an issue for the crown. We're here on a quest of our own." Tim hoped the prince understood he was saying they didn't mind helping, but it sure as shit wasn't going to be free, and doing so with enough respect to keep them out of a dungeon.

The prince thought about what to say for a moment, then visibly made a decision. "Maybe it's time we laid our cards on the table." He motioned to encompass the entire group. "I know that you've come for the stone."

"And?" Tim held Desmond's eyes.

The prince looked over the group and shook his head as if he still couldn't believe they were the right ones for the job. "I need something of grave importance done, but I can't hand this task to just anyone."

"Trust me. We're the ones to handle it." Cassie gave him a look that would have curdled milk at twenty paces.

Tim tried probing a little deeper. "What's stopping you?"

"Your level of training for one." The crown prince snorted as he looked them over. "You haven't progressed your classes."

JaKobi looked at Tim and held his hands up to the side of his head, then blew them up in the classic "mind blown" gesture.

Guess that settles what we're doing next.

Surprisingly, it was Cassie who wasn't having any of it. "Do you know what we had to do to get here? Now you want to send us back on repeat so we can save your ass? Forget it."

Desmond looked from her to Tim in confusion.

"Getting from the city through the three boroughs to your gates isn't an easy task." JaKobi moved so he was right next to Cassie. "I don't think any of us want to repeat the experience if we don't have to."

Tim filled the prince in on the details, brushing over the bribery they'd committed at the first gate.

There was a genuine rage in Desmond's eyes. "They go too far. He isn't dead yet."

The prince stood and moved toward the door with purpose. He stopped at the entry and looked back at the adventurers. "Here is your quest if you want it, but I suggest training up a bit before you take it on."

The prince stormed out of the room as a quest icon popped up.

Guess there won't be any more negotiating.

Quest Received: Saving the King

The king of Promethia has been cursed by the witch Isadora after stealing lands from the crown. She says they're owed to her because the crown seized her family home. Desmond looked into her claims personally and found them lacking anything of substance. The crown offered to lease the unused lands to her for the fee of one gold a year if she healed the king. The witch Isadora refused.

The kingdom will not negotiate with the Witch of Lies any longer. She needs to be stopped and the king restored to health. Secure the antidote but above all else make sure that the witch doesn't survive to attack again.

Reward for killing the witch: Twenty gold, an item from the treasury, and you will earn friendly status with the crown.

Reward for saving the king: The Stone of Immoratis.

The prince was gone. There wasn't anything to think about. It wasn't the perfect deal, but it gave them a chance to get the stone so he accepted the quest.

As soon as he accepted it, he realized they still didn't have an easy way back through the gates if they decided to take the prince's advice. He was in the process of kicking himself when the door opened again, and Brother Khalil came into the room and closed the door behind himself.

"The prince gave me this on his way out, said it would help you with your problem." The priest held out the crown seal.

Tim quickly pocketed the item as he looked over Brother Khalil with new respect. "So the prince isn't a bad guy?"

"Not that I've seen. Desmond is driven and unrelenting in his expectation of excellence, but never cruel." Brother Khalil spread his arms wide as if to say sorry for the deception earlier. "Will you be staying with us for the night or returning to the city?"

"Can you give us a moment?" Tim wanted to find out where everyone stood now that they had the quest.

"Of course. I'll wait outside." Brother Khalil exited and closed the door.

This time it didn't lock.

Cassie looked pissed. "Screw that fucking prince. I say we show him we can handle it."

"I wanted to go and fight before. Nothing's changed except my vote." JaKobi grinned as he kissed Cassie.

Lorelei looked torn. "I want to get back to Neema, but the way the prince looked at us makes me think we'd be better off completing our class change quests first. We're going to have to do them anyway, might as well make the fights easier on ourselves."

ShadowLily made sure she wasn't going to be casting the deciding vote this time. "I'm with Lorelei. We might as well go into our next big fight as stacked as possible."

This was why democracy sometimes sucked because at the end of the day, it still felt like Tim had to make the choice alone, and either way, it was going to disappoint some people. They both had points, and he'd been super gung-ho about going on, but now he wasn't so sure. What was the worst that could happen if they lost a fight?

It wasn't logical, but he wanted to get in another fight. Maybe Cassie was starting to wear off on him, or her addiction to loot was. Whatever it was, he was ready to see what the next level of fighting would look like, and he was sure they had the skills to take it on.

"I say we fight." Tim looked over at the two women he'd disappointed only to find them smiling.

Lorelei walked past him toward the door. "Better hope we pull this off."

The time for doubting his choice was over. The task before them was to kill the witch Isadora, and he aimed to see it done. The Blue Dagger Society never failed, and they weren't going to start now.

CHAPTER EIGHTEEN

Grant's carriage wasn't suitable for the dirt roads, so Brother Khalil had lent them horses.

Tim already missed the luxury of a padded seat as his balls hit the saddle for the umpteenth time. *Cowboys' balls must've been fucking steel.* Still, there wasn't really anything for him to complain about. They were following the map to the witch's hideout, and it felt good to be on the hunt.

If the only way to secure the stone was to save the king, merely killing Isadora was as good as failing. Cassie might lose her shit if they had to start negotiations again. Although with their status set to friendly instead of neutral, they might be able to secure the Stone of Immoratis as a quest reward instead of a bonus for completion.

Tim's mind kept playing out scenarios where they saved the king, and a happy, healthy royal family showered them with any additional gifts their minds could fathom.

A guy could dream, couldn't he?

They followed the coast until they turned toward the forest. None of them had ever been on this side of Promethia before. The main road leading out of the city led to Tristholm. Several smaller gates led to hamlets, but there was no easy way this far north without traveling through the king's land. It was much less daunting using the king's gate instead of spending a week going around.

The perks of carrying the royal seal were awesome, and he planned on taking advantage of them as long as he had the item in his possession.

Cassie slowed her horse to a walk. "We're almost to the spot marked on the map. Once we get there, we have to proceed on foot."

"I don't get why we couldn't have waited until the morning and taken a carriage outfitted for the wild." JaKobi yawned. "Are you sure you guys want to do this now?"

Tim tried for a little bravado. "Saving the day before going to bed is what we do for shits and gigs."

Lorelei grinned. "Plus, when Eternia has the stone, and the portal network is back up, I can go see Neema whenever I want."

"That's assuming things go smoothly with the king or the prince if we can't secure the antidote." ShadowLily shrugged. "Just being practical. Rulers aren't exactly known for their incredible honesty or keeping their word."

A smile started at the corners of Cassie's mouth. Then it burst into a full-on grin. "That's when we get to do things my way."

"Head-bopping time." Lorelei snickered, making all of them laugh.

There was a small clearing on the right and a place to tie up their horses. The trail ahead was lit by two giant crisscrossed torches. JaKobi cast his light spell anyway, and the rest of the party cast their buffs.

"Everyone ready to kick some ass?" Tim waited until he got a nod from everyone. "Then let's do this."

Cassie led the way past the torches, and they followed her in single file. The trail was narrow enough they couldn't walk side by side but wide enough the trees weren't brushing them. The forest didn't give them any opportunity to see more than a few feet off the trail in any direction. There could've been an army hiding just out of sight, and they would've never known.

The trail continued winding deep into the forest. By this point, Tim could've asked which way was north, and everyone would have pointed in a different direction, and he would've believed all of them. They kept moving forward regardless, and for the next hour, they didn't see a thing.

Tim was starting to think JaKobi was right and they should've taken Brother Khalil up on his offer of a room when he noticed the torchlight. "Anyone else see that light up ahead?"

"Finally, some action." Cassie looked like she wanted to sprint forward, but at the last second, she stopped herself.

She really is one hell of a tank.

The path they were on slowly widened until they could get in a more standard battle formation. Cassie led their group up to the gate with the confidence of Achilles outside the gates of Troy. She never missed a beat even when the woman dropped from the trees right into their path.

"These lands are off-limits, interlopers. Cross the next gate at your peril." A vine-like rope shot from her wrist into the treetops and the woman disappeared from view.

Tim stood staring at where the woman disappeared like Spiderman. "Well, that was some creepy shit."

"Like I'm going to let some little bitch with a magic rope stop us." Cassie twirled her staff. "Sack up, boys. It's time to ride."

They were all buffed up and ready to go. There was no reason to delay any longer. Tim nodded at the tank. "Lead the way."

Cassie moved forward. She crossed the threshold into the new area, and the rest of the group was right behind her. The path inside looked much like the path on the other side of the barrier, except this one was twice as wide, letting them spread out enough that a single attack wouldn't be able to hit all of them.

ShadowLily lunged forward. "Cassie, watch out."

Her arm closed on the tank's, and she yanked her backward, but it wasn't fast enough. Six foot-long spikes erupted from the ground and skewered Cassie so many times it looked like someone's perverted idea of a human porcupine. Tim cast his heals instantly, but it was too late.

Cassie was dead.

The spikes receded, dumping Cassie's body at their feet. Tim worked on healing ShadowLily's arm as JaKobi moved toward his dead girlfriend's body. He reached out to touch her, and the body burned away in a swirl of golden motes like one of the bosses.

Fire rippled across his robes, and JaKobi launched spells into the trees. "I don't care if I have to burn this whole fucking place down. I'm coming for you."

A small dart shot out of the trees. One of ShadowLily's throwing knives deflected it. "We have to move," she shouted. "Stay behind me and keep up."

The assassin ran, and Lorelei was right behind her. Tim chugged hard in third place, and JaKobi brought up the rear. The two nimble women pulled farther away, and it wasn't long before he heard JaKobi go down behind him. Lorelei and ShadowLily turned, ran back to help, and were punctured full of darts.

Both of them fell to the ground dead.

Tim dropped to his knees. The darts seemed better than missing one of the traps and getting skewered.

A lone female warrior walked down the path toward him. She had tattoos down one side of her face, and her ears were almost elven. Her feet and midriff were bare, and her dark green loose-fitting clothes, mixed with her very tan skin, would've made it impossible to track her through the tree's canopy. She pulled a light spear from behind her back.

The warrior tested the weight of her weapon for a moment and threw it with deadly precision. The spear hit him hard in the chest, sending him to the ground. Pain lanced through his body as the woman's face swam into view.

"Tell that spineless king, this land is mine, and I'll kill any who try to take it from me." She yanked her spear free, sending him into oblivion.

You have died.

CHAPTER NINETEEN

It had been a long time since he died in the game.

If dying didn't hurt so much, it wouldn't have been as big of a pain in the ass. Not to mention Tim had no idea where he was going to respawn. When he left Barbara's office, the game could dump him anywhere.

The last thing he wanted after being handed such a soul-crushing defeat was to have to walk back to the castle, then back to Promethia so they could do their class change quest. Tim looked back on the encounter and tried to think of something he could learn from it.

The only lesson he took to heart was one of humility.

The crown prince stood right in front of them and told them to finish their class change quests before taking on Isadora. Tim should have known as soon as Cassie was on his side he wasn't making the best logical decision. At the end of the day it had been his choice to make, and he led them right to their deaths. When he looked back on their successes, it was easy to see why they'd been able to string so many together. It was because they did things the right way.

Always be prepared.

"I won't make that mistake again." Tim made the vow to himself as his body solidified in the waiting room.

"I hear that," a mountain of a man in full plate grumbled. He pointed at his singed armor. "I will repeat this only once. No matter how much you drink, do not, and I repeat, do not ever take a bet to tickle a dragon's balls."

An older man with a bald head rumbled, "Imagine how you'd feel if you woke up to some stranger tickling your balls."

"At least your death was quick. I got stepped on and felt my insides go outside," a sorceress in a diaphanous gown replied as she tucked a bit of purple hair behind one ear.

Tim didn't hide his smile as he listened to people around the room talking about the way they'd died before coming to the waiting room. Some of their stories were funny, and some were tragic, but they all shared a common bond in their love for gaming and their hatred of dying for silly mistakes.

When it was Tim's turn to talk about dying, he shared with the same gusto as the others. "Our entire party was taken out in moments, and then." Tim grabbed his chest. "I took a spear right to the heart."

"A chick with a spear took you out? That sounds kinda hot." The woman with the purple hair looked intrigued.

Tim was about to answer when the door to the waiting room opened, and Barbara appeared. His bubbly caseworker pointed at her shirt. It showed him taking the spear to his chest. Then it flashed to a picture of the woman who killed him smiling as she walked away. "I'm ready for you, Tim. We gotta get you back into the action. People really can't get enough of you guys."

"That's Tim," a teenage elf whispered to his friend with awe.

His friend, a surly-looking half-orc, glared in Tim's direction. "Thought he'd look cooler in person. You know, more magical or something?"

"It has to be him. Look how fast his caseworker showed up."

The young man's voice cut off as they stepped into the hallway and the door closed behind Tim.

It was crazy to think that he might run into people who watched him play the game from back in the real world. With new gamers joining all the time, it had to happen eventually. It was a good thing he had ShadowLily and Cassie to bust his balls, or he might let something like this go to his head.

If nothing else, Barbara's shirts always had a way of reminding him that he wasn't quite so all-powerful as he liked to think. The shirts used to be a point of contention with him. No one liked to see a replay of their death unless the rest of their group pulled off an epic win.

It kind of felt like she was rubbing the defeats in his face until he realized it was her way of keeping people grounded in the fact that it was a game. It was easy to forget that things happening inside the game weren't real when your every instinct said they were.

Tim wanted to make sure Barbara knew he was over the whole shirt thing and kind of liked them. In short, he was tossing out an olive branch. "That's an awesome shirt."

"Do you like it?" She stopped and turned so he could see it again. "I also have this version." This time the scene showed their entire party getting killed in a matter of moments. "It didn't feel personal enough."

She stuck her tablet's stylus into her mouth and chewed on the end like a pencil before switching her shirt back to the version of Tim dying. "Let's get to my office and square away the details so you can get back into the game."

He followed her down the white hallway and into her office. With the door closed behind them, he felt safe. It was like they were in a little pocket dimension and nothing could happen to him here unless he made Barbara angry. By the broad smile on her face, that would be nearly impossible.

Barbara stuck her tablet into the docking station and tapped her pen on her monitor a few times before turning to face Tim. "Did I tell you that I spoke with your mother?"

Tim's mouth dropped open.

"She was a real handful with corporate. Wouldn't stop calling about the money in her checking account until she could speak with someone who knew her son directly."

The one thing he never thought of was his parents being suspicious of the deposits. "Sounds like you made a friend."

"I did." Barbara touched her shirt, and it flashed to a picture of her and his family at a barbecue. "I think they feel a lot better knowing someone is looking out for you."

He couldn't take his eyes off the image. It was easy to forget about his family because he was so busy with the game, but seeing them now made him realize how much he missed them. It was nice to know if he ever needed an update, all he had to do was die, and Barbara could give it to him.

"They're doing fantastic, by the way." Barbara hit the screen on her tablet and a few new pictures projected into the air. "Your dad said he was going to save the money and give it back to you when you got out, but I told them in no uncertain terms that you wanted them to spend it."

Tim groaned. "They probably hated that."

"They might have grumbled a bit, but they agreed to use the money." Barbara stopped the slideshow, turned her monitor back around, and typed on her keyboard.

The images of his family were gone, but Tim felt relieved knowing his little contribution to their bottom line was helping out. He trusted his parents to use the money for things they needed to fix around the house they'd been putting off for years. Sometimes all it took to make life easier was a new washer and dryer. His parents weren't fancy people. They would always spend extra money on practical things.

"I see here that we have your entire party under contract now."

She tapped her screen and turned toward Tim. "I signed them all up once you guys hit the top twenty."

Barbara pouted. "Maybe I shouldn't have ruined the surprise. The rest of your group is finding out about their promotions now. Their bank accounts haven't been debited for fees in some time, or they've received some of their fees back if they prepaid."

That was fucking awesome!

Money was one of those things you didn't talk about with your friends. You expected if they needed help, they would ask, and if they didn't, everything was probably fine. None of them mentioned struggling to stay in the game, and now he might know why. It was a huge relief knowing something as little as payments wouldn't break up their team.

"You just made my day twice in five minutes. If you ruined the surprise, I'll let it slide." Tim finally felt like he knew for certain he'd made the right choice when deciding to be a gamer instead of getting a regular job.

Something about gaming brought people together. It was like video games had this mystical power about them. Beyond the forum trolls and the clickbait articles written to stir up the community, there was a true sense of friendship among gamers that he couldn't explain. Once a person created a character, it was a fresh beginning and a great way to make new friends.

"Let's make it three times then." Barbara pointed at the screen. "You've received a small bump in pay, and if you accept the extension, your pay will look more like this, based on viewership, bottoming out here, and topping out here."

Tim looked at the numbers and nodded. If things stayed like this, he would come out of this game debt-free from the streaming contract alone. Any gold or items he sold along the way would be extra cash to start whatever the next chapter in his life would be.

Even if that chapter was right where he was now.

He placed his thumb on the screen and accepted the contract. "Thanks, Barbara, this is awesome. I hate dying so much, but every time I do, you give me the best news. Totally takes the sting out of it."

"Well, you keep earning me bonuses for finding unique talent, and I'll keep trying to get you more money." She stood from her desk. "Any other questions?"

His family was doing good, inside and outside the game. Tim couldn't think of another thing he needed to know about right then unless he could control where he was going to respawn. "Any way you can tell me where everyone respawned and send me to the same place?"

Barbara pulled up her tablet. "None of you had access to the bind points in the castle or beyond. Looks like everyone is going to respawn back in the center of Promethia."

"At least it will save us a walk." Tim wondered how long it would take him to complete his class quest when he got back.

The Blue Dagger Society had some payback to dish out.

"Buy a round for everyone on me." Barbara handed Tim a silver coin. "I don't want to see you back here until I get to try your mom's lasagna next month."

The portal back into the game world opened before him, and Tim pulled Barbara into a quick hug. "Thanks for looking in on my family."

"Stop being a big gushy baby." Barbara broke their hug and shoved him through the opening.

It felt like he was falling. Then there was a gut-wrenching twist like something hooked him around the midsection and pulled him toward his destination.

CHAPTER TWENTY

Tim always ended up on his knees after portaling, but at least he didn't throw up anymore.

He stood on the stone cobbles and tried to get his bearings for a moment. Then the world settled in around him. It took him about four seconds before he felt confident his first step wouldn't send him back to the ground, but then he was moving. He took the first step as gingerly as a newborn foal, but his stride evened out as he moved out of the courtyard and back into the city.

If the others spawned in the same location, they were probably waiting for him back at the inn.

A low rumble bubbled up from deep within his stomach as Tim walked. "I have the munchies." It was worse than the time Xander bought that hookah.

When he looked up at the sun, it was easy to tell why. It was just about midday, and he hadn't eaten since dinner on horseback. Not the kind of meal that would leave anyone full and satisfied. Knowing how hungry his fiery best bud got, Tim expected when he returned to the inn, there would be a feast from Joe's waiting for him.

Knowing that the others had probably handled the food situation, Tim started thinking about the next steps. Some of his skills might be replaced with better ones or might disappear altogether. It made sense to go over his list of current skills to find out where he stood before searching for his class trainer.

Tim pulled up his user interface, found the correct screen with a few mental clicks, and adjusted the size to read it while walking. Now that he had a fairly decent chance of not walking into the side of a building or one of the gas lamps, he continued his journey. Enjoying his newfound ability to multitask, he ducked around some refuse in the street and pulled up the first of his skill updates.

Skill Increased: Quick Feet

Rank: Apprentice two

Run, run, run. **No, this isn't a music video. It's you running away from things over and over again. Maybe start running toward things or leaping through the air while moving fast if you want this skill to progress quicker.**

Tim felt like that was a little unfair.

He used Quick Feet to run toward people sometimes. Not nearly as much as he saved the skill for a quick get-the-hell out-of-Dodge free card, though. On the flip side, he'd never considered using it while running around and jumping in the air while running two or three times his max speed seemed kind of dangerous.

Like the old pillowcase parachute.

The fact he could use the skill in ways he hadn't thought about yet intrigued him. If he ever needed to jump across a chasm now, he might have the skill to do it with as long as the gap was a small one. There was no reason to fall to his death like Neo would've done if his first jump in the matrix wasn't a simulation. Another trip to see Barbara wasn't the worst thing in the world, but Tim leaned toward practicing his jumping ability over something that wouldn't cause his death before going full Evel Knievel.

Skill Increased: Rectify

Rank: Apprentice two

Removing buffs from targets can be extremely beneficial. Who needs a monster dealing extra damage or pumping out enormous amounts of healing? Not you, that's who. When you see the enemy has a buff in place, use this skill to try removing it.

Tim really liked that his buff remover and interrupt were separated. Now he didn't have to make a hard choice in the middle of a fight to save the skill or spend it. He could already tell that interrupts would be a large key to their success moving forward, but if he could also stop an enemy from doing extra damage or taking less of theirs, this spell was worth using every single time it was off cooldown.

Skill Increased: Disturbance

Rank: Apprentice three

Thought you were going to get obliterated by the big whammy, but you didn't? This skill is almost always the reason why. Bosses get many useful skills to try killing you, and it seemed unfair that there was nothing you could do to stop it. Now all you have to do is watch the boss for a moment of opportunity. Land your interrupt or multiple interrupts at the right time, and you might not only stop an attack but create a window of increased damage for you and your party.

So if they stopped a boss' attack by coordinating their interrupts, there might be a chance the boss would take more damage for a small window of time. That was fucking awesome. It made interrupting an attack almost more important than doing damage. Not only would it stop them from getting hit by something nasty, but the chance to knock off a few extra percentage points could be the difference between victory and death.

Any time they could do more damage and take less, Tim considered it a huge win.

Skill Increased: Dodge

Rank: Journeyman three

Like your inherent knack for running away, you tend to avoid getting hit. At first, we thought it might be luck, but you've shown a real knack for staying out of harm's way. It's almost like someone is looking out for you.

Yep, right until I got corpsified.

Tim grinned as he kept walking toward the inn. Sure, he was lucky sometimes, like when the game put Lucy Briarthorn in his path, but two things contributed to his overall success, and neither of them was luck. He'd been putting in the work since his first day inside the game, and for the most part, he'd managed to do it with a positive attitude.

It was easy to turn any bit of adversity from a molehill into a mountain if he wanted to. Instead, Tim always tried to focus on what he could control in any situation. Right now, he loved his job, and it made working hard seem like the only smart decision.

Skill Increased: Behold My Power

Rank: Journeyman five

Sometimes you don't care who you hurt. Only a real sadist would constantly harm their friends to do a little extra damage. Just kidding, we don't care if you murder your friends to damage the boss. We created the skill, after all. Just make sure your heals are on point, or they may start to resent you for it.

Tim started cackling as he walked down the street. Anyone passing him must've thought he was nutso. He imagined what he must look like staring off to the right of center and laughing at something no one else could see. It was like the first time he passed someone with Bluetooth built into their sunglasses.

You talking to me?

Tim managed to stop drawing attention to himself but still wore a big smile as he thought about what Cassie would do to him if he killed her with his curse. *Oh, there will be pain.*

Of course, only he would pick a class where one of his skills as a healer required him to damage his party. It was counterintuitive to his role in the game, but Behold My Power did so much damage it was worth it.

Skill Increased: Divine Light

Rank: Journeyman five

ZAP! You've been struck by a smooth goddess. Seriously though, this is like your own little blast of Zeus' lighting. Point, shoot, and watch for the fireworks. When Divine Light reaches the master ranks it earns a bonus, so keep working at it. The proof is in the pudding.

Was it wrong that instead of delectable chocolate pudding, all he thought of now was Margot Robbie dressed as Harley Quinn? Mr. J probably wouldn't like Tim thinking dirty thoughts, but maybe ShadowLily could do the hair thing again, and he could buy her a bat. He might have to dust off his Dark Knight cap, but if he could indulge in his fantasies, it seemed only fair that she could too.

It took a few seconds for him to realize he was still walking down the street. He blushed so hard that anyone walking by probably thought he was about to stroke out. He pulled up the hood of his robes and continued his journey. There would be time for Harley Quinn and Batman later. Now he had to finish reviewing his skills.

Skill Increased: Healing Storm

Rank: Journeyman five

Everyone loves a little rain, and the fact that yours also heals them makes it even better. Sometimes healing one person at a time isn't enough or efficient. In those scenarios, call on the goddess' light to make it rain.

Tim felt like he was walking on air as he kept moving. This skill update didn't come with any snarky comments or hints on how to use the spell, just a nice little reminder that he was doing things right. Healing Storm was his go-to when they were all taking damage as soon as everyone had the Rehydrated buff from Healing Orb. It was a damn good spell and his bread and butter for AOE.

Skill Increased: Who Needs a Shield

Rank: Journeyman five

Seriously, someone in your group should have a shield, but none of you do. At least you have one spell handy for when things go sideways. Let's be honest about it. Things go sideways for your group quite a bit.

The snark filter apparently only lasts for one skill.

Tim snorted as he reread the description. It wasn't exactly, not true. The Blue Dagger Society tended to get into a lot of trouble, but they always made it out. Well, not always, but most of the time they made it out of things just fine. Reducing Cassie's damage and boosting her already inherently high dodge chance was like getting twenty seconds of damage reduction.

In a boss fight, twenty seconds might as well have been an eternity.

Skill Increased: Curse of Giving

Rank: Journeyman eight

We probably should've changed the title for this skill, but it's ironic, right? You've almost mastered this skill, which goes a long way to show you understand the basics and use the spell efficiently. Continue making this curse your bread and butter move, and you'll be a master in no time.

Curse of Giving was awesome, and it was the only skill he continually watched the ticker for so he could reapply it to the boss the instant it fell off. Having Rehydrate and the HOT from Curse of Giving on Cassie made his life easier. Each time she took damage, half of it healed almost instantly, and the next half when the spell ticked again. Anything the HOTs couldn't keep up with, he supplemented with Healing Orb or by blasting the boss with another damaging ability.

Skill Increased: Cleanse

Rank: Journeyman nine

No one likes a dirty mouth, and to use this skill, you don't have to buy a pack of Orbitz. Not to knock the wonderfulness

that is gum, but Cleanse has one up on a dirty mouth: it will clean your entire body. Feeling a little off, maybe a little poison on that blade that nicked your arm? You have the spell to take care of all your worries. That's right, one spell that does it all. Quick, clean, simple. Just the way you like it.

It was truc. There was nothing Tim hated more than when games filled up millions of keys with useless skills. Why should he need one cleanse for one type of damage and another for a different kind? Sure, it made sense from a lore or story perspective, but as a gamer it sucked, and it wasn't fun. There should always be one cleanse to rule them all.

He was happy *The Etheric Coast* recognized that healers had enough to do and didn't need to search through a list of possible spells while someone was dying from a debuff.

Tim clicked his interface again and realized there wasn't another update. He'd made it to the end of the list. The only thing that surprised him was that there was no update to his Healing Orb. He'd expected a jump in what it would take to level the skills in the master ranks, but not making any progress after he used a metric shit-ton of Healing Orb in an all-out heal-fest during the last fight seemed odd.

Game's just reminding me, I have to earn it.

There were no easy roads to success, so it wasn't a huge shocker that people who worked hard found it more often than those who didn't. Tim was a grinder. He liked to put his nose down and get shit done. Almost to the point where he couldn't stop himself from digging into a project until he finished it, even if he missed other things.

It was his nature.

So when the game said, you gotta step it up, not only was he ready, but he accepted the challenge with a smile.

Game fucking on!

CHAPTER TWENTY-ONE

The feeling of relief when a person sees home after a long day of work is palpable.

In this case, he hadn't quite reached the slums yet, but the familiar arch leading to his home was there along with the two guards. Chris and Barry weren't bad guys and seemed to like their positions at the newly renovated arch well enough. That didn't stop the two men from busting his balls every time he ran into them.

I swear they exist to keep me humble.

Chris tapped Barry on the chest. "Look who we have here. King of the Slums."

"Not so slummy anymore. Me and the missus talked about renting one of the apartments," Barry replied before he looked up to see Tim standing there. "Her mother would never hear of it."

Tim clapped Barry on the shoulder, startling the man. "If you're planning on moving into one of my buildings, let me know. I'll shoot a message over to Mr. Applebottom and get you fifteen percent off the going rate."

Before Barry could respond, Chris hinted, "Some of us get hungry from time to time."

Were they hitting him up for favors instead of giving him shit? There had to be a way he could work this to his advantage.

First things first, Tim had to lay his cards out on the table. "I don't own Joe's so I can't offer you anything there without talking to him, but I'm sure he'd be happy to offer something to two fine guardsmen such as yourselves. As for the inn, I'll have Liz set something up."

Tim leaned closer and spoke in a conspiratorial whisper so he could set the hook. "But I'm going to need something from you guys as well."

Barry and Chris shared a nervous glance.

"We can't break any rules, mind you." Chris glanced at the two medals on his chest.

Barry nodded. "Our duty will always be to the crown first."

"Nothing like that, guys." Tim tried to take the edge off. "It's not like I'm going to ask you to let me smuggle illicit goods into the city."

Lifting his fingers to the corners of his mouth, Tim pushed the edges up into a smile. "I want you guys to look happy. Our district is supposed to be inviting. I need people to come in and spend money, and that all starts with you."

No one wanted to spend money with armed guards giving them the death stare. Tim thought it might take a few minutes to get them on board with the idea of not being so stoic, but the two men were already taking his message to heart.

Chris grinned ear from ear. "Welcome to the slums."

"He said not to scare the people." Barry slapped him on the chest before trying on a smile of his own. "Welcome to the West-side Shopping District."

Tim had a moment of inspiration listening to the two men. Barry was right. What Tim needed to do was flip the script and change the narrative. The fact they still called this area the slums was a problem. They needed to rebrand, but was he allowed to do that? Surely, the slums wasn't the official title for the area. He would call it a shopping district until he heard otherwise, but what they needed to seal the deal was a sign.

Since entering the game, revitalizing the slums was his special project. Now that the buildings he purchased were being finished, Tim could funnel more of his gold into the side projects. They were already harnessing the rainwater to grow crops and feed a small pond one of the residents built a fish hatchery in. Next, they would expand the cobbled streets to the rest of the district. From there, his job would be to get out of the way and contribute where he could.

The people of the slums were hard workers, and now that they had easy access to a trading kiosk without an exorbitant fee attached, they were thriving. It amazed Tim that the kingdom had written these people off when their only crime was being poor. He knew exactly how that felt growing up, and the last thing he wanted to be a part of was being the guy who fixed up an area so the people who originally lived there couldn't afford to stay.

That wasn't revitalization. It was a hostile takeover.

While they needed to bring new blood into the area, they needed to keep everyone who wanted to stay in place. It was a tricky path to walk, but that was why he put Mr. Applebottom in charge. Since there wasn't a line of people standing outside the inn throwing tomatoes at him whenever he left, he assumed that things were going well.

He realized the two men were looking at him, waiting for him to say something about Barry's greeting.

"Sorry, I was thinking about what you said." Tim pointed toward the arch and then moved his hand from one side to the other as he spoke. "West Side Shopping District. I like it."

Barry was beaming with pride, but Chris looked a little crestfallen. Tim clapped him on the back. "The smile was great. Don't let this guy get in your head."

"Welcome to the West Side Shopping District." Chris motioned for him to enter.

Tim gave him a high five. "That was awesome, man!"

With both guardsmen in good spirits, it was time for him to have a little fun at their expense for a change. With a broad smile, Tim announced, "I'd love to have both of you guys living in the area. It would give us a certain sense of credibility having two of the King's Own living here."

Wiping the smile from his face in an instant, Tim focused a glare on Chris that would've peeled paint. "But I'm going to need you to lose the smile. Barry was right. It's a little creepy."

Chris lifted a fist and shook it gently. "Why, you little shit."

"That is Sir Shit, to you." Tim winked. "And don't you forget it."

Barry wiped some sweat from his forehead. "He has a sense of humor. Who knew?"

Chris nodded and looked at Barry with a deadly serious expression. "The magistrate of the slums strikes again."

"What happened to King of the Slums?" Tim mocked.

"That was before we knew you paid your taxes like everyone else," Chris admonished. "It's a good thing too, or you'd finally get to see us use these." He held out his halberd so the sunlight twinkled off the blade.

Barry spun his weapon in a neat arc and snapped to attention. "And we can." He gave a little bow. "I'll talk to the missus. When she finds out how much more she can spend a month, it'll seal the deal on the move."

"Sealing the deal is what got you saddled with her in the first place." Chris elbowed Barry in the ribs.

Tim chuckled as he moved past the two men on his way to the inn. Barry made a quip about quality over quantity, and the two were bickering again. He tried to keep his laughter to himself as their voices trailed away. Winning over the two men had taken some effort, but it was worth it. With the two guards on their side, there was no doubt the slums had better days ahead.

Once Tim stepped through the archway, the weather changed as it always did. Where it was bright and warm on one side, it was cold and drizzly on the other. There had been a time when the constant rain bothered him, but now it was a nice change of pace and only reminded him of home. It didn't take long for the inn to come into view, and seeing its sturdy wooden timbers made him feel better after being trounced by Isadora.

The healing shack was off to the side of the inn, and there was a small line waiting outside. He might not be here all the time, but when he was, it felt like his job to help with the healing as much as possible. After neglecting his duties for so long, it only seemed right to make an appearance before going inside.

He hit everyone who was waiting outside with a Healing Orb in rapid succession. It was amazing how many times he could cast spells when he was out of combat. Anyone who still had a problem after the barrage of healing, he Cleansed and healed them again. In a matter of minutes, the entire crowd dispersed.

The door to the healing shack opened, and a man came out looking relieved. He moved down the steps and past Tim without looking up. Judy was in the doorway a few moments later. Her smile considerably brightened when she saw who waited for her outside.

"What have you done with all of our patients?" Judy put a hand on her hip and gave Tim the kind of stern look only a mother or grandmother could.

He was about to respond when a young man poked his head out. "What did you say about the patients?" He looked past Judy to see no one waiting in line. "Now you see here," he began but stopped when Judy put a hand on his arm.

"This is Brother Gunther." She looked from the priest to Tim. "Gunther, this is Tim, founder of our little healing shanty."

The look on Gunther's face instantly changed as he marched down the three steps and pulled Tim into a hug. "Thank you for this. I've waited my entire life to get away from the temple politics and receive an assignment to a post where all I'm required to do is help others."

Wanting to get away from politics was something Tim understood completely.

Tim broke away from the hug and beamed at the young healer. He couldn't have been happier about the pick for the position. Still, only one opinion mattered on the issue since she had to work with him directly.

He turned to look at the woman who made his vision of a place to heal others come alive. "As long as Judy is happy, I'm happy."

"With the rest of the afternoon off, it's hard not to find a smile." Judy descended the steps and gave Tim a warm embrace. "It's good to have you back."

Sometimes, hearing a kind word was all it took to make him feel special. "Thank you."

He gave Judy another hug, and as they pulled apart, Tim spoke. "Probably no surprise that I'm in a hurry as usual, but if you need anything, I'll be in and out of the inn for the next couple of days. Or send me a message."

"What could I possibly need? Your Mr. Applebottom will hardly let me do a thing for myself these days." Judy looked exasperated.

What an interesting development.

God, he wanted the juicy details so badly, but it wasn't polite to pry. "As long as you're taken care of and happy." Tim put his emphasis on the word happy, letting Judy know he always had her back. "Then I'm happy."

"Oh, she's happy." Gunther grunted as he took an elbow to the ribs. "Maybe I'll head back inside." He shook Tim's hand. "It was a pleasure."

Being a complete gentleman, Tim ignored the fact that Judy

and Mr. Applebottom might've become a thing and pulled her into one last hug. "I mean it, Judy. You need anything, even funds for an assistant; all you have to do is ask."

"I'll keep that in mind," Judy replied with a little twinkle in her eye before heading back inside.

Turning to head for the inn, Tim couldn't help but smile from ear to ear. Sure, Isadora had murdered him, but the seeds he planted when he first started to buy properties in the slums were coming to fruition. There were people here he cared about, a community he wanted to be part of. It was like he finally found where he belonged in the world.

He expected the mood in the inn to be somber when he walked in, but there was a full-throttle party going on. Cassie was up on a table bellowing out some bawdy song while everyone clapped and danced around her. When she looked up and saw Tim, her eyes took on a fanatical gleam.

"There he is!" Cassie leapt off the table and charged straight for him.

Tim tried to curl up in a one-legged standing ball as he prepared for the worst. "Not in the face."

Instead of being punched, Cassie wrapped her arms around him in a bear hug and tried crushing him to death. "I got a streaming contract!"

Holy shit, he'd forgotten all about the contracts. No wonder they were celebrating. It was a good day to be alive when a person started getting paid to do what they loved. Their entire group was now playing the game for free and getting paid on top of it.

ShadowLily and Lorelei jumped onto Cassie's back, sending all four of them to the floor in a heap. "We all did!" they screamed together.

Strolling casually toward the pile of bodies on the floor, JaKobi sat on top as if his friends had become his throne. "Even I, your new leader, have received a most luxurious payday."

"I could do with a little less leadership right now," Tim wheezed.

JaKobi stood, looking as though he'd enjoyed his moment at the top no matter how brief it was. "Sure thing, boss."

They all climbed back to their feet, and he felt a rush of energy. Knowing that everyone had a future in the game even if they only kept playing together took a giant weight off his shoulders. The thought of replacing any of them now for someone new seemed absurd. They would rise or fall together.

"That's awesome, guys. No one deserves it more than all of you." Tim sipped the beer Liz pressed into his hand. "But we have work to do."

Cassie finished off her mug before slamming it down on the nearest table. With a belch that would have made Friar Tuck envious, she bellowed, "Hit me with a Cleanse and let's get down to business."

It didn't take him long to Cleanse the entire group and send out a wave of Healing Orb. He wondered how much people would pay for a service like this back in the real world. *Want to tailgate in the morning but get some work done in the afternoon? Call Tim for your hangover needs.*

He'd be a billionaire.

"No way to sugarcoat this. The witch ate our fucking lunch." Tim met each of their eyes in turn before continuing. "Our defeat was my fault. I ignored the prince, and it was a mistake each of you paid for."

Standing straighter, Tim continued. "We won't make that mistake twice. Let's split up and get our class change quests done. The prince is counting on us, and so is Eternia."

Fuck, even he felt inspired after that.

ShadowLily kissed him on the cheek. "I forgive you. That big brain of yours was bound to make a mistake eventually."

"None of us handled the fight well." JaKobi looked ashamed. "This time, I'm going to make her pay for hurting my lady."

Lorelei had the same fire in her eyes as the fire mage. "Payback is a bitch named revenge."

"Then let's get out of here and get to work." Everyone scattered, and Tim shouted after them, "If you won't be back by dinner, send a message."

He looked around and realized he was standing in an empty room until Liz emerged from the kitchen. He'd never had a request obeyed so fast in his life. He felt the same excitement all of them did, but damn.

Everything was about to change for them, and it was going to be amazing.

"Really cleared the place out, didn't you," Liz called from behind the bar as she wiped off a glass.

Tim smirked. "You know me. I have a special gift with people."

Liz tossed him a small sack. "Don't forget to eat something."

He snatched the bag out of the air and looked inside. "No, you didn't!"

"I did." Liz looked tickled pink with herself.

His eyes got huge as he pulled a dark chocolate peanut butter cup sprinkled with sea salt from the bag. He took the first bite, and they rolled back in his head as he tried not to drool. "It's like heaven."

"I knew you'd like it." She pulled out another bag and ate a peanut butter cup of her own. "So I took the liberty of ordering some for the bar."

Tim approved. "Wait until you try one baked inside a chocolate chip cookie."

"I don't even know what that is?" Liz looked like Tim had uttered a foreign language.

He walked toward the door. "Get with Roberto. He'll know what I'm talking about."

"I'd rather get with that carriage driver," Liz retorted, then looked shocked at herself.

Tim kept moving toward the door as if he hadn't heard a thing. When he was safely out of mug-throwing range, he called, "I'll send him a message and find out if he's available to give you a ride."

Beer mugs flew farther than he thought.

CHAPTER TWENTY-TWO

With Neema gone, Lorelei was happy to be getting some action.

As she walked toward her destination, she pulled up her user interface and looked up the class change quest to give it one more quick read-through.

Quest Received: So you want to be a Spirit Archer

You've experienced the animal side of things and decided to go in another direction. Congratulations on being bold. The spirit archer is the assassin of the ranged world. They're best used to deal a high amount of damage from medium range while harnessing the spirits of the dead to increase their dodge and damage-dealing abilities. Welcome to the big leagues. You've earned it.

To start your path of ascendance to spirit archer, find Felix Moonshadow at the Pepper Pot Flounder.

"It better not be a weird sex thing," Lorelei grumbled as she dismissed her user interface.

Her hands moved quickly across her weapons and trinkets, making sure everything was in place. She'd even managed to get her hands on a couple of minor healing potions because her healer wouldn't be there to bail her out if she made a mistake. Completing this quest on the first try was important to her on more than one level.

This was an opportunity to prove she could do things on her own. She'd been fighting with the group for so long it felt like she was losing some of her edge. If she wanted to be the best, Lorelei needed to stay hungry.

Have to be able to rely on yourself before you can count on others.

If there was one thing she was good at, it was counting on herself to come out on top. Sometimes to her detriment, but that was starting to change. Being part of a team made her feel like she had a place to call home. Even when she got pissed at the boys and their antics, it was only out of love. It was like she'd found two little brothers.

Ones that didn't care who she slept with.

Lorelei left the past in the past. This was her chance to forge a new beginning. Not only a fresh start, but when she signed her contract, they refunded her prepaid POD fees.

After all the bullshit she suffered with Tammy the Scammer, things were going amazingly well. For a game she never really wanted to play, signing up was quickly turning into one of the best decisions in her life. *The Etheric Coast* was letting her live the kind of life she always dreamed of.

If she had to pick her spirit animal, it would've been Erin fucking Brockovich crossed with Xena, and maybe a little of Ruby from *Ash vs The Evil Dead*. Sure, while not technically an animal, she was tired of everyone clinging to the, oh I wanna be a dolphin or something that flies. She didn't want to do any of those things. Lorelei wanted to kick ass and defend the innocent.

Maybe pocket a little coin along the way.

"That would be one badass bitch." Lorelei snickered as she picked up the pace.

It turned out she didn't have to worry about the Pepper Pot

Flounder being some weird sex term. Unless the picture of a giant copper pot with a spotted fishtail sticking out of it meant something different than we serve fish in a pot.

The squat one-story wooden building was right on the water's edge. Lorelei found a spot where she could lean against the wall of an older warehouse and watch the front door without being creepy. She had to pull out her bow and activate one of her skills to read the wording under the copper pot.

Fish stew so good, Eternia asked for the recipe.

"We'll have to see about that." Lorelei put her bow away and ran her hands over the handles of her knives as she watched the restaurant for signs of life.

The door to the restaurant opened, and a couple came out laughing and smiling. Their clothes were newer, marking them as slightly wealthy. The two of them had the walk that only people who overindulged in a meal could achieve. It wasn't quite a waddle, but it was so damn close it might as well have been.

The stew must be fantastic.

Seemed odd to her. Fish stew was something Lorelei would've skipped over on any menu. Her three staples when she went to any seafood restaurant were fresh lobster, gigantic shrimp, or a really good chowder. If they served the chowder in a fresh sourdough bread bowl, she would be a customer for life.

Based on the couple's happy look, she was about to broaden her horizons.

Inside, the restaurant smelled salty like the ocean. There wasn't a lot to see. In front of her was a small hostess station, and beyond it, a wide-open floor plan until her eyes found the kitchen entrance at the very back of the building.

"Welcome to the Pepper Pot Flounder. Table for one?" the hostess asked as she picked up a menu.

"I'm looking for someone. Maybe you could help me?" Lorelei turned up her charm to one thousand percent.

The hostess locked her up and down as if thinking about some-thing. "I've had worse offers."

Too much charm.

Lorelei played it off like she didn't hear a word. "Do you know anyone here named Felix?"

"Everyone's always looking for Felix. I don't get it. All the guy does is sit around here and eat stew." She tapped her chest where the name Maria appeared over her right breast. "I'm interesting. I want to do things besides eat stew."

Lorelei understood those feelings well. "I'm sure one day you'll find your passion."

If I didn't have Neema waiting, I might've helped you find it right now.

"For now, I need Felix." Lorelei tried her best not to look too cute, which probably only made her hotter.

Maria pointed. "He's over there, blue hat." She pulled out a small notepad. "He's going to want stew. Do you want some as well?"

"Two stews and anything else you think he would like." Lorelei knew dealing with a man when he had a happy belly was a million times easier than when he was hungry.

"Got it." Maria tucked her pad away and headed for the kitchen.

Lorelei watched her for a moment and zoned in on her target. Felix had his back turned toward her, but the electric blue hat was hard to miss. There weren't many people wearing bright colors, making her wonder if the cap was magical. Not wanting to scare him by walking up behind, she moved one row of tables over and continued her approach.

Felix spun out of his chair and dove to the side. He came up to a knee and disappeared. A second later, he popped back into exis-tence fifteen feet to the right and threw a knife at her.

"What the fuck?" Lorelei rolled to the side, came up with her bow in hand, and two arrows nocked and ready to fire.

Felix gave her a shallow bow. "Excuse the theatrics, but I had to see what I was working with." He motioned toward his table. "Please have a seat."

Circling the table slowly before taking her seat, Lorelei tried to think of something to say. She'd never run into a class trainer that threw a knife at her before. Well, at least not one that did it without introducing himself first.

"It was impressive how you were able to follow me even when I shifted." Felix looked excited by the achievement. "I can work with that."

Maria kept her tray in one hand and circled to Felix's knife stuck in the wall. She pulled the blade free and brought it back to the table with their food.

Setting down two bowls of stew and a small bottle of brandy, Maria admonished him, "Try not to poke holes in the walls."

"Don't get blood on the floor. Don't poke holes in the walls. How's a guy supposed to train anyone around here?"

Maria shook her head. "You're not training. This is a restaurant. You're supposed to eat."

"Oh, stew!" Felix looked delighted. "I can't get enough of this stuff."

Felix started to eat, and Lorelei looked down at the bowl in front of her. It smelled good enough, but she wasn't sure about it. Potatoes, carrots, celery, onions, and chunks of fish swirled around in the stock as she spun her spoon around the bowl. It seemed rude not to try a bite when the man she needed help from loved the stuff. She found a chunk of fish and lifted it to her mouth.

Steam drifted lazily up from the spoon so she blew on it for a second to cool it off. Closing her eyes and praying for the best, Lorelei put the spoon in her mouth and closed her lips around it. The initial taste of the broth was fantastic, and soon she was slurping away as fast as Felix.

"This stuff really is good." Lorelei was seriously considering ordering another bowl to go.

Felix tossed his spoon into his empty bowl and used a small

piece of bread to wipe up the last of the stock. "I take it you're as handy with your other skills as you are with that bow?" He lifted one eyebrow almost in a challenge.

"Better." Lorelei knew it sounded like a brag, but it was the truth.

She could run fast and dodge better than most and was talented enough with her hunting knife, but the bow was where her heart was. Practicing with the weapon took up most of her free time, but putting in the effort paid dividends when it came to dishing out the pain.

Lorelei still dreamed of being Robin Hood. She'd played out a little of the fantasy by helping the resistance in the desert, but at some point, she'd love to find a way to steal from the rich and give to the poor. Of course, she'd accomplish it all with a better sense of style and a healthy amount of flair.

What an adventure that would be.

For the time being, Lorelei was on a different path than Robin Hood, but an equally important one. As a spirit archer, she'd have to devote less time toward tracking and talking to animals and more time doing rock-solid DPS. Someone else could handle the tracking and talking to animals stuff. She wanted to shoot things and save the world.

Felix was watching her, hoping for more information, but when she didn't add anything else to the conversation, he continued. "I hope the bow talk isn't all bravado because what comes next is going to require you to do more than roll out of the way."

"What exactly is coming next?" Lorelei leaned back in her chair but was laser-focused on his response.

Felix poured a snifter of brandy, swirled it once, and swallowed the shot down whole. "The trials, of course. Enter and win; you'll leave as a spirit archer. Fail, and you die."

"Simple as that, huh?" Lorelei didn't like it when things sounded too easy.

Felix wagged a finger. "You're a sharp one, aren't you?"

Lowering the finger, eyes glittering with mischief, he grinned. "Of course, if you want to try again, you'll have to buy me more stew. I really can't get enough of this stuff."

Sounded fair enough.

At least this wasn't the type of situation where she got one chance, and it changed her future forever. She could retake the trial as many times as she needed to pass, but with her team waiting on her and the time crunch on their other quest, failure wasn't a realistic option. This time she was going to take a tip out of Tim's playbook and go for the slow and steady approach.

There was no reason to be hasty when she could one-and-done this shit.

Lorelei signaled Maria for the check. "I'm ready to go when you are."

Leaning back in his chair and resting a hand on his belly while sipping a freshly poured snifter, Felix chortled. "I'm not going with you."

He waved, and a prompt showed up.

Quest Updated: So you want to be a Spirit Archer?

The quest to become a spirit archer consists of one step, pass the trial. Failure will result in your death and having to purchase more stew. Your updated map shows the trial's location.

Good luck.

Lorelei looked at the spot on her map. The location wasn't far from here. At a brisk walk, she could be there in under twenty minutes.

The future was waiting.

"Next time we run into each other, I'll be a spirit archer." Lorelei felt confident she would nail this.

Felix rose and extended his hand. "When that happens, the stew is on me."

Lorelei grasped his hand and gave it a firm shake. "See you soon."

"I hope so." Felix sat, rubbing his belly. "I can't get enough of this stew."

Maria came with the bill, and Lorelei tossed her a gold coin. "Thanks for all your help." Without another word, she turned and left the Pepper Pot Flounder.

CHAPTER TWENTY-THREE

If she'd seen one giant warehouse down by the docks, she'd seen them all.

It wasn't like there was a lot to look at. Most of the buildings were giant wooden boxes with numbers painted on the side. A few of the buildings facing the water had stone or brick sides to buffer the water's effects, but otherwise, none of the structures had any adornments.

The warehouse district was all about function over looks.

At least it was for most of the buildings. One of these warehouses also housed her trial, and she doubted that would be her schlepping a bunch of boxes from one side of the warehouse to the other. If she had to guess, it would be a test of skill, something to do with her bow.

Obviously, it would be dangerous, or death wouldn't be a possibility.

She'd run from werewolves, fought against monsters, and started to fall in love. Whatever the trial threw at her, Lorelei was sure she'd be able to handle it. Running through an obstacle course like a ninja warrior was going to be a lot easier without six hundred pounds of angry furball chasing her. All she had to do was play it cool and take on whatever was presented to her one step at a time.

Thankfully, the warehouses were in some kind of order. She'd been to a few cities back in the real world where streets stopped and started again a few miles farther down the way. *Sorry, Sacramento Ave. For this two-mile stretch, you simply don't exist anymore.*

Lorelei looked up as she rounded the corner and found the giant One Thirty-One stenciled on the side of the building. This was it. She'd found the right place. There wasn't a guard outside or any indication this was anything other than a storage facility. Remembering how Felix had thrown a knife at her, she approached the door cautiously.

She moved forward one step at a time and kept her bow on her back, not wanting to disturb any of the dockworkers. The last thing anyone wanted to see in their workplace was someone with a weapon and a grudge.

Her enhanced vision didn't pick out any traps on her way to the door.

She was starting to think that her imagination was getting the better of her when the door opened. A bloody body flew out of the warehouse and landed at her feet on the cobbles. Large gashes in the man's side and neck were barely pumping out any blood. He held a hand up, reaching toward the door as it snapped shut. In the time it took her eyes to move from the door back to the man on the ground, he died.

His body disappeared along with the blood. The golden motes she was used to seeing when bosses died swirled up into the heavens. The only thing that was missing was a pile of big phat shiny loot.

The door opened again, and she had an arrow nocked as she dropped to one knee and spun toward the opening. At the last moment, she recognized Felix and pulled the shot a fraction to the right, where her arrow thudded into the door wobbling back and forth.

Felix plucked the arrow free and tossed it back to her. "Not bad. I have the feeling you will fare much better than he did."

As long as much better translates into alive at the end, I'm okay with that.

"How did you get here before me, let alone have time to finish him off?" Lorelei had walked straight to the warehouse. The only way to be faster would've been by carriage or with magic.

The bastard said he wasn't coming, but there he is.

Felix smiled. "The fun part about this is you don't get to ask questions." He turned toward the door. "Follow me."

The best part for him was that she didn't get to ask questions. It was the absolute worst for her. Lorelei might not be much for planning things out, but she also liked to know what she was getting into up front. A person couldn't make good decisions without all the information, and right now she had none.

Back in the real world, the thought of following a strange man into a dark warehouse would have filled her with dread. Inside *The Etheric Coast,* going into dark places with creepy people was par for the course.

Once she was inside the warehouse, the light adjusted and Lorelei could see clearly again. The door behind her snapped closed, and Felix moved farther into the room, heading toward a white circle marked out on the floor.

"This is where your trial starts. On the other side of the warehouse is a similar circle. Reach it, and we move onto phase two." Felix stood to the side of the circle waiting for her to enter.

Don't reach it and get tossed out of the building in a bloody heap.

"No one said this was going to be easy," Lorelei whispered to herself as she nocked an arrow and stepped into the circle.

The twinkle returned to Felix's eye. "Hit the targets for extra time, avoid the traps. Prove you can handle the basics, and I'll teach you something new."

"I'm ready." Lorelei lied. She fucking hated surprises.

Felix held up four fingers and stepped back. The entire room turned so dark Lorelei couldn't see anything at all. She heard things moving in the darkness but had no idea how to tell what they were. The lights snapped back on, and there was a maze of boxes in front of her.

Spike strips replaced certain spots on the floor. Pendulums swung across the gaps in other places. She might've been wrong, but Lorelei swore she saw some fire up ahead. All she had to do was make it to the other circle, but what did Felix mean about time?

She turned and noticed a wall of spikes behind her.

"Running out of time is going to be a real bitch." She prepared herself to run.

Felix smiled. "I wouldn't advise taking your time." He ticked the last finger down, and the wall of spikes started inching closer.

Lorelei took off like a rocket.

There wasn't time for her to plan a route. She had to run on pure instinct. A barrel in front of her would be easy to jump over, but if she could land on top and vault to some of the higher ground, it would be better. Without overthinking it, she vaulted into the air. It didn't take her long to realize she made a huge mistake.

The barrel didn't have a lid, and there was something inside it.

Her toes brushed the edge, and the object in the center of the barrel came into focus. Someone put a giant spike in the fucking middle. Anyone dumb enough to blindly jump in was going to have the worst rectal exam of all time.

While Lorelei wasn't dumb enough to dive into a barrel, she also didn't leave herself many options. In the next instant, she had to decide whether to leap forward and hope for the best or to push off to the side into a wall run before doing the same thing. The barrel shifted, and she let her forward momentum keep going until pivoting off and running along the side of a cargo container for three steps.

Then she was flying through the air again.

"Gotta stop being so reckless." She drew a deep breath as she pushed herself to run even faster as the moving wall behind her crushed the barrel to smithereens.

The spikes were coming at her faster than she anticipated. Even moving full speed, she was barely ahead. Lorelei kept her eyes up despite her increased speed, looking fifteen feet in front of her for the best direction to go. The spikes behind her continued to catch up. Slowly but inevitably, they would catch her if she didn't find a way to move faster.

What a girl wouldn't give for a haste potion right about now.

A target sprang up on her left, and Lorelei fired. The arrow flew straight and true, but her movement nearly made her miss. A small hole appeared in the side of the target, and she turned her attention back to the course. The wall behind her was slowing down.

Picking up speed to a full sprint, Lorelei leapt over a pit of scorpions, landing on a four-inch-wide beam. Nimble as a gymnast, she sprinted across as it rose over a pool of water like a bridge. Crossing the balance beam made whatever was in the water froth around in anticipation of a snack. She was so busy looking down that she completely missed the target that popped up on her right.

The wall behind her sped up to its original speed.

Lorelei ran like the very hounds of hell were nipping at her heels. This was her *Tomb Raider* obstacle course, the hunter grounds of *Horizon Zero Dawn*. In her moment of desperation, she channeled all of the hours she spent playing *Assassin's Creed* and put everything she had into making up time. She was reckless, and while she recognized the fact, she simply didn't care. The next three targets went down in unison, and the wall of moving death was so far behind her now that she could've slowed to a walk.

But she didn't.

The *whoosh* sound and the rustle of air across her clothes reminded Lorelei of the pendulums. Now she felt like the luckiest gamer in the world. How could she have forgotten about the giant swinging blades of instant death?

All of the normal hazards were still there, but now the chance of being cut in half accompanied them. The pendulums didn't care if the wall behind her was going to crush her to little bits. They swung on their timeframe to make her life more difficult.

She missed the next target dodging a pendulum and the one after that. Lorelei kicked herself for the sloppy mistakes. She slowed her pace to a furious jog as the wall of death started gaining ground. Hitting the next few targets was more important than picking up speed. The first two went down, and she kept her jog going to make sure she hit the next three. The wall behind her slowed to a crawl, and it gave her time to look ahead to the end of the course.

That was when she started to panic. Instead of a circle, there was a giant wooden wall with hand grips on it.

"The circle must be on the other side," Lorelei huffed as she looked around, trying to find the fastest way up.

She hoped Felix choked on a fishbone.

Lorelei's next target went down. Then she slung her bow over her back in one smooth motion and put all her focus into running. Her bow wouldn't be much help once she started climbing. Hopefully, hitting her last six targets in a row would buy her enough time to make it over the wall before the spikes got her. She leapt from handhold to handhold with reckless abandon, not even caring when the pinky finger on her right hand snapped when she missed one of the holds.

All that mattered now was survival.

Jumping, clawing, kicking, Lorelei made it to the top of the wall, but the spikes were closing in. Looking down, she saw the circle was inside a larger pool of water. The outer ring was full of giant eels, but the inner ring looked like a safe zone. The spikes were seconds away from tearing through the wall she was standing on. Lorelei found her balance and dove for the circle.

The wall shattered behind her as Lorelei hit the ice-cool liquid. When her head broke the surface, she was magically transported back to the first circle and dumped unceremoniously on her ass.

"What in the hell, Felix!" She glared at her class trainer. "Give a girl a little warning next time." Lorelei did a quick inventory swap of her clothes and armor to dry off.

Bending down to wipe a couple of drops of water from his boots, Felix smiled when he met her eyes. "That might've been a course record."

"I barely made it." There was no way her victory was the record. Anyone a second behind her would've been dead.

Felix winked. "I might've sped up the simulation a bit to see what you could do."

Lorelei wondered if she could complete the quest with Felix dead. "You smug little shit."

"You made it, and everything is fine." Felix burped. "Maybe I shouldn't have finished that brandy. It made me a little whimsical."

Ugh, she should have only gotten him the stew.

"Just don't turn anything up during Phase Two, and we'll be fine," Lorelei stated in a cold tone. "Or, you know, maybe I could skip the wall of death because I set the record."

Felix looked offended. "Skip Phase Two, unheard of."

"So is almost killing recruits because you sped up the system." She was getting exasperated.

"It's not as uncommon as one would think." Felix pulled out a little flask and took a sip. "Or maybe the simulation sped up because I'm running out of brandy and getting bored. I can't remember. I just love this stuff."

"Try to stay on point." Maybe she should've picked a class with a better trainer.

Wagging his finger, Felix continued, "No siree, no skipperoos here. Everyone has to take on the boss to win their spot as a spirit archer."

"At least tell me what I'll be up against." Lorelei nocked an arrow. "You owe me that much."

Felix raised his hand. "It's big, it's furry, and it's coming for you now." He disappeared, and the room turned dark again.

As the light filled the entire warehouse, there was a howl, and Lorelei knew precisely what she was facing. Another fucking werewolf. It was like the game couldn't give her enough of the damn things. After how things worked out in Tristholm, Lorelei would've been fine never seeing another werewolf again.

Everything about a Were's design made ripping a human into itty-bitty little bits as easy as possible. That was all fine and dandy when they were on your side, but when six hundred pounds of human-smart monster was charging right at you, it wasn't nearly as fun.

The werewolf was somewhere between her and the other circle. Despite its howl, the monster hadn't made an appearance yet. She didn't know if sneaking past the creature would count so Lorelei would have to figure out a way to kill it on her way to the other circle.

The entirely new layout of the obstacle course wasn't exactly helpful. It was like, oh hey, great job setting the course record and all, but here, enjoy dying a horrible death.

This was not the reward she was looking for.

Lorelei glanced behind her and realized the wall of spikes was closing in, but it wasn't moving nearly as fast as it had in the first part of her trial. In the bright lights of the warehouse, stealth wasn't much of an option anyway. She'd have to rely on her bow and her wits to win. All she had to do was figure out where the big bad beastie was so she could kill it before it got her.

"Easy peasy, lemon squeezy." Lorelei let out her nerves in a rush of air as she thought about the man tossed out of the warehouse before she entered.

A few deep breaths helped her to find her calm center. Then she ran like the wind. The werewolf had every advantage here. Everything in the building was wood, and the monster's claws would be able to cling to all of it. Until she got eyes on the creature, she had to assume it could come at her from any direction.

Wall run, barrel jump, zip line, tight rope.

Fuck, she was flying across the course. Part of her knew it was too easy but couldn't stop running full tilt. Lorelei leapt over a barrel, and something flew out of the shadows, slamming into her side. Werewolf claws tore deep gouges into her leather armor and the flesh beneath.

Her bow flew from her hands, but that allowed her to grab a knife.

A few quick thrusts of her dagger made the werewolf yelp as they hit the floor and rolled apart. The dagger wouldn't do any lasting damage to the monster, but it gave her enough time to recover.

Lorelei popped the first of her healing potions as she ran toward her fallen bow. The wounds in her side sealed as she ran, and her broken finger reset, making her wince in pain. The healing potions had cost her a small fortune, but they were worth their weight in gold right now.

She dove for her bow and let out a grunt of pain as her still injured ribs hit the floor. She spun, arrow nocked, but the werewolf wasn't charging. The beast had taken slightly longer to recover than she expected, but with a single growl, she knew her lead time was gone.

If the werewolf hadn't seen her running, maybe she could pull this off.

Not wanting to give anything away, Lorelei crawled away from the monster with her bow in one hand. She knew the wolf's killer instinct wouldn't let an injured target crawl away so she played it up a bit. The hardest part of her plan was waiting with her back turned toward the monster as the wall of spikes slowly closed on their position.

Playing the victim was her only chance.

The werewolf rushed toward her. Lorelei waited until she heard it leap into the air before rolling onto her back and firing.

"Split!" Lorelei screamed, and the arrowhead she launched split into six identical copies, all slamming into the werewolf's center mass.

"You'll have to do better than that." The werewolf landed past her and stood to its full height. It snapped the shafts off with a brush of its arm.

The werewolf charged, but Lorelei stood still and watched as six hundred pounds of claws and death bore down on her. "Trust me, I did."

Ever since her first encounter with a werewolf, she'd been terrified of being turned into one. When Ernie made his last batch of antidote, she'd secured a small stockpile and always kept a vial or two in her inventory. As the werewolf charged her, she drank the potion, clearing the werewolf virus from her system.

Halfway to her, the werewolf collapsed, and its body slid to her feet. "My potion maker is also fond of poisons."

With the threat eliminated, all she had to do was make it to the end of the course. Lorelei moved like the wind. She was living in the moment but also anticipating her triumph. The spikes were far enough behind she could take her time, but she found she didn't want to. One course record was nice and all, but two would be fan-fucking-tastic.

She landed in the circle, and as before, it transported her back to the front of the warehouse.

Felix bowed low and held out a scroll. "Welcome, spirit archer. You'll find everything you need to know about your new class inside."

Drawing deep breaths to calm herself, Lorelei reached out and accepted the scroll. "Thank you, I guess."

Part of her knew she should have felt grateful, but it was hard to thank a person who tried to kill her twice. "Did I get another record?"

"Sadly, you did not." Felix's eyes took on their usual twinkle. "Would you like to try again?"

Lorelei held up her hands in protest. "No!" Then a little less forcefully. "I think I'm good. Holding one record is just fine."

She opened the scroll.

System Message: Congratulations on ascending to Spirit Archer

Your health and mana pools have increased, and you'll receive two new skills. Keep an eye out for further opportunities to learn more about your class.

Skill Received: Spirit Walk

Call on the power of the spirit realm to move twenty feet in any direction. As you progress with this spell, it will obtain additional effects. Some of the benefits you might expect to gain later include decreased cooldown, decreased skill activation time, increased attack or defense after using Spirit Walk. As you can see, it's in your best interest to use this skill as often as possible.

All right, she was on board with this. It would be perfect for when she had to use an attack from behind or to get the perfect angle for one of her special abilities. Depending on how long the cooldown was, she could also use this as a defensive spell, much like Tim's Quick Feet. Except Lorelei got the feeling with this spell, she'd disappear and reappear instantly, which was even better.

Skill Received: Spirit Arrow

For the next twenty seconds, empower your attacks with the spirits of the fallen. All of your attacks will deal ten percent of their damage as unblockable spirit damage. As you progress in this skill, you can expect more of your damage to convert into spirit damage, and your attacks will also gain buffs, debuffs,

and damage over time effects. Spirit Arrow is the backbone of your new class. Use this skill every time it's off cooldown.

Lorelei jumped into Felix's arms and kissed the startled man on the cheek before dismounting. "This is so fucking rad. Let's get you back to the Pepper Pot and get you some stew."

"I would be delighted." Felix gave her a bow and escorted her to the door. "I'll meet you there."

The spirit archer went translucent and ghosted right through the door, leaving Lorelei standing in the warehouse alone.

She felt like a new woman when she stepped out into the sun. She'd completed her class change. After sending Maria a gold to keep Felix in stew for a few days, it was time to get back to the inn. All she wanted to do now was soak in the tub until the others returned. Maybe tonight she'd go into the basement training area and practice her new skills for a while. Then she'd take another bath.

If there was one thing she'd never get enough of, it was a good old-fashioned bubble bath.

CHAPTER TWENTY-FOUR

JaKobi felt giddy.

He loved spending time with the others, but sometimes a guy needed a few hundred hours and a library full of books to explore by himself. Not that he would get the chance to read today. If he managed to finish his quest fast enough, he might be able to swing by the mage's college on the way home, but he doubted it. Everyone was all about the go, go, go, but he wanted to curl up in his book nook for a bit.

Because his first class change quest was so easy, JaKobi expected this one to be a doozie. The only way to find out was to get there, so he pulled up his user interface, found the quest in his log, and selected it.

Quest Received: So you want to be an Ember Wizard?

There are people who like fire, and then there are people who *really* like fire. It's a wonder that buildings don't burst into flames as you walk past. You relish the control you have over the flames, but to become an ember wizard, you must give yourself to the fire completely.

Go to the Sinister Lion, and ask for Giuseppe Flamelicker. There, your quest will begin.

JaKobi read over the text again, wondering what he'd gotten himself into. He'd never met a Giuseppe before so at least he could check that off his list. So much for his dream of going to the library or a bookstore. The Sinister Lion sounded a lot more like a tavern. It made sense not to do the quest around books because when it came right down to it, he was pretty sure being an ember wizard was all about lighting shit on fire.

The map showed Giuseppe's location wasn't too far away. There was nothing written about the building on his map. Only a lion's head marked it. It kind of sounded like the name of a biker bar but had needed to add something more innocent to the title, like the bar in his hometown. Everyone knew the Bashful Bandit. Despite the bar's outward appearance and Sons of Anarchy-like cuts they wore, most of the guys there were pretty nice.

He had the distinct impression the Lion wasn't going to be the same kind of place.

"I never get the easy missions." JaKobi stopped walking and drew a few deep breaths.

Going into a situation with the wrong attitude could ruin everything. It didn't matter if his quest was harder than everyone else's or easier. What was important was leveling up his skills with fire. Being an ember wizard was worth putting in a little extra effort.

Time to get my grind on.

He picked up the pace and before long stood outside a bar. Fire danced from pillar to pillar at the entrance, and a woman danced in a cage of flames hanging in front of the door. At second glance, the woman had wings. Maybe she was some kind of flame demon.

This shouldn't have been his kind of place, but he liked the vibe quite a bit.

Marching up to the bouncer with confidence, JaKobi stated very matter-of-factly, "I'm here to see Giuseppe Flamelicker."

The bouncer's eyes widened, and he nodded as if receiving communication from inside. "Boss would like to see you."

"Is your boss Giuseppe?" Things felt a little off right now, but JaKobi couldn't put his finger on it.

The bouncer had a ring in his ear that let him talk to someone inside, which reinforced that anything electronic was also possible with magic.

The bouncer laughed. "That little weasel, not a chance." He removed the red velvet rope so JaKobi could go inside. "Just ask for Max. Someone will point you in the right direction."

Everywhere he went, people wanted to point him in the right direction instead of simply telling him where to go. It'd be nice if the game gave him a big flashing arrow to follow and dispersed with the chit-chat. Maybe this was a trial of his patience. As good as he was at controlling the flames, he was as bad at managing himself. When it came to lighting things on fire, he tended to be a bit overzealous.

This was quickly becoming one of those times.

Inside, the bar looked like he stepped into a chill layer of hell. All of the seats and tables had red velvet with gold trim. The floor was solid black onyx, and the bar top was on fire. Several more of the winged creatures danced in cages around the space.

He fucking loved this place.

A set of stairs led up to what appeared to be a separate lounge. He didn't know much about fancy clubs, but he did know that a private lounge was the kind of place he should look for the club's owner.

The bouncer at the foot of the stairs glared at him as he approached. "You're not on the list."

"The doorman told me to ask for Max." JaKobi tried to smile, but when the bouncer continued glaring at him, he tried Plan B. "I'm not sure why I have to find this Max person. I'm looking for Giuseppe Flamelicker."

The bouncer's eyes widened with the same expression as the

first man, and he motioned for JaKobi to go up the stairs. "Max is waiting for you."

What in the hell is going on?

He didn't see an alternative to going up the stairs so he got his ass moving. The upper lounge was even cooler than the downstairs. Red and orange silk sheets draped from the ceiling, and a magical wind blew through the room. The slight breeze ruffled the silks giving him the impression he was standing inside a fire. At the very back of the lounge was a large circular sofa covered in red and black velvet.

The woman sitting on the couch was like nothing he'd seen since entering the game. Her blue hair stood out in stark contrast to the rest of the theme, and yet he got the impression she owned the place. Her eyes roved over his body for a moment, then turned hard.

Cassie would love her.

"I heard you were looking for someone," Max purred as she poured two drinks and motioned for him to sit.

JaKobi felt the same as when he got stuck in a customer service loop at one of the major banks. Story, hold, transfer, repeat story, transfer, repeat story with various endings, usually with him eating the fee because he couldn't waste any more time. He knew how he felt wasn't Max's fault and that for some reason his quest was being a little hinky, but that didn't stop him from wanting to rage.

He took the offered drink and tried to relax. If nothing else, finding this cool bar was a big bonus. Everything didn't have to happen instantly as long as it all worked out.

"I'm trying to find Giuseppe Flamelicker." He sipped the cocktail.

It was quite good.

"Oh, this is simply delicious." Max chortled as she sipped hers.

"Do you know him?"

Max polished off her drink and stood. After a cute little

shimmy to get her thigh-high skirt back in position, she motioned for JaKobi to finish up. "I don't know him personally, but I know he's here somewhere. Let's get you on stage and ask. I'm sure someone here will be able to point him out to us."

They moved back down the stairs, and Max motioned the band to cut the music. People looked around in confusion until they saw her walking through the crowd toward the stage.

Then the whispers started.

Moving as if by unseen command, the crowd parted and they made it to the stage in a third of the time it would have normally taken. The singer reached down to help Max up, but JaKobi had to crawl onto the stage by himself.

Max had a magical microphone in her hand as she addressed the crowd. "My new friend here is looking for someone who may be here tonight, and he needs your help."

People in the crowd started looking at one another, wondering if any of them knew the man standing next to Max.

She handed JaKobi the microphone. "Tell them who you're looking for."

Something about this didn't feel right, but this was his chance to find out if Giuseppe was here. Looking out over the crowd, JaKobi moved to the front of the stage. "I'm looking for Giuseppe Flamelicker."

Max started to laugh, and one look at her told him he stepped in it worse than expected. It was too bad this couldn't have been a drinking contest, or better yet, a game of fire pong. If he could play a game of pong for his class change instead of doing this, he'd already be sitting at the library.

Someone screamed from the crowd. "You motherless cunt!"

JaKobi turned in time to see the fireball slam into him.

"Oh, take it easy on him," Max said as she wiped a cool cloth across JaKobi's forehead.

Giuseppe looked like someone shat in his Cheerios as he glared down at the fallen mage. "Where'd you hear that name, boy?"

JaKobi sat up and checked his arms and hands, happy to find out he hadn't burned to a crisp. "I received a quest titled, So you want to be an Ember Mage."

Max started laughing again.

"Ragnus, you blathering bastard, you know I hate that name." Giuseppe's eyebrows pulled together so hard he was rocking a unibrow of frustration.

A man floated out of the crowd, his red robes and wizard's hat setting him apart from the rest of the patrons.

He landed on the stage and spoke. "I'm sorry, old friend. Sometimes I can't help myself. Please forgive me."

"We'll see." Giuseppe stormed off the stage and back to his group of friends.

Max looked thoroughly tickled by the entire experience. "Thank you for a wonderful diversion, Ragnus."

"Think nothing of it, my dear." He turned to look at JaKobi. "Well, get up. We have work to do."

Ragnus walked toward the club's exit, and JaKobi ran to catch up. "Where are we going?"

"To see if you have what it takes to complete your trial." He looked at JaKobi's singed robes doubtfully. "Not a very auspicious start."

Quickly replacing his robes with fresh ones, JaKobi followed his new teacher. "I might be a slow starter, but I bring it home like a freight train."

"Less talking, more walking." Ragnus never slowed in stride or looked back. He expected JaKobi to follow his command.

JaKobi kept his mouth shut and got his feet moving.

CHAPTER TWENTY-FIVE

"Welcome to the Ember Trials." Ragnus raised his hands and the warehouse they were in lit up as if it were full daylight inside.

I feel like I'm about to be tossed into a maze.

JaKobi didn't think it would be the fun kind, more like the murderous ax-wielding madman kind, or worse yet, *The Maze* kind. Dealing with robots intent on killing him was a trope he wasn't ready to explore yet. On the plus side, if it ended up being a madman with an ax, he could always incinerate the idiot.

Looking at the boxes and crates stacked to the ceiling in some places, he felt more like a mouse in an experiment than a wizard.

"You bring me to all the nicest places," JaKobi mumbled.

Sometimes when he got frustrated, he lashed out.

"What was that?" Ragnus lifted an eyebrow.

JaKobi met his gaze with his best, I don't care which way this goes down, Dirty Harry look. "Only that I need to find an appropriate way to thank you for getting me nailed with that fireball."

"That's more like it." Ragnus clapped him on the back. "You're going to need that fire to beat these trials, boy."

"Trials? As in more than one?" JaKobi gulped.

Ragnus chuckled from deep down in his belly. "You think we give the title of ember wizard to just anyone? You're about to join an elite branch of spellcasters. You have to earn it."

"Are you sure I can't play you in a game of fire pong?" JaKobi tried to keep a straight face. "It's a true test of challenge."

When Ragnus didn't say anything, JaKobi continued. "You see, each side gets ten cups, and you fill them about a quarter of the way with beer."

"Enough!" A little bit of steam shot out of Ragnus' mouth. "You are here to do the same trials that have stood for all of time. Prepare yourself because soon you face the gauntlet."

Gulp.

"The Gauntlet?" JaKobi's mind retreated to an old-school video game.

"Steel your nuts, boy. It's not that complicated." Ragnus motioned toward the circle. "You stand there, keep everything out of the circle for as long as you can."

JaKobi played a few games like this before. Set up the guns to guard the fortress from the hordes of whatever the flavor of the month was for baddies. Only this time, he was the gun, and his future in the game was on the line.

Fuck that loser talk. He was going to win.

JaKobi wasn't going to be the only one showing back up at the inn without his class change completed. He deserved to be here. He earned his place in his group by carrying his weight. He even saved their asses by blowing a charging pack of werewolves to smithereens. If anyone could do this, it was him.

He really did love setting things on fire.

Ragnus was watching him with an amused expression. "Your ascendancy awaits." He pointed at the circle.

"How do I know when I pass?" JaKobi asked from just outside the circle on the ground.

Ragnus looked like he was enjoying this immensely. "When you die, you'll either wake up here or somewhere else."

"Die?"

With a hearty shove, Ragnus sent JaKobi stumbling inside the circle. "Three-two-one," he spat out in a single breath. Then the lights went out.

When the lights came back on, the warehouse in front of him was clear of everything. In the distance, he saw rows of something approaching. It reminded him of *Galaxiga* or *Centipede*. It didn't matter what was coming toward him. He had to destroy it before it reached the circle.

The calm of battle slipped over him, and JaKobi cast his first spell.

He started by blocking one side of the room with his Flame Wall. From there, he picked off the targets moving fastest with Fire Missiles before casting his Phoenix to wipe out the large swaths of target clumped together as they moved around his wall.

As the targets drew closer, he could finally make out what he was facing.

"Ragnus, you dirty fucker." JaKobi exhaled the words as he continued sending out bursts of magic at the wooden targets.

I can't believe I fell for that shit after the whole fireball at the bar thing.

Ten seconds later, the scene in front of him was too chaotic for JaKobi to concentrate on anything but blowing up as many targets as possible. The little wooden cutouts seemed to be coming at him in the hundreds now. If he could die in here, it would be from being trampled and crushed to death when they finally over-whelmed the circle and not from any kind of attack. With that in mind, he used his flame walls to try herding the targets where he wanted them.

As the clusters of targets emerged he did his best to destroy them all with wave after wave of punishing damage.

At some point soon, this would stop being a case of "could he hold them off anymore" and become one of "he didn't have enough mana left to cast a single spell." It wouldn't be too much longer before he found out if Ragnus was joking or if being trampled to death by wooden targets would be a thing.

Hoping that from a scoring standpoint all he had to do was destroy as many of the targets as possible, he continued firing off spells. The only thing that could screw him over now was if this ended up being an endurance test.

JaKobi waited until his mana hit the thirty percent mark, then he put his plan into motion. He cast flame wall ten times in a row. It ate up nearly half of his available mana, but the series of walls formed a funnel across the entire warehouse. All he had to do now was let it rip with as much damage as he could muster before his walls winked out of existence.

Activating all his gear's special abilities, JaKobi launched spell after spell at the tip of the funnel. The targets blew apart like paper instead of wood, but there were always more of them. His mana reached ten percent, and he saw the warning indicator off to the right of his vision. A quick look at his status bar confirmed his walls had about five seconds left.

"Time for the big one." JaKobi let fly with everything he had until the walls of fire winked out of existence.

With the walls down, there was nothing else he could do but go nuclear. JaKobi started casting his final spell of the fight. The last five percent of his mana disappeared in a single flash, almost sending him to his knees. He screamed in agony and frustration as he straightened his back to look over the enemy. There were thousands of targets bearing down on him now, but he could fix it with a single word.

"Inferno."

Two small tornadoes of flame burst from JaKobi's hands. The flames only extended about eight feet out so he moved to the front of the circle and swept his hands back and forth across the targets until the spell winked out.

"Aw shit." JaKobi ducked and waited for death.

The first target hit the circle, and they all disappeared.

"Well done, boy." Ragnus chuckled as he walked toward the circle. "We haven't had a showing like that in some time."

Brushing some ash from the shoulder of his robe, JaKobi stood and faced the man who controlled his destiny at the trials. "What's next?"

After his first bit of success, JaKobi was elated about his chances for coming out of this looking like a champion. All he had to do was complete one more challenge, and he'd earn his ember wizard status.

Time to buckle up, buttercup. We're about to go for a ride.

"Next?" Ragnus looked around, almost bewildered. "Next, you have to fight something."

Of course, I do.

"Care to give me any hints before you pull the switch?" JaKobi hoped the man would finally take pity on him.

Ragnus started the trial. "Try not to get wet."

Wet?

The warehouse went completely black again. When the lights came on the floor was flooded with water, and there were small stone circles just big enough for him to stand on scattered across the space. Fighting on those would be tricky, and if falling in the water was a fail, the task felt almost impossible.

Say one thing for JaKobi. He wasn't known for being fleet of foot.

"All you have to do is make it to me on the other side of the warehouse." Ragnus disappeared, then sparks shot up from the opposite end of the warehouse.

The sparks seemed miles away. How big was this fucking warehouse?

The circle JaKobi was standing in started to shake. It was time to move.

As he jumped from stone to stone, JaKobi started to think that maybe Tim was right and he should invest a few more of his skill points in his secondary stats. Yes, he was trying to be a glass cannon, but having a little better dexterity and strength would've made this trial a cinch. Having to fight when he could barely gather his balance long enough to jump to the next island was going to make this trial a real test.

"Aw fuck." JaKobi made it to the next island as he spied the first of his attackers.

Why was it always bugs with him? As if all the spiders weren't bad enough, but having to face off against giant wasps? That was wrong. The creepy bastards were fast as all get out, and the two-foot-long stingers promised that JaKobi would have a really bad day if he got hit. The water also wasn't safe based on Ragnus' hint, so he couldn't dive in to escape an attack. The only chance he had of surviving was if he could take the damn things out of commission.

Time to summon his inner Delbert McClintock and kill some pests.

JaKobi didn't have a bug sprayer, but he did have a fireball, which would work just as well. The first wasp went down easy, giving him time to skip forward. The next two came at him simultaneously, providing more of a challenge, but one he handled easily. When the next batch was three wasps at a time, he started to get worried.

It was quickly becoming apparent that if he wanted to make it across the islands before he was overwhelmed, JaKobi would have to risk it for the biscuit.

JaKobi started leaping from island to island with a single bound. It took all his strength and concentration, but by the time six wasps were coming toward him, he was three-quarters of the way across the room. The seven-wasp challenge almost got him, but he managed to regain his feet as the last one died.

There was no way he could handle eight of them, so JaKobi jumped forward with reckless abandon. He was almost there. He could make it if he went a little faster. A buzzing filled the air. It didn't sound like eight of them. The noise sounded like hundreds of them. He stopped on a stone, looked up to find out how fucked he was, and saw what must have been the queen coming right for him.

She was one bad-looking bitch.

Her hair was neon yellow in a way that screamed, better run the fuck away, little girl. The queen hovered between him and the end of the trial. JaKobi felt like all her beady eyes stayed locked on him as he jumped closer.

This wasn't the kind of thing a simple fireball would take care of. He needed something bigger to kill the queen, something special. Inferno was out of the question. With the six-foot-long stinger, she might be able to kill him before fiery tornadoes killed her.

Fireballs, missiles, and the Phoenix.

It was all he had, but did he need more? JaKobi wobbled as he fired off spell after spell. The queen shrugged off the first couple of hits, but now she was pissed and coming straight for him with vengeance in her eyes. This was the moment he had to take her out.

Or did he?

JaKobi thought about the purpose of the first trial and what it tried to teach him and decided to apply the same rules here. With a thought, he spent the rest of his mana boxing the queen in a ring of fire and leapt right past her to sweet, sweet victory.

JaKobi stepped into the final circle as the queen broke free.

The room reset, and Ragnus appeared. "Again, you impress. Not every victory is achievable with brute strength alone. That isn't a lesson everyone learns on the first try."

Bowing low, Ragnus held out a scroll. "Welcome to the rank of ember wizard. May your flame burn ever brighter."

JaKobi accepted the scroll and grinned. "Thank you, Ragnus."

He gave the mage a little bow as he unsealed the key to his class change.

System Message: Congratulations on your ascension to Ember Wizard

Your health and mana pools have increased, and you will receive two new class-specific skills. Keep an eye out for further opportunities to learn more about your class and obtain new spells as you progress.

JaKobi couldn't have been happier. He was sure there was an entire library section dedicated to ember wizards, and he could probably find a few new spells there. When in doubt, look in a book. The philosophy had yet to serve him wrong, so why stop using it now? It wouldn't be much longer before he had more skills than he knew what to do with.

Skill Received: Sunbeam

Ever wonder what it would be like if you could shoot a beam of pure sunlight from your hand? Now you don't have to. This spell will work from a distance, but everything in its path will take damage, reducing the spell's effectiveness against the final target. As you level this skill, expect to receive additional benefits, returned health, increased speed, multiple target damage, etc.

JaKobi broke out in his latest dance move leaving Ragnus stunned. His new skill was awesome. The fact he could enhance it by using it was even better. If he had to think of a reason he liked the skill so much, it was the throughput behind it. He'd have to line up a shot to the boss with no other enemies in the path to do the most single-target damage, but if he wanted to hit multiple enemies, he could do that with a little additional finesse.

He loved Sunbeam and couldn't wait to try it out.

Skill Received: Ember Empowerment

Being an ember wizard isn't only about the flashy spells or the wicked cool robes. It's about doing a shit-ton of damage. For twenty seconds, all your fire-based skills will deal ten percent

more damage, and any skills under the ember wizard umbrella will also apply twenty-five percent of their single target damage as an unblockable DOT.

"Hells to the yeah. Bow-chica-bow-wow." He started dancing again.

Not only did he pick up a badass new damage-dealing ability, but he also got a skill that let him kick things up a notch for a full twenty seconds. Of course, he would have to figure out the best way to work his rotation to maximize those twenty seconds, but the spell itself was pure gold.

He stopped his dance and bowed low to Ragnus. "Thank you."

The man looked thoroughly amused as if this encounter would keep him in free drinks at the bar for a long time. "Let's get you out of here before you pull a muscle, and I have to call for help." Ragnus led the way to the exit.

JaKobi watched him go for a minute before calling, "Come on, man, my moves aren't that bad."

CHAPTER TWENTY-SIX

ShadowLily left the inn faster than anyone.

While she loved her time playing with the group, it had been a while since she'd been able to take a contract and hunt down her prey like the assassin she was. There was something she loved about stalking someone who had done bad things and making them pay for it.

What a wonderful life.

She dropped into stealth to avoid talking to people and pulled up her user interface while she walked. It took her a few seconds to find the right screen, but she only had a couple of open quests so selecting the right one was easy.

Quest Received: So you want to be a Mist Slayer?

Fuck yeah, I do!

There are three main types of assassins—those who hunt from stealth, distance, and behind. Then there are those who want to truly stand out, to become a master of blending stealth with exceptional dagger work. No longer will you be forced to fight from the shadows. You will weave in and out of enemies

like mist. Find Cassandra Killington at the Finicky Lady and start your quest for ascendance.

"Killington, that's a little on the nose. I like it." ShadowLily dismissed her user interface and pulled up her map.

The Finicky Lady was in a seedy part of town like most assassins' hangouts were. It was funny how quickly the slums changed, but with that change, the guilds had taken over other parts of the city. Gaston had brought most of them in line, but smart people stayed away from the areas controlled by assassins.

Dropping out of stealth, she picked up her pace. ShadowLily wanted to get to the location with enough time to scope it out before going inside.

Twenty minutes later, she slowed and turned down an unmarked alley. It felt like hostile territory, and she immediately dropped back into stealth. The alley in front of her went from a six-foot-wide strip to a twenty-foot-wide thoroughfare in a blink, not leaving very many places to hide.

This place looked like a shithole. So far, ShadowLily wasn't impressed.

This alley might as well have been the one from behind their diner back in the real world. Instead of large trash cans, there were crates and boxes. The difference being this alley had three people that she could spot waiting to ambush anyone walking by.

There was also a fourth man lying at the foot of the steps leading up to the bar's entrance. There was vomit splashed all over his shirt and a wet stain on the front of his pants.

She wrote off the unconscious man for the moment and focused her attention on the others. Killing everyone out here might not endear her to the folks waiting inside. As much as she hated having to suck up to others until she had her class change quest complete, Cassandra was the most important person in the world to her.

The real question was should she take the risk to sneak past them or knock them out as she went?

She'd spent most of her time at the inn in the training room. She'd also been fortunate enough to be trained by a grandmaster at the top of his game. So, her skills were sharp, and if she stayed focused, getting by these three wouldn't be any issue.

If they had any talent, I wouldn't have seen them in the first place.

It was easy enough to avoid the first man. He'd buried himself so much in his hiding spot she would've been surprised if he could climb out fast enough to make an effective attack. She wasn't taking any chances after their defeat at the hands of the witch Isadora, but her odds of walking right past him without stealth were fifty-fifty. In stealth, the idiot never had a chance.

ShadowLily hit him with a knockout dart. "Never had a chance."

The darts weren't cheap, but it never paid to leave an assassin at your back. If something inside went terribly wrong and she had to fight her way out of this, leaving enemies at her back was a big mistake. Getting surrounded was probably the only way they could take her out.

As if she'd let that happen.

ShadowLily might make fun of Tim for his plans, but she never went into an assassination without one. Part of why it was so easy for her to be with her man was that their mindset was similar despite their styles of play being opposite. Scouting and killing weren't just how she paid the bills. It was how she lived her life.

And then there were two.

ShadowLily crawled under a pipe and through a crack in a crate to come up behind the second lady. When the assassin fell from the knockout dart, she caught the body and gently lowered it to the ground. The next guard was close enough to hear a body drop if she made a mistake. If he raised the alarm, the jig was up.

One second.

She drew a deep breath.

Two seconds passed, then three and four. Her ears burned as she listened for any indication that the third guard heard anything, but there wasn't a sound to speak of. Slowly she let herself breathe again as she inched forward.

And then there was one.

The third guard was also a woman and more skilled than the previous two. Her eyes were alert as she scanned the surroundings for uninvited guests.

She even looks behind herself from time to time.

Sneaking up on people and knocking them out was so much harder than killing them. ShadowLily could've killed all three guards without batting an eyelash, but this felt like it was taking forever. She wasn't nearly as precise with the knockout darts as with a knife, so she took precautions to make sure she never missed. When most of her fights revolved around dealing the most damage and not throwing knives from stealth, it was easy to see why her skills with the darts lagged a bit behind.

Getting closer would be risky, but so was missing.

Nothing said, hey someone is here, than a dart sticking out of the wall an inch in front of their nose.

ShadowLily crawled across the dirty alley like a worm in a spring garden, inching forward until getting any closer would've put her directly in the guard's line of sight. The shot she was about to take was ten feet farther than she'd ever attempted, and she'd have to wing the toss. If she fucked it up, ShadowLily would have to kill the woman.

Whoever ran this place should've hired someone better.

Thinking of all the times she'd spent hitting the center of the target with her knives, ShadowLily lifted the dart in her hand to check the weight. She thought about what happened over a distance when she threw her knives and realized the dart would drop as much if thrown properly. She had her plan in place, and her backup was to sprint at the guard as fast as she could and hope for the best.

Nothing to it, but to do it.

She lined up her throw and felt that moment of clarity where she knew it would be perfect. When those moments came to her in life, she didn't question them. She simply acted. The dart flew from her hand, and as she watched its progress, ShadowLily was up and sprinting across the space, daggers in hand.

The guard turned, and the dart hit her right in the center of the chest.

Spinning her daggers around before slamming them back home in their sheaths, ShadowLily strutted toward the door. "That's how I get shit done."

The man at the base of the stairs didn't move so much as a muscle as she approached. He could've been dead, or he could be faking. One thing she learned in college was that the drunk slept like the dead. If it was a trap, she didn't want to let on that she figured it out so she kept her pace even as she approached the steps to the bar.

The bastard tried to sweep her legs out from under her. While she was climbing the stairs.

Dick move.

It was easy enough to avoid the kick. The assassin telegraphed it from a mile away. What he probably hadn't expected when she jumped was that he'd be enjoying both feet slamming into his chest. The man flew back, clutching his chest as if a horse had kicked him.

Not missing a beat, ShadowLily moved forward and grabbed the guard by his hair as he gasped for air. Then she slammed his big fat melon into the cobbles until he stopped fighting. Ugh, she had vomit on her clothes.

The front of her clothes smelled like shit. "I gotta give it to him. That's some real commitment."

A quick flash of her armor through the good old inventory trick and most of the stink was gone. The last thing she wanted to do was go into a new place smelling like she spent the past week on a bender. She wished there was something she could do about her arms.

Maybe they could help inside.

With her armor looking fresh, ShadowLily kicked the bar doors open with confidence. "Who's going to get me a fucking towel!" She swaggered in like she owned the place.

A raucous cheer went through the crowd until a woman stood at the far end of the bar. "Who are you?"

The room went silent instantly, and she heard the sound of blades leaving sheaths.

ShadowLily knew this wasn't the time to back down. "I'm the one who took out four of your people." She looked at the bar. "I'm still waiting on that towel."

"Donovan, check them. She doesn't move an inch until I say otherwise." The barman swept the room with a hard eye, and the men tightened into a circle around ShadowLily.

Flipping the latches off her sheaths, ShadowLily prepared to take on everyone in the bar. Her user interface wouldn't show any of their names, but the woman giving orders had to be Cassandra. Maybe there was a way she could get out of this before the situation got away from her.

"My instructions said to seek out Cassandra. That she would be able to help me ascend." ShadowLily met the woman's eyes.

"Bold." Cassandra nodded. "But not too smart if you killed my people on your way in."

Donovan reappeared in the doorway. "They're only unconscious, but Earl got his head cracked open pretty bad."

"Sorry about that. It was the smell." ShadowLily glared at the barman and held her hand up, hoping he would throw her a towel to wipe the gunk off her arms.

Not seeing him move, ShadowLily marched to the bar and grabbed one on her own. She dunked it in a man's beer to get it wet and wiped off her arms before tossing the towel back.

"That was my beer." The man had some eye daggers of his own going on.

ShadowLily grabbed the mug and swung it at his head. The

glass stopped an inch away from the man's head as it shattered around the blade of a small sword. Cassandra had moved so quickly she didn't even see it until the woman blocked the attack. The realization that Cassandra could've killed her but instead only blocked her swing washed over her like a cold shower.

Note to self, do not fuck with Killington.

Cassandra smiled as if nothing was wrong in the world. "Join me for a drink."

"Of course." ShadowLily knew it wasn't a request.

As they walked back to Cassandra's private alcove, all Shadow-Lily could think about was how much she would pay to see her and Gaston duke it out. Her gamble of swinging the mug at the man's head paid off, but it almost cost her everything. She was still trying to find her calm center as they sat.

"You've earned five minutes of my time. Why are you here?" Cassandra poured herself a drink and waited for a response.

Now didn't feel like the right time to be humble, and saying something like she was only here to learn from the best felt trite. Now wasn't the time for bullshit. She had to own this moment. "I'm here because I want to learn how to deal more damage, and I heard becoming a mist slayer is the best way to accomplish my goal."

"It will be if you're worthy." Cassandra eyed her for a moment, then decided. "Are you ready to start the trials?"

Was it going to be that easy after doing all the work to sneak in here? Almost killing a man at the bar seemed to have earned enough of the woman's respect that she was going to give her the quest without making her jump through a bunch of hoops.

"Of course I'm ready." ShadowLily went with the flow.

Taking a sip from her drink, Cassandra smiled contentedly. "Normally for a woman like you, someone who wants their kills to mean something, I find them a nice juicy innocent to take down. Being an assassin isn't about moral fiber. It's about killing who needs it."

Eyeing her over the rim of her drink Killington grinned. "Luckily for you, I've had a contract come in that will be right up your alley."

"So all I have to do is kill someone?" This was going to be easier than ShadowLily thought.

"Yes, that's all you have to do." Cassandra stood and put her drink down. From inside her inventory, she produced a letter. "All of the details. When you come back, try not to hurt any more of my people."

It was easy to tell Cassandra had dismissed her, and one thing ShadowLily never liked to do was overstay her welcome. "I'll see you soon."

Cassandra winked. ShadowLily gave her a curt nod and turned for the door. The mask of business slipped over her features. From here on out, it was go time. Whoever's name the woman had sealed inside the letter was about to have a really bad day.

CHAPTER TWENTY-SEVEN

Now that ShadowLily was safely away from the Finicky Lady, she took a moment to open the letter Cassandra gave her.

Quest Received: Assassinate the Assassin

A key member of our guild has gotten a little too big for his britches. Sneak into the estate of Hugo Mendoza and do what assassins do. There is a price for betraying the honor of the guild, and you are its deliverer.

At least he's not royalty or innocent.

"What is with these guys who own estates? All of them feel like a bunch of jackwads." She thought about the last estate they visited and the ritual that was going on behind the house and shuddered.

Tucking the letter back into her inventory, ShadowLily pulled up Hugo's house on the map.

She was going to need a ride.

It was a good thing they'd hired a carriage driver that had a crush on Liz. With him hanging around the inn more often, Grant was always a message away. She fired off a quick letter, and the carriage pulled to a stop next to her a few minutes later.

Jumping down from the driver's seat, Grant opened the door

with the smooth precision only a lifetime of repetition can give to a person. "Where are we off to today?"

ShadowLily gave him the address. "You should come by the inn tonight. We'll be having a celebration."

"I will one hundred percent take you up on that offer." Grant closed the door and hurried back to his seat.

As soon as the carriage started moving, ShadowLily leaned back in the plush interior and tried to relax. Part of her still expected Cassandra to jump out at any second and murder her. Not exactly the vibe she'd ever gotten from a class trainer in a game before. Normally they were all, oh thank you for coming, you're the best and super special, here's your class.

Not in *The Etheric Coast*. Here, the class trainers moved so quickly they could kill in the blink of an eye. It was like the game reduced her superpowers to one, and she was starting over again. It was a good thing for little Miss Killington that she enjoyed a challenge.

"I can't wait to move like she did." With that kind of speed, ShadowLily could throw ten knives before someone took a step. "This is going to be awesome."

Pulling up her user interface, ShadowLily looked for any available information on Hugo's estate. There was a dot on the map, but as usual, there wasn't a lot of information about the place. The map did have a topographical view of the property. It wasn't the best resolution, but she could make out a massive house and a whole lot of trees. The legend on her map showed an apple over the swath of trees so it must be an orchard.

"A lot of places to hide and to hide guards." ShadowLily closed the map while thinking about her next moves.

The situation wasn't ideal.

It was daytime for one thing, and she couldn't walk through the front door and start executing people. That would be a sure way to get herself killed before she ever reached the target. If ShadowLily was going to do this right, she needed to wait and watch for the right opportunity to strike. There was always a way to win. She had to stealth her way there and kill it.

She fucking loved this stuff.

The carriage stopped, and Grant opened the door for her. "We're still a block or two away. I figured you would prefer to make the final approach on foot."

ShadowLily jumped out of the carriage and flipped him a coin. "How did you know I had a job to do and this wasn't a social visit?"

"Just had that kind of feel to it." Grant tipped his cap to her and closed the carriage door.

Turning back toward ShadowLily, the carriage driver met her eyes. "Would you like me to wait here for you, or will this be an extended visit?"

"Probably better if you don't, in case things go south." Shadow-Lily stroked Ripley's flank. "I expect to see you at the inn later."

Grant hopped back up into the driver's seat, and she could tell he was already thinking about spending time with that cute little bartender.

"If you need me I'm a message away. Otherwise, I'll see you tonight." Grant tipped his cap one last time and swung the carriage back out into the road.

As he slowly pulled away, ShadowLily got to business.

Bright and sunny. Of course, it was. Why wasn't this guy's house in the slums where it was dark and rainy all the time? Breaking into someone's house in the middle of the day to kill them was sketchy at best. She thought about channeling her inner Agent 47, but knocking someone out for a disguise seemed like a lot of work when killing someone was so much simpler.

Not to mention that while my elf ears are sexy as fuck, they tend to make me stand out a bit.

If disguises were out, her best bet was to move quickly and decisively. If anyone found a body and raised the alarm before she reached the final target, there wouldn't be a celebration tonight. It was time to focus up.

From one step to the next, she dropped into stealth so smoothly a person one foot away would have only glimpsed a shimmer. This must be what it felt like to be a *Predator*—stalking her prey like the alien in the movie. Only her stealth could break a lot easier. Especially in the daylight.

When she reached the estate, it was easy enough to scale the twelve-foot-tall wall that surrounded the property. She thought about what it would have looked like if anyone had seen her do it. It wasn't every day a person walked down the street and saw a woman run two steps up a wall and vault on top like a cat. Thankfully her stealth kept any prying eyes from seeing anything worth mentioning.

Staying in a low crouch, ShadowLily moved along the wall taking in the sites and sounds of the property. There wasn't time to do a full circle of the place. She'd have to settle for only seeing this small slice before trying to move inside.

The only real dilemma she faced was knowing if leaving a trail of bodies behind her would hinder her progress. It wasn't like the alarm would be any quieter if others found the guards were only unconscious.

Maybe it's time to get a little ruthless.

ShadowLily swore silently and shook her head. She wasn't the kind of person who killed innocents because it was easier. Killing the guards of a master assassin was one thing. Those men and women knew what they signed up for.

Some of the people working the grounds and kitchen probably didn't have a choice. If her dad didn't have the diner, she was sure she would've been working wherever would have hired her.

Sometimes people needed work, and the job and employer didn't matter.

I need more practice with my darts anyway.

A guard came around the corner of the house as he had three times before. She followed him along the top of the wall until he was close to a tall bush, then dropped from above. Unlike the mythical assassins in games, she didn't have an assassinate from above skill. Instead, she landed behind him, looked at his solid metal breast plate, and decided to strike somewhere a little more splashy.

In a lot of movies, when they slashed someone's throat, they got it wrong. It was like the special effects guys couldn't decide between an avalanche of blood and a dribble. The reality was the shit shot everywhere when you slit someone's throat, even if you damn near cut their head off. It made a noise, and the person didn't die instantly.

That was why every quality assassin needed an even better poison master at her back.

The poisons Ernie made for her were the best on the market. The poison was already working as his blood splashed the lawn, making the guard too weak to struggle. ShadowLily grabbed the man's feet and wedged him into the bush as best she could.

Hiding the body that way wouldn't fool anyone for long, but at least he wouldn't be out in the open. No one else had come in this direction since she'd been scouting, but that could change at any time.

The clock was officially ticking.

Dropping back into stealth, ShadowLily checked to make sure that her boots weren't leaving a trail of blood before she poked her head around the back side of the estate. Her feet were clear of any red splotches, and no one blocked her path so she moved. The rows of beautiful apple trees threatened to steal her attention from the task at hand, but almost bumping into an unexpected guard sobered her up instantly.

This man didn't go down as smoothly as the first one, but he did go down quietly.

One of her daggers went up through the bottom of his chin and into his skull. The other stabbed into his belly. The guard doubled over, making it easier for her to guide the body to the ground silently. There wasn't a great place to hide this corpse so she made sure it was off the main path and hoped for the best.

Two men guarded the back door, and there was nowhere for her to hide. This was the perfect opportunity for her to work on her throwing knives. It didn't take long for her to line up the shot. The first guard went down with a blade in his throat, but the second guard moved to catch him, throwing off her knife's trajectory.

Instead of hitting him in the neck, her second throwing knife *bonked* off the guard's leather helmet. He went down on top of the first man but not without making a considerable ruckus.

ShadowLily bent to retrieve her knives, making sure to cut the second guard's arm before straightening. The poison on her blades would make sure neither of the guards would get back up, but if anyone heard her, ShadowLily would be having tea with her caseworker in short order.

Waiting to see if anyone would come storming out of the back door was killing her. It was like her entire body was electrified, waiting for the scream from inside to set her sprinting like the starter's gun at a race. Ten seconds went past, then a minute. The scream never came. It was time to get moving before someone discovered one of the corpses she left behind. Being an assassin was walking a fine line between hurry the fuck up and slow way the hell down.

The large mudroom off the back door was empty.

It took a little bit of doing to shove the two men into the empty storage bins under the long benches, but ShadowLily got it done. Leaving two dead men in the doorway seemed like a bad idea. It was too bad she couldn't do anything about the blood on the floor. Quick use of the inventory trick cleaned her clothes off instantly. Then she moved toward the interior door.

A quick peek through the doorway confirmed she would be walking into the kitchen. Probably the busiest room in the entire estate. It would take a lot of cooks to feed the entire staff and guests.

Sneaking through the kitchen to the stairs she saw at the back of the room wasn't ideal, but it was the only plan she had. Finding a different entrance would only increase the risk of someone finding one of her kills.

What she needed was a distraction.

Even in stealth, the number of people in the kitchen and the heat would make it nearly impossible for her to stay hidden. ShadowLily's best bet was to stay low and behind whatever objects she could until she was close enough to tag one of the women with a dart.

Moving through the kitchen at a snail's pace felt like it was taking forever, but soon she stood so close to one of the women she could've reached out and brushed the hair behind her ear. Instead, she jabbed the knockout dart into her leg and pulled the weapon free before moving back into hiding.

"I don't feel so good." The woman went down in a heap, scattering silverware all over the floor.

The rest of the room moved toward the fallen woman to see if she was okay, giving ShadowLily the freedom to move around unmolested.

A few moments later, she was out of the kitchen and into the main house. The timer in the back of her head was ticking down faster now. Every part of her was screaming to sprint forward. Ignoring the impulse, ShadowLily stayed in a crouch as she moved up the stairs. Just because she wanted to move faster didn't mean she had to give into that temptation by sprinting down the hallway naked and screaming, here I am, here I am.

Yet her feet were picking up the pace.

Moving right past the second and third floors, ShadowLily stopped on the landing before floor number five. There were two guardsmen at the top of the stairs. They were the first ones she'd seen since entering the building. Both wore the metal breastplates and helmets made famous by the Conquistadors.

Watching the two men, all she could think was this was going to be loud. Throwing a knife from here wasn't worth it, and the same went for her darts. Her best bet was a stealth attack, but that would only take care of one guard. Surprise might win the day if she moved fast enough, but even so the sound of two men rolling down the stairs would speed up her killing process dramatically.

She dropped out of stealth and slammed both of her daggers into the femoral arteries of the first guard. He fell screaming as ShadowLily sliced the tendons in the back of the second guard's leg before stepping past him, and smoothly kicking him down the stairs.

As if on cue, Hugo Mendoza stuck his head out of the wide double doors and started shouting. "What in the bloody hell is going on out there?"

When Hugo saw the guards, all the color drained out of his face. His eyes darted around frantically until they settled on ShadowLily. She must have been one hell of a sight dressed from head to toe in black leather, dripping blood from her arms like the serial killer in a slasher flick.

Hugo ran back into the room, but she wasn't going to let him get away. She had one throw before he would be out of her reach and able to close the door. Instead of going for the one in a million kill shot, ShadowLily aimed for the door jamb. Her dagger slammed into the wood, and Hugo tried to slam the door shut. The dagger wiggled back and forth as he slammed the door again and again.

Before Hugo's antics could dislodge her knife, ShadowLily sprinted toward the door and threw her entire body into it. Her target stumbled back, falling on his ass as she rolled to her feet with daggers in hand.

Hugo was skittering backward on his hands and feet like an upside-down crab instead of going for a weapon. Not much of an assassin unless he was using the cat to lure her into some kind of trap.

ShadowLily started throwing knives like Mariano Rivera tossed fastballs. By the time she finished, Hugo looked like he was the victim in a *Saw* film. It was like shish kebobs gone horribly wrong. Or looking at an hors d'oeuvre that needed one toothpick and instead had fifteen.

Now that Hugo was dead, she could scan the room for traps without worrying too much. This wasn't her highest-graded skill, but it worked well enough to single out one wonky floorboard with a pressure switch. She disarmed the floorboard, unsure of what would've happened if she tripped it.

Assassins were normally required to bring back proof of their kills, and while Cassandra hadn't specifically requested proof, it was safer to take something with her in case. Looking over the body took her less than a second. The only thing that stood out was a necklace. She pocketed that, but would it be enough? Not wanting to have to come back, ShadowLily also cut off his right index finger.

"Taking heads is last century." She dropped back into stealth and ran. All that mattered now was getting out of the estate and back to the Finicky Lady in one piece.

She took the stairs down four at a time and thundered through the back door, over the wall, and back into the street. Once she was out on the road, ShadowLily changed out of her leathers and into a very respectable dress. She even had one of those fancy little parasols and a hat to match.

When she'd covered a block with no one screaming bloody murder, ShadowLily called for a ride. Grant slowed as he moved next to her, and she hopped inside with no one the wiser.

"Thanks for coming." She tapped the roof of the carriage.

"Just doing my job. We'll have you back to the Finicky Lady in less than five."

She changed into her leathers, sat back, and tried to relax. The hard part was over. All she had to do now was claim her reward.

This time she snuck past all the guards except for Vomit Boy. That asshole got a dart right in the chest. If anyone were holding a grudge, it would be him, and the last thing she wanted to do was try to get another towel from the barman.

This was her time to celebrate. She was returning as the conquering hero. All she wanted now was her prize and not another fight. The other guards watched her as she walked up the steps, but they'd already missed their opportunity to stop her. When Stainy didn't get up to stop her, she heard a gasp from behind.

Just adds to my mystique.

Once again, ShadowLily entered the bar like she owned the place. "One of you lazy fucks get me a beer."

The bar went silent again.

"Guess that only works at my local bar," ShadowLily mumbled as she made her way through the silent stares to the back of the bar and Cassandra's booth.

Rising from her seat, Cassandra held out her hand. "Proof of the deed?"

This was exactly why she liked to plan.

Holding out Hugo's necklace and finger, she dropped them into Cassandra's drink. "I think you'll find everything in order."

"Then all you have to do is throw to win." Cassandra dumped the contents of her glass on the floor. "Bring out the target."

The room burst into cheers as the center of the bar was cleared of tables, and three women moved in to set up a large target about fifty feet away from them.

"All you have to do is beat my throw, and ascension is yours."

Cassandra held out the class change scroll and tucked it back inside her vest.

ShadowLily pulled out one of her throwing knives. "This would have gone better for you if you let them serve me that beer."

"From here, then." Cassandra tapped her toe on a floorboard and tossed her knife with a simple flick of her wrist.

The blade flew across the room and hit the target just off center. It was a bullseye, but there was room for improvement.

Moving to the same spot Cassandra had been standing, ShadowLily lined up her throw. She let everything fall out of her mind, and when she saw the target and nothing else, she let the blade fly.

It hit the target dead center.

"I'll take that scroll now." ShadowLily held out her hand.

Pulling the rolled parchment free from her inventory, Cassandra passed it to her. "Welcome, mist slayer. If you ever need our services, all you have to do is ask."

A man pressed a beer mug into her hand, but ShadowLily knew when not to push her luck. Drinking a beer in a den full of assassins would've been a mistake. What in the hell had she been thinking?

She set the mug down on a table and headed for the door. She knew Cassandra was staring daggers at her back, but she didn't care. She had what she came for.

Grant was waiting for her return. "Back to the inn?"

"And step on it." ShadowLily climbed inside and finally started to relax.

ShadowLily was getting used to riding in style instead of running everywhere. Plus, it gave her time to look over her class advancement.

System Message: Congratulations on your ascension to Mist Slayer

Your health and mana pools have increased, and you'll receive two new class-specific skills. Keep an eye out for

further opportunities to learn more about your class and obtain new spells as you progress.

Skill Received: Mist Strike

Tired of always having to stand behind your target to deal world-class damage? Now you don't have to. You must be standing before the target to use Mist Strike, but the attack receives all the same bonuses as if you were attacking from stealth and behind. This skill can proc any skills that also activate from behind.

At higher levels, this Mist Strike will provide buffs to damage and critical hit chance, place a debuff on the target, and a DOT. Continue leveling this skill to unlock all the benefits.

Holy shit, that skill was fucking awesome. Backstabbing from the front, who knew that could even be a thing. She also had a few buffs that only activated when she landed an attack from behind. Knowing she could keep those buffs in place by using Mist Strike in the front opened a whole new world of possibilities for her. When the time was right, she could stand next to Cassie and deal out a metric shit-ton of DPS.

Skill Received: Slash and Dash

Kind of like that time you were a mega asshole in high school and ran out on your bill; this is a way to deal some serious damage and get the hell out of Dodge. Slice and Dash is three strikes to the boss followed by a ten percent increase in movement speed for five seconds.

At higher levels, the Slice part of the spell will add a DOT to the target, and the Dash part of the spell will provide additional benefits such as increased healing and dodge chance after performing a critical hit. To unlock the skill's full potential, keep using it.

ShadowLily grinned as she flipped her daggers around and caught them over and over again like someone tossing a coin. Both of her skills were awesome, and both of them would increase her DPS. It was so easy for the ranged classes to sit back and hit things without worrying about getting stomped on. These two skills would shrink the gap in DPS.

All she wanted now was for everyone to get back to the inn with their new classes. Then they could find that bitch Isadora and dish out some payback. It still embarrassed her how easily the Witch of the Woods had cut through them. It wouldn't happen again.

ShadowLily would see to her death personally.

CHAPTER TWENTY-EIGHT

Cassie watched JaKobi go off in the direction of the library.
No big shocker.

Unlike most of the others, she was going to miss having her group around. It wasn't because she was afraid of dying like Tim probably was. It was simply because her fights took so damn long without them.

Part of being a tank was doing a lot less damage than the DPS, and the one place that difference showed up was in solo fights. Her class hit a little harder than the average tank, but the tradeoff was if she took a direct hit from the boss, she got punished big time when a more traditional tank could probably shrug off the damage.

Tanking wasn't a job for the faint of heart. A tank was the front of the line, the bastion of safety in a world ruled by evil monsters. Her job was to take the hits so her team didn't have to.

Or avoid the hits in my case.

Being out in front gave her a certain weight of responsibility the others didn't have. She not only set the tone for the fight but had to lead the way there. Knowing how much they relied on her to perform, she knew she had to ace whatever this next challenge was. The group wouldn't be waiting because of her.

Cassie opened her user interface and pulled up her quests. After a second, she found the right one and selected it.

Here we go, baby!

Quest Received: So you want to be a Shadow Dancer?

I'm not super-sold on the name, but the class sounds awesome.

Standing on the front lines and not wearing a giant pile of metal and carrying a shield the size of a house is dangerous business. One wrong step and your health disappears faster than a social security check at a casino. Avoiding those nasty hits and moving with a dancer's flexibility and agility is the essence of shadow dancing.

Find The Leaky Spoon and Kevin "Ledfoot" Mcgrath to start your ascendance to Shadow Dancer.

"Ledfoot doesn't sound like a great nickname for a dancer." Cassie snickered. "But it's a great name for a tank."

She looked up the Leaky Spoon and was pleased to see it wasn't too far away. The bar was on the fringe of Tim's sphere of influence inside the slums. Apparently, old Ledfoot had fallen on hard times. That or no one wanted to be an avoidance tank when big bulky armor looked so much cooler than her leather duds.

Most people probably thought she was a leather DPS of some kind, but screw them. Cassie dressed this way because she needed to be able to move. It was probably fun for some people to stand there and soak up damage like a big metal sponge. She liked to be more interactive with her targets.

Hitting things also helped with her anger issues.

The walk to the Leaky Spoon didn't take longer than ten minutes, but ten minutes in the slums was enough to get soaked to the bone with rain. Not that she minded much. After being in the desert, the near-constant rain felt like a gift from Eternia herself. It was funny how being deprived of something for a while made it seem that much better when she finally got it again.

Cassie spied her destination in the distance and came to a complete stop. She looked at the building for a few more minutes, wondering how this could be right, then started walking. As far as she knew the location on quests was never wrong.

The Leaky Spoon was a total shithole.

She spotted the holes in the roof as she walked down the hill toward the location. The rain pouring inside the building didn't seem to stop the customers from flooding in and out of the place. Warm laughter and the sound of people drinking reached her every time the door opened or the wind shifted just right to carry the sound through the holes in the roof.

At least this won't be boring.

As far as she could tell, the people moving in and out of the building were normal folks. At first glance, she would've marked this place as a location frequented by those who enjoyed drinking a lot but not paying an arm and a leg for it. Sometimes a girl only wanted a beer. She didn't want to pay fifteen dollars for a fancy glass and an even fancier address.

Fuck all that nonsense.

For her, drinking was something she did socially, and she always had a ton of fun with it. Even if the next day tended to suck. This looked like it would be her kind of place to throw one back, minus the hole in the roof. She liked cheap drinks, not getting pissed on while she drank them.

The Leaky Spoon also needed to hire a band to play some righteous tunes, even if it was just background music. As she thought that, the most beautiful voice rang out as a band started to play. She was so ready for this.

Cassie marched up the steps like she was going to her favorite watering hole and stepped inside like she owned the place. There was a stage in the back right corner where the band with the female singer was rocking out. On the left side of the bar was a small alcove with beaded curtains in front of it. The rest of the place was a wide-open space with people milling about and drinking.

Except for the very center of the room. A giant copper spoon balanced on a bronze triangle dominated the entire space. All of the water from the roof went down copper funnels and emptied into the spoon. When the spoon was full, it dipped and dumped the water into a bronze funnel. The bronze funnel continued as a tube that led under the bar and outside. It was super fucking cool, but it probably would've been cheaper to fix the roof.

She turned away from the rain catcher and moseyed up to the bar. When the bartender turned her way, she motioned for a beer. "I'm looking for Ledfoot."

The bartender handed her a glass full of amber-colored delight. "I wouldn't call him that to his face. He gets a bit sensitive." He pointed behind her to a small alcove in the back of the room.

"Thanks for the tip." Cassie tossed the man a silver coin and turned to hunt down Kevin.

Ledfoot's little alcove wasn't much better than the rest of the place. There was a grimy couch in one corner covered in clothes. A small round table with seating for two occupied the rest of the space. A man wearing very bright colored clothes and one monster of a hat currently sat in one of the two chairs.

Maybe it wasn't the hat that was big, but the giant-ass feather sticking out of it.

For the first time since she entered the game, Cassie was starting to doubt the AI's decision-making process. Out of all the possible characters she could have gotten stuck with for a class trainer, this was the best the game could do?

A drunk guy sleeping in a chair.

Ledfoot had propped himself up against the wall on the chair's back two legs. He'd pulled his hat down over his eyes. It only made him look more absurd because every time he took one of his deep, lumbering breaths, the feather danced around.

How can he even sleep in here? It's louder than a Metallica concert.

Not wanting to get too close, Cassie pulled out her staff and poked Kevin in the chest. "Wake up."

Jumping to his feet, Ledfoot pushed the staff out of the way and then thumped back down into his chair heavily and started adjusting his boots. "So you've come to see me perform."

"Not exactly." Cassie stopped when he cut her off.

"Don't be shy, girl. It's fine to admit you've come to see the one, the only, Kevin Mcgrath. I dominate the stage here nightly. No one goes home unsatisfied." Ledfoot turned and yelled into the bar, "But it would be nice if these bumpkins appreciated a little culture."

A chorus of drunken jeers cascaded back from the bumpkins.

Cassie was dumbfounded as Kevin continued to ignore her as he prepared for some kind of dance routine, and she was starting to get pissed off. "Listen, are you the shadow dancer guy or not? I'm kind of in a hurry."

"The theater waits for no one." Kevin tossed an electric blue silk scarf over his shoulders and brushed past her, heading for the stage.

"I just want to be a better tank," Cassie shouted after him, hoping the desperation in her voice would sway him to come back.

As Kevin climbed on the stage, Cassie grumbled to herself, "Bet those sword and board bastards don't have to deal with this shit."

There was nothing she could do now but grab another beer and watch the show.

Ledfoot did a couple of stretches, limbering up his body before he motioned for the band to start playing. The woman who'd been singing was sitting at the bar next to her. Was Ledfoot going to sing?

This was going to be bad.

The band started playing some kind of Broadway show tune, and Kevin strutted around the stage like a peacock. When he started singing, it became apparent that his adherent dance moves weren't the worst part of his routine. How was it possible that someone who couldn't even dance was the shadow dancer class trainer?

The crowd was starting to get pissed off as he preened around the stage, daring them to do something as his voice grew more out of pitch by the moment. The dance moves slowly degraded into something that made the JaKobi shuffle look like a routine created for *Hamilton*.

With a wave of his hand, the song changed, and Ledfoot belted out, "Hop in my carriage, it's as big as a whale and about to set sail."

The first mug of beer flew at him a moment later, and Ledfoot dodged it without missing a beat. "My carriage seats about twenty, so come on, and bring your beer money."

"Bang, bang." The backup singers from the other stage sang as the mugs started flying faster.

Ledfoot managed to dodge every single one as he shouted, "On the door, baby."

Cassie couldn't knock his choice in parodies, or the fact not a single mug of beer had touched him during his entire performance was fucking impressive. The shadow dancer ducked and wove through the onslaught of mugs. Even though the floor was sticky and covered in broken glass, Kevin never lost his footing. At one point, four men teamed up and threw their mugs at the same time.

A wall of shadows flew up in front of Ledfoot. All the beers smashed against it before he spun out of the shadow wall like it was mist. "It's the beer shack, baby!"

With his performance over, the bar simmered back down to its normal pitch. Everyone looked happy except for the bartender, who worked furiously to replace all the beers. The two guys sweeping and mopping up the stage also didn't look too thrilled, but Kevin seemed tickled pink as he jumped off the stage and headed back to his private alcove.

Cassie paid for her beer and moved to follow him with a

genuine smile on her face. "Kevin, I have to tell you, that was something else."

"These heathens don't understand what it takes to be an artist." Ledfoot changed out of his beer-splattered pants and searched for a fresh pair as he addressed Cassie. "I have something I need you to do for me."

"How about you put those pants on first?" The tank grabbed a pair off the couch and tossed them at Kevin.

He snorted as he snatched the pants out of the air. "As if, girl. You see, you have a P, and I'm into big dangly D's."

"That makes two of us then." Cassie hoped he understood what she meant.

Ledfoot pulled on his new pants as he giggled delightedly. "Then let's get to business."

Quest Received: Rejection only makes my heart want to break your face.

Head to the warehouse district and look for the building marked 537 Paper Street. Let's just say the owners find my particular brand of fighting not as interesting as they'd like. Show them that dodging attacks can be equally fun to watch. In every fight, you must dodge at least five attacks before winning. Return with the champion's belt, and you'll ascend to the ranks of shadow dancers.

"Wait, I get to go somewhere and hit people?" Cassie watched Ledfoot's face for any sign of hope.

"Yes, but you also have to—" Kevin stopped speaking when she slammed into him like a rocket and pulled the trainer into a giant hug.

"Thank you." Cassie almost felt like crying.

It felt like it had been forever since all she had to do was kick ass.

Ledfoot disentangled himself. "Dodge the attacks before you get to bashing, or you'll be doing the quest again."

"Oh, don't worry, I like to see them angry before the fall." Cassie couldn't stop smiling. This quest was her kind of thing.

Ledfoot motioned for her to leave the alcove. "A girl needs to get her rest before the next performance."

"See you soon." Cassie ducked through the beads and headed out of the bar.

This was it. She was on her way to being stronger. No one was going to get the drop on her again.

CHAPTER TWENTY-NINE

assie stopped outside the warehouse numbered 537 Paper Street.

It didn't look like much as far as buildings went. It was about three stories tall, made out of a sturdy wood frame and paneling. The side of the building facing the water had a thick coat of tar applied to it. The roof appeared to be in good repair, which all in all made it a huge step up from the Leaky Spoon.

There wasn't any foot traffic coming or going from the building. She stood watching the entrance for about ten minutes before moving toward it. If she was going to get in a fight, she wanted to control the situation.

The tank was the one who decided how the battle started and had to own everything that happened until it was over. Move the boss here, point an attack there, don't get fucking dead. All of it was her responsibility, and she loved that part of her job. It was also kind of nice being the first person to hit every boss they faced.

Hitting things is what I do best.

Cassie moved forward. Waiting here longer wasn't going to open the door and magically tell her what was inside. The second part of being a tank was having a big set of brass fucking lady balls. Running into danger when everyone else was trying to get away was par for the course. She was kind of like her own superhero.

"Super Cassie," she trumpeted. "Fuck no, that's lame."

Where was JaKobi when she needed to come up with a cool nickname?

Maybe it was better if she didn't give herself a superhero name. When it came right down to it, Cassie would probably call herself fluffy bunny lady to throw them off, then kick the shit outta them. *That's not very heroic.* Holy shit, maybe she wasn't a superhero, but an anti-hero. Just good enough that you had to root for her, but bad enough that people questioned her methods on the regular.

"Oh well, at least I'm fun." She'd much rather hang out with guys like Deadpool and the Punisher over morally superior tools like Daredevil any day.

Every team had a place for a Wolverine. She was theirs.

Cassie opened the door, and the sounds of fighting and cheering reached her ears. It was like she found a home. If there was ever a quest she was built to take on, it was this one. Fighting, drinking, blood, and scantily clad people everywhere. It was like *Fight Club* met the *Fast and Furious*.

"Oh, I'm so fucking down." Cassie let her eyes move across the space as she stepped inside and closed the door behind her.

It didn't take long to track down the fight master. He was a huge man with arms that made Arnold's look soft. He had long greasy hair, and the right side of his face was tattooed blue. The look in his eyes said he was as likely to try to kill her as schedule a fight for her, but he was the only option.

"I'm here to fight." Cassie stayed loose, ready for anything.

Pulling the cigar from his mouth, the man blew a puff of smoke at her. "I'm not in the business of murdering little girls for money."

"Maybe I'm in the business of smacking that smug fucking look off your face," Cassie growled.

Before they got into a tussle, she tried to inspect the man. It only gave his name. Roco? It wasn't much to go on, but if there was anyone who should run a fight club, it was a guy named Roco.

Fight Master Roco was already pushing her buttons. One of her triggers was when people didn't take her seriously because of her size. As if being six feet tall made a person special. Sure, if their job was getting stuff off a tall shelf shorter people couldn't reach, then yes, they were super duper spectacular. Otherwise, size didn't mean dick.

"You've got a little fire. Who's your sponsor?" The fight master watched her thoughtfully.

Ugh, Kevin didn't say anything about having to name-drop him. Normally when she name-dropped, it was to add credibility to her situation, not to take it away. It made sense she'd have to divulge who she was working for at some point, or else Kevin wouldn't have sent her here to earn some respect.

"Ledfoot." Cassie said it with as straight a face as she could muster.

Laughter erupted from the fight master's lips, and his cigar fell to the floor, sending sparks everywhere. "Had to ban that guy cause he wouldn't stop singing during the fights. His voice is like two cats fighting while a baby screams in the background. People aren't going to pay to hear that shit no matter how good a fighter he is."

Roco's expression turned hard. "You're not going to sing, are you?"

"Never been much of a singer. I'm more of a punch you in the face kind of girl." Cassie was starting to like the man despite their first moments together.

He nodded as if that made all the sense in the world. "You're going to have to start at the bottom and fight your way up. Can't have you taking on the champ without proving your chops."

"Point me in the right direction, and let me know if I'm allowed to bet on myself to win." Cassie understood the real reason she couldn't face the champ straight away was that it would ruin the betting.

The fight master pulled out a fresh cigar and clipped off the end. "Just don't get greedy, or the house reserves the right to kill you and keep the money."

"Seems fair to me." Cassie thought about it for a second. "Can you tell me what greedy is so I don't step over the line?"

Lighting the fresh cigar, the fight master smiled. "You're in ring three."

So that's a no on the helperno.

"Ring three it is." Cassie knew when someone dismissed her for asking too many questions.

She wanted another beer, but it didn't feel right to be drinking when there was so much at stake. It was going to be hard enough dodging attacks in the small confines of the ring. She didn't want to add to her stress level by having a buzz. As far as she knew there was only one drunken master, and she wasn't it.

Ring number three might as well not have been a ring at all. They'd driven four metal posts through the floor, and a single blood-stained cloth was looped lazily around them to indicate the border.

"I guess it's better than the basement under a bar." Cassie dropped into her fighter persona. "You don't know where I've been, Lou."

"Who's Lou?" When the speaker didn't answer right away, he continued. "You wanna make a bet or what?"

Cassie almost punched him in the balls, but she reminded herself she had to save it for the ring. Plus, it wasn't his fault she was talking to herself, and he happened to overhear. She'd save the anger caused by her momentary embarrassment for whomever she faced in the ring. It was going to suck for them and be cathartic for her.

"Listen, beefcake." Cassie poked a finger into his chest and pulled up her user interface to see his name.

"I'm here to fight, Viktor. So tell me who I'm facing and what the odds are so I can bet on myself to win." Cassie stared into the bet master's eyes and dared him to make the odds low.

After looking over the assembled fighters, the gambler pointed at a rail-thin man with a bald head and chiseled arms. "Shoeless, I've got a fight for you."

Turning his attention back to Cassie. "Ten to one."

Don't be greedy.

Reaching into her inventory, Cassie pulled out eleven silver coins. "Ten on me to win. Use the rest to buy yourself something nice."

She stopped herself from reaching out and patting his cheek at the last second, which probably stopped a fight before it started.

Holding up the silver coin, Viktor smiled and turned to the male fighter. "I'm putting this on you, Shoeless. It'll earn you a bonus if you win. I'll double it if you make it a good show."

"You're on, and add ten silver for me. You know I'm good for it." Shoeless turned to face Cassie. "Try not to bleed all over the floor."

"Try not to lose all your fucking teeth," Cassie growled and snapped her teeth shut with a *click.*

Viktor muttered, "I don't get paid enough for this shit." Then screamed, "Get it on."

Shoeless moved in quickly, closing the distance and trying to use his superior reach to his advantage. She couldn't risk that the guy had a glass jaw so she had to dodge five of his attacks before taking a swing. The fastest way to accomplish her goal was probably to antagonize him.

"I've heard of some gimmicky shit, but not wearing shoes?" Cassie shrugged. "Unfortunately, you're that guy."

Shoeless came at her with a quick series of punches, followed by a flurry of kicks. She was blocking and deflecting all the attacks, but her counter for dodging had only gone up once. Did dodging mean she couldn't get hit at all?

It was the only logical explanation.

Nothing really changed in the sense of the fight. She'd taken Shoeless' measure during their first exchange, and the only way he could beat her was if she injured herself napping on the mat. Cassie had this fight all sewn up. Shoeless just didn't know it yet.

Channeling her best Lawrence Fishburne, she held out her hand and made the come get some gesture. "If you think you can win, show me."

Shoeless came at her hard this time, which made it easier to weave around his attacks. She almost felt bad that it was this easy to set him up, but if he wanted to be a real fighter, he would have to learn some control. Like she was showing by not throwing a single punch.

When her counter hit five, she waited until Shoeless overextended himself and delivered an uppercut that started from her knees and ended with her jumping a foot off the floor. Shoeless' head snapped back like he got whiplash, and Cassie smiled as she watched him topple over like a house of cards. It took a few moments for the feeling to start returning to her hand, but by then, the fight was over. She'd won in a single punch. Shoeless wasn't getting back up, and she scored a cool gold.

"Gold, please." Cassie turned to face down Viktor with a cocky smile.

The gambler reached into the purse tied at his waist and tossed her a gold coin. "I'll take my satisfaction when you see what's waiting for you next."

"You giving ten to one again?" Cassie quipped.

Looking at her as if he were trying to evaluate cattle for breeding, the gambler walked in a slow circle around her. "Ten to one."

With a smirk of satisfaction, Cassie pressed the gold coin in his hand. "I don't take IOUs."

"Go back to Roco. He'll get you squared away for your next fight." The gambler was watching her like a rat watched a piece of fallen hotdog.

It's like he knows he already made a bad bet.

"Someone scrape Shoeless off the floor and wipe up that blood. We have fighters that want to rumble," the gambler shouted from behind her as Cassie worked her way through the crowd.

537 Paper Street was really hopping now. There was even a band set up at the very end of the space. A buffet was forming along one wall, and the bar was pumping out drinks like there were a hundred thousand people in the warehouse instead of only a couple hundred.

She snagged a shot off one of the passing trays, downed it, and flipped the empty glass onto another tray in one fluid motion as she followed the cloud of cigar smoke to Roco's new location.

Roco saw her coming, and the fight master waved her forward. "Should have known better after you told me you were working with Ledfoot, but I have something special lined up for you this time." He leaned in closer, dropping his voice a bit. "If you think you can handle it."

"Already put a gold on me to win." Cassie winked. "Think you can stomach the loss?"

Narrowing his eyes, Roco pointed at the second ring. "Just remember what I said about getting greedy."

Cassie figured she probably reached her limit on bets if she won this fight, or she'd have to dial it back down for the third bout. It wasn't like it really mattered. This wasn't about making money. All she had to do was win these fights to get her class change accomplished. Pocketing the extra gold was merely icing on the cake.

The second ring was better than the first one, but still not that great. A canvas mat covered the floor, and the poles had two sets of ropes tied around the edges. The setup was almost starting to look professional. The thing Cassie loved most about the second ring was that the size of the fighting space nearly doubled. After the last match's cozy quarters, this space was going to feel downright comfortable.

This wasn't the right time for her to get cocky, but anyone who lost to the last chump didn't deserve to step inside the door, let alone get their class upgraded. It almost felt like a waste of time. Any idiot who hit level twenty could've taken on Shoeless, but Cassie knew the next fight would be tougher, and the final one would be a doozy. At least this time she got to dodge the attacks instead of having to get punched the entire time.

It was go time!

Cassie slid into the ring and stood with a flourish, lifting her fists in the air and shaking them. "Yeah!"

She was basking in the attention and the crowd shouting back at her, so when they stopped, Cassie noticed instantly. The widest man she'd ever seen was coming toward her. A quick inspection showed his name as Dean "The Brick" Hippowitts.

Wide as a hippo, hits like a brick.

The bigger they were, the harder they fell, and this guy wasn't nearly as big as some of the bosses they faced. If they wanted her to be intimidated, he would have to sprout tentacles or an extra set of arms. Standing toe-to-toe with a man didn't scare her anymore. Plus, with his wider body and her smaller size, she could probably avoid most of his attacks by strafing.

"I see they brought me a snack before my next fight." The Brick chortled at his joke. "Or maybe you're here to warm my sheets."

Cassie laughed in his face. Getting to her wasn't as easy as making a crude sex joke. She'd been to plenty of frat parties. The Brick's line wasn't even original.

If there was one thing Cassie loved, it was shutting down a guy who thought he was hot shit. She knew how to make it sting. "If you can tell me the last time you saw your dick, I'll consider touching it."

Just like that, the fight started.

The Brick was faster than she expected. Despite being huge and wide, he moved with elegance. Every team in the NFL would've paid this guy quarterback money to play on the line. It almost seemed unfair that someone could be that big and still move so quickly.

His punches whistled as they snapped near her head as she rolled and dodged out of the way. The wider ring gave her every advantage as long as she didn't let The Brick pin her down. If one of those punches connected, it was going to rock her world.

So far, she'd managed to dodge two attacks. It was too bad she didn't get points for deflections because she'd already have a hundred of them. Half of her fighting style was diverting the other person's attacks instead of flat-out avoiding them. Changing things up with a big angry man chasing her around wasn't exactly easy, but she'd manage.

The kick came out of nowhere.

She wasn't even sure if The Brick could do more than waddle around the ring and dish out death with his two gloves. The fact his big ass could balance on one leg and manage a kick shouldn't have surprised her with how he centered his balance. He might be big and fat, but there was a load of muscle under there.

Cassie hit the mat hard but rolled out of the way instantly. The Brick came down hard in the spot she'd occupied. His ass created a crater in the mat where her head would have been. If he'd landed on her, that dent could've been her face. The last thing she wanted to have happen on her first day of streaming was to die with some ginormous bastard sitting on her face.

Talk about embarrassing.

Luckily for her, The Brick over-committed with his attack, trying to end the fight early, but now he was having trouble trying to get back up. Cassie darted forward and started landing unblockable punches to the back of his head. She landed four hits before he started to wobble. The fifth glanced off his shoulder as The Brick finally found his feet.

Hippowitts swayed gently from side to side, but that didn't stop him from coming at her.

Not wanting to get in front of that speeding freight train,

Cassie made herself look like she was bracing for impact and rolled to the side at the last second. As her roll took her wide of The Brick, she kicked out with one foot, tripping the giant.

There was a second where she thought her kick hadn't done enough damage to trip him, but then The Brick went down in a heap. Her first instinct was to run forward and finish it, but the fight was already over. The big bastard wasn't getting up. She'd done it. Now she was going to get a chance at the champ.

It was too bad Tim wasn't here to heal her up. Taking that kick hurt more than she'd like to admit. It was like getting gut-punched by a horse. At least she was able to get out of the way when he tried to smash her. If one more boss farted on her, Cassie was going to lose her shit.

Enough was enough already.

It wasn't the right time to gloat. She took her ten gold from the bookie with little more than a nod. "For the next fight." She handed him ten silver.

"Not feeling quite as confident this time?" Viktor didn't have the same problem with gloating as he looked her over to set the odds for the next fight.

Cassie smiled the slow-time grin of a low-down killer. "Just trying to make sure I don't upset the house." She nodded toward Roco. "No one likes it when someone wins too much."

"Fair enough. I'll still give you ten to one." The bookie turned and raised his voice to the crowd. "Five to one, the Firecracker here gets her ticket punched."

For a split second, she thought he was about to make her the favorite, but then came the sucker punch. Nothing like a little reality check to the ego to make her focus up. These last two guys had been chump change, but no one was giving her the crown so easily. She knew this next fight was going to be on a whole different level.

Roco was motioning for her to join him. "Not bad, but the fun stuff is over. It's time you faced our champion, Juan 'The Rocket' Grubinski."

"Point me in the right direction." Cassie cracked her knuckles.

"First things first." Roco pulled a red vial from his belt. "Dink this, I can't have you starting the fight all nicked up."

Taking the little red vial, Cassie chugged the contents and immediately felt all her wounds heal. "Thank you."

Roco leaned back, trying to look like he didn't care one bit. "Just trying to make sure the gamblers get a good show. This business doesn't run on cupcakes and daydreams."

"None of them do." Cassie gave Roco a warm smile. "Thanks again for the potion. I'll make sure I earn it."

Roco nodded and pointed at the third ring.

The third ring was the real deal. The ring itself was elevated from the floor, making it easier for people to see the fighters. White cloth covered the rough hempen ropes, and now there were three of them. The space inside the ring was slightly larger than her last fight, but size wasn't a factor in her fighting ability unless she felt confined.

It felt like all of these fights would have been pretty simple if all she had to do was win, but having to dodge the attacks first made it harder. Skilled fighters didn't miss as often. The Rocket was going to be the toughest man in this place. It was time for her to channel her inner Ledfoot and dodge, punch, and kick her way to victory.

Sans the singing, of course.

There were seats around the final ring so more people could watch. Normally doing something in front of a large crowd would've paralyzed her with fear. It was her one weakness. Cassie liked being a badass, but she liked doing it better on the sly. When she was fighting, everything else around her fell away, and all she cared about was what was right in front of her.

The Rocket was already waiting in the ring. He was smaller than she expected. Her experience was that the bosses in games tended to get larger as a player progressed and not smaller. This was a welcome surprise that put her on a more even footing for the fight.

She walked up the six steps to the edge of the ring and waited while they announced Juan. He took off his robe and danced around, throwing a series of punches. The only thing that stood out to her was the large silver bands over his wrists. She didn't know what they were, but she'd heard Tim call out enough of this stuff in fights to know they were worth paying attention to.

The attendant motioned for her to enter the ring. "Fighting on behalf of Ledfoot, we have Cassie!"

There was scattered applause, nothing like the outpouring of love that Juan received. The only way to explain how she felt was that picture of Michael Jordan leaning back in a chair saying, "and I took offense to that." It didn't matter what a person had to do to psych themselves up for the big moments, even if it meant taking imaginary slights to an entirely new level.

Sometimes I dream that he is me, like Mike. If I could be like Mike.

She stepped into the ring as though she owned it.

If these idiots were dumb enough to bet against her, they deserved to lose their money. This was it. Cassie was five dodges and a knockout away from obtaining her class change. The calm of battle slipped over her, and she waited for the one thing that could release her.

"Fight!"

The Rocket came at her slowly, watching for any sign of weakness. He closed the gap and feinted a few quick jabs as if he were sizing her up. Then he started working the distance. Cassie wasn't exactly sure how it happened, but there was a twinkle in his eye, and she knew she was totally fucked.

The Rocket's hands flew off, adding an extra two feet of reach to all his punches.

How was this possible?

The fists flew at her again, and she dodged one before the other skipped off her shoulder. Getting hit didn't hurt any more than she thought it would, which was a pleasant surprise. Cassie quickly adopted a new plan. Each time he attacked, she dodged one of the fists and blocked the other.

At least Ledfoot didn't say they had to be consecutive attacks.

Rocket's fists flew at her relentlessly. She hated to admit it, but the magic was kind of elegant. Part of her wondered if there was a damage-dealing class with the same magical abilities. It'd be like being a warrior monk, but with fucking rocket fists.

The hits she was blocking were starting to take their toll, but Cassie finally dodged the fifth attack. As soon as she saw the counter in the lower right-hand corner of her vision hit five, she changed things up by using her feet. The Rocket wasn't expecting her to block an attack without harm before roundhousing his other hand into the crowd.

The Rocket looked at his hand in a woman's lap and pointed his wrist at the limb, willing it back onto his wrist.

"Should've tied a rope to it," Cassie shouted as she delivered a brutal kick to the back of The Rocket's head.

Landing next to the unconscious body of the fighter, Cassie whispered. "And never take your eyes off your opponent."

The arena broke out into furious applause, and Cassie bowed, loving every second of their adoration.

Viktor entered the ring and tossed her a gold coin. "Great fight kiddo, when you come back, we're going to make some real money together." He winked at her and made room for Fight Master Roco.

"Defeating the champion grants you a single request." Roco handed her a letter. "Here is a testament to your achievements in the ring."

Cassie took the letter. "You're not going to like what I ask for."

Roco grinned. "I rarely do."

"Give Ledfoot another chance to fight here. He's dying at the

Leaky Spoon. He needs this." Cassie smiled. "That's my only request."

Roco thought about it for a moment. "Cheap for me, not a lot of effort required. You will have your boon." He handed her a second letter. "Now get out of here before one of these other ruffians gets the balls to take you on."

Snatching the second letter from his hand with nimble fingers, Cassie turned and headed for the door. She had a quest to turn in.

Ledfoot was waiting for her with a hopeful expression on his face. "Tell me everything that happened."

Cassie accepted the drink he offered and sat. After taking a sip, she pulled the two letters from her inventory and set them on the table. "The long and short of it is, I won, and you're back in."

"What do you mean I'm back in?" Kevin downed his glass and stared at the letters, unable to pick them up for fear of what they might contain.

Cassie smiled and polished off her drink before holding out the glass for a refill. "I mean you can fight again."

Ledfoot jumped up and pulled her into a hug. "You did it!"

"I did, but if you want to keep your spot, I'd suggest less singing during the fights." Cassie returned the hug. "Even if it's kind of growing on me."

"They'll learn to love it eventually." Ledfoot sounded elated. "Oh, and I have something for you. Welcome to the ranks, Shadow Dancer."

Kevin reached inside his shirt and pulled out a sealed envelope. With a flourish, he bowed and handed it to Cassie. "Congratulations."

"Thank you." She gave Ledfoot one last hug before turning to leave.

Once Cassie was outside in the quiet, she opened her class change information, and started to read.

System Message: Congratulations on your ascension to Shadow Dancer

Your health and mana pools have increased, and you'll receive two new class-specific skills. Keep an eye out for further opportunities to learn more about your class and obtain new spells as you progress.

Skill Received: Here and There

When you need someone to think you're in one place when you're really in another, activate this skill. Select a location within ten feet of your current position, and you'll move there instantly while a magical look-alike of you will remain in the spot. When your opponent destroys the mirage, you will transport back to the original location.

Cassie smiled again and thought of the last time it happened this often in such a short time. This skill and all the fights were so awesome she couldn't stop her elation. Getting new and shiny things, badass skills, and a streaming contract was like the best day of her life. She couldn't wait to get back to the inn and find JaKobi to celebrate.

I'm going to rock that fiery little wizard's world.

While she couldn't use Here and There during sex, it was the kind of skill that would save her ass when she was close to death. Mirage out, let Tim top her off, boss destroys the mirage, right back to kicking ass. It was nice to have an emergency *don't get eviscerated* button.

The only thing Cassie would have to watch out for was that she didn't use the skill and transport back into danger when the boss destroyed the mirage. There were some downsides because of the positioning, but once she mastered this skill, it would be a huge bonus for them.

Big upgrades are the eBay kind of upgrades, baby!

Skill Received: Dance Dance You're Dead

This is the skill to use when you need something flashy to get the boss' attention. The series of attacks generated by this move are so fluid people often refer to it as dancing. If all eight attacks are successful, the skill increases threat by three hundred percent. All other outcomes increase threat by one hundred and fifty percent.

This was going to come in helpful when one of the DPS deliberately tried to make her life hard.

Cassie looked over her new skills for a few more minutes and couldn't wait to try them out. She closed her user interface and walked back to the inn with a lighter step.

That bitch Isadora wasn't going to know what hit her.

CHAPTER THIRTY

Tim stood on the inn's front porch watching the drizzle and people running from shop to shop.

It was time for him to work on his class change, but he wanted a moment to regroup his thoughts. They'd been through a lot in the last few weeks, and sometimes it paid to take a few moments to soak it all in. He was living in a game, getting paid to go on adventures. The closest thing he could think of in the real world was an archaeologist, or maybe a mercenary treasure hunter.

Sadly, back in the real world it felt like a lot of the great discoveries were already made, but there was always the chance for something new and interesting. Maybe space would be the next great adventure or the colonization of Mars. While he might not get to be a part of that next great adventure as a businessman, here he was part of a new and exciting adventure every day.

For Tim, coming into the game and getting to experience a new world for the first time was part of what made the adventure special. There was a good chance that they were some of the first people to tread in a few of the places they'd been. It was a super cool thought to be an explorer. It was like their group was the

Daniel Boone of the game, forever pushing into new territories and learning new skills.

He stepped off the porch and started walking when a woman called to him from across the street. "Excuse me, are you Tim?"

Since his encounter with the man with the orange sash, Tim always took caution when meeting strangers.

He walked across the street, prepared to activate Quick Feet if he needed to get away. "Yes, I am. How can I help you?"

"I wanted to thank you for my new store location and the wonderful pricing." She blushed and looked slightly embarrassed. "I seem to have run into unforeseen trouble with my last establishment."

It took him a minute to catch on, but this must have been Watch Commander Brennen's sister.

"Sarah." She gave a small curtsy. "Thank you again. No one else would give me the time of day."

Tim was starting to feel like a real schmuck. Yes, he helped her secure a new shop with fantastically reduced rent, but he did it for his progression, not because he cared about her plight. When he thought about the situation, he probably would've helped her anyway. He was always a sucker for trying to right as many wrongs as he could, but in this particular case, he wasn't much better than the people who blocked her from keeping her old place or finding a new one.

Not wanting Sarah to think of him as a benevolent benefactor, Tim tried to think of a way to phrase what he'd done gently. "I hate to ruin your opinion of me, but I needed a favor from your brother, and helping you seemed like the best way to secure it quickly."

"Thank you for being honest, but I already knew." Sarah flipped a small dagger out of her sleeve and tucked it away again. "He told me to watch out because he didn't know you. I thought I'd come and get a look at you for myself."

She appraised him for a moment longer. "You seem like a good man, Tim. Not everyone would have been as honest." Sarah gave a slight curtsy. "I hope that when the end of my lease expires, you think enough of me to keep me around."

Tim nodded. "All I ask is you treat people right, and you'll always have a place here. Oh, and try not to stab anyone who doesn't deserve it."

"Done." Sarah turned to head back into her shop and stopped. "Stop by and take a look around. I'm sure I have at least one item you'd be interested in."

"I'd be delighted to." Tim looked up at where the sun should have been. "Unfortunately, I have other pressing business to attend to."

He gave her a cheery wave as he headed out of the slums. This new relationship might work out better than he expected. Granted, he still had no idea what Sarah sold so it could end up being a total disaster. The knife up the sleeve was an interesting surprise, and like with Lady Briarthorn, he reminded himself never to underestimate Sarah.

It didn't take him long to get out into the city proper. Then he pulled up his quest log to find out exactly which direction to head in.

Quest Received: So you want to be a Hex Witch?

Wouldn't it be nice if you could click a button and *whoosh*, you were exactly what you wanted to be? Of course it would, but that isn't what's going to happen. Before accepting your new class, you must understand it. The road to true knowledge begins with a single step. Your first step is to seek out Joaquin Thunderhawk and convince him to show you the way.

This time his map had a little icon next to it showing the location of his class trainer. Sadly, it wasn't far enough away for Tim to need the carriage so he put one foot in front of the other and hoofed it toward his destination.

Tim expected to find Joaquin at a tavern or an inn. Out of all the places he could've pictured, it would have never been a bakery.

Not only was he working at a bakery, but based on the giant sign with his name above it, he owned it.

Joaquin's Bakery: healing through the power of food.

At least there was a healing tie-in. Tim was starting to worry that the game was dicking him around sometimes. What was with the last name Thunderhawk anyway? Sounded like some kind of crazy DPS, not someone inclined to the healing arts. Healers always had boring names.

Like Tim.

He laughed, earning a couple of stares from the people waiting in line outside the shop. Maybe he should've named his character something sexier like HealzBot420 or MrWaffles, but he still felt better being him.

Not sure if he should cut to the front or wait in line, Tim grabbed a number and took his spot in the back of the queue. The last thing he wanted to do was offend Joaquin by cutting off his paying customers when his quest said he'd have to convince him to help. So he waited patiently as the line moved forward at a steady clip.

As he got closer, Tim noticed a different sign, Today's Offerings.

Bust that Ritis Biscuits
Get up and Go Chocolate Cake
Need Some Relief Croissants
Couch Locked Cupcakes
Today's Special: Berry Inspirational Cobbler
Have your order ready when you come inside. Peace be with you.

Everything sounded fantastic, but also like each item served a specific purpose. He looked over the list again and saw cures for arthritis, low energy, bound bowels, and pain relief. If he had to take a wild stab at it, the last item wasn't exactly for healing unless the person had writer's block or needed to have a great idea come to them. How Joaquin wove his magic into food was something he'd love to learn.

The line kept moving quickly, and now he knew why. With only five things to choose from it wasn't tough for most people to make a quick decision. He wished there was something like this in the real world where people could go and get instant relief from their issues without having to ingest another prescription.

When it came right down to it, life was easier with magic.

Tim made it in the door and listened to the orders before him to know how he was supposed to do it. He wasn't exactly sure how to fit the whole "will you train me" thing in, but he'd find a way.

"How can I help you?" the woman at the counter asked. Her name tag indicated he should call her Sharron.

Tim put on his best, I'm not trying to be difficult face. "I need to speak to Joaquin for a moment."

"He doesn't see customers. People aren't really his thing." Sharron pointed at the lady behind him. "What can I get for you, ma'am.?"

As the lady rattled off her order, Tim's anger started to boil over. He didn't come here for her to dismiss him. This was something he needed to accomplish for his group to progress, and a gatekeeper wouldn't deny him.

The woman who ordered shoved past him to pick up her food. As she reached for it, he acted like the shove made him stumble and bumped his arm into her order, scattering it everywhere. Sharron glared daggers at Tim as she came around the corner to clean up. As soon as her eyes were on the food on the floor, he vaulted the counter and pushed through the swinging doors into the kitchen.

A lightning bolt slammed into the tiled floor at his feet.

"Kitchen's off-limits," Joaquin stated.

Tim finally got his first look at the man. He was short at five-five but covered in lean ropy muscle like a fighter. He'd dyed his hair electric blue. It was long on top and shaved underneath. Blue energy crackled across his fingertips as he waited for Tim to back up.

"Sorry for the intrusion, but I hear you're the man to talk with about becoming a hex witch."

The energy disappeared from his fingers, and Joaquin motioned for Tim to come in so they could talk. "I am the trainer, but wouldn't you be happier being one of those rain splashers? Healing by doing damage isn't for everyone."

"It is for me." Tim loved his class, and expanding on his curses was what would set him apart from the other healers.

Joaquin moved toward the brick oven, shot lightning from his fingertips until it was hot enough to melt a tire, and put in another batch of cupcakes.

"What's up with that?" Tim held out his hands like he was zapping something.

The hex witch closed the oven and turned toward Tim. "We all start life somewhere. I started mine as a DPS."

"Explains why you would be the perfect teacher." Tim wasn't trying to butter him up. He loved learning from people who were already successful at their craft.

Joaquin nodded. "It certainly gave me a unique perspective when it came to healing." He motioned for Tim to join him over by the sink as he started washing dishes. "I've always found that the best teacher is one's own experience."

Looking up, the baker locked his gaze onto Tim's. "In that regard, I have something I need you to do for me."

Quest Received: The Most Luscious Fruit You've Ever Seen

There's a small orchard on the outskirts of the city. They have the sweetest fruit in the entire kingdom, but everyone I send to collect an order never comes back. I need the fruit to make my latest creation, and I need you to get it for me. Find out what is happening with the Sisters of Eternal Bliss, and get me that damn fruit.

The quest seemed simple enough, but nothing in *The Etheric Coast* was truly simple.

Tim accepted the quest. There was no turning back now. He

needed to become a hex witch, and this was the way to do it. He'd find out what in the hell was going on and bring back as much fruit as he could carry.

"Do you have any tips for getting past Sharron? Last time I kind of made a mess, and if I do that again, I think she might kill me." Tim looked at the front of the store and the glare she gave him had him rethinking his life choices.

Joaquin motioned for Tim to follow him. "When you return, come to the back door. Knock three times, then once. I'll let you in."

"Thanks, man, you're a real lifesaver." Tim hurried out the door.

"You say that now, but you don't know where you're going!" Joaquin called after him and slammed the door shut.

Tim walked down the alley until he found a junction that took him back to the main thoroughfare. A quick check of his map showed he would need Grant for this trip. Now that he knew where he was going and how he would get there, Tim turned his mind toward the problem at hand.

What was it that made this fruit so damn special?

CHAPTER THIRTY-ONE

Grant opened the carriage door. "Hate to break this to you, but this is as far as we can go."

Tim stepped out of the carriage and looked off into the distance. He couldn't see the farmhouse. He didn't know why the game wouldn't allow the carriage driver to enter the farm's boundaries, but it sure set an ominous tone.

He wouldn't press the driver to take him farther. This was a quest, after all. There had to be some challenges involved. "I'll call you when I get out of there."

"Are you sure you have to go in?" Grant looked hesitant to continue but found his courage. "Not that I'd ever speak ill of the Sisters, but there have been rumors."

Well, that didn't sound good.

"What kind of rumors?" Tim watched the man in earnest. The carriage driver never steered him wrong.

Grant hopped back up into the driver's seat after closing the door. "Just don't eat or drink anything."

He turned the carriage in a slow circle and shouted back over his shoulder. "And certainly don't smoke anything."

What in the hell kind of farm is this?

There wasn't even a fence around the damn place, only an arch made out of beautifully hand-crafted wood. Carved out of the same wood as the arch were the words The Sisters of Eternal Bliss. It was a boundary where no other boundaries existed.

Miles of beautiful orchards and fields stretched as far as the eye could see. It was like looking at a slice of paradise, the kind of place he wouldn't mind retiring to someday. People were milling around, and a river cut through the back corner of the land twinkling in the distance.

A man walked past the archway smoking something in a pipe. He looked through the arch, shook his head, and continued walking. It was the weirdest thing Tim had ever seen. It was like the man had looked right at him and hadn't seen a damn thing.

Going onto the farm was going to be trouble. Still, the quest had to be completable so there was a way off as well. Tim had to keep his wits about him. What was it Grant said, don't eat, drink, or smoke anything? It almost sounded like he was going into the fairy realm or the island of the lotus-eaters.

Tim looked through the wooden archway. "Keep your head, no touching. Everything will be fine."

Muttering the reassurance helped as he stepped toward the archway. When he walked under the arch, he expected to feel a zap or some shift in the energy around him, but Tim was still just Tim. He took a few more steps, and nothing jumped out and murdered him. The farm didn't turn into another realm where all the people he saw were demons. As long as this wasn't a *Midsommar* remake, he would be fine.

What's better than being a world traveler? Being alive.

With each step he took into the Sisters' farm, he felt more at ease. Several people waved and said hello. All of them wore smiles, even the ones who didn't wave.

There were all kinds of activities going on. People were working on the farm. Others were doing yoga under the apple trees. Scattered throughout the property were little hookah stations, with piles of some kind of purple and pink dried flower next to them.

Now and then, he passed a station where someone was enjoying a puff. Each time, the clouds they exhaled smelled different although the flower looked the same. It also wasn't the pot or plant smell he expected.

The last little cloud he walked through smelled like an old-time mint ice cream milkshake. His feet started to turn him toward the hookah station as he thought about digging the chunks of mint out of the bottom of the metal milkshake mixing glass.

"Whoa." Tim shook his head and tossed a Cleanse on himself. "Haven't even made it to the sisters yet and they almost got me."

He continued down the path. Thankfully it only moved in one direction, or else he'd be lost as well as tempted. The first mile went by slowly as he took in the sights, but the second one went at double the pace. By the third mile, Tim could see the farmhouse in the distance nestled between two small hills. It was painted in a myriad of bright colors and had colored silks blowing from rows of fishing line tied across the roof.

If he didn't know any better, Tim would've thought he walked onto a hippie commune. Everything felt right. Free food, free love, and piles of drugs that smelled like anything you desired. The food here was probably the best anyone ever tasted. Why would anyone want to leave?

Could they leave?

That was a scary thought. If this was anything like the island of the Lotus Eaters, a person could leave if they ever gained enough of their sense back to want to. Navigating this quest was going to be tricky business, but he was up to the task.

Tim passed a man with a clipboard in his hand snacking on an apple between hits from a little pipe.

"Do you mind?" Tim held out his hand for the clipboard.

He wasn't sure he would get any straight answers from the

Sisters, so he needed to pay attention to little clues like the man in front of him before reaching the farmhouse. He probably should've used a little more tact when he was asking, but the man was in such a pleasant mood he didn't wonder why Tim wanted his clipboard or how he asked for it.

"Sure thing, bud." He handed his clipboard over with a shrug.

It didn't take long for Tim to realize this was one of Joaquin's missing delivery men. The man wasn't a hostage unless endless bong rips and free food counted as kidnapping. Maybe the delivery guy just said fuck it, why have a job when everything here was free. There was a certain sense of pride in being a part of a self-sustainable community.

Or maybe he liked getting stoned.

"Do you mind if I hang onto this?" Knowing what Joaquin wanted delivered would certainly make Tim's job easier.

Taking a long pull off his pipe and blowing out a cloud that smelled just like a Double-Double with onions, the man waved away his concerns. "Knock yourself out." He held out the pipe to Tim. "Care for a hit?"

"Sure thing." Tim reached for the pipe.

Even knowing that one hit off the pipe might be enough to keep him trapped here forever, it was a tempting offer. Part of him wondered if they tasted the smoke the same way he smelled it as he walked by. Tim smiled as instead of taking a pull, he cast Cleanse on the man and set the pipe back down on the tray next to the dried flower. "How do you feel now?"

Standing up kind of wobbly, the delivery man blinked a few times. "Where am I?"

Blasting him with another Cleanse, Tim replied. "You're at the Sisters of Eternal Bliss. Joaquin has been looking for you."

"I had an order to get. Did I send it back already?" He blinked a few more times.

Tim didn't know if he could do anything more for the man until he was ready to leave himself. The best he could do was to get the man moving and hope he made it out. Now that some of his senses had returned, the delivery man had a fighting chance.

"Joaquin is waiting for you, and the order is on the way." Tim gripped him by the shoulders, shaking him gently to make sure he had his complete focus. "Don't stop for anything until you're back at the bakery."

The delivery man walked away slowly at first, but then he picked up speed. Before long, he was running.

"That wasn't very kind of you," a female voice said from behind him.

Tim turned and stared at what must have been one of the Sisters. She was wearing a white gown and had a green circlet of an olive branch around her head like a crown. Her feet were bare as she glided closer to him.

"Not everyone is made for the stress of the outside world. Here they can be at peace for as long as they like." She motioned toward the hookah. "You could find that same peace of mind if you wanted it."

Tempting, but he had a world to save.

"As much as I'd like to take you up on your offer, I have people waiting for me out there." Tim pointed toward the clipboard. "And I have a client who would like to buy some of your fruit."

Taking the clipboard from his hands, she looked over the list. "We can arrange this for ten percent more than he offered, and we will only carry the fruit to just inside our borders."

"As for the safety of our men that must carry the fruit the rest of the way?" Tim didn't know if it was an appropriate question to ask, but he felt like it was one that he needed to.

Smiling warmly, the Sister nodded as if his concern were foolish. "This isn't a prison. We don't kidnap people. You might have noticed we don't have chains or even walls."

Tim pointed toward the flowers. "There are other kinds of chains."

"The men you send for deliveries will face no less temptation. Pick them well." She extended her hand. "Do we have a deal?"

All he could do was say yes and tell Joaquin to be careful. There was no way he'd risk coming back here himself. It was too tempting. A life where he could grow organic food while improving his mind and body seemed too good to be true. It was the perfect low-stress lifestyle. All he had to do was give up everything.

Wasn't going to happen.

Tim shook her hand. "Deal."

There was a small jolt of power as their hands broke apart. "Before you go, you should see the river." The Sister pointed off in the distance.

"You know, I think I'd like to see that river." Tim almost couldn't believe the words coming out of his mouth.

Part of him was screaming to turn around and walk away, but there was a chorus of voices telling him to go to the river. That not seeing the river after coming all this way would be a huge mistake.

"The river is beautiful this time of year." The Sister smiled warmly. "I'll leave you to it and hope to see you again at our first delivery."

Everyone was so nice here.

Tim wished everywhere could be like this. They had plenty of free food and some kind of mystery flower to smoke that always smelled amazing. People were relaxing, working out, tending to the plants. It was a utopia.

The fact there was a river where he could go to cool off and relax was amazing. Even though his quest here was complete, it seemed like the right thing to do. His group wouldn't mind waiting for him a little longer. In fact, he'd finished this quest so quickly he earned a little downtime before heading back to the inn.

Maybe someone down there had a fishing pole.

Tim followed the path through the trees for a mile or two and came out of the grove on top of a small hill. Below him in the valley was the most beautiful blue river he'd ever seen. There didn't even appear to be anyone down there. It was like he had the entire place to himself. He couldn't remember the last time he went somewhere, and there wasn't another person.

It was like a slice of heaven.

Taking his time walking down the hill to soak in all the scenery was the right choice. The countryside was so beautiful. How was it that a farmhold this big could be tucked so close to the city without him noticing?

Magic was a crazy beautiful thing when used the right way.

The cool blue burbling water called to him like a pool in the summer heat. Tim walked toward the water, unaware of anything else around him. A fish jumped out in the center of the river, and it was the most beautiful thing in the world.

Once ShadowLily saw this place, there was no way she would question his choice to give up adventuring. He could probably even keep streaming. Tim would have to change the channel's name to Chilling by the River.

Something was rising out of the water.

"Make that three somethings," Tim said as he counted the three heads that appeared in the water.

The long hair marked them as women, but there was no way to be sure until he saw more of their bodies. As their shoulders rose above the surface, there was no question about their femininity. All three women wore gossamer-thin gowns, and he saw their darkened nipples through the wet fabric as it clung to their bodies.

Something isn't right.

The panic side of Tim's brain kicked in, and oddly enough, it was the thought of what ShadowLily would do to him if she found him with three nearly naked ladies more than the fact his life might be in jeopardy. Tim activated the special ability Clarity from his shoulder guards, and the world snapped back into focus.

One of the Sisters had lured him down to the water to what, feed him to the women in front of him? Tim wasn't a fucking snack. He was a healer, damn it. When the situation called for it, sometimes he was a DPS.

Before any of the women shambling out of the river could figure out that he regained his senses, he cast Curse of Giving on all of them. The women howled as the pain hit them, but he didn't care. Without even considering what the negative consequences might be if he killed these three, Tim blasted them with Divine Light. As they finally made it out of the water, he finished them off with a channeled cast of Flame Burst.

"Must have been overly confident her handshake put the hoodoo on me." Tim smiled. "Because that fight wasn't shit."

There wasn't a moment to waste. It was time to get the fuck out of there. He turned and started jogging. Ignoring the path and making a beeline for the archway would be faster, so that was what he did.

As much as he'd love to deal with the Sisters now, that seemed like a task he would be better off handling once he had his entire group with him. Once they had the Stone of Immoratis safely back in Eternia's hand, maybe he could convince them to come here, and they could get to the bottom of what was going on. The Sisters couldn't be allowed to go around trying to kill anyone who wouldn't eat, drink, or smoke their way into becoming snacks.

The Blue Dagger Society would come back and set things right!

The way out of the farm took him three times as long as the way in. By the time he dipped under the archway and placed his call to Grant it was already evening. The entire day had slipped away in what should've been a two-hour trek. If they ever came back here, they were going to need to track down some pretty strong resistances to mind magic, or they wouldn't be able to handle whatever was going on inside.

When Grant opened the door for him, Tim slipped into the carriage and laid back against the seat, trying to get some rest. "Back to the bakery, then to the inn."

"Let's try to make this quick. Everyone is back there already, and I have a beer with my name on it." Grant started to close the door.

Tim stopped the door from closing with a gentle push. "Do you know if they were successful?"

"I know at least one of them was." Grant closed the door, and the carriage gently shook as he climbed into his seat. "Let's get your quest finished up, then you can ask them for yourself."

Tapping the top of the carriage to signal he was ready to go, Tim stared out the window. Despite how easy the final fight had been, it was a close one. Joaquin had some big-time explaining to do.

The line outside the bakery was gone, but the gas lamp next to the door was lit, and bright light streamed through the windows.

Tim didn't know if he needed to use the back door with the bakery closed. It would make sense that Sharron was gone, but Joaquin would still be there. At least the bastard better be there after all the shit Tim went through to get his precious order filled. If he had to track down the class trainer, the game might have one less of them by morning.

The quest he'd sent Tim on was ridiculous. Tim was still bristling about how little the man had told him upfront. The quest wasn't even a proper test of his healing or damaging abilities, merely something to help his business and damn the consequences.

Tim marched through the door, slipped around the counter, and stormed into the kitchen. "You slippery little fuck!"

The words died on his lips as he took in the families eating dinner together. All he could do now was stand there with his mouth hanging slightly open, waiting for someone else to say something to save him from the embarrassment.

"The man of the hour!" Joaquin lifted the delivery sheet. "You did it."

Tim activated Quick Feet, crossed the room, and had Joaquin's throat between his hands as he growled, "You could've warned me."

"It all turned out for the best." Joaquin gasped as he held up Tim's reward envelope.

Tim snatched the envelope, shoved the man to the floor, then healed his neck. It wasn't like him to get so worked up. Maybe it was the thought of the Sister trying to sacrifice him to those women in the water. What in the hell was that shit? Knowing Joaquin was willing to trap him there forever to get some new fruit must have sent him over the edge.

He was better than that.

Tim extended a hand to help Joaquin back to his feet. "I'm sorry about that." He brushed off the baker's shirt. "I seem to have lost my head for a moment."

The rest of the room was deadly silent as they waited for Joaquin's answer. "Would you care to join us for dinner?"

It was nice of him to offer, but after his recent display of aggression, Tim thought he better let them enjoy their meal in peace. "I think your family would agree I've overstayed my welcome."

Tim backed out of the kitchen. "Just make sure whoever you send to do the pickups going forward knows what they're getting into."

"I'll be handling them myself." Joaquin lifted a glass. "Until next time."

When the kitchen doors closed behind him, Tim let out a deep breath. When he was standing outside and halfway back to the carriage, his heart stopped hammering. What in the hell had he been thinking? He attacked the one person everyone cared about in a kitchen full of knives. Not to mention the man could shoot lighting out of his fingers, like Darth Malgus. Joaquin might've deserved it, but Tim had the distinct feeling he'd been about two seconds away from having an unexpected visit with Barbara.

The gentle motion of the carriage moving through the city took the edge off. He poured a drink and opened the envelope.

System Message: Congratulations on your ascension to Hex Witch

Your health and mana pools have increased, and you'll receive two new class-specific skills. Keep an eye out for further opportunities to learn more about your class and obtain new spells as you progress.

Yeah, buddy!

Here it was, the moment of truth. These two new skills would influence his entire journey through the rest of the game. Closing his eyes for a moment, he thanked Eternia for watching over him. Then he moved onto the next screen.

Skill Received: Curse of Sacrifice

Nothing worth doing comes without sacrifice. That includes DPS. Every time you use this spell, you'll sacrifice one percent of your health to do double that as damage to the target of your choice. The inflicted damage will return as health to the target/targets of your stance.

Continue leveling this spell to see what additional powers it can unlock.

Tim hoped for another damage-dealing ability he could use to heal at a higher rate than his Healing Orb. The whole point of his class now was really to do as much damage as possible to heal the tank while using his other healing abilities to keep the group up. This gave him even more flexibility during fights, and he needed to start leveling the skill as fast as possible.

More power, more damage, no more problems.

It was time to scroll down and figure out what the next skill he received would be. Tim was so ecstatic with the first pickup that even if the next skill were a total bust, he'd be happy.

"Please don't be a bust." Tim crossed his fingers and looked down.

Skill Received: Hex of the Shattered Beast

This skill places a buff on the target for five seconds. Any damage done to the target during the buff window will trigger the Hex Hound effect. A spectral hound will appear next to the person being damaged. At the end of five seconds, the hound will attack, returning a percentage of the damage done back on the attacker.

At higher levels, the Hex Hound effect can apply debuffs to the target of its attacks, provide increased healing, hit multiple targets, and a few other fun surprises. Continue leveling your hound to figure out what special abilities it will gain next.

Did he just get a dog?

Hey, it might not count when it came down to being able to rub bellies and go for walks, but his dog was going to fuck some bosses up. The best part was he could cast this on Cassie, let the dog do a big burst of damage, then wham Cassie was back at full health because of his stance. He knew a spell like this would have a decent cooldown on it, but it was powerful enough that it was worth saving for when it would really count.

Both of his new skills were awesome.

A wave of relief flooded over him. Despite how well the game had treated him so far, there was always the chance he could've picked a stinker of a class. Knowing that wasn't the case eased some of his worries. If everyone had the same kind of luck he did, Isadora's days were numbered. Sometime tomorrow, they'd restore the king to full health, collect the Stone of Immoratis, and be on their way.

He loved it when a plan came together.

"I'm the fucking queen of the world!" Cassie downed a shot and dove off the balcony, landing on a table harder than a Buffalo Bills fan in the heart of winter.

The table cracked like an egg as she slammed into it. Tim would've been worried, but this was her third time doing the stunt. Everyone was still so pumped about the day's victories that they were overdoing it a bit.

"That's going on your bill!" Liz shouted from behind the bar as JaKobi incinerated the remains of the table.

Before Cassie could respond, Tim healed her. "We get it. You're damn near indestructible now. Try to save some of that for the morning."

"And save some of the tables for the guests," Liz shouted again, making her point about the destruction of furniture known.

"Listen up, wizardly hex man." Cassie swayed on her feet. "Just do your *whoosh* no hangover thing so I can go to bed."

Lorelei tapped her beer against Tim's and downed it. "Me too. I'm ready for bed."

Maybe they weren't in as celebratory a mood as he thought.

That was probably a good thing. While they'd come out ahead so far, getting a good night's rest before taking on the boss that eliminated them was probably a good thing. With the royal seal, they could have Grant take them straight back to Isadora's hideout.

Then it was boss fight city, baby!

Despite how fun it was to go out on his own sometimes, Tim wanted to kick the crap out of people with his besties. Taking down the bad guys and restoring order to the world was what he did. Some people eviscerated others in fiction. He liked to do his in games.

Tim sent out a round of Cleanse. "Meet down here at nine for breakfast." He turned toward his girlfriend. "Try to keep the jokes to a minimum until I finish my coffee."

"How about you keep the coffee in your mouth instead of spraying it through your nose?" ShadowLily winked and linked her arm through his, pulling him gently toward the stairs.

There was no way Tim was going to get the last word on this fight. Spraying coffee out of your nose had a way of shifting victory quickly to the other party. Instead, he settled for getting the last word in a different way.

"Grant, you too. Breakfast at nine. We'll need a ride afterward." Tim let ShadowLily drag him up the stairs.

In reality, dragged might have been an overstatement. It wasn't like he didn't want to go upstairs with his beautiful girlfriend. Having their inn room back at their disposal was nice. The room was soundproofed and located in one of the safest buildings in the city. It was the perfect place for a love nest or to build a home.

And the sex, don't even get him started.

When they reached the top of the stairs, Tim saw Eternia's door cracked open. "I'm going to go check on her. I'll be right back."

ShadowLily looked up and down the hallway. Then her gear flashed away to be replaced by an outfit made out of leather straps and buckles. "If you hurry, I'll be wearing this."

He snapped his mouth closed in time to stop the drool from leaking out. It was a good thing he had robes on because no one wanted to stand in front of a goddess with half a chubby in their pants. This was like a best-case, worst-case scenario. There was only one thing he could do.

Hurry the fuck up.

"I'll be like lightning." The hardest thing he ever had to do was turn away and go into the room next door.

Eternia was sitting in her chair by the fire. "I would have understood if you waited until the morning. She had quite the outfit on."

Tim's cheeks burned. There was a simple rule of thumb to follow when working with a goddess. It was to assume they knew everything, all the time, and to act accordingly.

"Your door was open. I wanted to check in." Tim tried to think of anything but ShadowLily so he could focus on their conversation.

Eternia gave him a knowing smile. "I wanted to let you know that the others have reached Tristholm safely and will be returning soon."

"Neema and Khalid will send word once they reach the deserts." Eternia rose from her seat. "How goes the quest for the stone?"

He wanted to say it was going perfectly, but that would be a lie. "We've run into a few complications, but we should be able to secure the stone tomorrow."

"Before you leave in the morning, I will place a blessing upon you." Eternia rested a hand on the mantel as she looked into the flames. "We must wrap things up here quickly and return to the desert before things spiral out of control."

Tim dropped to one knee. "We will do our best to see this through."

Turning away from the fire, she slid her hands under his shoulders and lifted him back to his feet. "You've never failed me, Tim.

I'm counting on you to rise and see your duty done until completion."

He nodded, feeling the weight of her words. "I understand."

"Now go to her and make her wildest dreams come true." Eternia winked.

Holy shit, did Eternia just make a sex joke? Rise and satisfy her to completion? Not exactly what he expected, but Tim appreciated the goddess trying to keep the mood light. They all knew what was at stake, but dwelling on the consequences of actions untaken was a fool's errand.

"Breakfast is at nine." Tim bowed low and exited the room.

With Eternia next door, Tim kind of felt like he was trying to sneak a girl into his room back home. Of course, it was damn near impossible there with the creaky floors and nosy siblings. Not to mention what would've happened if his parents found a girl in his room.

Although Tim didn't doubt if anyone could sneak past his bratty brother and sister and right under his parents' noses, it would've been ShadowLily.

Tim stepped into their room and unequipped all his clothes. "Here's Johnny!"

"You know what they say about writers, all work and no play." ShadowLily rose from the bed, and he couldn't take his eyes off her. "Makes Johnny a dull boy."

She grabbed him by the manhood and pulled him toward the bed. "Now, let's find out how dull Johnny really is."

God, he loved it when she used horror movie talk to seduce him. Tim let her pull him toward the bed. Then his mind went blank as the moment consumed him.

***

The scent of coffee tickled his nose.

Tim had no idea how he'd ever function without Liz. She ran

this entire place from sunup until well past sundown and still found time to make sure his coffee was waiting for him as soon as he woke up. That kind of excellence wasn't easily found and wasn't replaceable.

The delicious scent of full-flavored coffee followed him as he took care of his morning ritual in the bathroom. With his business concluded, Tim donned his robes and took his first sip of the deliciously dark liquid. He already knew today was going to be a good day.

It was nice to wake up knowing all he had on his plate for the day was a dungeon crawl. Knock off the witch and get the stone back before dinner. Everyone was happy. Then they could get back to work taking care of the real problem.

Vitaria.

For the first time in a long time, he wasn't sleepy as he walked down the stairs. Say what you wanted, but a productive day and good sex always made him sleep like a baby. Last night he'd slept like the dead.

Everyone was already downstairs, which was no great surprise, but they all looked a little shocked to see him. Tim had cultivated the reputation for waking up late and grabbing something to eat on the run to make up for it. Today he was down thirty minutes before breakfast should have even started.

It was one of those mornings he woke up feeling like everything was going to work out for the best. Cassie wasn't cannonballing tables, and JaKobi was reading a book while stirring his coffee. Lorelei was gossiping with Liz at the bar while ShadowLily and Eternia chatted by the fireplace.

Tim's heart clutched for a second. Seeing his girlfriend and the goddess chatting was worse than the feeling of bringing a girl home to meet his mom. They could've been talking about anything, about him, about sex. His heart started beating faster, and he sipped his coffee, which didn't help things.

The front door opened, and Grant walked in. "Ready to go

whenever you are, boss. Including something I think you'll all appreciate later."

Tim looked at the man with his mouth hanging open for a full three seconds before his brain registered that he had to respond. "Breakfast first. It never pays to adventure on an empty stomach."

Eternia and ShadowLily shared a look, and they both smiled.

At least if they were talking about him, it appeared to be good things only. He could handle that. It was one thing to be worried about people talking behind your back when it was bad things. When it was good things, Tim thought they could talk as much as they wanted.

"Tim, join us for some stimulating conversation before Roberto brings out the food." Eternia beckoned him to join them as ShadowLily blushed.

Before going to join the goddess, Tim clapped Grant on the back. "I trust you can look out for yourself for a few minutes."

The carriage driver's eyes darted toward the bar. "I do believe that I can."

Tim watched the man for a moment, wondering if Liz and he were going to become a thing. No reason they couldn't be, but he tried to stay out of matters of the heart when it came to his friends' decisions in love. Love wasn't always logical or perfect, but no one wanted to hear disparaging remarks about someone they cared for. So no matter what his personal feelings were, he gave his friends space to figure things out on their own.

Even if he really wanted them to work out.

There was no further use in delaying. He had to join them by the fire. "Good morning, goddess. Hello, hon."

"You call her a goddess, and I'm just hon?" ShadowLily's eyes blazed.

"Not a good move," Eternia chided.

Tim looked from his girlfriend to the goddess and back again. "But she is a goddess."

"The goddess has a name!" Cassie shouted from her spot next to JaKobi.

He was about to start freaking out when he realized they were all screwing with him. "Not cool, guys."

"Ah yes, but I have so little to occupy my time these days." Eternia was clearly enjoying herself. "Maybe if I had the stone back in my possession, I would have less time for all the delicious stories I've been hearing."

As if on cue, Roberto entered the room with a box full of burritos in his arms. "I have food to go."

A waitress joined him with mugs. "And juice if anyone wants it."

"I thought we could avoid another incident." ShadowLily snorted.

Tim would have been offended, but he was choosing to own his schnozzle-rockets like a boss. "Listen, baby. I can blow just about anywhere."

JaKobi laughed so hard he fell out of his chair. "It's too easy. I can't do it."

Eternia looked at ShadowLily. "Are you sure he's the smart one?"

The mist slayer rose to her feet and kissed Tim on the lips. She lingered long enough to let him know she meant it. "I'm sure."

"Burritos and sexy talk, are you sure I haven't died and gone to heaven?" Tim made his way to Roberto to collect the package with his name on it.

Eternia pulled a book from the table by her chair. "Don't worry. If that happens, I'll be sure to let you know."

JaKobi grabbed his burrito. "Dude, she has a sense of humor, and it's awesome."

"Before you leave, let me bless you." Eternia lifted her arms in the air, and a wave of energy washed over the group.

It felt like Tim was getting kissed by a rainbow.

Tim was starting to pick up on the fact Eternia wasn't only a goddess but a funny one. It must've been nice for her to take a small break from watching over the entire world for a few moments. Sure, she was still fighting her sister and trying to regain her powers, but this gave her a chance to see and feel what she was fighting for. For the briefest of moments, she was one of them.

And everyone still loved her.

"Grant, my man, I guess we're leaving early," Tim called to get the driver's attention.

Roberto held out an extra bag. "In case you haven't eaten yet."

The carriage driver grabbed the bag on his way out the door. "Thanks, Roberto!"

As the rest of the group said their goodbyes, Tim took the time to fill up his coffee. This was it. They were a carriage ride away from taking on the witch and powering up the goddess.

He didn't know how things were going to turn out, but he felt like it would be a win. All of them were powered up and wouldn't be attacking in the dark. With enough forethought, they could avoid the traps and claim their victory.

Win baby, win, all I wanna do is win.

CHAPTER THIRTY-THREE

The king's seal moved them through gates without an issue. Even the duke, who wanted a word, didn't refuse to let them pass. The castle quickly faded into the distance, and they were moving toward their destination. Tim was so busy planning that he didn't question still being in the carriage. At least they'd seen the beginning of Isadora's camp. The information they gleaned on their first visit would give them the scraps to make a rudimentary plan.

Mostly they needed to avoid the traps.

It felt like every game tossed the players a segment in a dungeon or a raid where they had to complete some kind of jumping puzzle or movement objective. Normally he hated those because even players who could dodge the boss and knock off the last three percent solo died doing the easy stuff. Their next encounter started with a crazy run, but now that they'd seen it, hopefully no one would die.

"We're going to need ShadowLily or Lorelei to point out the traps." Tim looked around the carriage at his party members. "What do we do about the darts?"

Lorelei poked JaKobi in the stomach as if he was chubby and out of shape. "Some of us were doing fine running."

"Some of us died trying to keep up." JaKobi looked as if he were playing the scene back in his head. "Maybe because I fell too far behind."

ShadowLily looked over at him. "We died when we turned around."

"So stay together and don't turn around." Tim shrugged. "It's not much, but it's better than what we had going in last time."

Cassie was watching Tim like he was the last Atkins peanut butter cup at a Weight Watchers meeting. "How did you die?"

"Me?" Tim pointed at himself, feigning innocence.

"Yes, you." Cassie wasn't buying it for a second.

He looked around the carriage, knowing they all shared their embarrassing defeats, and it was time for him to share his. "I got on my knees, and she threw a spear through my chest."

"Got on your knees, huh?" ShadowLily quipped.

Tim's cheeks reddened, but he went for it anyway. "Please, you know I have a silver tongue. If I were down on my knees doing anything else, I never would have died."

"So avoid the darts and the traps, and watch out for spears." ShadowLily summarized, doing her best to pretend her boyfriend hadn't spoken.

Just like that, they were back on track.

JaKobi's hand was shaking slightly. "I promised to burn that place to the ground. Just get me to Isadora and get out of the way."

Cassie pulled him into a hug. "I know you want to kill her for hurting me, but she's a sneaky bitch, so we need to follow the three C's."

JaKobi's hand stopped shaking, but now one of his fingers was on fire. "Cool, calm, and collected. I'm calm enough."

"Save it for Isadora, big guy. We'll be there soon enough." Tim felt pretty good about how things were going.

They had an idea of what they were facing, they just had to execute, and they would win.

With their new classes, they should have the situation well in hand. "So we're agreed, Cassie and ShadowLily take the lead, JaKobi and Lorelei in the back. I'll stay in the middle and try to call things out as we move. When we reach Isadora, Cassie is in charge, so watch her for the changes."

ShadowLily looked at Cassie. "Take it slow. I don't want you to be a tank kebob."

"Please, as if her traps could stop me now. I can take a two-story fall through a wooden table without blinking." Cassie winked. "But slow seems like the right call."

The carriage stopped, and all of them grew silent. Tim looked out of the window at the path they would take to Isadora's location. Instead of feeling dread, he felt energized. This was it. They were one step closer to fulfilling their quest to Eternia. Soon they would be back in the desert, putting Vitaria down, and setting things right.

Looking over the anxious faces staring back at him, he only felt a sense of pride. Tim had the best friends in the world, hands down, and he knew it. There wasn't a single one of them he wouldn't die to save. If he played his cards right, none of them would die, but part of being a good leader was knowing when your team needed a pep talk.

Tim held out his hand in the middle of the carriage like the center of a huddle in football. One by one, the others laid their hands on top of his, and he spoke. "I don't know what's going to happen out there today, but I want you to know that I believe in you. All of us are here because we're the best at what we do. No witchy tricks are going to stop us because we got this shit!"

"Goooooo Shit!" Cassie did it with the same inflection as someone would normally say, go team, and they all lifted their hands in the air like they were breaking the huddle.

JaKobi sighed dramatically. "Listen, guys. I don't think we

should be called The Shits. They already did that in *Accepted,* and my skin doesn't go all that great with brown."

"How would you like to break the huddle, big guy?" Tim replied casually, but he was excited to see what his main man had in store.

The ember wizard thought about it for a moment, then thrust his hand into the middle of the carriage. Everyone piled on top of his. Looking at each of them in turn, JaKobi addressed them with energy. "What are we going to do today? Win, that's what. Now say it with me on three. Blue Dagger for life."

JaKobi lifted all their hands in the air. "One." He let them drop and lifted them again. "Two." One final time. "Three."

All of them shouted in deep, barking voices, "Blue Dagger for life!" as they tossed their hands in the air and broke out laughing.

Lorelei laughed the loudest despite herself. "I've never played sports, but if they're this much fun, I missed out on something."

"Sports are a great way to learn life skills, but you can learn a lot of those same lessons playing video games with your friends." Tim grinned. "So you probably didn't miss much."

The carriage door opened, and Grant poked his head inside. "This is as far as we can go in the carriage."

"My man, the ride was a million times better than the ball-smashing one we endured on our first trip here." JaKobi flipped him a golden coin. "For all the extra trouble."

Grant pocketed the coin. "Not a problem." He helped JaKobi down. "It's nice to get to try out these off-road wheels finally. I bought them years ago but never had cause to leave the city once the routes to Tristholm dried up."

"On the plus side, travel to Tristholm should start to pick up again shortly," Tim said as he climbed out of the cart. "We already solved the werewolf problem."

Grant stepped back as all the ladies nimbly jumped down from the carriage without needing his assistance. "How long should I wait for you?" He looked up into the bright mid-day sun.

"If we're not back by sundown, it's safe to assume we're not coming back, and you should head to the inn." Tim felt a wave of confidence rush through him. "In reality, we should be back in a few hours."

Grant extended his hand to him. "Best of luck, sir."

"See you soon." As Tim spoke the words, he knew they were true.

They'd prepared better for this fight than the last time. With their increased health, Tim was pretty sure Cassie could survive eating one of the spike traps. Not that having all those spikes shoved through her would be a pleasant experience. Still, it gave him a certain sense of peace knowing one small mistake shouldn't be the end of them.

Cassie took the lead as they followed the winding path back through the forest. As soon as their senses were good and scrambled, the forest opened, and they saw the familiar torches marking the start of Isadora's land. When she reached the torches, Cassie stopped.

"ShadowLily, grab my belt and steer me from behind." Cassie took her stance, ready to face any threats that might appear.

Lorelei snickered. "I thought we weren't making sex jokes when Tim had a drink in his hand."

"Oh, I'm ready for them now." Tim took another sip of his coffee, daring them to make him spray it out of his nose, and slipped the canteen back in his inventory.

ShadowLily moved up behind the tank and took hold of her belt with her left hand. "I've got you, girl."

Tim moved into position behind the two women. "Follow the plan, stay together, and execute."

"Talking ain't doing." Cassie took the first step into the zone.

Together, they moved as one. ShadowLily kept Cassie from running into any of the traps, and as long as they didn't get too spread out, the darts seemed not to be a problem. Just like in most games, it felt like this dodging and moving segment went on for way too long, but that was probably the tension he felt, knowing those darts could ruin their day in an instant.

ShadowLily tugged Cassie around a trap and let go of her belt. "We're all clear."

"I'm going to keep moving slowly. You see anything, shout." Cassie stayed in front of the group, and the rest spread out in their standard battle formation.

The path continued for a few hundred more feet before abruptly opening into a wide clearing. Black scorch marks dotted the grass leading up to the small cabin at the back of the space. Smoke lazily drifted out of the cabin's chimney, but there were no other signs of life. The clearing was easily big enough for a boss fight so this had to be the right place.

Trying to sound bolder than he felt, Tim shouted, "Isadora, by order of Crown Prince Desmond, your life is forfeit. Come out and face the consequences of your actions."

Isadora appeared in the cabin's doorway and strutted down the steps. "I thought maybe after our last encounter, you would've been smart enough never to return, but if you insist on dying again..."

The Witch of the Woods' face pulled into a jack-o-lantern-like grin. "I'd be happy to help you along."

"You might find things go differently this time," Cassie growled.

Tim dropped into his Way of the Boulder stance. "Stop wasting time. We aren't here to negotiate."

"God, I love it when you speak my language." Cassie spun her staff and squared herself to charge at Isadora. "I'll ask Eternia to take pity on your soul."

Growling like a feral dog, Cassie charged across the clearing. Tim half-expected her to die instantly in some new kind of trap, but that didn't happen. Instead, Isadora pulled her spear free and went toe-to-toe with the tank. It was weird seeing a boss that stayed the same size as them, but not everything could be a giant monster.

Tim cast Curse of Giving to make sure he had a periodic heal going and immediately followed up by casting his newest spell, Curse of Sacrifice, to bring Cassie back to full health. With the opening salvo out of the way and the tank not dying, it felt like the right time to drop Behold My Power.

A few rounds of Healing Orb erased the feedback damage from the curse and gave him time to scan the battlefield. Thankfully there wasn't anything charging at them, and he didn't see any land formation or objects they would need to use during the fight. It appeared this was going to be an all-out slugfest—last person standing wins.

ShadowLily entered the fight with a backstab. Then she did something Tim had never seen her do before. She rolled from the boss' back to the front and launched into a new attack before rolling back behind Isadora to continue dealing damage. If his girl found a way to do backstab-like damage from the front, the bosses were in real trouble going forward.

His heals would have to be spot on if she slipped up. Cassie could afford to eat a cleave from the boss. If the wrong attack hit ShadowLily, she was dead. Even a normal hit from Isadora would be devastating. Tim didn't have to worry, though, because every time she launched into the new skill, she seemed to do it at the right time.

The boss' health was dipping quickly, and that had Tim worried. They couldn't burn through her this fast. The last fight before getting the stone would never be that easy. There had to be a catch. He hoped they were ready for it when Isadora sprang the trap.

Behold My Power hit, and Isadora's health dropped to sixty-five percent. The boss wasn't looking so confident now, but again, that made Tim think they were falling into some kind of trap. There was tank and spank, but this felt more like a bait and switch.

At fifty percent, a vine launched out of Isadora's wrist plate, sweeping them all back to the clearing's entrance. "Enough!"

Magic flowed up from the forest floor, enveloping Isadora in its power. She doubled in size, and her leather armor turned into hardened steel plates. The worst thing for them wasn't the witch's new size or armor. It was the fact her health had reset to one hundred percent.

"I hope you didn't think I'd be so defenseless inside my domain." Isadora grinned and charged back into the fray.

Cassie was there in an instant. The tank launched into a series of moves that were so fluid it almost looked like she was dancing. Isadora turned her attention back on the tank completely, and the fight was on.

With a blink, Lorelei disappeared and popped back into existence a moment later, twenty feet to the right. She fired off a series of arrows. Then her bow flashed translucent, almost as if it was something from the spirit realm instead of a regular bow. Then the spirit archer moved into a series of her most brutal attacks as Tim turned his attention back to the tank and the boss.

There wasn't anything fancy for him to do yet. Tim kept his Curse of Giving on the boss, and whenever Cassie took too big a chunk of damage, he cast Curse of Sacrifice and looked for the next most injured person to cast a Healing Orb on. The Rehydrate effect from Healing Orb was enough to keep his health topped off.

This phase of the fight was a little more challenging, but so far, they hadn't run into a major mechanic yet. The increased damage the boss put out kept him busy but didn't tax his resources in the way he expected after instantly being slaughtered the first time. Upgraded Isadora hit seventy-five percent health, and everything changed.

Magic shoved them to the edge of the clearing again. This time the ground rumbled, and the clearing split into four distinct sections. The effect made Tim feel like he was standing on the biggest spin-to-win wheel there was. The section of the clearing around Isadora flashed green, and a moment later, roots burst from the ground. They thrashed back and forth, filling the entire quarter of the area with insta-death.

"Cassie, get her in the center so it's easier for us to switch sections!"

The tank ran at Isadora using her special attack to jump to the top of the aggro table, and then she started pulling the boss toward the center of the clearing.

A green light flashed under Tim's feet. "Run!"

Tim activated Quick Feet and made it to the next section before the roots would've gotten him. Now that he was safe, he started dishing out the heals. Healing Orb on the others and damage to the boss to keep Cassie going strong.

JaKobi found out the hard way that the root attack didn't only rotate in a clockwise pattern. The ember wizard had locked in on his DPS rotation so much that he missed the roots landing in the same zone twice.

"Watch your feet!" Cassie shouted as she yanked him to safety with the chain around her waist.

JaKobi started casting the second he landed back on the ground. Every few seconds he looked down to see where the roots were or if the green light might be flashing, but he never stopped casting.

While it was great that JaKobi wasn't going to fuck up again, his small blunder was already eating into Tim's mana reserves like a college football player at an all-you-can-eat buffet. The roots hadn't gotten him too badly, but they'd put an incurable debuff on him that was doing a metric shit-ton of damage. Tim had it under control, but it cost him.

Isadora hit fifty percent health, and a lot of things happened at once.

The witch started to grow again. He didn't know how it was possible, but Isadora was now four times her original size and ripped like the Hulk. She didn't have a spear anymore, but the fist of her gauntlets had blades on the ends. This was like facing the big green guy, but adamantium armor covered him from head to toe.

Cassie was the only person in their group who looked happy to be facing down the equivalent of a Sherman tank with a stick. "I wondered when things were going to get interesting."

As her health started to reset to one hundred percent, Isadora laughed. "After I kill you, tell the prince what comes next is on his head."

Two of the sections started flashing green, and they all had to run.

Tim gritted his teeth as Cassie and the witch clashed together. This wasn't like the other round of the fight. Cassie was getting torn apart. He didn't have Behold My Power to call on again, but he did have Hex of the Shattered Beast to use for the first time. He didn't have to think about how to do it. With a thought, Tim cast one of his newest spells and dropped right back into his normal healing rotation.

At this low level, the beast didn't absorb any of the damage Cassie was taking. However, it was storing it all to rebound that damage on the boss. His tank was getting beat to shit, but she was taking the hits like a champ. It wouldn't be long now before the beast did its thing.

When the five-second countdown ticked to an end, Tim looked away from the boss and focused on the giant golden retriever running toward her. The beast was a semi-solid red mist that held the shape of his favorite furry companion. With a flash, it crossed the space fast enough it left a streak behind it as it slammed into the boss. When the two collided, there was a piercing howl, and Isadora staggered as she took all the damage instantly.

That was cool as shit.

Tim checked his cooldown and saw that he'd be able to use the spell more than once in a fight and was excited about it. It wasn't something he could toss out every time he wanted, but he'd be able to call on the beast enough for it to make a difference. That fact it happened to be his favorite breed of dog was the icing on the cake.

He wondered if the beasts were like Patronuses. Everyone's was different.

Lightning crackled from the sky. Tim noticed a small circle of red flashing on the ground by his feet and instinctively threw himself to the side. Rolling back to his feet in a decently smooth move, he never missed a beat in his healing rotation.

"Watch out for lighting!" Tim cast a blast of Divine Light at the boss to emphasize the point.

"Like we don't already have enough to do," Lorelei snapped as she fired an arrow.

Tim couldn't argue with her logic. It was hard enough to rotate around half of the area covered in deadly vines at one time. Now they also had to worry about lightning strikes. He wasn't sure how they worked in the game, but lightning strikes in the real world were pretty deadly if taken directly.

Hulkadora was kicking their asses. It took everything Tim had to keep them going, but it was enough for now. When they crossed the fifty percent threshold, he was surprised to see the boss didn't change again or go back to full health. Her health kept dipping, and as long as he could keep up with the heals, they had this.

At twenty-five percent, ShadowLily ate half of a cleave, and it almost broke them completely.

Tim cast Who Needs a Shield on Cassie to buy himself enough time to get ShadowLily back up to full health. It helped that Cassie also picked up the Hydration buff, and Curse of Giving was ticking away, doing just enough to keep her health dipping slightly instead of going down in big chunks. The way things were going, they were fine, but if Lorelei or JaKobi made one misstep, they were totally fucked.

Tim activated the Orb of Clarity's special ability to increase his mana regeneration and did what he could as the boss' health kept ticking down.

Ten percent.

All he had to do was hang on a little bit longer. It didn't matter if he burned through all his reserves or not. Tim threw his hands up and channeled Healing Storm.

Five percent.

They were really going to do this. Tim almost didn't think it would be possible, but they had it. His mana was starting to bottom out, but it didn't matter now.

Isadora's health hit zero percent, and she screamed. "No! It shouldn't be possible."

The witch's health reset to fifty percent as she shrank back to half her size. The quarters of the area started rotating like a wheel, the roots moving with them. Now they had to keep moving all the time to make sure they could stay out of whatever two slices were full of the deadly roots. The lightning was still coming down sporadically through the space, forcing them to scatter whenever it got too close for comfort.

Tim's mana was in the shitter. There wasn't anything he could do about it except cast sparingly and hope to stay in front of the curve. If he could get his bar to refill a little, he'd feel a lot better about whatever twist was coming up next.

"Conserve your energy for when she changes back to her original size. That's the real burn phase." Tim kept running, trying to watch the ground for the changes.

"Oh, I have something special ready. No one hurts my girl and gets away with it." JaKobi pointed his hand, and a beam of pure sunlight flew from it.

Running, dodging, healing, everything was a blur of motion as Tim tried to keep his head about him as he kept everyone alive. This was the shitty part of healing when a few missteps and he'd be responsible for their downfall. It was also why he loved healing.

Pressure pushed him to greatness.

Isadora's scream was barely a whisper as she shifted back into her normal body. The witch's leather armor was torn and ripped.

Even her spear appeared to be blunt. Blood dripped from several wounds as she glared at them. It was easy to see they'd almost broken her will, but something forced her to carry on.

"How is this possible?" Isadora asked as a third section of the ground started flashing.

"Run!" Tim screamed.

They were so close to victory but one fuck-up now and they'd be trying this fight for the third time. Tim hoped the random number gods were on their side. One bad lightning strike and this phase was over before they got a chance to win.

It wasn't all bad news, though. During this phase, they were taking way less damage and dealing even more. Like the first round of the battle, they were making incredible progress, but the shifting landscape kept the tension rising. They all felt it. They were close, and no one wanted to be the one to screw it up.

The hit points were melting off Isadora in droves. Tim's heals weren't needed as much so he started to focus on upping his DPS output. He cast Divine Light repeatedly until Cassie needed a burst of health. Then he switched to Curse of Sacrifice.

The lightning stopped being random and targeted all of them. As they scattered to avoid the new wrinkle, everyone kept doing their best to keep Isadora's health moving down. When the boss' health hit ten percent, JaKobi let out an incoherent scream of rage and walked toward her as he blasted her repeatedly with fireballs.

The ember wizard froze in place and cast the one spell he'd been keeping in reserve. He turned bright red, and his robes burst into flames as his buff went into effect. Then his hand shot out and channeled a burst of Sunbeam that would've made Iron Man super jelly.

Tim quickly cast Hex of the Shattered Beast on Cassie again as Isadora unleashed the last of her fury on the tank. Knowing it would strip Cassie of some of her protections but confident he could handle the additional healing. Tim switched from Way of the Boulder into his Way of the River stance. Now that his damaging heals would reach the entire party, Tim focused on blasting Isadora with every spell he had at his disposal.

Casting Curse of Sacrifice again and again hurt him, but it was hurting her more. Tim kept blasting away until he saw the red streak of his hex beast, and he knew the fight was over.

Isadora was down. The Blue Dagger Society was victorious again.

CHAPTER THIRTY-FOUR

Beautiful golden motes filled the clearing.

There was an elaborate golden chest where Isadora's body had been. Not only were they going to get loot when they turned in the quest, but the witch also dropped something. There was nothing better than that feeling of hope right before he put his hand on the chest. It was a moment in which anything was possible.

"Dude, that was some epic healing." JaKobi clapped Tim on the back with enthusiasm.

Tim felt pride welling up inside him. The fight was one of his better efforts as a healer in the game so far, but what really saved their asses was how the entire group aced the mechanics. One or two extra missteps, and he wouldn't have been able to heal them through it.

"I'd like to take all the credit, but Cassie kept the boss right where we needed her to avoid most of the trouble." Tim gave her a little bow.

"Damn right I did!" Cassie strutted toward the chest. "Ain't nobody do it better." She started to JaKobi shuffle instead of walking. "Ain't nobody do it better than meeee!"

The tank placed her hand on the golden chest and turned toward the group looking ecstatic. "Grappling Hook of Wicked Intent. This is what's going to help me save your ass, slowpoke."

"Hey, not all of us are built for running." JaKobi winked at her. "But you can grapple me anytime, baby."

Lorelei rested her hand on the chest. "Leather Pants of Spirit. Increased resistance to earth and lightning damage, and a small increase to damage when using my new skills. All in all, a pretty damn good upgrade."

Moving forward to place his hand on the chest, JaKobi chuckled. "Say what you want about Isadora, but she sure had some nice loot."

"That's almost like starting a joke with three men walked into a bar." ShadowLily brushed past him and put her hand on the chest.

Tim put his arm around JaKobi's shoulders and squeezed. "It's okay that your jokes are shitty. You're one hell of a dancer."

"Ain't that the truth." JaKobi brushed Tim's arm off and broke into a jig.

ShadowLily was grinning at his antics as she donned her new boots. "Slayer's Boots of Reckoning. Bonus to attacking while in front of the enemy, and increased defense against cleave damage."

Keeping his jig going, JaKobi danced closer to the chest before putting his hand on it. "Staff of the Sunbeam. Clearly just something to make me more badass, and the rest of you jelly."

"I'm so gel-in," Tim quipped like he was in a bad Dr. Scholl's commercial. "But seriously, guys, that was one hell of a fight."

Reaching out, Tim ran his fingers against the top of the chest.

Item Received: Hex Witch's Armament

The greatest hex witch of all time was Maximus Rittenhower. The damage he dealt while keeping his companions alive was legendary. Maximus was known for fighting on the

front lines as close to his tank as possible. Because of this, he shunned his robes for a more traditional leather breastplate.

The Hex Witch's Armament provides a bonus to defense when standing within fifteen feet of the target or targets of your stance.

+2 Endurance +2 Dexterity +6 Intelligence +8 Wisdom

Tim unequipped his robe and put on his new chest piece. The leather armor was solid black, with blue stitching. The leatherwork was awesome, and he was continually impressed with how much the items looked cooler the higher they progressed in levels.

The new chest piece had everything he could ever want when it came to stats and special abilities. It was nice when the special abilities activated independently, and he didn't have to do it manually. Less work during the fights was always a welcome relief.

"Fancy duds, man!" JaKobi slapped his hand against the new armor. "But now I'm the only one in a robe."

Lorelei laughed. "You should be ecstatic. You basically get to wear a snuggie to work. Looking this fine takes a lot more effort."

"You know it, girl. Men don't know how easy they have it." Cassie gave the spirit archer a high five.

ShadowLily came back from the cabin as they spoke. She must have snuck off while he was getting his share of the loot. "The entire place is empty. Hopefully, killing Isadora was enough to heal the king because whatever she was keeping inside disappeared with her death."

"You know when we get to the castle, they're going to give us more work." Cassie's shoulders slumped.

I hate to admit it, but I think she's right.

"Let's get back to the castle and find out." Tim started walking back the way they came when Lorelei coughed.

The spirit archer pointed off in the distance. "Portal."

He loved it when game developers put a portal to the front of the dungeon or raid at the end. No one wanted to run back through that shit. Especially in this game where they didn't have quick travel spells outside the portal network. If they had to walk back to Promethia, it would have taken them a month, and it would be boring as hell. Sometimes he was okay with a little suspended reality as long as it made his experience in the game batter.

"I second that," ShadowLily purred. "I'm pretty sure we left a cask of beer in the carriage, and I could really use a drink."

"Did you say beer?" Cassie wrapped her arm around her bestie and dragged her toward the portal. "Let's hurry the fuck up."

The carriage stopped, and Grant opened the door. "There seems to be a problem."

Of course, there was.

Tim climbed out of the carriage. "What's going on?"

"He says we can't go through the gate." Grant pointed at the guard.

Why are the easy parts of the quest never so easy?

"I'll take care of it." Tim marched over to the closed gate and held up the royal seal for them to see. "Why are we being delayed?"

The guard snapped to attention at the sight of the seal but made no move to open the gates. "I'm sorry, sir, but the king has stopped all travel through the royal grounds."

"For how long?" Tim tried to keep the anger out of his voice.

Not only was the king alive, but he banned them from the castle grounds. This meant they weren't getting the stone even though they fulfilled their half of the bargain. It was total bullshit, and he wanted to scream.

Instead, he kept his cool.

When the guard didn't answer, Tim took it to mean he didn't know how long it would take before his orders changed. They weren't going to get through the gate anytime soon by the looks of it. He wondered what the problem was. If the king didn't want to pay them, the very least he could do was facilitate their quick trip home. He turned away from the guard and made his way back to the carriage.

"We might be stuck here for a while." There wasn't anything else to say. Tim had no idea what else they could do.

Grant hopped back up into the driver's seat. "I'll be here when you need me."

"Thank you." Tim meant every word. Since Grant had come into their lives, things on the travel front had grown considerably easier.

He turned to climb back into the carriage when a notification flashed across his vision.

System: You Have One Urgent Message from Prince Desmond

Tim opened the message.

The king has awoken, but he's a changed man. Something is not right with my father, but I can't put my finger on the source of my unease. Needless to say, he isn't willing to part with The Stone of Immoratis and is upset I made such a bargain for his health. I'll meet you at the gate and ride with you back to the city as soon as I can. There is much we need to discuss.

"That little rat bastard." Tim felt a flush of anger as he closed out the message.

Then his mind started working on the problem. It would be nearly impossible for the prince to openly defy the king, even if he was acting strangely. While they might not have the stone yet, he had the distinct impression they were about to get another quest that would finally deliver the stone into their hands.

Epic quests aren't called epic because they're short.

Tim opened the door and climbed back into the carriage. "Guys, I have some news."

A chorus of grumbles met his ears, and Cassie pressed a fresh mug of beer into his hand. Tim certainly had worse days in his life, like that time he'd missed the first half an hour of his calculus final. That was a cause for panic. This was a bump in the road.

Tapping his beer against Cassie's, Tim lifted his glass high. "Blue Dagger Society!"

List of Tim's Current Stats and Skills

"Tim" level twenty Hex Witch
    Primary Stats
    Strength: 14
    Endurance: 28
    Dexterity: 25
    Intelligence: 55
    Wisdom: 63
    Perception: 6
    Vitality: 4
    Revitalization: 4
    Luck: 7

Notable Gear
    Weapons
    Simple Dagger of Dexterity, +1 (X2)
    Greater Staff of Yin +3 Endurance +7 Intelligence +7 Wisdom
    Orb of Concentration, +5 Intelligence +4 Wisdom

Armor
    Circlet of Divine Wisdom, +1 Endurance +3 Intelligence +5 Wisdom
    Shoulder Guards of the Spotless Mind, +1 Intelligence +2 Wisdom +1 to Perception, Vitality, Revitalization, and Luck

Hex Witch's Armament, +2 Dexterity +2 Endurance +6 Intelligence +8 Wisdom

Jerkin of Fortuitous Solitude, +1 to all base stats, and bonus to healing when standing twenty feet away

Paul's Gloves of Mending, +7 Intelligence +4 Wisdom

Belt of Divine Inspiration, +1 Endurance +2 Intelligence +4 Wisdom

Hermit's Pants for Special Guests, +2 Endurance +2 Intelligence

Boots of Tranquility, +2 Endurance +2 Dexterity, Increase mana regeneration by 2%

Jewelry and Accessories

Leather Wraps of Divergent Health, 10% chance for single target healing spell to jump targets and heal the secondary recipient for 50% of the value

Wristband of the Faithful, +1 Endurance, ten seconds of double mana regeneration

Ring of Luminosity, +1 Endurance +2 Intelligence +3 Wisdom

Necklace of Hydration, +1 Endurance +2 Intelligence +5 Wisdom

Trinket of the Smiling Monkey, +1 to random stat

Skills

Curse of Sacrifice: Novice rank one

Hex of the Shattered Beast: Novice rank one

Appeal to the Goddess: Novice rank five

Night Vision: Novice rank eight

Quick Feet: Apprentice rank two

Rectify: Apprentice rank two

Disturbance: Apprentice rank three

Backstab: Apprentice rank four

Throwing Knives: Apprentice rank four
Sneak: Apprentice rank six
Shadow Master: Apprentice rank six
Small Blades: Journeyman rank one
Snare: Journeyman rank one
Dodge: Journeyman rank three
Flame Burst: Journeyman rank three
Behold My Power: Journeyman rank five
Divine Light: Journeyman rank five
Healing Storm: Journeyman rank five
Who Needs a Shield: Journeyman rank five
Curse of Giving: Journeyman rank eight
Cleanse: Journeyman rank nine
Healing Orb: Master rank one

Stances
Way of the River
Way of the Boulder

Buffs
Weaken Undead: Journeyman rank two
Armor of Eternia: Journeyman rank five
Attacks of the Faithful: Journeyman rank five

Open Quests
The Stone of Immoratis

CHAPTER THIRTY-FIVE

Prince Desmond hovered over his father's bed, wishing he could do something to make him better.

The High Priest's adventurers failed on their first attempt to slay Isadora, but on their return through the crown's land, he'd sensed a great change in them. Since they rode past, he'd been by his father's side, waiting for the curse to break. It would be nice to end the day with some good news.

They had to succeed this time. They just had to.

"The duke is here to see you," the familiar voice of his manservant Thurstan called from the doorway.

Desmond looked down at his father's pale skin and wondered how much time he had left in this world. The man who raised him looked so frail, lying unconscious on the bed, but he would always remember his dad in his prime. They used to spend hours training and studying together. So much so that his mother put a firm stop to some of their shenanigans lest the kingdom suffer from his father's inattention.

He would never forget the times they snuck off to the city so his father could glean the heartbeat of the people. His father used to tell him that a wise king must not only listen to the nobles but the men and women working the land. The burden of keeping the kingdom running often fell on those at the bottom, and their voices mattered greatly to him.

No one cared for the people of Promethia like King Rasmus. He made sure that the crops got planted and the mouths of the hungry filled with bread. During his reign, the kingdom benefited from a stable peace with the desert kingdoms.

Peace was a wonderful thing. When they had it, the minds of men and women flourished. The arts and inventions that came out of times of great peace were the things Rasmus wanted for his legacy.

Thus the entire kingdom found themselves living in a golden age of magic and art.

While it was nice for the rest of the kingdom, the success of his father's rule put a great burden on Desmond. The prince spent most of his childhood knowing he had to be the best at every discipline to have even a chance of living up to Rasmus' legacy. How did one follow the greatest king in a hundred generations without looking like a blundering idiot? The last thing he wanted was for others to remember him as the king who squandered his father's hard work. He refused to be known as Desmond the Dummy.

So while other children played, he studied.

The one art he never mastered was politics. The art of lying to someone's face to get what he wanted eluded him to this day. His honor had cost him more than one friend, and the unyielding nature of his will burned even more bridges. It wasn't simply good enough for him to be the best.

He had to be better.

Desmond sighed. If the Duke was here, it could only mean trouble.

Keeping her waiting would only make whatever giant piece of

horse shit she was going to drop into his lap today worse. "Tell her I will be there momentarily."

"Of course, sir." Thurstan disappeared as silently as a ghost.

His mother rose from her chair, crossed the room, and clasped his hands. "Don't worry. I'll stay with him."

"I'll make sure this doesn't take long. I want to be here when he wakes up." Desmond kissed her on the cheek and dropped her hands.

He felt her eyes on his back as she called, "It takes as long as it takes. Make sure not to let her take advantage of you."

Of course, she was right. The duke was a strong-willed woman. Anyone should've been able to guess that by the way she claimed the title for her own. That didn't mean the duke could do whatever she damn well pleased. Her first duty was to serve the crown, and if that didn't happen more frequently, there would be dire consequences. The least of which was stripping the title she fought so hard for.

Walking out of the room was the only signal his two guards needed to follow. They trailed behind Desmond day and night whether he willed it so or not. It seemed with the king in ill health, no one was taking chances with his. What they didn't know was that the king would wake up soon. When Isadora died, the adventurers would have the cure, or better yet, her death would break whatever spell the king was under.

It just had to.

The guards entered the audience chamber with him and positioned themselves to either side of the door as he walked into the room. Duke Ravenstorm was sitting at the head of the table eating grapes off a silver tray and drinking a glass of wine. She could never make things easy. Everything had to be a power play.

Don't let her take advantage of you.

Desmond moved to the table and stood by his chair until she got up and moved to another seat. When she moved, the duke also sat in her new seat before he had the chance to claim his. So even in his tiny victory, she slighted him. Today wasn't the day to let it get under his skin.

Today was going to be a good day.

A small part of him wanted to give into the game completely and call her duchess when he addressed her. If she wanted to push the issue, he'd have her stripped of her lands and titles so fast that she'd be cleaning the chamber pots of a tavern by nightfall.

"What can I do for you today, Duke Ravenstorm?" Desmond poured a glass of wine.

This was going to suck.

"A carriage rode through my lands today, carrying the crown seal." Stephanie's body language looked bored, but her eyes were intense.

Desmond shook his head and set down his glass. Maybe drinking wasn't such a good idea right now. "You mean someone traveled through the lands you manage for the king while bearing his seal? I don't see how that's a concern of yours."

"It concerns me because the people riding in that carriage crossed my lands once without my leave already." She stared at him, daring him to correct her. "Last time, they carried the family crest of one of my men."

Oh, that must have really chapped her buns.

Desmond tried not to smile at the thought of a lowly adventurer having the guts to face down the duke. "This time as they crossed the king's lands, they carried a seal I handed to them personally."

He could play the power game as well as she could. The difference was that he was the one with all of it in this situation. As the acting king, his word was law. If he gave someone the royal seal, they acted with his voice and could go wherever the fuck they wanted. She was dangerously close to crossing a line.

Or maybe trying to get him to cross one.

"How am I to protect the crown when I don't know who is coming and going?" The duke leaned back in her chair. "It's almost as if you don't care what happens to the king." Her eyes moved toward the doorway he entered from.

This was why he hated politics.

This entire meeting was to set the stage for her trying to seize power when he became king. What Duke Ravenstorm hadn't figured out yet was that she would be crushed between three armies. He'd already promised her position to the marquess and the marquess' position to the earl. All they had to do was continue supporting him if it came to battle. Seeing sense in any given situation wasn't the duke's strong suit.

Desmond kept his voice even when he spoke, which under the circumstances should've earned him an award for best performance of the millennium. "Actually, they have the seal because they're heading to slay the witch Isadora. I wonder what kind of correspondence they might find there."

He played the card not knowing how close it would strike to home, but he instantly knew when it landed. Was she so stupid as to side with the witch over the crown? Maybe the real question was if it was ambition that drove her or something else.

The duke's eyes widened slightly at his remark. "Surely, I have no idea what you mean."

"If there isn't anything else, I have my father's recovery to attend to." Desmond took a small sip from his glass of wine.

The wine tasted like fruity piss in his mouth, but he swallowed it just the same. It was his nerves that were getting to him and not the quality of the wine. He was playing a dangerous game right now, but he was past caring. If his father didn't make it through the day, the first thing he would have to do was bring the duke to heel. So he might as well get a head start.

"No, I guess that's it." She rose and swaggered out of the room.

He was going to count that interaction as a win in his book. She'd slighted him at every turn, yet he found a way to make it through the conversation without losing his temper. Not only that, but he found out some useful information. He'd never considered her a direct threat, but now their cards were on the table. He was happy to have prepared for this day.

The only way they might avoid bloodshed now was if the adventurers found a way to save the king. He stayed seated for a moment drinking the wine whose flavor had only slightly improved. Appearances mattered. Even here in the heart of his castle, there were always eyes watching and gossip spreading. It wouldn't do his reputation any good to be seen storming away.

After finishing his glass, Desmond stood and slowly made his way out of the room. The guards followed him in lockstep until he made it back to his father's chambers.

His mother looked up from her seat by the bed. "No change."

"Damn it!" Desmond smashed his fist into his palm. "What's taking them so long?"

His first instinct was to pour another glass of wine, but with the duke lurking and his father's fate hanging in the balance, it was better to keep his wits about him.

Turning away from the wine bottle on the table, he focused his attention on his father in time to see one of his fingers wiggle. "Mom!"

The queen turned and grasped the king's hand in hers. "Rasmus, I'm here for you."

Desmond was standing behind her in an instant. "Me too, Dad."

Slowly the king's eyes fluttered open, but the once faded blue was now slightly red. "Water," he croaked. "I need water."

Fully dressed and sitting on his throne, the king looked strong and hearty.

Watching him now, no one would've guessed he spent the last four weeks in a coma. His back was straight, and his head held high. There was a bearing of command Rasmus easily carried that Desmond knew he would never master in the same way.

He was so happy to have his father back, but there was also something wrong.

Rasmus wasn't acting like himself. Gone were his gentle ways. His normally jolly tone had been replaced with brusque efficiency as he issued orders. The red tint to his eyes still hadn't faded. This new version of his father was almost worse than having him in a coma.

No one could openly defy the king, not even his son.

"Father, before you retire for the evening, I have one last matter to bring to your attention." Desmond looked at his mother, and she gave him a slight nod to continue.

Looking down from his throne, Rasmus smiled. "For my son, I will always make time."

It sounded like his father and looked like his father, but Desmond wasn't exactly sure it was his father. Something was off. It could have been residual blowback from the curse, or maybe something else still had its claws in him. There was no way to know.

But he couldn't ignore it.

"There is the matter of the adventurers who slew Isadora and released you from her curse." Desmond lowered his head. "I promised them a reward from the treasury."

The king didn't look concerned. Their kingdom was wealthy enough he could afford to part with almost anything.

"What exactly did you promise them?" Rasmus' voice had an edge that didn't match the calm expression on his face.

This was going to be the hard part. It wasn't strictly in Desmond's power to offer the stone, but in times of dire need, it seemed a petty trinket. "I offered them the Stone of Immoratis if they could wake you."

"I'd rather have them killed!" the king bellowed as he rose to his feet. "What in the hell were you thinking?"

His mother tried to place a hand on the king's shoulder, but he brushed it off and marched toward his son until they were standing eye-to-eye. "That stone is not yours to barter with, and now you've put me in a terrible position."

Desmond didn't understand. Yes, the stone was a powerful magical object, but it was only one of the hundreds inside their vault not doing anything. Giving it up to save his father's life had seemed like a no-brainer. This cemented the fact for him that something was terribly wrong.

The real king would never kill someone they owed a favor to. That was more the duke's kind of sabotage.

"I'm sorry to have disappointed you." Desmond lowered his eyes to the floor as he tried to think of his next move.

Rasmus barked harsh laughter. "Then you have a hard way of showing it. How much of my life must I spend cleaning up your messes?"

Just this once, if I recall correctly, was what he wanted to say.

"Then let me clean this one up for you." Desmond placed a hand on his father's shoulder and looked him in the eye. "It wouldn't be right for us to kill someone to whom we owe a favor."

Rasmus' hand came up, gripping the opposite shoulder and squeezing tightly. "I know, and that's why I'm so upset with you. Having to give this order dishonors us, but it must happen for the good of the kingdom."

"Oh yes, Father, I know." Desmond lowered his voice conspiratorially. "I suggest we let one of our oldest enemies do the deed for us instead."

Smiling wide, Rasmus looked over at his son, beaming with pride. "You mean to send them after her?" He licked his lips, knocking his son's arm away and pulling him into a hug. "It's genius. I love it."

Now I have to sell it to the adventurers.

"Of course, I'll send a detachment of men with you." Rasmus winked. "In case we get lucky, and they refuse the quest."

It sounded like a good way to lose a lot of men. "Splendid idea," was what Desmond managed to croak out.

"You go and see to it immediately." The king's red eyes were hard to read. "Don't let me down again."

Desmond bowed. "Your will is my command." He rose, turned, and strode out the door with purpose.

He had to find the adventurers and quickly. They needed to get out of the royal lands as quickly as possible. The thing wearing his father's skin could change its mind at any moment and have the adventurers killed. Now Prince Desmond had to get the group of adventurers to agree to a quest for a reward they should have already received.

No one ever said being a leader was easy.

As soon as he was out of the throne room, he sent a message to Tim. The gist of it was simple. "I'm coming."

CHAPTER THIRTY-SIX

Grant's carriage was big and comfortable, but it wasn't the kind of place a person spent an entire day in.

Waiting in the carriage was kind of like lying in bed all day. After a while, even the soft memory foam hurt Tim's ass. He opened the carriage door and stepped out into the cool night air. If Desmond didn't show up soon, they would probably have to concede the fact he wasn't going to show up. At some point, they'd have to give up and make the long circle around the king's lands back to Promethia.

As it stood, he'd give Desmond until breakfast to make it right.

Stretching his back until it popped, Tim stood straight and looked around. There were still two guards at the gate, but the men had gone back to mostly ignoring them as they waited for new orders. With his stretching done, he felt the familiar urge to pee. What was it with sleeping that made a person run to the bathroom to make water the first thing upon waking?

Wandering off into the woods alone was never a great idea, so he moved to the wall, and once he was out of sight of the guards, he let it rip.

Once he finished peeing the letters of his name on the king's wall, Tim tied up his pants. "Just keeping it classy."

Chuckling, he turned back toward the carriage and saw the others emerging. "What's up, guys?"

Cassie shrugged. "I don't know. ShadowLily said something about a commotion at the gate."

"I think the guards were running around screaming something like pee on the walls." JaKobi snickered. "They were all looking for buckets and rags."

Lorelei stopped about ten feet from the wall. "You can see here where the early-stage pubescent male has left his marking on another man's territory." She pointed and moved her hand like she was tracing something. "As you can see here, there is a pattern."

She turned and looked at Tim. "By God, I think we've solved the case. The markings spell out a name."

"Bitch." Tim coughed into his hand.

"No, that wasn't it." Lorelei smiled demurely. "I'm not impressed because you can write your name on a wall without paint."

Cassie's eyes lit up. "What if I could do it?"

"I'd buy that shit on pay-per-view." Lorelei busted out laughing as soon as she spoke.

They all got a good chuckle out of the joke, but then Shadow-Lily pointed toward the gate. "Someone is coming. Maybe we should show them the marking and see if they can determine what caused it."

"Got it, don't pee your name on things." Tim winked at her. "Let's find out if this is the prince.

Together they moved to stand by the carriage.

A carriage stopped inside the gate, and Desmond leapt out. The prince tapped his hand against the side of the carriage, and it turned and left. He motioned for the guards to open the gate and walked forward with efficient purpose.

"I'm sorry to have kept you waiting so long. Things in the castle have been rather chaotic since the king woke up." Desmond didn't look very happy about his dad taking a turn for the better.

Cassie got in the prince's face so quickly one of the guards gave a startled shout. "We're not in the business of working with welshers."

"In the most respectful terms, of course." JaKobi eased Cassie back a few steps.

Tim almost sighed in exasperation. They'd gone over this moment a hundred times while they were waiting for the prince to show up. It was plain as day something else was going on, and they'd agreed to give the prince the benefit of the doubt until they heard his side of the story.

This wasn't the plan.

"Would you care to join us for a drink, Desmond? We have one keg left, and it's a long ride back to the inn." Tim motioned toward the carriage.

ShadowLily didn't miss a beat. She strung her arm through Desmond's and led him in the right direction. "We'd be delighted to have you."

One of the guards looked uncertain about letting the prince ride off with people barred from entering the grounds by the king's orders. "Sir?"

Desmond pulled his arm gently out of ShadowLily's and turned to face the man. "It's fine. Go back to your post."

"Yes, sir." The man ran back to the open gate.

Holding out his arm for ShadowLily to take, Desmond smiled. "Tell me more about this beer."

As soon as they were all in the carriage and underway, Cassie turned her frown back on the prince. "Someone's got some explaining to do."

Tim was impressed she wasn't screaming or punching him. The normal Cassie defaulted to solving problems by hitting things hard until they relented or broke. So far, they were marked safe from causing a royal incident, but that could change at any moment.

Turning his attention from Cassie to the prince, Tim took the lead. "I think that's what he's here to do."

Prince Desmond told them everything that had happened since the king woke up from his coma. It was one hell of a story. The king was either under another spell or not the king at all. How something or someone could've replaced him was anyone's guess, but with magic, anything was possible.

"The bastard wanted to kill us," Cassie raged, not concerned for a single second with the bigger picture.

JaKobi was smiling as though he was in the middle of a great fantasy novel and was ready to sink his teeth in. "The king might not be the king?"

"I'm worried the imposter thought Desmond's idea was a good one. If the fake king is on board, it has to be a trap." Lorelei looked at ShadowLily for confirmation.

The mist slayer nodded in confirmation. "Agreed. Before we can help, we need more information."

That's why I love her.

Tim was grinning as he addressed the prince. "Tell us about this quest you want us to take on."

"First things first." Desmond pulled out five pouches of gold. "While I might not be able to secure the stone for you yet, I can and will honor the rest of your quest rewards now."

Everyone accepted their twenty gold as the prince continued. "As for the item, I've sent you a list of what we have available, you merely have to select the item, and it will be messengered to you immediately."

Cassie smiled for the first time since laying eyes on the prince. "It's a start."

Desmond bowed his head. "I promise you this, young warrior, if completing this next task doesn't free my father, I will steal the stone for you myself."

Cassie saw the sincerity in his eyes as he lifted his head and heard it in his words. "Don't let us down, and we won't let you down."

Desmond bowed his head again in respect. "I swear it."

"That's good enough for me." JaKobi clapped the prince on the back and handed him a mug of beer.

"You're also right." Desmond met each of their eyes in turn. "It's probably a trap."

Tim felt his smile growing as he thought about their previous victories. "Against the odds is kind of what we specialize in."

Desmond nodded. "I'm starting to see that." He waved. "These are the details. You don't have to take on this task, but the fate of the kingdom hangs in the balance."

Quest Received: The Veil of Madness

Something is wrong with the good King Rasmus, and the problem lies hidden within the Veil of Madness. Travel to the location, enter the veil, and stop whatever is happening there. The only additional information I can provide to you is the witch living there is named Cronos. The villagers gave her the title to mock Sonos as she grew older and more powerful in her magical arts.

Since then, she sealed off those lands, and any who enter have been cast out and driven mad by the experience. Now the entire village serves at the whim of Cronos, and she delights in taking her slow revenge. Isadora was her greatest apprentice, and she'll seek vengeance for her death.

Reward: The Stone of Immoratis, even if I have to steal it myself.

Tim gazed around the carriage, seeing what everyone thought of the quest. As far as he could tell, everyone looked on board so he accepted the quest. "We'll find out what's going on, and if something is controlling your father or has replaced him, we'll take care of it."

The relief in Desmond's eyes was palpable. "Thank you." He

turned slowly. "All of you. I know I've asked much from you and delivered little, but I will not forget your service to the kingdom."

"You better not," Cassie growled.

They all broke out in laughter.

Desmond was looking at Tim but pointing at Cassie. "I really like this one."

"She grows on you, that's for sure." JaKobi gave her a quick kiss.

Desmond tapped on the roof of the carriage, signaling for it to stop. "The royal seal should be effective for you again, but I ask that you not return until you complete the deed."

The carriage stopped, and Tim opened the door for the prince to exit. "Be safe, Prince Desmond. If all is as you say, your life might also be in danger."

Cassie added, "You can't pay if you're dead."

Nodding, the prince left the carriage. "Do not underestimate Cronos. She is as deadly as she is old."

The door to the carriage closed, and a few moments later they were moving again. Tim fired off a quick message to Grant to let him know they needed to get to the inn, leaned back, and waited for the chaos to ensue.

"The balls on that guy," Cassie stated bluntly.

Lorelei laughed. "Were they spectacular? I didn't even notice."

"Can balls be spectacular?" ShadowLily laughed. "I mostly ignore them."

Tim pretty much did the same thing. "Hey, unless we're going to sing the song, let's get back on track."

"So this is what we know." ShadowLily took over the conversation, not wanting to hear one word about that dreaded song. "If we want a shot at the stone, we have to try and defeat this next dungeon or storm the castle."

Cassie sipped her beer. "You know what I've been saying from the beginning. We need to take that shit."

"I'm willing to give Desmond one more chance, but if he lets us down again…" ShadowLily smirked as she pointed at Cassie. "I'm with her."

Tim raised his hand. "All in favor of giving Desmond one last chance?"

Three more hands shot into the air.

"Then we give him one more shot." He turned to Cassie. "If we end up doing it your way, you call all the shots, and I'll back you one hundred percent."

Cassie looked mollified for the moment. "Fine, but I want dibs on the killing blow."

"Done." Tim was confident he didn't need to check with the others to meet that particular demand.

"Oh, and I don't want to have to tell Eternia that we don't have the stone," Cassie added quickly.

A chorus of "not it" rained across the carriage.

Tim took a fresh beer from JaKobi. "Fine, I'll tell her about our setback, but I want all of you to use this ride to go over your skills and get them updated. We need to make sure we go into the next fight prepared."

"Don't forget to check the auction house for supplemental gear or potions. There are some really good deals, and all you have to do to complete an order is go to Tim's kiosk. He waived the fees for all of us, so use it when you can." ShadowLily *clinked* her glass against his.

Lorelei tapped hers against the two of theirs. "I'll send a message to Roberto and tell him we're coming in hot."

"If I were into dudes, I'd be all over that." JaKobi was clearly thinking about the endless breakfast options that came with marrying a master chef.

Cassie's face turned serious for a moment. "Wait, I'm into dudes. Should I be getting all up on it?"

"How good is the discount on pancakes?" JaKobi mocked as he tried to suppress a laugh.

Cassie dove into his lap. "I think they'd be free but are you willing to give all this up for a few free pancakes?"

"Humm." JaKobi pretended to think about it. "They are really good."

Cassie socked him in the stomach. "And I'm not?"

"Nah, baby, the point is you're so good we'd be rolling in free packers for the rest of our lives." JaKobi held onto her tightly. "Of course I'd never trade you for anything."

"I'm starting to like this free pancake idea. Maybe I could even get Roberto to throw in some breakfast sausage." Cassie laughed at the look of shock on JaKobi's face and nestled back into him.

Tim finished his beer and set the mug down. He hated to be the vibe killer, but they were going to be busy tomorrow, and he wanted to get the grunt work out of the way so he could enjoy their newest dungeon crawl without feeling guilty about not updating his skills.

"Time to focus up. Update your skills, and try to stay quiet until everyone finishes." Tim looked at Cassie.

"Why are you looking at me? I might play a tank on TV, but in real life, I'm a college graduate." Cassie winked. "Me try read book now."

"Finally, someone speaking in a language I can understand." JaKobi beamed from ear to ear.

Tim laughed as he leaned back in his seat to get comfortable.

This was going to take a while.

CHAPTER THIRTY-SEVEN

Tim watched for a moment as everyone pulled up their interfaces to check their skills.

Normally this part of the process felt a little daunting even though it was incredibly rewarding when he received a tier upgrade, but today it felt like a breath of fresh air. He needed to take his mind off the task in front of them for a bit, and this was the thing to do it.

Doing this next quest for the same reward was rubbing him a bit raw, but the loot they picked up while handling all these side missions was adding up. Everyone in the party had really good gear stacked, and if they kept rocking these boss fights, they would always have top-tier loot. Sometimes it felt good having that shiny thing everyone else was dying to get their hands on.

System Message: You have gained a level.

You have been awarded one skill point.

Tim couldn't help but smile as he started making progress to level forty. Some people hated leveling, but he kind of loved it. It was just like the endgame grind, but instead of gear progression, the player was always chasing the next skill unlock or dungeon they would have access to. For some reason, he couldn't get enough of it.

Like the mouse who only pushed the pleasure button.

He dumped the one stat point in strength, bringing his total to fifteen. The first thing Tim wanted to do was get all his stats to a baseline of twenty. Then he would start stacking Wisdom like he found a pallet of the skill points at a going out of business sale. He sipped his beer and moved onto the first skill update.

Skill Increased: Hex of the Shattered Beast

Rank: Novice three

Good doggy, good doggy. Interesting choice on the manifestation of your beast, but a Golden Retriever can do the job as well as any other breed. To level this skill, you need to keep using it, get creative, and show us you can use it to maximum effect for larger increases.

Tim was already thinking of ways he could use this skill to boost healing. If he didn't heal during Behold My Power and switched to Way of the River right before the hound hit, he might be able to top off everyone's health without having to cast an additional spell. It was never a bad idea to save as much mana as he could so it was there when he needed it. That was one of his highest priorities during fights.

Things started with a bang. Tim hoped they kept going as well with his next update.

Skill Increased: Curse of Sacrifice

Rank: Novice six

No pain, no gain, takes on an entirely new meaning when it's your health stripped away as you deal damage. Still, you used this skill repeatedly, and it's already paying dividends. It won't be long now until you make the apprentice ranks and this skill receives its first perk. Keep up the sacrifice.

Just like with Behold My Power, this curse required him to pay a price for using it. Having the same thing happen with his previous skill made it so Tim didn't feel the pain anymore. The only thing he had to be careful about was losing too much health attacking and then not dodging quick enough to avoid an attack. At that point, he might as well have been throwing himself off a cliff. The way he used the skill now, his worst-case scenario still left him two or three mistakes away from being dead.

Tim didn't make a lot of mistakes.

Skill Increased: Night Vision

Rank: Apprentice one

It never ceases to amaze us how much time you spend wandering around in the dark. Your eyes are adapting, and at the apprentice ranks, you're more likely to see things in low light conditions. Obtain higher ranks to see when there is no light at all.

Tim used this skill without even thinking about it most of the time. So far he'd noticed that the skill made the light from JaKobi's floating orbs cover more ground. If it was totally dark, he still couldn't make out more than his hand in front of his face, and even then, it was only an outline. If they kept having to fight in caves, this skill would continue leveling all on its own.

He loved having as many passive abilities as possible. It was nice sometimes not to have to think about every minor detail. If he could see, he could see, and if he couldn't, he was leveling the skill. It was the perfect harmony for the player who wanted to do as little work as possible.

Skill Increased: Rectify

Rank: Apprentice four

When the boss wants to make you go splat, but first they wanna supercharge, this is the skill you need to use. You can't remove every boss buff, but the ones you can, will have a green icon. Use this spell whenever it's off cooldown, and the boss has a buff you need to remove.

Tim loved this skill. The bosses in games were a bunch of tricky bastards and tended to buff up before dealing swathes of big, painful damage. Stopping their ability to do increased damage or shield themselves from it was paramount to their group's success. The line between a boss hitting the enrage timer and winning in time was often down to stopping the boss from buffing up.

Skill Increased: Disturbance

Rank: Apprentice five

Wham, bam, you're dead, but not if you use this skill in time. Bosses will have some interruptible attacks, and it's in your best interest to stop them from happening at any cost. Larger attacks might take more than one interrupt to stop. At the journeyman ranks, this skill receives additional benefits.

He loved nothing more than stopping the boss from doing damage and causing them to fumble their attack and take increased damage for a bit. It didn't happen all the time, but when the boss took that extra damage, it really helped them out. This was a skill he needed to use more. The higher the level, the more it would help his group.

Skill Increased: Quick Feet

Rank: Apprentice Five

Run, run, Rudolph, but try not to choke any more bakers. Yeah, not your finest moment. On the plus side, you used the skill leading to an attack, which you haven't done before. Keep using this skill when you need to move fast, and it will level up quickly.

Hey!

Tim already admitted he wasn't proud of how he acted and made amends with Joaquin. There were all kinds of ways he could justify his actions to himself, but he knew when he'd screwed up even if he didn't like to admit it. The Sisters of Eternal Bliss hung in the back of his mind like a hangover he couldn't shake. He'd get back there one day and find out the truth of what they were doing to the people trapped there.

Skill Increased: Dodge

Rank: Journeyman six

He runs, he jumps, he falls flat on his face. That pretty much sums up your use of this ability. We wish your technique was super cool or clever, but you normally throw your body around like it's a ragdoll and hope for the best. Have a little more respect for yourself.

Tim wanted to argue, but it was truc. When he saw trouble coming, he didn't think about *how* to get out of the way. He just did it as quickly as possible. Any damage he took by tossing his body around would be less than what would happen if he ate an attack from the boss. And normally, something Hydration would take care of automatically. Until his last piece of loot, he'd never really had any serious protection and managed to stay alive just fine.

Now he not only looked badass, but he could probably take an extra hit or two before dying. He wasn't exactly sure what direction his class would take him when he started the game, but Tim was ecstatic with where he ended up. This game was so much fun, and they had more crazy fights in front of them to look forward to.

He was ready to find out what was on the other side of the veil of madness and defeat the evil residing there.

Skill Increased: Flame Burst

Rank: Journeyman six

It's kind of amazing how well you use this skill when you don't use it all that often. Come on already. Lighting stuff on fire is cool. Ask your pyrotechnic friend. Continue using Flame Burst, and it'll reward you when you hit the master ranks.

Lighting his enemies on fire was pretty fucking cool, but he also used this skill to keep people away. Sometimes creating a little distance was all he needed to let Cassie take control of the situation. Plus, he could totally make a mountain of s'mores at one time, and not everyone could do that.

Skill Increased: Behold My Power

Rank: Journeyman seven

It's okay to have a pain fetish. Lots of people do. The fact you

like to share your pain with your friends is a little unique, but who are we to judge? You're almost at the master ranks with this skill. Keep on hurting your friends and your enemies to level it up.

If they didn't want him hurting his friends, they shouldn't have made the skill so damn appealing. It was one of his favorite skills, and Tim liked to use it to start or end most fights. It was his largest single target damaging ability, and it had saved their ass more than once. They could say what they wanted, but he embraced his class's philosophy on dishing out pain to himself and others to do even more to the boss.

Doing damage to heal was fucking awesome.

Skill Increased: Who Needs a Shield

Rank: Journeyman seven

At least it's not all about hurting your friends. Sometimes you even save them from damage. Who Needs a Shield is your bread and butter for deflecting damage, and you tend to use it at the right times. You've almost reached the master ranks. Get ready for this spell to gain a new perk when you get there.

As if blocking damage and increasing the target's dodge chance wasn't enough. If this skill received an additional benefit, it would be the bee's knees.

Did bees even have knees? Who came up with this shit, anyway?

Tim chuckled as he took another sip of beer. Truth be told he might need a Cleanse, but he would let it ride until they got back to the inn or he finished updating his skills. This wasn't quite the party he expected to be having tonight, but he was doing just fine.

Skill Increased: Divine Light

Rank: Journeyman eight

So now we know why you don't use your Flame Burst as much as you should. You're addicted to shooting light from your fingertips. We get it. It's a cool skill although it can be hard on the mana pool when the fighting gets intense. You use this

skill well and are almost at the master ranks. Keep up the good work, and you'll get there shortly.

Tim didn't know why but it felt like the game was being nice to him today. These skill updates were super helpful and encouraging and not exactly what he was used to when he got them. Normally the game was a little more judgmental of his talents. Maybe it was the beer, but it felt like everything was going to work out just fine. In the morning, he'd get to put these new updates to the test.

Skill Increased: Healing Storm

Rank: Journeyman eight

Just like Pacman Jones, you like to make it rain. Okay, so you don't exactly do your thing at the strip club, but imagine how cool it would be if you did. This is your go-to AOE heal, and you know how to use it well. Watch the channeling cost so it doesn't leave you in a pickle.

No kidding.

Tim knew he'd become too reliant on channeling Healing Storm at the end of fights and that needed to change. It wiped out all his mana, and if they were in another situation like their fight with Isadora where zero percent didn't mean the fight was over, it could be trouble. He vowed to make sure when he channeled the spell the next time he did it at the right time, for the right length.

Skill Increased: Cleanse

Rank: Master one

Welcome to the master ranks, again. It must feel good being a master of more than one skill. Cleanse will now automatically cure any debuff at the journeymen ranks and below. With each move you take up the master ranks, your ability to cure master-level debuffs will increase. Right now, you have the base thirty-three percent chance for success.

Cleanse can now also be cast as a group cleanse for an additional mana cost.

Some days it felt like the game was raining down love on him. He knew other people joining the master ranks were probably getting similar benefits to their classes, but this increase felt especially good. Not only did his chance of cleansing master-level spells increase, but the fact he could cast Cleanse on his entire party for an additional cost was huge.

It's going to save me a shit-ton of time.

Tim read over the update again to make sure he understood it. Then he tried to cast the spell. Just like that his buzz was gone.

"What in the fuck, man?" JaKobi poured himself another beer. "Not cool, not fucking cool." He chugged it and poured a second.

ShadowLily laughed. "Let me guess, new spell?"

"She got it in one." Tim touched a finger to his nose. "Sorry, guys, didn't mean to kill your buzz."

JaKobi handed Tim a mug. "Easy enough problem to fix."

Lorelei accepted a fresh drink. "Since we don't have to worry about calories, why not have another."

Tim sipped his new beer and went back to reading his updates.

Skill Increased: Curse of Giving

Rank: Master one

Curse of Giving is becoming one of your favorite spells to use. It provides periodic damage to the boss and periodic healing to the targets of your stance or stances. The increased damage you received at the journeyman ranks has increased to five percent, and that percentage is now unblockable. At the master ranks, each cast of Curse of Giving places a stack of Shattered World on the target. When the target receives three stacks of Shattered World, the skill will activate and deal a burst of single target damage.

System Message: Achievement Title Granted

This is your third skill to make the master ranks. That's quite an achievement and should be celebrated. You've earned the title "Triple Threat." This title is a display-only achievement and provides no additional benefits.

Did that mean some titles did give bonuses? If so, there was an entire secondary path for gear he'd have to dig into. How to get certain titles with the right benefits would be something they could look into soon. For now, he was excited about the title, and more importantly, the update to Curse of Giving.

Holy shit, that was one hell of an update.

Tim almost spilled his beer as he tried to stand. Then he bumped his head on the roof of the carriage and sat back down, only spilling a small bit. How was a guy supposed to celebrate when he couldn't stand up to dance properly? Asking Grant to pull the carriage over so he could break out the JaKobi shuffle seemed like a crazy idea, so he kept his mouth shut and hoped no one noticed.

"Smooth move." Cassie giggled.

So much for no one noticing.

ShadowLily rubbed his head. "Don't go smashing that pretty little head of yours. I like it the way it is."

Feeling his cheeks turn red but unable to stop it, Tim embraced his mistake. "Sorry, forgot where I was for a second."

"Update was that good, huh?" JaKobi lifted his hand for a high five. "Right on, man!"

Lorelei smiled as if she was indulging children. "You guys mind? I have a few more things to go over."

"Sorry." Tim had a few skills he needed to go over as well.

The last thing he wanted to do was reach the inn and have everyone done with their updates but him. It didn't set a great example when the person in the leadership role didn't get the job done because he was too busy goofing off. Tim set his empty mug to the side and got back to work.

Skill Increased: Healing Orb

Rank: Master three

Splash, splash, splash. Man, you would be a hit at summer pool parties. Not only would you win every water balloon fight without balloons, but you'd heal all the people while doing it. Healing Orb won't receive another major update until you hit the grandmaster ranks, but with each tier increase

inside the master ranks, the spell will provide increased healing.

Tim couldn't have thought about a more fitting end to his skill updates. Healing Orb was his oldest skill and his most used talent. Nothing he did kept his group alive more than casting this single spell as many times as possible. If the skill kept getting boosts, he'd make up for some of the power it lost during the update.

Sometimes when things were going right, they turned into a freight train of good luck.

Buffs

Skill Increased: Armor of Eternia

Rank: Journeyman seven

Armor of Eternia will only receive small tier increases until it reaches the master ranks. Don't forget that while your buffs last for eight hours unless specifically stated otherwise, it never hurts to do a buff check before a fight.

That was probably the most considerate reminder he'd ever received in a game. His skill received a slight bump, and he couldn't have been more pleased. It wouldn't be long now until his buffs reached the master ranks and became even more substantial.

Tim couldn't wait.

Skill Increased: Attacks of the Faithful

Rank: Journeyman seven

Like your other buff, this skill will only receive small increases until it reaches the master ranks. That doesn't mean this buff isn't worth its weight in gold. Helping your entire group do more damage is always a winning strategy.

Tim liked to think the easiest way to win a fight was with unrelenting brute force. It wasn't always the best way, and sometimes not everyone made it, but just going ham and trying to destroy the boss as fast as possible got him through more fights than it didn't.

As long as the group could keep up.

The Blue Dagger Society was the best group of gamers he'd ever had the pleasure to game with. None of them were flawless, but they all knew how to excel and didn't make the simple mistakes that would've wiped out many other parties. He loved every single one of them like family and would do anything for them.

Even buy them more beer.

The carriage stopped, and Tim looked over his group. "Drinks are on me tonight. Let's have some fun and take on tomorrow with everything we've got."

"Like we'd ever do anything less." Cassie *clinked* her mug to the others.

ShadowLily opened the door to the carriage. "Let's hurry up and get inside before he makes us do a cheer again."

"Hey, that was fun," Lorelei groused as she followed her out.

Tim motioned for the others to exit. "We'll save the cheer for tomorrow."

"Bro, they need to see our new moves." JaKobi grinned like a madman. "As soon as we take down Cronos, we should bust them out."

"This is going to be epic." Cassie jumped out. "Girls, we're in for a real treat."

Tim looked over at JaKobi with a huge shit-eating grin. "They aren't going to know what hit them."

They climbed out of the carriage and headed for the inn.

CHAPTER THIRTY-EIGHT

"I sense a great disturbance…"

In the force, say in the force.

"At the castle," Eternia continued smoothly. "There is a dark cloud hanging there, but it isn't my sister's influence."

Tim hoped for a *Star Wars* line in there, but he wasn't disappointed. In fact, he felt relieved Eternia was confirming Prince Desmond's fears. While it might suck for the kingdom, it meant the prince wasn't dicking them around and could be trusted. The stone was almost in their hands now. One more day and this would all be over.

Turning away from the fireplace, Eternia locked eyes with Tim. "You should be careful when confronting the evil in the castle. There is powerful magic at work. It isn't safe."

"What else can we do?" They both knew there wasn't another way forward except to fight Cronos and whatever was lurking in the castle.

Eternia took the seat by the fireplace in her room and slipped into thought. "Maybe you will find something beyond the veil that will help in the final battle, but even my sight cannot penetrate Cronos' realm."

"So we're in for a real fight then." Tim knew he should've been nervous but pushing into a new dungeon was what he needed right now.

Eternia looked worried enough for the both of them. "Adventurer, it will be the fight of your life."

Tim dropped to one knee. "Thank you for your help."

"You are the one helping me." Eternia motioned for him to rise. "Now go and have fun with your friends. The fight for *The Etheric Coast* continues tomorrow."

He was never one to turn down a good time. "Thank you. Will we see you in the morning?"

"I'll be down to see you off." Eternia flicked her hand, and the door to her room opened.

Tim turned to leave. "Then I'll see you in the morning." The door closed gently behind him as he stepped into the hallway.

He tried to think of something he could do to make a great entrance, but as he started down the stairs, Tim couldn't come up with a single thing he could do that was cooler than Cassie diving off the balcony and through a table. It was one thing when she could do it and not get hurt, but if Tim did it and broke his back, it wouldn't be nearly as funny. So he settled for strolling in and grabbing a beer.

"How did things go with the boss?" JaKobi screwed up his face as if he were expecting bad news.

At least on this front, Tim had nothing but good news. "She understands our difficulties and accepts them."

"I don't accept them. The prince better have something nice for us after all this hassle." Cassie took a swig of her beer.

Lorelei shrugged. "He sure did last time, and you know Cronos is going to drop something epic."

"I could do with a new offhand weapon. I just haven't found

anything worthwhile yet." JaKobi looked excited. "Are you sure we can't leave now?"

Gaston strutted into the middle of the bar like he hadn't ever left. "I'd kind of like to have a beer with my friends before we leave again."

"Stop all that foolish talk this instant," Ernie grumbled as he walked past, heading to his secret rooms at the back of the kitchens. "Goddess or not, I'm too old for this shit."

ShadowLily moved to stand next to her favorite assassin. "Sounds like you guys had one hell of a trip."

"Oh, you know, what happens in Tristholm stays in Tristholm." Gaston accepted a beer from Liz. "Your new friends should be safely back in the desert by now."

"Thank you for getting them home safely." Lorelei hugged Gaston. "I'm going to send Neema a message. See you guys in the morning."

Gaston looked rather put out. "Really? No welcome back party?"

"I promise we'll throw you a huge bash tomorrow, big guy." Tim clapped him on the back. "But we had one hell of a day, and we're going to chillax for a bit."

Gaston took a swig of his beer. "Had a few of those days myself recently. Tomorrow night will be fine, but I expect it to be big. Like, blowing off the doors big."

"Only if we win," Tim replied casually. "Or I should say when we win."

Gaston nodded. "Naturally."

"That guy at the bar with Liz is Grant, our new carriage driver. Be nice." ShadowLily scolded Gaston like a loving older sister as she slipped her arm through Tim's. "I have a quest for you to accomplish upstairs."

Tim felt the grin spreading on his face. "That's my kind of quest." He cast his group Cleanse and let her drag him away.

How people woke up without the fresh scent of coffee in their nostrils always mystified Tim.

Seriously, try it one time, and every day becomes like those old Folgers in your cup commercials. The scent of fresh-brewed coffee gently stimulated the nose and lured the sleepy family members into the kitchen. Somewhere deep inside, he wondered why there wasn't a *Family Guy* parody of that but where Stewie lured them all into the kitchen and killed his family with one of his ray guns. Sure, it might be a little dark, but if the little guy really wanted world domination, he had to start somewhere.

He didn't touch the coffee yet. Instead, he crawled out of bed, surprised to see ShadowLily was still there. After a quick trip to the bathroom, he came back to find ShadowLily enjoying his cup of coffee.

"What?" She shrugged, and the sheet dropped dangerously low. "If you wanted it, you should've taken it with you."

Tim smiled as he headed toward the door. "Trust me when I say those are two smells that should never combine."

The pillow came at him out of nowhere.

"See you downstairs soon," Tim called as he closed the door, chuckling the entire time. "See if she steals my coffee again."

It would be a few minutes before ShadowLily joined him for breakfast. The rest of the group was going to be blown away by how early he was up. It was dangerous to set this new kind of precedent, but when he woke up early, he liked to get up and go with it. As for how Liz always knew when he'd be waking up, he'd never had the courage to ask.

Wait, did she decide when he woke up?

The thought totally blew Tim's mind. She could drop off a cup of coffee at two am, and the smell would wake him before he realized what time it was. Maybe all of this was some kind of sick experiment to make him wake up early. Did ShadowLily put her up to this?

Tim shrugged as he started down the stairs. "At least the coffee's good."

Liz ran around the bar when he appeared. "Good, you got my note."

"What note?" Tim felt a little befuddled. He hadn't had his coffee yet.

"The one on the bottom of your cup, knucklehead." Liz glared at him. "Where is your coffee anyway?"

Tim felt a little embarrassed not to have the steaming cup of joe in his hands after Liz clearly went through some extra trouble this morning. "Um, about that, we might start needing two cups of coffee."

"She's drinking it?" Liz gasped. "Let's hope she doesn't see the note."

For a second there, he thought Liz had been trying to poison him and was upset she poisoned ShadowLily instead, but now he was intrigued about what this note was and why ShadowLily couldn't see it.

Tim reached out and put a comforting hand on Liz's shoulder. "I think you better tell me what's going on."

"Joe's back." She gave a nervous laugh, and her hands flew into the air in exasperation. "Surprise."

Before Tim could respond, Liz continued. "The note was asking you to keep her busy for a bit. Joe wanted to make her something special."

Tim pulled his hand back, held it in front of him, and mimicked pouring into a glass. "If I'm going back up there, I need my cup of coffee."

"Dick!" Liz slapped his arm but went to get his coffee anyway.

With his strength to face the day in hand, Tim ascended the stairs and tried to think of a good distraction. If he wanted to distract her without it being too suspicious, he was going to have to pull out all the stops. He started looking through his inventory until he had on the perfect outfit and equipped it before walking through the door.

Tim had decked himself out in a fully Renaissance look. He was either Sabastian Stann as the Mad Hatter or the infamous Dorian Gray. Whoever he was supposed to be, he looked fucking pimping, and ShadowLily was going to eat him up. She loved all those romancy novels and movies so this was her kind of thing. All he had to do now was set the proper mood.

He walked into the room and dipped his incredibly tall top hat. "Baby, I'm ten-sixths hard for you."

ShadowLily's towel fell to the floor. "Just don't tell my boyfriend, Mr. Hatter. He gets awfully jealous about these things."

"You might as well say that I see what I eat is the same as I eat what I see." Tim unequipped all his clothes and rushed into the arms of the most beautiful woman he'd ever seen.

Liz nudged Tim. "I said buy me some time, not make her late for breakfast."

"What can I say? Things got a little carried away." Tim tried not to laugh at the shocked expression on Liz's face. "Look at the two of them. It all worked out."

Liz topped off his coffee as she watched Joe and ShadowLily chatting. "It sure did."

He felt a bit of sadness coming off her and didn't want to ask what it was about so he pulled her into a side hug. "You'll always have a place here with us. You're part of our family now."

"Thank you." Liz returned the hug, but when she left, there were tears in her eyes.

JaKobi pointed at him. "What was all that about?"

"You know me, always a hit with the ladies." Tim downplayed the situation, mostly because he had no idea what sparked the moment.

If Liz ever needed their help, she would have it in an instant. Tim hoped she knew that whatever it was they were there for her. Maybe he could have ShadowLily or Lorelei find out what was going on and get to the bottom of it. It could be as simple as she needed someone to talk to.

Joe let out a burst of laughter. "No, he didn't."

ShadowLily giggled. "You should see the look on his face when he runs."

Joe slapped his thigh and then looked up at Tim. "Speak of the devil."

"Hey Joe, welcome back." Tim accepted the hearty plate of food and sat.

Joe grinned. "Won't be here for more than a day or two. Just checking in on my girl and Roberto."

"Roberto is the man!" JaKobi decreed.

Cassie was a little more helpful. "We all love him."

"That seems to be the consensus." Joe smiled. "Which is good because I'll be spending more time in Tristholm with Seraphina."

He turned and looked at his daughter. "Just get those portals back up, so I can come to see you more often."

"You know we will." ShadowLily took a bite of her blueberry pancakes. "If you stay another day or two, you could probably avoid the ride back altogether."

Joe looked from her to Tim. "Do you think so?"

"As long as the prince holds up his end of the deal, it's a foregone conclusion." Tim winked at his girl. "ShadowLily could probably handle this one on her own, but we're tagging along to make sure things don't get out of hand."

Cassie slammed her juice down. "Let's fuck this bitch up!"

"Language," Joe chided. "This is a breakfast table, not some bar."

Lorelei grinned. "Actually, it's a breakfast table inside a bar. So swearing is optional but not required."

Joe started laughing. When his belly brushed against the table, the entire thing shook with the depth of his mirth. "Then I'm going to have some more fucking pancakes."

"Not your best work, Dad." ShadowLily poked him with her elbow.

Joe ignored her as he drenched his pancakes in syrup. "What do you expect? I spent the last twenty years not swearing so I could keep you out of the habit. I'm outta practice."

Cassie patted Joe on the leg. "We'll spend an afternoon together sometime, and I'll catch you up to speed with all the new slang."

"I'd be delighted." Joe took a big bite of his blueberry pancakes.

Tim laughed. "Maybe he's not cut out for it. Don't feel any pressure, Joe. You can sit here and not swear too. Some of us like to keep things a little more dignified."

"Damn straight!" JaKobi barked, and the entire table started laughing.

This was what it was all about, saving the world and great times with the people he cared about. He didn't know what would happen today, but he did know there was no one he'd rather experience it with than the Blue Dagger Society.

Eternia missed breakfast, but she met them at the carriage.

"A final word before you leave, adventurers," the goddess called as she walked out onto the covered porch.

Surprising them all, it was Cassie who dropped to one knee first. "Get down, you ungrateful bastards. The goddess is going to give us her blessing."

All of them dropped to a knee in a line, and Eternia moved toward them. She stopped over each adventure touching their heads and saying the words of blessing. When she finished the task, the goddess stepped back and motioned for them to rise.

"Today you face an unknown danger in an unknown land. Take my blessing of protection, and bring home a great victory." Eternia looked as if she were enjoying herself quite a bit.

ShadowLily gave Joe one last hug. "See you soon, Dad."

"Don't do anything crazy." Joe fretted over her.

JaKobi tapped Joe on the shoulder. "Crazy is kind of her specialty."

"I used to like that one." Joe glared at JaKobi's back as he followed Cassie into the carriage.

ShadowLily slapped him playfully on the arm. "You still do." Then she turned and followed the others.

Lorelei pulled Eternia into a hug. "We'll have you back to full strength soon."

"I know you will." The goddess returned the hug warmly and smiled as she watched Lorelei get in the carriage.

Joe pointed at Tim. "You bring my girl home safe."

"I'll do my best."

Joe brushed past him, walking into the inn. "Do better."

Now he sounds like one of my parents.

Turning to face the goddess, Tim couldn't help but smile. "Thank you for seeing us off. We'll return with good news, I promise."

"I see great things in your future adventurer, but first you must conquer the task at hand. Even with my blessing, the victory will be hard-fought." The goddess bent so she could look directly into his eyes. "I believe in you."

Tim's heart almost leapt out of his chest. The goddess believed in them. In their chance for victory. His spirits soared, knowing that the most powerful being in this world was on their side. They could do this. They just had to have a little faith.

Limp Bizkit-style.

"We won't let you down." Tim turned and headed for the carriage.

As he climbed inside, he heard Eternia's voice. "You never do."

This was it. They were about to tackle a brand new dungeon.

He lived for this shit.

CHAPTER THIRTY-NINE

It was a surprise to find the king in the hidden chambers leading to the family vault.

Since Rasmus awoke from the curse Isadora placed upon him he'd been acting differently. There were times Desmond almost doubted himself when the king acted as he normally would, but then he would miss something simple, and his suspicions would be confirmed all over again.

The secret passages were one of the things the king had seemingly forgotten until now.

Desmond knew his duty, and if this thing wasn't the king, he couldn't let it access the family vault. Their greatest treasures resided within, including the Stone of Immoratis. He'd promised the stone to the adventurers, and he'd be damned if he let the imposter tarnish his reputation again.

Sliding his sword free, Desmond followed the imposter.

It was clear the creature had no idea where it was going, which made following it dangerous. At the same time, he couldn't risk letting the thing get to the vault out of his sight. So Desmond settled for waiting farther back when he saw Rasmus make a mistake. The last thing he wanted was to provoke a confrontation when there might not be a need for one quite yet. It was better to know an enemy completely than to jump into battle without a plan.

The winding, turning, cursing rampage went on for hours until finally, they reached the vault.

The ancient door blocking the way into the royal treasury was made of two things, metal and magic. If he had to guess, Desmond would've said magic played the more significant part. Nothing could open the vault except the blood of a royal, a secret not shared with any due to the possible ramifications.

The last thing they needed was people bumping off the royals to try and break in.

Desmond waited around the corner and watched as the thing tried to open the vault. The key fit in the lock, it even turned, but the door wouldn't open. It had to be incredibly frustrating for the king as he tried to figure out what the problem was.

"The problem is, you're not my father." Desmond gritted his teeth instead of screaming in frustration. Now wasn't the proper time or place to confront the creature.

He slid his sword safely back into his scabbard and watched the king rage as he plotted his next course of action.

The adventurers had deployed to deal with Cronos. Their victory might end all his problems, but it could take days. Longer if they continued dying. They might not have that kind of time before this creature grew impatient and started taking more drastic measures.

The king already threw half the damn castle into the dungeons for some perceived slight or another. Desmond had been sneaking people out for weeks, and the king hardly even noticed. It was almost as if he couldn't tell the difference between one person or another. That or the thing didn't care. The rash actions of the imposter were driving more of the nobles into the open arms of Duke Ravenstorm. It was a nightmare.

If only ending these threats was as easy as waking up.

"Why do you deny me?" King Rasmus slammed his hand against the vault door.

Prince Desmond ducked his head back around the corner as he listened to the thing that was wearing his father's body continue to rage. It was horrible looking into the face he'd loved for so long and seeing someone else. The thought of lifting his sword against his father, even knowing that it wasn't him terrified him. He wasn't sure he would be able to do it unless driven by some desperate need.

What he needed now was the support of the nobles, and he'd never have it with the duke spreading honeyed whispers in their ears. Instead, he'd have to rely on himself and the ones he'd hired to take out Cronos if they could only succeed where all other adventurers had failed.

Then it really would feel like waking up from a bad dream.

"I pray to the goddess to grant strength to the adventurers and let them return to the kingdom quickly," Desmond whispered as he turned away from the king and headed back toward his rooms.

The vault was secure for now, but he had to make sure his mother knew the truth. It took him five minutes to work his way through the maze of corridors before he reached the secret entrance in his chambers. When he exited his room, Prince Desmond's guards fell into step behind him, and he went to see the one person he knew he could still trust.

Mom.

If she didn't know what to do, his mother would at least be able to calm his nerves. While he didn't always listen to her counsel, he always appreciated it. It wasn't often he had someone in his life he could count on to tell him the unvarnished truth. That kind of truth was what he needed right now.

The guards who would normally be waiting outside the king's chambers were gone, and the door was open. Desmond pulled his sword free, letting the steel sing its song of death as he raised the blade high above his head.

Desmond pointed at one of his guards. "Go for backup." He turned to the other. "You're with me."

He moved inside the royal chambers, and that was when he saw the foot. It wasn't like the guard had been knocked unconscious, and his foot was out in the open. Something had ripped the limb off, and the bone was sticking out without a body to be seen. The edges looked gnawed-upon.

"Search the rooms. Look for the king and queen." Desmond knew where the king was, but it wouldn't do him any good to tell his guard what was happening.

The guard grunted his acknowledgment and headed down the corridor to the right. Desmond turned left, making his way toward his mother's room. There was another guard down and two of her servants. He wanted to have hope, but this much death could only mean one thing. He just wasn't ready to believe it yet.

There was a body wedged into the doorframe of his mother's room. Almost as if the woman had been trying to hold the door closed when the top half blew apart. His heart went out to her. It was something truly special when an average person became a hero. Desmond would find out her name and remember it always.

He pushed the door open, and the lower half of the unknown woman's body fell over with a *thud*. The prince stepped around her corpse and entered the room, searching for the thing he most feared to find. His mother's welcoming chamber was empty save for the destruction. People tended to forget that his mother was one hell of a sorceress, and it looked as though she'd brought her entire arsenal to bear. There were holes in the stone where her magic had ripped free large chunks. If the fight lasted much longer, she might've brought the whole damn place down on top of her attacker.

Maybe that was what she was trying to do.

He saw the signs of her magic everywhere as he moved through the space. The attacks grew more frantic, and in her panic, it looked like more of them missed their mark. There was blood on the wall and now on the floor.

If whatever attacked his mother was powerful enough to hurt her, they were in real trouble. Desmond wouldn't be able to kill the king alone, he needed to rally more men to his side, but first, he had to know the truth.

There was only one room left, the queen's bedchamber and entrance to the secret tunnels. The door to the room was gone, along with half of the wall that held it. There was black ichor splattered around the room, but it was nothing compared to the blood. Red felt like it was quickly becoming the only color he could see.

The queen was dead.

Not only was she dead, but she'd been savaged like when the hunting hounds caught a hare. Still, even in death, she left him a message. The door to the secret entrance was open, and there was only one person he'd seen down there for hours. Part of him already felt guilty for not being here, but by the time he saw Rasmus, this horrible deed had already happened.

Desmond wanted to fall at his mother's feet and weep. Instead, he pushed the secret door closed and called for help.

The king ran into the queen's chambers, flanked by several guards. "What happened here?"

Desmond met the king's smiling eyes and looked down at the scorch marks on his robes. "Maybe you should tell me."

The scorch marks disappeared, and the smug expression on Rasmus's face changed to predatory. "The prince has killed the queen. Throw him in the dungeon."

Clutching his sword tight, Desmond prepared to fight. Then he looked back at his mother's body. Instead of wading into battle, he sheathed his sword and unlatched his sword belt. He tossed the weapon to his guard.

"I'll come peacefully." Desmond turned his eyes back on the king. "You'll never get what you came for."

Rasmus motioned for the guards to take him away. "I guess we'll see."

It was too late to fight back now, and he might have missed his only chance to do so. Striking the king might have forced him to reveal himself, but it would have also given credence to the tale that he killed his mother. Desmond didn't mind others remembering him as a lot of things, but the prince who killed his mother wasn't one he was willing to live with.

The guards shoved him from the room as they left the queen's chambers and headed toward the dungeon.

"Sir, what should I do?" John, his guard asked, clearly wondering if he should try and attack to free the prince.

Desmond stilled his sword hand with a look. "Go tell Brother Khalil what happened and that the kingdom is counting on his friend now more than ever."

"I will do so." John sprinted away as fast as he could.

This wasn't exactly how he'd expected the day to go after his father had awoken. A celebration, a feast, maybe even the announcement of his marriage to a woman he'd never met. The thought of a monster replacing his father and killing his mother never crossed his mind.

The worst part was he might've brought all of this on himself. If the adventurers hadn't killed Isadora, the thing wearing his father's skin might've never woken up. It would've been easier to live with the thought of his father dead than it was to think of himself as alone in the world as he was now. All his hopes rested on the shoulders of five brave adventurers.

It was too late to offer them more help now. He'd have to hope they had what it took to free everyone from this madness.

The bars closed on his cell. Desmond took a seat, feeling the bittersweet sting of injustice. There was only one thing he could do now. He dropped to his knees and prayed.

"Eternia, please shine your strength upon those in need." He looked toward the ceiling of his cell. "If you can carve out a little free time, I wouldn't mind some assistance in whatever form it can be delivered."

CHAPTER FORTY

The veil wasn't what Tim expected.

The shimmering surface that separated Cronos's land from the rest of the world looked like a wall formed out of the aurora borealis. Tim had expected something much more sinister than some nice shiny lights. If Cronos was such a monster, why did the borders to her land scream, come right in. We have wonderful and tempting things inside?

It could be a trick, like the Sisters of Eternal Bliss, yet he didn't think it was.

He watched the shining lights ripple across the sky. Behind them, he saw nothing. It was almost as if he were looking into a mirror. Whatever Cronos was hiding beyond the veil, they wouldn't be able to figure it out from this side. They could be walking straight into hell itself and wouldn't be able to tell until they were trapped there.

"I'll give her one thing, Cronos doesn't skimp on the theatrics." Cassie huffed as she looked up into the sky.

JaKobi walked toward the veil and tapped his staff against it. The shimmering wall of light clung to it almost like liquid. The ember wizard shook off his staff, and the droplets floated back into the veil.

"The real question is, who wants to go first?" JaKobi looked back at Cassie with hopeful eyes.

The tank rushed forward and slung JaKobi over her shoulder. "Why don't we go in together?"

Then they were gone.

"Catch you on the flip." Lorelei ran to catch up.

ShadowLily gave Tim a quick kiss. "We've got this."

"You know it, baby." Tim took one last look at the outside world and stepped through the veil to join his friends.

The sensation of moving through the magic was more like swimming than walking. The veil clung to him in big thick drops, but he could still breathe like normal. It was almost like he stepped inside a lava lamp as the bright colors of the aurora darted past him.

What felt like an eternity passed before he stepped out on the other side. In reality, he'd probably only been inside the veil for ten or twenty seconds, but with the magic pressing in all around it felt longer.

"Holy shit!" Tim breathed as he took in the valley below them and the sky above.

The aurora rose around them like a dome, but it wasn't the flashing lights that caught his eyes. It was the giant wings flapping in the distance. "Is that a dragon?"

JaKobi turned and started walking toward the exit. "Nope. Not going to happen."

"It'll be fine." Tim turned his buddy back toward the dungeon. "Just don't touch his balls."

Lorelei laughed. "Do dragons have balls? You think they'd get in the way with all the flying and the landing."

In his head, he saw a dragon with great big balls trying to land and rolling onto his back to try and protect them with a giant chat bubble over his head saying "ouchie."

"All I'm saying is, I met a guy in the lobby who died trying to figure out the answer to that question. Didn't ask him how successful the attempt was." Tim laughed at the absurdity of it.

"My guess is this one is a lady." ShadowLily grinned. "Maybe even Cronos herself."

JaKobi looked worried. "Why do you have to say stuff like that? You know if you speak it into existence, it can become true."

Cassie laughed. "That's an old wives tale, and lizards don't have balls on the outside. They have them tucked inside like lady parts."

When everyone stared at her, Cassie shrugged. "What, I passed basic biology."

"There goes that dream." Tim was grinning like an idiot. "You know what I think is weird? No one ever talks about dragon shit."

JaKobi laughed. "That's because if it falls on you, there's no one left to talk about it."

"I mean if the things are eating flocks of sheep and entire towns, the poop problem has to be epic." Tim's face took on a serious mien. "I'm sorry we have to raise taxes again. It's just the kingdom cannot keep up with all this dragon shit."

JaKobi grumbled, "Kill the dragons, down with the shit tax!"

"That's how wars get started." Tim finished his little act and turned to see all three women staring at them with their mouths hanging open.

Cassie was the first one to speak. "I can't believe it's me saying this, but focus up, we've got work to do."

"The poop wars, can you imagine?" ShadowLily shook her head at the thought of it. "This is what my entire life is going to be like from now on. I've decided to live with the man who invented poop wars."

Tim kissed her. "You know you love me."

Lorelei laughed and stopped when she realized everyone was looking at her. "Sorry, I had an image of this happening back in the real world and being on the news."

The spirit archer dropped her voice into a smooth news

reporter tone. "Samantha thought today would be like any other day. Then her life changed forever. When poop falls from the sky, tonight at nine."

ShadowLily was laughing but shaking her head at the same time. "You guys are too much."

"I used to be the reserved one." Lorelei snorted. "Guess that ship has sailed."

Cassie pointed into the sky. "Not sure if you noticed, but the dragon is coming back."

The tank was right. The dragon took a wide banking turn and glided straight for them. The monster's feet were the size of cars. Its legs might as well have been school busses. This wasn't only a dragon. It was a giant among dragons.

The megalodragon.

As it landed in front of them, the dragon's claws tore huge chunks out of the land. The trenches were deep enough they'd have to crawl down into them and up the other side if they wanted to continue. The dragon took a few steps forward, shimmered briefly, and a woman in flowing blue robes edged in white replaced it.

"This is my kingdom. You are not welcome here." Cronos looked over the group of adventurers with disdain. "Leave now, and I will spare your lives."

JaKobi elbowed Tim. "See, this is what I was talking about."

Ignoring his friend completely, Tim addressed Cronos. "We've come on behalf of Prince Desmond to end the trouble plaguing the king."

Cronos laughed. "The king suffers a fate of his making. My offer stands unchanged."

Tim didn't know what offer she was speaking about, and he didn't need to consult the group. They all knew what the stakes were. "Then we refuse."

Cassie stepped to the front of the group. "I'm ready to rumble."

The briefest hint of anger flashed across Cronos' face revealing some hidden rage behind the illusion of serenity. "You've been warned. I will see any further advancement into my realm as hostile, and my forces will attack you on sight. I doubt you'll make it past my defenders, but if you do."

Cronos turned away from them and ran. The ground shook as she changed from a beautiful woman into a terrifying dragon. Fire belched from her mouth as she took to the air, igniting the wet grass and trees before she flew off into the distance.

"Well, that went well." Cassie grinned. "Must not be all that if we're not dead."

Lorelei put an arm around the tank's shoulders. "Or she finds the task beneath her. I mean, look at that."

Even in such a brief visit for Cronos to taunt them, the devastation to the clearing they stood in was immense. Tim didn't want to think what one of those claws would do to him, or the fire for that matter. They couldn't have to face down a dragon to win the dungeon, did they? It didn't seem like a fair test of skill, but he knew if the game put an obstacle in their path, there had to be a way to win.

All they had to do was find it.

"Since they know we're here, Cassie in the front, standard battle formations for everyone else." Tim looked down at the ground. "Until we know there aren't any traps, we take it slow and steady."

There was a path leading through the grass and into the trees of the forest. The logic was simple enough for all of them to follow. Going down the path would lead them to their next fight. There would be time to worry about Cronos if they made it that far. For now, they had to focus on what was right in front of them.

"You got it." Cassie took command. "Stay behind me, and don't get fucking dead."

JaKobi nudged Tim. "That's some award-winning advice right there."

Tim nodded. Staying behind the tank was gaming one-oh-one.

If you didn't want to go splat, there were certain rules to follow. While merciless devs could break all rules, they tended not to break that big one unless it led to a devastating mechanic.

He took his spot at the back of the group. This was it. They were finally on their way.

CHAPTER FORTY-ONE

The clear shimmering dome of the boss area was right in front of them.

Cronos' realm was different from the way they normally fought bosses. Most of the time, they could see inside the area and were given a small advantage in the terrain before the fight started. This time they couldn't see a thing. It was like they were looking into a mirror, and Tim didn't like it one bit.

Cassie looked over her shoulder. "Buff and ready check."

"It's like we're pros." Tim couldn't help but smile.

There was a point when a person started gaming with people long enough they didn't check their companions' buffs anymore. They assumed they were in place. Even then, after a close win, some of the best gamers would make a statement like, "We did that without the crit buff." Everyone cringed at first. Then they realize they beat a boss while missing out on a five percent bonus the entire time.

Thus making them completely badass.

When they first entered the game, Tim was always the one calling these minor things out, but now Cassie was taking over, and he loved it. So he didn't have to look at his user interface to check, Tim cast all three of his buffs. He felt the other players' buffs increasing his stats as well.

"Follow Cassie. I'll try and call out the changes as they come." Tim looked at everyone. "If you see something weird, say something."

Cassie walked into the shimmering mist. "Don't fuck this up. Mama wants to leave this dungeon with a new pair of dragon skin shoes."

"That's cold." JaKobi gave Tim a high five and went through the barrier.

Tim followed the ember wizard through the mist and ended up standing in a clearing much like Isadora's. The ground wasn't littered with scorch marks so they had that going for them, but there was blood on the closely shaved grass.

Was that shit?

"I thought we were kidding about the dragon shit." Tim looked at the rather large pile of droppings and knew they were too small to have come from the dragon.

Lorelei kicked a pile with the toe of her boot. "It's probably a bear."

"Bear?" ShadowLily looked worried, like she was having a *The Revenant* flashback. "Are you sure?"

Lorelei bent and looked at a couple of different piles. "I guess it could be a werebear or something mixed with a bear, but yeah, for the most part, I'm pretty sure."

She stood with the expression on her face saying she was about to wreck their day. "There's also more than one."

"This is going to be interesting." Cassie started moving forward. "Might as well find out what we're in for."

Tim kept his head moving from side to side, but there was nowhere a giant-ass bear could be hiding, let alone two. There was a pillar of rocks to their left, but while they could hide behind it in ones and twos, it wasn't big enough to hide a bear unless it was a cub.

A man walked into the clearing wearing simple overalls with a wide-brimmed hat. The man had the look of a farmer. If it wasn't for the two bear cubs at his side, that's exactly what he would have been. Maybe it was more like he was a breeder. A quick look at his official title said bear farmer, whatever that meant.

"Mistress said you'd be coming." He spat on the ground. "Ain't normally old Eli's place to be getting involved with the killing. I'm a farmer by nature, but Mistress says do a thing, and it's best get done before she comes back to check on it."

The two small grizzly cubs rubbed against his legs like cats. "Now it ain't my place to be offering you a deal, but walk away from this. It'd be in your best interest. You seem like good folks. I'd hate for you to die."

Tim appreciated the deal, but they couldn't walk away. No matter what Eli thought of Cronos he was pretty sure she was as evil as they came. It was like someone saying they grew organic when really they were out there spraying their GMO with pesticides. Most of the time, when things sounded too good to be true, they were a scam. Whatever Cronos offered wouldn't change what she'd done to the king.

Good people didn't fight dirty.

"We'd love to take you up on the offer, but first, you'd have to tell us what she did to the king and how to fix it." If Cronos guaranteed the real king or the death of the imposter, maybe they could work something out.

Eli pulled a Bermuda grass seed head from the tip of his cap and started chewing on the end. "All that's above old Eli's pay grade. If you're spoiling for a fight, then it's a fight you'll have."

The bear farmer stepped back and easily doubled in size. The two small scythes the boss held appeared to be all the weaponry Eli needed, as long as you included the giant bear trap strapped to his back. Tim wasn't sure that counted as a weapon, but it could be deadly in the right situations.

Tim had no idea what direction this fight was going to go in, but for now, he decided to be happy he had three targets to cast Curse of Giving on instead of one.

"I can't wait to try bear for the first time." Cassie charged into battle with a scream that shook the ground.

Tim immediately noticed that his curse on the bears wasn't doing any damage but didn't know what he could do about it. Eli and the bears weren't showing any buffs he could remove, and his curse was ticking away on the boss himself. This was going to be a long fight if they couldn't kill the bears. He wasn't crazy about Cassie taking all the extra damage.

"The bears aren't taking damage. Focus on Eli!" Tim shouted as he fired a blast of Curse of Sacrifice and followed it up with a quick Healing Orb on himself to spread Hydration to anyone that had taken damage.

Cassie seemed to have things in hand so it gave him time to look around. Maybe now that the fight had started, there would be some clue about what they had to do to harm the bears. It was amazing what details the devs would slip in as a fight progressed. As for now, he wasn't picking up anything new, but that didn't mean it wouldn't happen soon.

Tim normally hated fights where the bosses had pets that players couldn't kill. In those situations, the players usually had to deal with an additional mechanic from the pet. On the plus side, in those fights, the pets didn't do a lot of additional damage, and all they had to do was beat the mechanic and kill the boss. It didn't get much easier than that.

Unless there was a twist.

ShadowLily was having a hell of a time trying to dart in and out of the two bears and the boss while doing damage. So far she'd managed to be nearly flawless, but it was a risky game that she couldn't win forever. She might have to take a back seat on the

DPS until they figured out what mechanics the boss had in store for them.

The words to Behold My Power tumbled from his lips effortlessly, like he'd said them a million times before. As the first shockwave of damage tore through his group, Eli met his eye and smiled. For the first time in a fight, Tim had the feeling he fucked up, and it was going to cost them.

Eli grunted when Cassie hit him, but he wasn't taking damage anymore. With each blow of her staff, he grew slightly larger, and the bears took on a red hue. Tim was pretty sure he'd figured out the game. If they hit Eli when he wasn't supposed to be taking damage, he got a little bit bigger, and the bears got a little bit more enraged. If they hit the bears at the wrong time, they would also get bigger, and Eli would get enraged.

It was a hell of a tightrope to have to walk.

Paying attention in this fight was going to be a huge deal. Their entire success or failure depended on how quickly they could manage the switches. By casting Behold My Power before knowing what the fight's mechanics were, he was putting them in a hole. When his spell hit, the bears were going to get a huge enrage boost, and Eli might grow a foot.

How had he been so wrong about the mechanics early on?

At least the mistake was early enough in the fight they would recover, but Tim had to warn the others. "No long-lasting spells. If we miss a change, it's going to suck."

Behold My Power hit and didn't do a damn thing to Cassie's health, but Eli grew a little bit larger, and the bears were doing slightly more damage. They were still in Phase One so everything was manageable, but they sure weren't making things easy on themselves.

"You were saying!" Cassie let out an evil laugh as she redirected an attack from one of the bears into Eli.

Eli was taking damage again. There wasn't time for fancy talking. The changes came too quickly. There was only one thing that would get them on track fast enough. He had to make the calls.

"Switch!" Tim watched as everyone followed Cassie's lead and started damaging Eli again.

The boss was down ten percent in health, and the bears were slightly behind him. When they switched damage back to Eli, the animals he controlled stayed enraged and larger than when the fight started. So the effects of their missed attacks were cumulative for the entire fight.

This was going to be rough.

Tim knew that he couldn't stop some of his attacks from having their DOTs linger on the boss, but then he noticed during the next switch that all of the DOTs only ticked once then faded away. It meant they could use spells with DOTs, but they would risk either the boss or the bears taking one tick of damage if they didn't time the switch right. He wasn't going to tell the others what to do yet, but for now, Curse of Giving was off the table.

Tim needed to stick with the pure healing of Healing Orb and Curse of Sacrifice for now. He wasn't willing to keep putting stacks on the enemy only to make them stronger. Divine Light would also work to boost healing and DPS, but only if he timed it right. The spell did his most single-target damage, and landing a hit at the wrong time wouldn't help their cause any more than casting DOTs would.

"Switch!" Tim cried as Eli took a zero percent fireball to the head.

The bears were still small enough they were taking a good amount of damage per attack. The real question he had to face now was, did they have to kill the bears simultaneously to avoid a larger enrage or could they pick them off one at a time?

"Focus on one of the bears until it gets to ten percent, then switch to the other." It'd be a waste of time if they didn't need to kill them at the same time, but if they did, it was the only way they had a chance.

"Switch!" All their damage went back to Eli.

Tim blasted the bear farmer with Divine Light and Curse of Sacrifice on repeat until he needed to use Healing Orb. Then he kicked himself. Early in the fight, he should've used his Hex Beast instead of Behold My Power, but he couldn't do it now. Not until the next switch.

Eli hit eighty percent health and sent out a blast wave that dropped them all to fifty percent health instantly. Thankfully his Healing Storm didn't cause any damage, and Tim could use it as long as his mana was in a good place. Before he could cast the big heal, he had to cast three quick Healing Orbs to get Hydration on everyone. Then he put his hands in the air and called down Eternia's healing rain.

Their health was back in a good place and climbing rapidly. Tim cut off the costly spell and let the HOTs finish carrying them to full health. So far, nothing too crazy happened, and the fight was going well. There were a few nicks to heal with ShadowLily, but Lorelei and JaKobi had gone relatively untouched until the boss' special attack at eighty percent.

ShadowLily had a look of frustration on her face that melee characters get when the boss is always moving around, and getting the proper positioning sucks ass. It was hard not to get hit with four claws, two scythes, and two sets of big-ass bear jaws all striking simultaneously. It was a wonder they hadn't gutted Cassie yet, but the tank was redirecting blows and dancing from side to side to keep them guessing.

Watching the tank do her thing was impressive. He'd never have the courage to stand close and eat all that damage. Getting hit in *The Etheric Coast* still hurt. Getting ripped apart by bear claws might not have the same sting it did in the real world, but she was feeling every damn hit. Tim had never been more impressed with their tank's fortitude than he was now.

Not that Cassie's constant movement made things any easier for ShadowLily. The mist slayer had to sync her attacks to Cassie's rhythm, and it was throwing her off. While she was frustrated, he was happy she wasn't going YOLO and taking a bunch of damage just to get her numbers back up.

The first bear hit ten percent health, and they all switched over to the next target without being told. In some groups switching off the target they wanted to be kept alive would have felt like a minor miracle, but not with Blue Dagger Society. They managed to burn another five percent before the animal stopped taking damage and they needed to switch back to the boss.

"Switch!" Tim called as he sent Curse of Sacrifice straight at Eli.

A blast of pure sunlight rocketed past him and through one of the bears before striking Eli. The bear's health didn't move, but the red tint around Eli grew a fraction darker.

"Shit, sorry guys!" JaKobi called as he blasted Eli again, this time making sure not to hit the cub.

The attack dropped the boss' health to seventy-five percent, and he let out a roar of rage. With a single motion, he swept them back to the far side of the clearing. Tim tried to move, but he was stuck in place while Eli used one of his scythes to cut the palm of each hand before placing them on top of the bear's heads.

The bear at ninety percent health snarled and growled as it stripped his health away, while the bear at five percent looked content as its health bar started to fill back up. When the boss stopped his cast, one bear was sitting at fifty percent and the other at forty-five.

They needed a new plan.

If Eli could equalize the bears' health, then two things were probably true. They needed to kill the bears simultaneously to avoid an enrage mechanic, and it didn't matter if they split the damage as long as they didn't kill one of them. He was trying to think of a plan when Eli called to them.

"Nothing I hate worse than vermin that won't take a hint." The bear farmer pulled the giant trap from his back and set it on the ground. Then he wound it up like a set of clacking teeth and let it go.

Tim couldn't believe Eli's big move was one wind-up bear trap. Seriously, they wouldn't even have to try and avoid it. This was like asking an NFL running back to dodge a parked car. When something was that easy, it had to be a trap.

"Get ready for it," Tim called.

The twinkle returned to Eli's eyes as he clapped his hands. Then the one trap turned into ten, then a hundred. They were clacking toward them in waves, but there were gaps in the pattern. All they had to do was move into the empty spots without getting hit.

Tim was pretty sure each of them could survive being hit by a single trap. One wasn't a problem. The real issue was they were coming in waves, so if they couldn't get the person out in time, they'd keep getting hit by them until they looked like the victim in one of the *Saw* films.

The only person that their group needed to worry about was JaKobi. Tim was pretty sure he could handle this, but he wasn't going to fare too much better than his fireball-hurling buddy. Everyone else in their party might as well have been a ninja-like dodge master. It was too late to get the entire benefit now, but if this attack came again later, it would be the perfect time for Who Needs a Shield. The extra dodge percentage would give the ember wizard a fighting chance.

"Son of a—" JaKobi let out a startled cry as Cassie used her chain to yank him toward her.

She pulled JaKobi onto her back and dodged the next set of traps with ease. "Don't you worry about a thing, baby. I've got you."

It was awkward seeing the five-foot-nothing girl giving a piggyback ride to the six-foot-tall man. His chest towered over her shoulders, leaving his arms free to cast spells if he needed to.

"Good morning, Vietnam!" JaKobi cried in his best Robin Williams voice as he started blasting fireballs toward the boss.

The fire stopped two feet short of the boss, and ash washed over the three of them like a cool autumn breeze. "Totally unfair."

"Only person who should be saying that is me." Cassie dumped JaKobi on his ass as the last of the traps went clacking past them.

Eli stepped forward with his hand scythes at the ready. "What are you waiting for?"

"Just seeing if that ugly corn-fed mug of yours was up for round two." Cassie swirled her bō staff around her like a tornado.

"Attack!" Eli sent the bears running toward them, his eyes gleaming with malicious purpose.

Tim had a sinking feeling in his chest just like the seconds after casting Behold My Power in the first phase of the fight. "Check who's taking damage before going wild!"

As he finished screaming the order, he saw a fireball launch into the sky.

"Couldn't be sure," JaKobi called as he waited to see if the bears took damage from the tank before attacking again.

Lorelei fired an arrow, just nicking one of the bears. "It's Eli!"

Cassie picked up the bears as the rest of the group transferred their attacks to the boss. They had to make a push here. The internal clock in Tim's head was screaming that the fight was taking too fucking long and if they didn't speed things up, they would get stomped at the end. Two enraged bears and a boss would be a huge problem. One he didn't think they would survive for more than a few seconds.

"When he switches back, try to kill one of those bears." Tim knew they would be pushing their luck, but the healing was light, and their DPS was pretty on point to make a big push.

Lorelei tried to be the voice of reason. "Eli isn't even at fifty percent yet."

Cassie laughed out loud. "I can't believe I'm the one saying this, but we should wait."

"Come on, where's your sense of adventure? Tim called. "Let's get a little reckless."

JaKobi blasted Eli with his Phoenix. "Uh oh, my man Tim's got one of his crazy plans, and I'm totally on board."

"Is it the 'we're all going to die' kind?" ShadowLily mocked as she rolled in front of the boss and slashed him three times before fading behind him and landing a critical backstab.

Tim laughed. "Only one way to find out."

"Switch!"

As one, the entire group pivoted to the bear on Eli's right with forty-five percent health. With every single one of them focused on the bear, it went down quickly. Thirty percent, Tim cast three Healing Orb. Twenty percent, he cast Curse of Giving on the other bear. Ten percent seemed like the right time to drop Who Needs a Shield.

The bear on the right died, and the remaining bear instantly turned into a full-sized grizzly. There was a bright red shine to it, and Tim knew it was fully enraged. He looked over at the creature knowing this next part was going to hurt. The buffs on the bear said it was doing three hundred percent increased damage, and they were about to switch into a phase where they couldn't even hurt the damn thing, let alone kill it.

Maybe this wasn't the best plan he ever had.

"Switch!" Tim screamed like he was a Roman general. "I want this bear fucker hurting!"

He felt some of the tension lift as the group laughed at him as much as what he said. Tim hit Eli with Curse of Giving. He figured that if he hit him right at the beginning of a switch, then the timing would be about spot on or close enough that he was willing to risk it. His DPS during the fight wasn't going to be an issue. The real problem was going to be keeping Cassie alive.

There were a few seconds left before he could activate his plan. If he did it too soon, they'd miss the switch, and Eli would also get a huge boost in DPS. If he acted too late, they wouldn't get the big chunk of the bear they needed to take it out. He fell into a rhythm of casting Curse of Sacrifice on repeat until he executed the next phase of his new plan.

Tim cast Hex of the Shattered Beast on Cassie. He never considered that the beast might attack Eli when this was over because he was the boss. He'd hoped that it would go after the thing doing the most damage, which right now was the enraged grizzly.

Cassie was taking so much damage it was all he could do to keep up with it. Tim made a mental note that if he wanted to try this fight again, they needed to wait at least one more phase before hitting the crazy and killing one of the bears early as he asked them to do this time. That was a move they should've only pulled when they out-geared the dungeon and not during their first attempt at the fight.

"Switch," Tim screamed as his beast started to move.

The red-blurring Golden Retriever slammed into the bear and burst out the other side in a sea of red mist. Even being enraged and taking less damage than usual the single attack stripped away half of its health. The beam of pure sunlight that hit it next cut that number in half again. Five seconds later and the enraged grizzly hit the ground as dead as its twin.

Eli waved his hand again, sending them back to the beginning opposite side of the clearing as he started pacing back and forth. "You monsters killed my babies!"

Eli kept screaming the words at them. Each time he did, the boss grew in size. The small farmer was now over twelve feet tall, and his skin was tinged a pinkish color. "Those bears were my fucking family!"

Instead of bear traps, Eli started spinning in a circle, and hand scythes flew out from him in intervals. Tim tried casting Disturbance out of desperation, but it didn't stop the attack. There was still a pattern to the scythes, but they came on twice as fast as the bear traps had, and all of them were getting nicked. When they came out of this phase, the only thing that mattered was burning the boss down until he lay dead at their feet.

They wouldn't make it through another round, especially if Eli kept getting stronger now that the bears were dead.

"I want you to light this guy up like the Fourth of July. Every attack, every buff, anything you have, we need it now." Tim sent out a small burst of Healing Storm and a round of Healing Orb.

Eli didn't wait for his scythes to stop flying before he charged at Cassie. Tim's world turned into pure madness, but he shut out all the distractions and focused on what mattered. The healing. It was nice that he had a single-target spell for damage that didn't cost a boatload of mana. He could cast Curse of Sacrifice almost all day, as long as he didn't let it zap too much of his health before topping himself off.

The boss hit fifteen percent health, but there wasn't a switch to save him this time. The group continued hammering away, and the bear farmer didn't have a chance. ShadowLily rolled in front of the boss and leapt up, jabbing both of her daggers deep into Eli's stomach. She ripped them out wide, splattering herself in gore. As Eli fell to the side, clutching the horrible wound, he gave one final gurgle before the rest of the group finished him off with ease.

The body disappeared in a beautiful swirl of golden motes, and the blood on ShadowLily slowly did the same. It was crazy to watch the red drops lift into the air and burst into golden globes of light before drifting to the heavens.

ShadowLily let out a battle cry. "We did it!"

All of them raised their weapons into their air and screamed!

Let Cronos hear their cries and learn of their victory. They were coming for her.

CHAPTER FORTY-TWO

"That was something else." Cassie looked at Tim. "Have you ever seen anything like that?"

Tim shook his head. "You mean bear traps acting like The Joker's teeth? I've never seen anything like that in a game."

"Dude, that was awesome." JaKobi pumped his fist, looking at the chest longingly before turning to look at his girlfriend. "Except for when you had to carry me."

Cassie kissed him. "If the choice is between you getting killed and me carrying you, you better climb aboard."

"I plan on doing that later." JaKobi winked.

Lorelei moved toward the chest. "If I can't get laid, I'm getting loot first."

No one objected.

Tim was looking forward to returning to the desert, if for nothing else so Lorelei could spend some time with Neema. Their spirit archer deserved to be happy, and right now, she was the only one having to struggle without their significant other around. It was funny how he never really liked being in a relationship until it was with the right one. Then he couldn't imagine his life without her.

"Bow of the Slaughtered Bear." Lorelei turned, firing a series of arrows across the clearing to test the new weapon. "Adds a DOT and increased endurance."

The old bow disappeared off her back, and the new one replaced it. "Normally, I'd pass, but the base damage is so much higher, it doesn't matter what the other stats are."

Tim had found a few items like that in games. Sometimes it was on purpose, and sometimes his new favorite weapon got hit with the nerf hammer. Nothing sucked worse than logging into the game he loved and seeing his stats reduced drastically. Thankfully that hadn't happened in *The Etheric Coast*, and he hoped it never would.

Instead of going to the chest, Tim hugged Lorelei. "We'll be back in the desert soon."

"Ain't had nothing 'twixt these nethers that don't run on hand power in a good long while." Lorelei looked dead serious.

JaKobi was grinning. "I could stand to hear more."

Cassie slapped him in the chest. "You forgot Mal's part."

"No, I didn't. I just wanted to hear more." JaKobi snickered.

Tim felt the oomph when Cassie hit the wizard in the stomach. "Don't you ruin my *Firefly* with your lecherous ways."

"I'll lech if I want to." JaKobi laughed and pulled the feisty tank into his arms. "Just maybe out of earshot." He rubbed his stomach and winced.

A quick Healing Orb took care of the worst of JaKobi's damage. "I thought it was kinda funny."

"I was impressed you got Lorelei to watch it with you." ShadowLily looked around at the group. "What? She doesn't strike me as a science fiction kind of girl."

Lorelei laughed. "I wasn't until these two snuck me into a video session. Kind of breaks the game immersion, but the show was worth it."

He'd never even thought about trying to stream outside content inside the game. Things seemed too chaotic for something as simple as watching movies. Plus, he kind of liked stepping out of the real world for a bit. Sure, he missed watching his old favorites, but when he wanted entertainment, all he had to do was go downstairs and find Gaston. The assassin was always up to something.

"*Firefly* is awesome. Of that, there is no doubt." Tim motioned to the chest. "Ladies first."

Cassie tapped him on the chest as she passed. "This is what being a gentleman looks like, JaKobi. Take notes."

"I brought chocolate." JaKobi held up a small bar wrapped in waxed paper.

Cassie snatched the chocolate out of his hands. "I take it back. You're doing just fine."

ShadowLily nudged Tim. "What, no chocolate for me?"

"Nope, just that good loving," Tim replied, cool as a cucumber.

Laughing, the mist slayer moved toward the chest. "I think I'll settle for what's behind door number two."

"Sick burn!" JaKobi doubled over with laughter.

Tim clutched his back, looking wounded. "Et tu, JaKobi. Et tu."

Ignoring the two men, ShadowLily placed her hand on the chest and turned, looking excited. "Hat of the Dubious Farmer."

ShadowLily equipped the hat, but with her leather armor, she looked more like Anne Bonny than a farmer. "Increased dexterity, and dodge. Plus, I kind of like how it looks."

"That's because it's hot." Tim liked a woman who didn't take shit from anyone, and no one represented that like his favorite female pirate.

Cassie ran toward the chest. "Let's hope three is still the luckiest number."

The tank placed her hand on the chest. "Leather Pants of the Dancing Bears." She equipped the new pants and smiled wider than a kid at summer camp getting their first delivery from home.

"Increases bonuses to all my new skills, and a huge boost to dexterity."

"Man, this loot is all awesome." JaKobi walked toward the chest. "Book of Burning Shadows."

He cast a fireball watching the trail of flames it left in its wake. "Seriously makes my fireball leave a trail that does damage to anything it hits. I love this game."

Tim's excitement built as he laid his hand on the chest. He felt a small surge of power, and the familiar message appeared.

Item Received: Bearhide Wrist Guards of the Faithful

Dalton Red was a priest in the western woods. For a time, he lost himself in nature and lived among the bears. When he returned from the wild, he was a changed man, a healer who damaged the guilty to heal the needy. Eventually, the villagers drove him off, but his memory lives on in these wrist guards through those who wear them.

+1 Endurance +1 Wisdom

Special Ability: The Bear Necessities

If you take damage that would've normally killed you, you will reset to one hit point. The price of this miraculous ability is the low, low cost of seventy percent of your remaining party members' hit points.

Not exactly the piece of gear he was expecting, but the special ability was ridiculous. It was almost like a resurrection spell. The only difference was that not only would he need to be able to heal himself immediately, but everyone in Tim's group would need a huge amount of heals to get back in the fight. One wrong move while any of that was going on, and they were all dead.

Still, the wrist guards would give them a chance when everything else failed.

"Guys, you're not going to believe this." Tim gave them the lowdown on his new item.

JaKobi gave him a wicked high five. "That's fucking awesome, bro!"

"Let's see if you're saying that after he zaps you to thirty percent health." Cassie laughed, but her expression turned serious as she looked at Tim. "If you think that gadget of yours is going to activate, try and give me a little warning so I can pop a cooldown."

Tim nodded. If there was time, he would give her all the warning he could.

"Are you guys ready to move out?" Tim looked around at the group, wondering if anyone needed to take a break.

No one said anything, and Cassie moved to the front of the pack. "Follow me, but I don't think you're going to like it."

"What do you mean?" Tim looked around the clearing and the path leading to their next destination and didn't see anything amiss.

"You have to look up." Cassie pointed into the distance.

Lorelei blinked a few times and whispered, "Is that a fucking castle?"

"Of course Cronos would have a floating castle." ShadowLily's eyes narrowed. "I doubt she's flying supplies up there on her back so there has to be another way in."

Tim looked up at the castle and at the expectant faces of his group. "My guess is we'll find the way up at the end of this path."

"And another boss to go with it." Cassie was grinning as she thought about the chance for more loot.

"All right, Cassie, lead the way." The tank turned and led them into the forest, and Tim followed.

If Eternia told him he'd be fighting in a castle in the sky by the end of the day, Tim would've called her a nutter. Maybe not to her face, mind you, but he would've thought it. Castles in the sky felt like endgame stuff, not the kind of thing you took on while climbing the ranks. Still, it was beautiful, and Tim was happy Cassie pointed it out to him.

The group started walking, and he knew that this was their day. Nothing would stop them now.

"Whoa," JaKobi said with wonder in his voice.

Tim felt the same way. They were closer to the castle in the sky now, and while it was magnificent, it was the magical lift in the town below that claimed their attention. A disk the size of a city block rose into the air carrying carts and people to move the supplies. Then after twenty minutes, it descended again, right into the shimmering mist of the boss dome covering the building.

"At least we know right where the boss is." Cassie sounded ready to rumble.

Tim looked down in the valley and couldn't disagree, but it was the long trip down and through the town that had him worried. With no trash mobs between the entrance and the first boss, this might be the only place they would run into some unless the castle was full of them. His best guess was still that they wouldn't reach the boss without fighting something else first.

Moving down the switchbacks into the valley didn't trigger a fight or a boulder chasing them, so things were going relatively well so far. The pine trees faded, and orchards of citrus and fruit replaced them. The farmland was empty, which seemed odd in the middle of the day unless they expected trouble or were luring them into a trap.

"It's a little too quiet." Lorelei had her bow out as she scanned the horizon for threats.

JaKobi bounced a small ball of flames between his hands. "It's like that moment in horror or action movies right before all hell breaks loose."

"Thanks for calming my nerves." ShadowLily gave the wizard a dirty look before dropping into stealth.

Tim tried to ease the tension. "What you can't see is her putting a sign on your back that says, eat the wizard first."

When no one laughed, he continued. "Come on guys, when

have we ever been stopped by a little trash? It's not like Cronos is going to appear and slaughter us."

"I hate it when he's right." Cassie picked up the pace.

On the outskirts of town, they saw their first two people. The men were huge, and their arms looked like the kind of things Mr. Olympia would be jealous about. When Tim noticed the giant axes slung over their backs, he realized why their arms were so big. The axes weren't Paul Bunyon big, but they were larger than anything he'd seen at the hardware store by far.

"Those ax heads have to be three feet long." Cassie whistled. "Let's hope they only know how to use them to fell trees."

Tim nudged her forward. "I'm dying to find out."

Cassie moved forward and whistled to get the lumberjacks' attention. "How many fucks, does a woodchuck fuck, when a woodchuck chucks fucks."

"Say it again, sister!" JaKobi let loose with a massive fireball.

Tim cast Curse of Giving on both of the lumberjacks and couldn't stop from smiling. Sure, she replaced some of the chucks with fucks, but for some reason, he was cracking up. He wondered what the lumberjacks must be thinking. Both of them might be questioning if it was okay for them to cut someone in half who was clearly mentally challenged.

Cassie answered that question for them when her staff brushed aside their wild swings with ease and conked them on their heads. Fire washed over them, and arrows started to appear in their arms as if they ran into a rabid porcupine.

Curse of Sacrifice wiped out most of the damage Cassie had taken so far, and the lumberjacks were already under fifty percent health.

ShadowLily appeared behind one of the targets, slamming her daggers into the lumberjack's back before rolling under a swing aimed at Cassie and making the same attack from the front. When the lumberjack staggered forward, she slit his throat and danced away.

One of them was down. Now it was mop-up duty.

Seeing the other man fall enraged the remaining lumberjack and he started swinging his ax in wide arcs, forcing them to retreat. His skin was pulsing red, and Tim felt lucky that his health was only at fifteen percent.

Cassie and the remaining lumberjack clashed, and despite her new class, she was staggered by the increased damage. It was everything Tim could do to keep her alive as the rest of the group finished off the target.

"You were saying something about trash being easy?" Cassie looked at the two dead lumberjacks as their bodies turned into golden swirls of light.

Tim nodded. It was a fair assessment of the fight. "Looks like we shouldn't kill them when their health is too far apart."

"You think?" ShadowLily quipped.

"Yeah, I'll watch out for that next time." Cassie laced her words with sarcasm that would have made Denis Leary proud.

I just want coffee-flavored coffee.

They lived so everything was fine, and they figured out that the health thing might be a recurring mechanic in some of the upcoming fights. All they had to do was learn from the first couple of trash packs, then clean them up in a rinse and repeat fashion. These fights weren't there to stress them out but to teach them mechanics and give them a little coin since the bosses mostly just dropped loot.

All they had to do now was keep their wits about them, and they'd make it to the boss without an issue.

The next group was two lumberjacks and a man with brass knuckles. "Remember, try not to kill any of them until they're all under ten percent. Then we should try and AOE them down."

Cassie pointed at Tim. "Get that shield thing ready."

He wanted to cast his Hex Beast, but it was too unpredictable in this scenario. If the beast took out one of the men early and two of them enraged, they would be in trouble. Instead, he had Who

Needs a Shield tucked away in the back of his mind if things turned sour.

Three Curse of Giving casts were enough to keep Cassie at full health, letting him have the option of using other skills for fun. Curse of Sacrifice and Divine Light were his skills of choice for the moment, and doing lots of damage was the name of the game as Tim used his tracks to try and balance out the enemies' health. At around fifteen percent health ShadowLily blinked out of existence, and Tim knew one of the men would die in the next five seconds.

"Blast 'em." Tim started channeling Flame Burst at all three targets like he was the pyrotechnics director at a monster truck rally.

JaKobi hesitated. "I thought you said ten percent?"

"Just go," Tim yelled as ShadowLily appeared and started her attack.

"Oh shit!" The ember wizard caught on to what was about to happen and fired his Sunbeam.

Lorelei was moving forward with a dexterity that would have made Legolas jealous as she pounded arrows into the last target.

Just like that, the fight was over.

"That went much better." Cassie grinned. "I didn't feel a thing."

Lorelei pointed in the distance. "How do you feel about a little five on five?"

"Not as good as I felt about three on five," Cassie grumbled.

It turned out five wasn't much harder than three as long as Cassie could keep control of all five of them herself. If one of them got away, it turned the fight into a bit of a mess. Thankfully with five Curse of Giving casts on her, Tim had plenty of time to use Snare or do straight DPS to even out the enemies' health.

They moved through the town picking off groups of two, three, and five until they reached the building housing the magical lift and the boss. He'd almost expected the doors to open and for ten men to stream out as the final battle before the boss fight, but nothing as exciting as that occurred. They stood in an empty square facing the building. There was nothing left for them to do but open the door and get to work.

"Buff up bitches." Cassie cast her buffs on the group.

Tim reapplied his buffs to the party and moved into his spot behind the tank. "Lead the way."

Cassie smashed her staff against the giant wooden doors. "Open Sesame."

The doors swung open, and she turned to look at the group. "That's never worked before."

"I don't think it was the words." Tim pointed past Cassie to a man standing in the center of the circular room.

He was beckoning them to step inside.

Cassie looked back at Tim. "I have a bad feeling about this."

"That's my line." Tim winked at her. "Let's go kick that little guy's ass."

JaKobi leaned in. "They said that when I had Oddjob and Proximity mines, it didn't work out well for the big guys."

"Encouragement, you big oaf." ShadowLily elbowed the wizard in the ribs like Cassie would have.

JaKobi rubbed the injury smiling. "What? It's not like my girl ever loses a fight."

"Damn right, I don't." Cassie stepped into the building. "Hey Shorty, I got something for you."

The boss' laughter filled their ears.

CHAPTER FORTY-THREE

"Please come inside." The gatekeeper beckoned.

The boss stood before them, all of five feet tall as he hunched with age. His walking staff was more of a cane the way he clung to it with quiet desperation, and yet he beckoned them inside with open arms.

Cassie led the way, moving slowly and looking for traps, but Tim doubted she would find any. This was their next boss fight, and while the gatekeeper might not look like much now, that didn't have to last forever. Or he'd have help as the farmer did with the bears. Whatever was going to happen, Tim knew they weren't going to be facing down a little old man. Heroes didn't go around kicking the crap out of senior citizens.

"I just need to see your token, and we'll get you straight up to Mistress Cronos." The gatekeeper held out his hand.

Cassie looked back at Tim and mouthed, "Token?" When he gave a slight shake of the head, she addressed the boss. "Think of us as uninvited guests."

"Oh, that simply won't do." The gatekeeper snapped his fingers, and the doors to the lift closed, sealing them all inside the room.

He pulled a pair of reading glasses from inside his robes. "Cronos only accepts *invited* guests. As for the uninvited?" He motioned behind himself. "I have help."

Two men walked out from hidden rooms on either side of the gatekeeper. The fuckers were gigantic. If the members of their group were midsized compacts, these two brutes were Greyhound buses. They made Shaq look like he was an itty-bitty little guy, and anyone who played *Shaq Fu* knew that wasn't the case.

Tim would've called them monsters, but they were giant humans with biceps the size of semi-truck cabs. Before the doors closed, Tim spotted huge cranks in each room. The gatekeeper's helpers must've lifted the platform by cranking it like Arnold at the beginning of Conan when his captor forced him to spin the wheel of pain.

There wasn't a lift?

Magic was a real trip sometimes. His mind started wondering if the cranks were necessary or if whatever moved the platform up to the castle was illusioned so they couldn't see it. If the cranks were only for show, the two men could be highly trained fighters. At this point, he wouldn't put anything past Cronos.

"Normally, I'd offer the ill-informed a chance to leave, but the bear farmer was my friend." The gatekeeper's eyes glowed red for a moment. "I am not adjusting to the news of his passing well."

The older man snapped his fingers again. He lifted into the air on a small disk of pure magic, where he hovered over the shoulders of the two giant guards. Sledgehammers with heads the size of a small SUV appeared next to the men, and they lifted them with practiced efficiency.

"Don't go splat," Tim whispered to Cassie.

The shadow dancer turned to glare at him. "I'm the one who makes them go splat."

"She said it." JaKobi chuckled.

Cassie let out a growl of frustration and charged into battle. "Just be happy these aren't your nuts." She swung her bō staff in a wicked arc right at one of the giants' loin cloth-covered under-carriages.

Tim winced even though the giant wasn't on his side.

The first giant went down in a heap, exhaling a great breath as he tried to control the pain. If there was one thing every man universally appreciated, it was how much taking a hit right to the boys hurt. Sure, it was also good for a chuckle, but deep down, they were all thinking of a time it happened to them.

"Now that's just rude." The gatekeeper sent a blast of energy from his staff at the tank.

Cassie rolled out of the way, and the fight started in earnest. Blasts of magical energy from the gatekeeper's staff kept the tank off-balance enough that the second guard had time to recover. Tim pulled up his interface and almost expected it to say Master Blaster, but instead, the hulking twins were Dee and Dum. It was just their luck that they had to face two huge guys named after the creepiest things from his childhood.

If he never had to think of the Walrus and the Carpenter again, it would be too soon.

Tim shook off the shock of their names and got to work casting three Curse of Giving. He was happy to see that all three targets were taking damage, so they weren't going into another fight that would force them to switch targets constantly. That was fun for a battle or two, but having to work between multiple targets for an entire dungeon could get tedious. His guess was there was a shared health pool here, and they needed to time things right or face the consequences.

"Don't kill any of them until we see if their health balances out or if they have some other trick up their sleeve." Tim cast Hex of the Shattered Beast on Cassie as the hammers started to fall.

The real trick here would be trying not to kill one of them too early. If they let two of the three get enraged even for a moment, it would mean they fucked up and were about to take a trip to see their caseworkers. Of course, that strictly depended on if he was guessing the mechanics of the fight correctly. So far he was making a lot of assumptions based on the trash they faced on the way into the boss fight without any kind of concrete evidence to back them up.

Cassie and ShadowLily had their hands full dodging the two massive hammers and blasts of energy from the cackling gate-keeper as he whizzed about on his disk of magic. Tim tried to think of which one they should take out first, but he didn't have an answer yet. The damage seemed to be coming in pretty even incre-ments so he wasn't feeling overwhelmed on the healing front.

Waiting for confirmation he was on the right track was killing him.

Tim's Shattered Beast ran across the room, leaving a red streak in its wake. Before hitting the boss, it split into three, and each target took the damage it had done to Cassie. The spell was freaking awesome, and he hadn't nearly given the developers the praise they deserved. The spell was more versatile than he'd given it credit for, and he needed to use it every time it was off cooldown.

Feeling like the momentum was on their side, Tim cast Behold My Power on Dee because he was the brute with the highest health and blasted Dum with Curse of Sacrifice to top off Cassie's health.

So far the fight was going well, but that normally meant things were about to change. Tim kept casting heals as he watched the three enemies' health plummet. The three of them were taking pretty even damage, but they weren't making any real progress yet. Maybe what they needed to do was focus all their energy on a single target,

"Everyone focus on Dee," Tim called as he switched his attacks over to the same target.

JaKobi fired one last fireball at Dum before switching. "What? I didn't want the big guy to feel left out."

Dee's health was at seventy percent, while the other two were hovering around eighty-five. With the group's full attention focused on one target, the hit points started flying off the sledge-hammer-wielding guard in huge chunks. Sixty percent flew by, but when they hit fifty percent, a wall of energy slammed into them, and they all began to take periodic damage.

Tim tried to cast Cleanse, but nothing happened.

The gatekeeper continued to cackle as the trio pushed the adventurers back to the entrance, and the two guards moved to stand under his hovering disk. With a wave of his staff, the gatekeeper cast a spell, and Dee's health rose.

Tim almost cried out in anger, but he realized the other two members' health was dropping. This was the best-case scenario for them because they could figure out which of the targets took the most damage and focus on them until the health reset. Then they could rinse and repeat until the fight was over.

As long as there weren't any other big wrinkles.

The floor started to spin in a slow counterclockwise motion. *That's a new twist.* The real question was if the entire room was turning or only the outside walls as a way to disorient them. Overall it was an odd effect. His best guess was that they were spinning, and the walls were static. What was happening in the room didn't matter. All they had to do was focus on the task at hand and kill the damn boss.

Red lines appeared on the floor, and Tim moved until he was standing outside them. Apparently, what was happening in the room did matter. The lines on the floor started pulsing with magical energy and flames erupted from the crevices. When the blasts of magical fire receded, the floor was whole again, and they could move without being worried about being damaged.

Until the effect happened again.

Tim made sure Healing Orb blanketed the group. "Watch your feet for the fire, and let's see what kind of damage Dum takes this time."

"If he gets to ten percent, switch to something else." Cassie ran back toward the bosses. "The last thing we can afford to do is kill one of these guys early."

At that moment, he felt like Cassie was channeling his energy, and Tim felt a sense of pride knowing they were on the same page.

The second phase of the fight went much like the first except for the occasional fissures of fire that erupted at their feet. The healing was more intense due to the constant movement slowing down his casting. The flames erupting from the floor didn't help with the movement problems, and whenever anyone tried to eke out a little too much DPS, it cost them. He wanted to scream, keep moving, but getting burned tended to serve as its own best reminder not to slow down.

In short, the battle with the gatekeeper was a chaotic mess, and Tim loved it. Dodge, heal, damage, heal, it was all a blur as he kept his feet moving and his party alive. He wasn't even watching the bosses' health bars anymore unless it was a quick check to make sure he wasn't going to kill one of them.

After all his fussing, he wasn't going to be the one to screw this up.

Dum hit twenty-five percent health, and a wave of energy and the DOT that came with it hit them. Every third pulse, the DOT hit them with a double-tap of damage. The healing wasn't the worst he'd ever had to deal with, but it stopped him from being able to recharge his mana the way he wanted to during the downtime. The bosses' health equalized again, and now all three were sitting at sixty percent.

"What do you think, time to pick on the little guy?" Tim kept casting as he watched the gatekeeper zip around.

"Let's do it." JaKobi's eyes were tracking the gatekeeper as he wove around in the air.

ShadowLily huffed. "I'll stay on Dum."

Tim hadn't thought about her not being able to target the gatekeeper in the air effectively. It was a good plan though, albeit unintentional. If they could get two of the three's health down to ten percent, they might be able to push for the win during the next phase. All they had to do was survive this one first.

It was going to be a wild ride, but they were ready for it.

Along with the fissures on the floor that spat fire, now there was a beam of light that shot from the center of the room to a fixed point on one of the outer walls. As the room spun, they had to jump over the ankle-high beam as they passed it. Tim didn't want to find out if the magical beam did damage or was only a stun. Either way, it would be bad. Getting stunned into a sledgehammer or having a firepit open beneath them would make for a bad day.

"Watch your feet." Tim made the call as second nature as breathing.

He doubted the group needed another reminder, but it was his job to say the right things to keep their focus sharp. So after the call, he didn't check to see what the others were doing. He did what he did best and kept healing.

Cassie used her chain to try and pull the boss down closer for ShadowLily to get a hit in, but the gatekeeper wiggled out of her grasp before he was in the mist slayer's range. Not perturbed for a second, she kept working on Dee, as the others used the distraction to do some serious damage to the little old guy. The gatekeeper's health was nearing fifteen percent.

"Remember, don't kill him. Switch to Dee or Dum when he's at ten." Tim leapt over the beam, and threw himself to the side to avoid a burst of fire from the floor, then rolled into a crouch laughing maniacally. He could dodge attacks with the best of them.

Holy shit, were his pants on fire?

Tim quickly stood and doused the flame with a Healing Orb before sending another two orbs flying into the scrum. Now that everyone had the Hydrate buff, he returned his attention to the bosses and reapplied Curse of Giving to each of them. Cassie's health looked perfect, and everyone else's was ticking up nicely as

Hydrate did its thing. He almost ate another set of flames as he cast Divine Light on the gatekeeper but got lucky.

It was time to tighten things up.

"I've had about enough of that!" the gatekeeper roared. Bolts of magical energy flew out of the bottom of his disk, striking all of them.

Right when things had been going so well.

Tim cast Who Needs a Shield, hoping that Hydrate and the heals from his three curses would be enough to lift Cassie's health back to full while he dealt with the rest of their party. A fresh round of Healing Orb and a burst of Healing Storm got their health looking good, but his mana was in the shitter. Big time.

Time to use those special abilities.

With his mana regeneration doubled for the moment, Tim tried not to cast a single spell to get the full benefit of the regeneration. With all the healing over time spells he had going, everyone's health could handle a few seconds of inattention as he scanned the room for any sign of what would come next.

The gatekeeper's health was at thirteen percent, and Dum was at fifty percent. Dee had gone mostly untouched during this phase and was sitting at fifty-nine percent health. There was no way they were getting out of this phase with a chance to win in the next one unless they sped things up. With the gatekeeper's DOT doing more damage during each stage and Tim's mana taking the hits from the additional ground AOE damage, they weren't going to last forever.

If they couldn't find a way to pick up the pace, they would face an enrage, and he hated the idea of dying that way worse than if they made a simple mistake. Things were getting intense, but so far, it felt like they were still in control.

With his mana bolstered, Tim got back to work by topping off Cassie's health. Then he focused his energy on Dum. The only way this would work was if they got at least two of them so low that pulling the extra health from Dee didn't matter. Sixty percent health only went so far when spread between three people.

The gatekeeper hit ten percent health, and Dum was at twenty when the phase changed. Once again, they were swept to the back of the room and hit with the DOT effect. This time every second and third pulse had a double-tap of damage. The damage over time effect was a real pain in his ass. It continually stopped him from being able to recharge his mana while the others were getting a breather. It would have been nice if the attack was interruptible, but it looked like it was one of those things built into the fight they would have to keep dealing with.

If they made it to a fourth phase, He'd try to use his interrupt anyway. Otherwise, he'd save it for the nasty AOE from the bottom of the gatekeeper's disk. That particular attack was devastating and would probably happen quickly during this phase because of the boss' lower health.

Dee screamed as his health ripped away before stabilizing at twenty-five percent. Dum's health was almost the same at twentyish percent, while the gatekeeper managed to pull a little more from the twins and was sitting at thirty percent health. They'd done a number on the trio during the last phase, but did they have enough to bring it home now?

Tim had a distinct feeling that this was it. If they didn't win during this phase, the bosses might enrage anyway. Facing three enraged bosses at sub-five percent didn't seem like a good way to win. If they didn't kill them all before the phase change, they would have to drop at least one of them and hope for the best. The risk was doing it soon enough and potentially facing all three bosses versus only the two. If they were flawless, maybe they could kill two of them first.

It was a lot to process.

Now there was also a beam coming at them below shoulder height. So while they were trying to kill the boss, they would be jumping over one beam, ducking under another, and avoiding fire that shot up from the floor like the infamous fire swamps of the

Princess Bride. It was going to be chaotic, but they had this if they stayed calm.

Tim called his final instructions. "Keep your wits about you. I want the gatekeeper under ten. Then we kill Dum."

"That's not very nice!" Dum roared and charged.

Holy shit, they can hear us.

Cassie intercepted the giant with the sledgehammer before it could hit him. Then his world devolved into a series of small tasks. Heal. Jump. Heal. Duck. Heal. *Oh shit, my pants are on fire.*

Despite all the craziness of the fight swirling around him, Tim found his calm center and focused on his job. He couldn't worry about what the other members of his group were doing. His only task was keeping them alive. His mana pool was as dry as the Mojave desert, but he had enough juice left to see them through this if they went a little faster.

The gatekeeper flew above them, ready to release his shower of magical sparks, and Tim screamed, "Interrupt the boss!"

Almost as one, the entire group shifted and blasted the boss. It was a frivolous call for him to make when every second of DPS counted, and he had no idea if it would work, but it was worth the risk. If they ate another round of damage that dropped the entire party under fifty percent health, they wouldn't be around to finish the fight.

Instead of the sparks, the gatekeeper's disk surrounded him with energy like a shield. The interrupts worked to stop the attack, and his health was now at eight percent. Dee was at twenty-five percent, and the edges of his hammer were pulsing with red light. Dum's hammer was pulsing as well, but his health was at fifteen percent.

Was this their moment?

Tim thought the pulses on the hammer might mean the phase was about to change so they had to push it now, or else they'd be facing three enraged bosses with over ten percent health.

He sucked in a deep breath and made the call. "Get me a couple of DOTs on the gatekeeper and kill Dum!"

The gatekeeper's health dipped as Tim reapplied Curse of Giving. His hope was the DOTs would shave off another percentage or two while they dealt with Dum. Jump, roll, duck, dodge—finally he blasted him with Curse of Sacrifice. Dum's health was taking a relentless beating. The giant tried to fight them off, but he didn't have the strength to stop their relentless assault.

When Dum died, ShadowLily and Cassie switched their attacks to Dee while the rest of them focused on the gatekeeper. With five percent health left the boss didn't stand much of a chance, but they'd almost tapped out their resources. A beam of sun and a cluster of glowing arrows did most of the work. What the gatekeeper hated was Tim's Divine Light.

The gatekeeper went down in a cry of anguish.

Dee let out a roar of rage and swept his hammer across the room, sending them all back to the entrance with ten percent health. The phase changed, but without the gatekeeper to summon any new magic, the floor and the beams stayed the same. What didn't stay the same was Dee. He doubled in size, and the top of his sledgehammer sprouted spikes like a bat from a zombie flick.

Ten percent was a better number than Tim hoped for when it took them so long to defeat the first of the three. That said, a full ten percent seemed like a big ask from his crew when Dee was fully enraged, and they were running on fumes. At least there hadn't been a DOT to worry about with the gatekeeper being dead, so he was getting a little breather before making the final big push.

An invisible barrier held back Dee, but the hate in his eyes promised nothing but pain as soon as he was released.

Tim pulled Cassie into a quick hug. "Just live."

"I plan on it." The tank kept her eyes on Tim's for a moment. "You know what they say about giants, right?"

She let out a little giggle as she turned her attention back to Dee. "Little cocks."

Dee let out a growl that shattered the barrier, and the fight was on.

Cassie rushed to meet the enraged boss head-on as the rest of them got to work doing whatever DPS they could manage.

The first thing Tim did was cast Hex of the Shattered Beast. The one thing he was certain of was that the boss would do a shit ton of damage. If he could send some of that back his way, even better. After that, his only concern was keeping Cassie alive. He reapplied Curse of Giving, cast Healing Orb, and put Curse of Sacrifice on repeat as he fell into a rhythm.

Run, dodge, curse.

Cassie was getting hammered despite blowing all her cooldowns, but the boss was at three percent health. Tim's Hex Beast activated. His favorite Golden Retriever slammed into the boss, bursting out of his back in a shower of red mist. Dee's health dropped by a full two percent as ShadowLily rolled in front of him. The mist slayer slammed her daggers into his stomach three times before rolling back behind the boss and repeating the attack until he was dead.

Dee fell to the floor, and Tim stared at his corpse as the beam of light that was about to cut him in half disappeared. He was so involved in the fight that the fact they won took a few moments to settle over him. Then he screamed in pure joy.

They'd done it. The gatekeeper was dead.

CHAPTER FORTY-FOUR

Cassie sat in the middle of the room. "I'm going to need a gym membership."

"Tell me about it. I can barely move." JaKobi flopped down next to her.

Tim blasted the entire group with a Cleanse and topped off their health. It completely refreshed his weary muscles, but his brain was still in fight mode. They'd won the battle, but it had been a close thing.

If they had to go back through the dungeon, even with the power of foresight, he wasn't sure they could've handled the fight any differently. The reality was that even knowing the boss's moves, the fights could've easily gone either way.

One of the tricky things about leveling was the players never got a chance to balance their gear before moving to the next challenge.

In fact, for most of the leveling process, players were normally in a mismatch of crappy gear and goofy colors. *The Etheric Coast* had one up on most other titles when it came to gear because the drops came so frequently it always felt like they were moving forward. It sure didn't hurt that all their drops were character and class-specific, either. The group was always getting rewarded with what felt like quality loot. Tim couldn't count the number of MMOs he'd played where he hit max level and didn't have a single piece of gear that he didn't want to toss in the trash instantly.

That was when the real struggle started, the loot grind.

Normally players were forced to progress through a series of events to get the best gear—solo and small group content, followed by dungeons, followed by raids of increasing difficulty. There was a gear progression at each level. Raids got the best loot, but the least of it. Then the next raid came out, and the loot was a little better, and yes, sometimes there was even a story associated with the new instance. Not that the loot-hungry minions noticed.

Who cared about a good story when there were shinies and world firsts to claim?

Tim always kind of liked the story element in raids, but it was hard to watch cutscenes when some guy was in your headphones screaming about how cool his dick looked wrapped in purple cellophane. He didn't know what it was with gamers, but the odder the character, the better the player. Not always, but he'd seen it enough to say it was more than a trend. Still, when a gamer wanted to listen to a cinematic about how to save the princess from the evil baddie, the last image they wanted floating through their mind was a big purple dick.

Like a summer sausage gone wrong.

Tim shook his head, clearing out the images of bad gaming experiences, and took a moment to thank Eternia for his new friends. Without them being inside *The Etheric Coast* with him, the game wouldn't be nearly as enjoyable. It was true when they said what made gaming special was the people. Reaching down, Tim pulled Cassie and JaKobi back to their feet.

"Cassie, dodger of hammers, I think you should go first." Tim pointed at the golden chest. "Show us the way."

The tank walked toward the treasure chest with a good deal of swagger. "Don't mind if I do."

ShadowLily appeared next to Tim. "You know I had to dodge those hammers too."

"Let her have this. It's her favorite thing," Tim whispered back. "Don't think for one second I wouldn't always pick you for my team first."

"Don't you forget it." ShadowLily poked him in the ribs as the tank laid her hand on the chest.

Cassie turned, the glow on her face radiating elation. "Hammer Staff of the Reckless."

The tank equipped her new staff and swung it around. A small sledgehammer head capped each end of the two-inch-thick shaft. It was the kind of thing she could use to put a dent in a big set of heavy armor.

"It feels different, but the bonuses are awesome." Cassie motioned toward the chest. "Come on, who's next?"

It didn't look like anyone wanted to go next after such a great roll. Say one thing about gamers. They were a superstitious bunch. Like everyone knew the football player who wore the same socks all season, gamers had all kinds of weird rituals. Take a sip of Code Red, a bong rip, and a bite of pizza was his best friend Xander's favorite pre-fight ritual. Tim normally closed his eyes for a second and hit his newest music mix so the perfect tunes played in the background while he kicked ass.

He moved toward the chest and rested his hand on the top.

Item received: That's not a Brown Spot Leather Pants

What in the fuck was that? His new pants better not have a big gross brown spot over the ass because some healer a long time ago shit himself during an intense fight. Tim wasn't a coward. He was proud to say that his bowels stayed intact every single time he got smashed into itty-bitty bits.

Ivan wasn't the best healer, and he was an even worse soldier, but he did one thing well. Ivan could run as if the devil

herself was chasing him. The man could dodge and roll away from trouble with the best of them. Their problem was Ivan was always running in the wrong direction. It got to the point where if they needed something done, they'd teleport Ivan to the front, knowing he'd be back in a minute. While the healer never actually shit himself, he earned the name brown spot because he always ran away from trouble.

+3 Endurance +2 Dexterity +4 Intelligence +3 Wisdom

Special Ability: Flee

Whenever you're running away from danger, you'll receive a five percent bonus to speed.

Whoa.

Those pants were pretty freaking awesome. Yeah, Tim didn't like the idea of being associated with a coward, but he did like the special ability and the stats. If he was honest with himself, there were a lot of times he had to run away during fights.

Sometimes he activated Quick Feet, but other times he was running because he didn't want to get trampled. The extra dexterity and Flee ability should make surviving a little easier, even at the roughest of times.

"Leather pants, with a bonus to running away." Tim left out the name of the pants on purpose.

Lorelei let out a very unladylike giggle that ended in a couple of snorts. "Running away, huh? Okay, Mr. Brown Spot."

He was never going to live this down.

"Why don't you go next? Maybe you can pick up a pair of yellow crotch panties of the ruthless." Tim wasn't bitter, not one bit.

Lorelei smiled at him but wagged her finger. "I swear to Eternia if there is something yellow in here, I'm going to shoot you."

"Not if I run away." Tim laughed with her.

Placing her hand on the chest, Lorelei let out a squeal of glee and turned. "Leather Gloves of the Spirit Archer. Bonuses to everything I care about and a special ability to add ten percent critical hit chance to my next attack."

"Gimme some of that." JaKobi looked at the gloves with envy.

ShadowLily pushed the wizard forward. "Be my guest."

"Don't mind if I do." The robe hid his strut, but they all knew he was walking as proudly as Cassie had.

JaKobi put his hand on the chest, turned, and an instant later did a fist pump that would've made Tiger Woods jealous.

"Necklace of the Ember God." A solid gold chain set with a ruby at the center appeared around JaKobi's neck. "You don't even want to know." The wizard's eyes said he was dying for someone to ask him about it.

Tim felt his curiosity bubbling and couldn't stop himself. "Spill the beans."

"Lets me double-cast a single spell, once per fight." JaKobi brushed off his shoulder. "Shit's about to get real."

It was an amazing skill. Tim thought about the damage and healing he could do with a double cast of Behold My Power. Using the special ability at the right time would be a big bonus for their group. There was no doubt in his mind that the ember wizard would figure out the right time to use the skill and exploit it to its full potential.

"Man, I only get to run away from stuff." Tim might have sounded disappointed, but he was thankful his new pants didn't have a brown spot.

Lorelei shrugged. "It's still useful, especially the way you play."

"Tell me about it." ShadowLily laughed. "For a guy who hates running, you sure do a lot of it."

The mist slayer walked toward the chest and settled her hand on it. She looked smugly satisfied when she turned to face the group. "Earrings of Critical Slaughter. Boosts to all the right stats, but the special ability is the kicker."

Pulling her daggers free, ShadowLily launched into a series of complex-looking attacks. "After three critical hits, the next critical hit receives an additional twenty-five percent damage boost. It's a persistent skill, so it's active all the time."

"That's huge!" Tim ran to her and pulled her into a hug. "You're going to destroy Cronos."

Cassie coughed. "*We're* going to destroy that dragon bitch."

"Damn right we are," Lorelei and JaKobi said in unison and stared at each other.

Tim laughed. "It's entirely possible we're spending way too much time together."

The chest burst into beautiful golden motes and drifted toward the heavens as the doors to the gatehouse opened into the castle's courtyard.

"Looks like we won't have to look for a way up." Cassie moved toward the door, and the rest of the group followed.

"It doesn't feel like we're floating in the air." Lorelei looked over the edge.

JaKobi was standing at the edge of the castle grounds peeing into the air and watching as it fell hundreds of feet below them to splatter on the rooftops. "It sure is a long way down."

Laughter burst from Tim's mouth before he could contain it. He knew he started all of this by peeing his name on the king's wall like a little boy in the snow, but he still couldn't resist throwing a dig at his friend. "Way to keep it classy."

JaKobi dropped his robes back in place before turning to face the group. "I don't like having magic used on me without my consent."

"Consent is key." Cassie slammed her elbow into his gut. "But next time you have to take a leak, try and do it with a little more style."

ShadowLily was squatting by the edge. "I could try, but I'm not sure I could get it over the edge."

Lorelei slapped her forehead. "You guys are too much."

"Just making sure my bud doesn't feel awkward being himself, even if it means peeing off the side of the castle on the poor little town folks." ShadowLily winked.

Tim was about to break out in the JaKobi shuffle when he saw a lady walking toward them. "Cassie, eyes front."

"It's not Cronos." The tank dropped into her fighting stance anyway.

JaKobi moved into position, flames rippling across his hands. "Nope, it's Trashnos."

It was Tim's turn to be exasperated. "Let's not make calling the trash Trashnos a thing." Dropping his voice so only Cassie could hear. "He's probably right, and this is our first battle."

Cassie laughed. "Let's call them Trashions. It's self-explanatory."

"Or we could call them trash like normal." Tim dropped into his stance. "Put on your game face. It's time to roll."

The woman wore all-white fabric with the edges dyed a deep purple color. "Mistress Cronos isn't accepting visitors."

"She's expecting us." Cassie flashed a feral grin. "Although I'm surprised she's too scared to show herself."

Deep rich laughter rumbled from the woman in white's belly. "Cronos isn't scared of anyone. She merely deems your presence not worthy of her attention."

Cassie snorted. "Tell that to the gatekeeper and bear farmer."

"No reason to rub her face in it," Tim chided. "It's gotta be hard being staked out like the sacrificial goat."

JaKobi motioned toward the woman. "The way behind us is clear. You can leave whenever you like."

The purple jewel set at the top of the woman's staff pulsed along with the matching jewel on her necklace. "The time for talk is over."

A blast of pure magical energy ripped from the jewel at the top of the staff. It sprayed all of them with its power. The DOT hit hard, and Tim got to work fixing the damage as Cassie charged into the fight.

Instead of dropping into his traditional stance, Tim used Way of the River instead. Now the damage he dealt would be returned to the entire group as healing. He started with his usual Curse of Giving and cast Hex of the Shattered Beast on Cassie. Then it was up to his single-target damage and healing abilities to carry the day. Curse of Sacrifice and Healing Orb would be what he needed to ensure the outcome ended in their favor.

Cassie didn't seem too worried about the magical damage. Her protection against that particular type of damage must've been a lot stronger than his. The single blast they'd taken at the beginning of the fight hurt a lot more than he expected, and it had him starting to think about boosting his resistances.

Now that Cassie had control of the woman, he wouldn't have to be worried about taking damage unless the Trashion used the AOE again.

The purple mage's health was going down at a decent clip, but she put up more of a fight than the previous trash they faced. When Shattered Beast returned the damage it absorbed, his target's health dropped to under fifty percent, and something unexpected happened.

The mage turned into a bear.

Purple energy rippled along the bear's claws, and the staff itself seemed to have turned into wooden bracers to protect the bear's forepaws. When the giant grizzly roared, Tim saw the purple energy extended to the bear's teeth, and he knew getting bitten would lead to a bad day.

"Hey Boo Boo, I think I saw a pic-a-nic basket," Cassie growled as she slammed her staff into the bear.

Tim gritted his teeth. "Stick with the nose boops."

The bear brought with it a ton of extra damage he hadn't expected. The magical claws ignored Cassie's armor. He switched to Way of the Boulder and cast Who Needs a Shield. The trash fights were supposed to be easy, but the bear lady would've wiped out an unprepared group rather quickly.

They worked together until the woman was lying on her knees before them gasping for air as the last of her hit points bled away.

"It shouldn't be possible." She reached to her neck and ripped the necklace free. "You promised me freedom."

The dragon dropped soundlessly out of the air and bit her in half as it landed. "And so you have it."

Cronos changed from the dragon back to the woman and spat a bit of bloody flesh onto the ground. "I do hate when things get caught in my teeth."

Before Tim could speak, she lifted a single finger to silence him. "If you still wish to face me, meet me in the Garden of Roses, and try not to kill any more of my people along the way."

Cronos turned into a dragon and took flight.

"We killed her? Like we were the ones who bit the lady in half. What is with these bosses and blaming everyone else for their problems?" JaKobi looked at the woman's legs lying on the ground with the guts spilling out and tried not to barf.

Lorelei looked kind of sad. "It's the way of the world. The strong eat the weak."

"Not today." ShadowLily Lifted her fist in the air. "Today, the weak get to take one back."

Tim grinned. "Then let's go win one for the little guy."

As they walked down the path toward the castle, more of the women in white and purple appeared, but none of them tried to bar their way. Instead, they filed in behind the group and followed them toward the castle's Garden of Roses. This was it. They'd almost arrived at the final battle and would be one step closer to getting the Stone of Immoratis for Eternia.

CHAPTER FORTY-FIVE

The Garden of Roses was one of the most beautiful things Tim had ever seen.

Neat beds of purple and white roses formed a football field-sized circle outside the castle. Inside the large outer ring were five smaller circles of roses, each with a massive rosebush at the center. Then three smaller circles without anything at the center, and finally at the precise midpoint of the garden, there was a twenty-foot square of meticulously kept lawn—just the kind of place to set up tables for a party.

Or for a dragon to luxuriate on.

"This puts the botanical gardens to shame. It must've taken generations to cultivate." JaKobi looked at the garden in wonder.

Lorelei huffed. "Or a shit-ton of magic."

"Why would she want to meet us here?" Tim looked around the space. "We're going to mess up her roses."

ShadowLily looked at the plants, then up at the castle. "She doesn't want us to go inside for some reason."

Cassie wiggled her fingers at the castle. "Presto chango."

When nothing happened, the tank shrugged and turned back to

the group. "Seriously, what if it was some little hut magicked up to look like a castle?"

"That would be one hell of a trick." Tim looked over the gardens and up at the castle. "When the fight starts, don't take anything for granted. We already know she's a powerful mage, but Cronos has also proved to be tricky."

JaKobi grunted. "When you can turn into a massive dragon and eat people, I don't think you need to be very tricky. She strikes me as the confrontational type."

"Yet she's part of what happened to the king." Tim let it hang out there.

JaKobi grinned at him. "Touché."

Cassie stepped between them. "Before you guys start to bro down, let's deal with her." She pointed up into the sky.

Cronos spiraled down toward them from above. Each circle she made was wider and slower until she landed on the grass square at the center of the garden. Slowly the dragon blurred, and the evil witch Cronos appeared.

There was no mistaking the change of clothes. Cronos had come ready for battle. Her dark purple robes turned white depending on how she moved, but it wasn't the colors that got Tim's attention. It was the spikes. On her wrist guards, shoulder pads, even the back of her boots. Everything about her outfit spoke of aggression and violence. This wasn't some simple talk to lure them into a trap. This was the final fight.

"Like most adventurers, you weren't smart enough to heed my warnings. Now I must make an example out of you so no one will be so foolish again." Cronos planted her feet and glared at them with hatred.

Tim stepped behind Cassie. "You wrong us with your words, Cronos. You know full well that we wouldn't be here if you hadn't conspired with Isadora against the king. It's time to face the consequences of those actions."

Cronos almost doubled in size as her anger consumed her.

"You lecture me on the consequences of actions. Have you met the nobles? Do they inspire you?"

"About as much as a politician," Cassie whispered.

Tim tried not to laugh or to get distracted. "They might not inspire me, but I also don't go around killing them."

Dark, murderous laughter filled the space. "Is the king not alive? Does he not walk the halls of the castle at this very moment?"

That confirmed Prince Desmond's fears. The king in the castle wasn't the king at all, or at the very least was under Cronos' total control. He doubted they would be able to convince her to part with an antidote or reverse the spell so they were down to their last option, kill the evil bitch and hope for the best.

"We both know he doesn't." Tim let the words hang between them for a moment so she could feel the weight of them. "If it's not us, it will be another group of adventurers. Now that Desmond knows the truth of it, you'll never see peace."

Cronos screamed, "Peace is a lie." She turned away from them and walked to create some distance. "If you insist on a fight, I am feeling rather peckish."

With a roar, she changed from a woman back into a dragon.

"Oh shit." Tim looked into the monster's eyes and wondered if this was how a seal felt when the water shifted beneath them as a great white went in for the kill from below.

Cronos rose into the sky, and Tim called, "Get ready for it."

The dragon turned and banked in a lazy circle, belching out fire. The only areas untouched were the grass at the center of the garden and the center of each smaller circle. Flames consumed everything else as Cronos continued to fly in lazy arcs across the entire space.

"Into the grass." It might not be the best place for them to go, but it was the closest, and it was a safe zone so Tim made the call.

The group piled into the grass square as Cronos finished her circle of flames. Tim looked around the battlefield, trying to figure out what he missed. Would it be better for them to try and pile inside the smallest circles or maybe the larger circles with single plants at the center? He didn't know yet, the fight was too new, but he knew those areas would come into play eventually.

The dragon quickly spiraled higher into the air and descended at the grass square like a falling rock. The only choice they had to make now was to jump into the flames or try and absorb the damage from the boss's attack.

"Everyone stack on Cassie!" Tim squawked as he ran toward the tank.

They dove into a pile under Cassie's protective shielding as Cronos slammed into the grass. The shockwave was enough to leave Tim feeling woozy, but he was on his feet in an instant. There wasn't time to check if they had negative status effects so Tim cast a mass Cleanse and followed it up with a trio of Healing Orb. With everyone's health moving in the right direction, he felt better about the situation.

They couldn't afford to make that mistake a second time.

"My vote is next time we stay out of the grass. Find a way to make that happen," Cassie snapped as she moved to engage the boss.

She was right. He was the mechanics guy. At least they weren't facing a full-on dragon anymore. As soon as Cronos hit the ground, she turned back into a woman. Being in human form didn't seem to make the witch any less formidable as her magical claws made her as deadly as Freddy Krueger rocking two gloves.

Cassie and Cronos tangled, staff against magical claws. The fire trapping them in the rectangle of grass slowly extinguished, and Tim knew it was time for the group to get moving.

"Get us close to one of those big circles." Tim cast Hex of the Shattered Beast and followed it with Curse of Sacrifice.

Cassie didn't waste any time as she used her attacks to position the boss. A good tank was worth its weight in gold, and watching Cassie work now was like watching Michelangelo paint the Sistine Chapel. Trailing behind the pair like an artist of death, ShadowLily wove a deadly tapestry of destruction with her daggers. The assassin was pushing herself this fight, and the numbers spoke for themselves.

Traditionally it was easier for ranged DPS to top the charts. A ranged player could get into optimal position faster, and they normally didn't have to move as much to dodge attacks. One of the biggest luxuries of playing from range was the ability to see the entire battlefield and cut loose until they had to move. When the DPS played up close, they moved as much as the tank while doing the same DPS as the players standing still.

The mist slayer handled the challenge like a pro. No one was going to tell her she couldn't top the charts on every fight. It meant pushing herself to the limit. As Tim watched her work, he felt inspired. She was a fantastic player, and they were lucky to have her in their group. Not to mention it kind of made him hot seeing her dart around wreaking havoc in those tight leather pants.

Like having his very own half-elf Mila Jovovich.

As the group moved closer to the circle with the rose bush in the center, the top of the bush started to wiggle. Tim didn't have to be a deep thinker to know movement normally meant nasty things were about to happen. So far, his ideas for this fight led them from one spot of trouble right into another. They wouldn't be able to win this fight eating the damage from Cronos' slam, the fire, and whatever the rose bush was about to do to them.

The rose bush burst from the ground. It was some kind of plant monster wearing the bush as a hat. Loose roots dangled around the face of the mandrake-like creature as it opened its mouth. Instead of a scream that could've stunned them, a stream of thorns sprayed from the creature's open mouth dealing damage to the entire party. The thorns also applied a DOT to the group.

Tim was about to tell Cassie to back up when the rose bush

creature slipped back into the ground. Cassie barely noticed the increase so she didn't start moving the boss away from the circle on her own. The damage they were taking right now, even with the DOT, was easily handled by Hydrate, but if the DOT stacked and they stayed put it would become a problem.

What were they going to do?

They needed to find a way to stay close enough to the circle to run in when Cronos turned back into a dragon but far enough away not to trigger the AOE attack. It was a tricky tightrope to walk, but they could do it if they tightened things up. This was the final fight. Of course, it was going to be hard.

Tim's Hex Beast slammed into the boss, but she hardly even flinched. He wanted to cast Behold My Power but couldn't risk wasting it if Cronos would change back to her dragon form soon. Instead, he settled for casting another round of Healing Orb as he prepared to tell Cassie what he wanted her to do next.

She was going to be so pissed.

The bush started shaking again, and there wasn't going to be time to get out of the way. His mana was dipping with the early damage they took from Cronos' opening salvo and again when he made the mistake of asking Cassie to get close to the rose bush. Not knowing if there was another way out or if it would even work at all, Tim cast Disturbance and hoped for the best. When the spell hit the bush, it stopped moving.

The real question was for how long?

Never one to let an opportunity go to waste, Tim called, "Cassie, let's move closer to the center again."

Until they had an active bush to test the range of the attack, there was no reason to get her riled up with useless commands. For now, he'd settle for not getting hit with the DOT again, and then he could explain to her what happened when Cronos did her dragon thing. At some point, they'd have to make a run for the rose bush and the protection of the circle, but until then it was easier to stay away.

"We just got out of the damn center," the shadow dancer grumbled as she started to move.

Tim laughed as he reapplied Curse of Giving. "Tell me about it."

Cronos roared as she hit seventy-five percent and her body shifted back into dragon form.

"Everyone in the circle," Tim called as he ran.

Cassie grunted. "Into the circle, out of the circle, make up your damn mind already."

Cronos took flight as they entered the ring, lighting the garden on fire again as she flew in a slow circle. While the fire raged outside, the rose bush creature seemed content to stay below the surface.

"At least we got to rest for a minute." Tim watched his mana bar replenish as he filled Cassie in on what they needed to try during the next phase.

Cronos decided they'd had too much time to rest. As she reached the pinnacle of her flight, she again descended with all the deadly power of a meteorite. When she hit the grass, the ground quaked, and Tim was grateful they skipped out on a big chunk of damage.

When the fire in the center of the area died out, the ground beneath his feet pulsed red.

Red means dead.

"Everyone out." Tim made the call as he started running.

When JaKobi didn't move, Tim tapped Cassie on the shoulder. "Get him for me."

Her chain came out, and she yanked the ember wizard forward as the circle burst into flames.

Tim looked at the circle for a moment, trying to decide what they should do next. "That's our enrage timer. As long as we don't burn two of the circles at the same time, we have four more chances to knock out the last seventy-five percent."

"Just tell me where to stand." Cassie ran toward Cronos and

made sure she had the witch's full attention before she started moving her toward the circle Tim pointed out.

"When you see that bush start to shake, back it up a few feet." Not eating an attack was important this time, but not as important as making sure they had the right distance down for the rest of the fight.

Lorelei broke out in peals of laughter. "I kinda like it when a girl's bush has a little shake. That's my call to move in, not to back it up."

JaKobi shot a beam of sunlight at the boss. "Preach it, sister."

Tim tried not to think about what these two got up to before he knew them and tried to focus on the fight. He quickly reapplied Curse of Giving and cast Behold My Power. From there, he dropped into a holding pattern. He didn't know when it would happen, but the second phase normally added a little something extra to the fight. While the wrinkle hadn't shown up yet, he was determined to be ready for it when it did.

Cassie moved the boss toward the next circle, and when the bush started to shake, she moved slightly farther away. The rose bush stopped shaking, and just like that, they found the perfect distance. The group quickly fell into the guileless rhythm of battle. Each of them worked as hard as they could to push Cronos to the next phase as quickly as possible.

Tim watched as the boss' health dipped to sixty-five percent, then sixty. They still hadn't been blasted by an extra attack, and he was getting worried. Not having an extra mechanic pop up didn't feel right. Something big was coming, and it would be coming soon.

Cronos hit fifty-five percent, and now his nerves were simply dancing.

The boss' magical claws started to turn into real ones, and Tim knew they were about to get scorched again. This time they were in the perfect position to move into the circle when the fire started. So far they'd done everything right, and when the dragon took off, they would step out of the circle into phase three of the fight.

This time they would come out with full health and mana and higher spirits. Maybe he'd been wrong, and they had this fight under control all along.

Then disaster struck.

Cronos broke free from Cassie, stormed into the middle of their party, and spun in a circle using her massive tail to send all of them flying in different directions. The lucky ones got knocked closer to the safe zone, but the unlucky were scattered further away from a haven. Tim made a mental note that if they survived this, to change their positioning so JaKobi would get knocked closer to safety instead of farther away.

The ember wizard was the slowest member of their group, which of course meant the mechanic's first use knocked him the farthest away. That didn't stop JaKobi from leaping to his feet and putting every inch of his strength and dexterity to use as he rushed toward safety. Tim watched him for a moment and began his mad dash toward safety, hoping his friend would be fast enough to make it.

"Lorelei, use an interrupt." Tim almost just shouted interrupt, but at the last second, he remembered everyone might cast simultaneously and settled on the closest player with the longest range.

The spirit archer executed the interrupt as Cassie stepped into safety. The rose bush monster stayed hidden as ShadowLily and Lorelei entered the circle of roses.

Hearing the fire roaring behind him as it drew closer was the most horrible sound Tim ever heard. It was like death was screaming at him, and no matter how fast he ran away it was always getting closer. At least he wasn't trapped in a burning building. All he had to do was make it to the circle instead of deciding whether to jump.

Tim activated Quick Feet, putting on a burst of speed that left the ember wizard trailing in his dust.

Entering the protective circle of roses, Tim turned back to watch JaKobi. "Run, Forressst!"

"Damn, that's cold." Lorelei snickered.

JaKobi tried not to smile as he put everything he had into running. "I'd totally trade a box of chocolates for a movement spell."

"You don't need one." Cassie threw her chain, and it wrapped around JaKobi's waist as the flames hit his heels.

With a solid yank, she pulled the ember wizard out of the fire and into safety. Tim got to work healing. As soon as JaKobi was at full health, Tim pulled up his user interface to look over the entire group's status. Everyone was at full health, and the boss was sitting under fifty percent. The new wrinkle seemed to be a knockback before the flames. That particular skill was easy enough to manage, but there would be a new wrinkle coming out of this phase. There always was.

Probably something that's going to make me run. I hate that shit.

"JaKobi, switch places with Lorelei during the next phase. We need you getting knocked closer even if it means you stop DPS early to get in position." Tim looked at the group and shrugged. "That's all I've got until we see what the boss has in store for us."

Cassie pointed as Cronos started rising higher in the sky, preparing for her slam. "Get ready for it because she's coming."

When Cronos hit the grass, the ground shook, their protective circle burned away, and it turned into an attack as they fled. The new twist didn't present itself right away, and Cassie stood in front of the group ready to intercept the boss.

Tim felt super tense, but maybe that was his default reaction to doing well. It was like he was always waiting for the other shoe to drop.

Sometimes it never did.

Cronos charged toward their group with her magical claws extended, ready to rip them to pieces. Cassie rushed in from the side, cut off the boss's charge, and started moving her into position. Tim cast Curse of Giving and Curse of Sacrifice as Cassie led the boss toward the next circle.

A glance to Tim's left confirmed JaKobi was in the right place. Things were going smoothly, and with their adjusted formation, they should be able to make it into the circle during the phase change without any last-second heroics. The way things were going, they might even make it out of this fight with a circle to spare. After losing their first battle with Isadora, they were playing at the top of their game.

Tim cast three Healing Orb to spread Hydrate, and started interchanging Curse of Sacrifice and Divine Light. Cronos hit forty-five percent, then forty. At thirty-nine percent, she started to glow. At thirty-five, a circle formed under the boss' feet and let out intermittent bolts of energy they had to dodge. So now they had their first real big movement problem to deal with.

"Oh fuck," ShadowLily swore as she rolled forward at the wrong time and right into one of Cronos' energy attacks.

Who Needs a Shield was the first thing Tim cast. As soon as he saw the spell take hold, he flipped the target of his Way of the Boulder stance from Cassie to ShadowLily. The next five seconds disappeared in a flash as he did damage to the boss. When the mist slayer had her full health, it was easy enough to flip his stance back to Cassie.

A round of Healing Orb topped off the group, and it was like the mistake never happened.

Letting out a deep breath, Tim looked at Cronos' health and realized she was at twenty-eight percent. While he'd been stressing out, the rest of his group had kept working. The trust they had in his ability to pull them out of the fire was humbling.

I won't ever tell them how close they came to death.

At twenty-five percent, something new happened.

Cronos ran to the grassy area and started to cast a spell.

"I have a bad feeling about this," Tim shouted as they started moving toward the circle of protection.

Cassie grunted. "You always have a bad feeling. Try lightening up a little, dude."

"Don't worry, be happy," JaKobi sang.

ShadowLily slapped him on the back of the head. "Not the right time."

"Winds of the East, I call upon you!" Cronos shouted as she pointed her hands up to the heavens.

A tornado formed from the tip of her finger and grew before doubling almost instantly and again equally quickly. Tim didn't think the rose bush trick would protect them from this so they had to wait for the spell to take effect and find some way to use the aftermath to their advantage.

One by one, the tornado sucked them off their feet and pulled them into the grassy area. Cronos continued her shift into a dragon as the tornado spat them out at the corner farthest away from the three remaining circles. As they landed on the ground, the dragon took flight.

"Run!" Tim cried.

Cassie didn't hesitate. She picked up JaKobi and slung him over one shoulder before taking off. "I might have to talk with Roberto about how many burritos you've been eating." She slapped his ass and kept moving.

"Hey, you can't gain weight in this game." The ember wizard bounced along on Cassie's shoulder.

They were going to make it. Everything was going to be just fine.

The tornado pulled JaKobi and Cassie back toward the grass area while the rest of them kept running free. Tim watched them land before turning in time to see ShadowLily stun the rose bush creature in the circle they'd been heading for. Lorelei made it into the circle next, and he stumbled inside a moment later.

Cassie and JaKobi were separated, and there was no way the tank could reach him and run to safety. She sprinted toward the next big circle hoping she'd be fast enough not to be deep-fried.

"JaKobi, get in the nearest big circle, don't forget to interrupt." Tim turned toward Cassie. "You gotta get in one of the small ones."

Cassie slid to a stop outside the closest big circle, her toes inches away. "A little heads-up would've been nice."

"Just trying to make sure your boyfriend is safe," Tim quipped.

"Why do I have to run way over there when this one is right here?" Cassie scuffed her toes on the edge.

"That circle is the only thing stopping us from having to get back in the grass with Cronos," Tim shouted back.

The choice was up to Cassie, but they would all know if she made the wrong one and they had to start the fight over. If she got in the small circle and it didn't save her, all the blame was on him. She got in the circle.

It was the safest bet.

"I better not die a fiery death," Cassie grumbled as she glared at Tim.

The flames washed over Cassie's area and didn't touch her. Then they moved past their group and JaKobi. Thankfully Cassie didn't make the selfish play, and they had their safety net in place if they failed to kill Cronos during this phase. If they somehow managed to squeak their way into a fifth phase, the boss would probably be enraged. The last thing he wanted to deal with was an enraged dragon, so they had to kill her now.

Stomp, dead. Fire breath, dead. Tail whip, dead. Razor teeth, dead. That was a whole lotta death and not a lot of winning.

This wasn't the time to start worrying about what would happen if they fucked up. It was time to focus up and see this fight through to the rightful conclusion. A Blue Dagger Society win. Cronos was sitting at twenty-four percent health, and all they needed to do was find a way to maintain their DPS.

They didn't have to improve, only hold the status quo.

The flames disappeared, and so did their protection. Cronos did what any cornered animal would do and found the weakest target and tried to take them out first. JaKobi tried to put up a wall of flames, but the boss ran through it.

At the last instant, Cassie managed to get her chain around Cronos' leg, and that one simple action might've saved their asses. JaKobi only took half of the swipe intended to end his life, which meant he was down but not out.

As long as Tim could reach him in time.

Heals poured out of Tim as if he existed only for this moment. Seeing his best friend lying on the ground in a pool of his blood tended to have that kind of effect on him. This was one of those never leave a man behind moments. He was willing to risk it all to save his friend. They were going to win this fight together.

How very poetic.

At least he didn't only have to heal his buddy back to full health. Tim got to deal out a little retribution while he was doing it. Most healers would have to wait for their friends to do the damage, but he didn't have that problem.

He switched his stance from Cassie to JaKobi and repeatedly blasted Cronos with Curse of Sacrifice, only stopping when the ember wizard was at one hundred percent. Then he switched his stance back to Cassie and duplicated the process.

Switching the target of his stances was a nice feature, and his DPS while JaKobi was out of the fight might be enough to keep them on track. The light under Cronos' feet was flashing again, and now she sent out multiple bursts of energy every time she moved. With a wave of one hand, the witch called forth swarms of bees. They flew through the garden in solid swarms that the group had to dodge or be overwhelmed. Now they not only had to dodge the bursts of electrical energy but roving clouds of stinging death.

"I fucking hate bees." Lorelei fired a flaming arrow into one of the swarms with no effect.

Tim pointed at Cronos. "Kill her, and they all go away."

"Now you're speaking my language." The spirit archer ran

forward, dove into a roll, and came up firing as if her very life depended on it.

Maybe it did.

Cassie had the boss now and was dragging her into position as the rest of them put everything they had into destroying the rest of her health. The bees swarming around were slowing them down, but there was nothing they could do about it. Life turned into a deadly game of dodge bee, which wasn't nearly as fun as dodgeball.

If you can dodge a bee, you can dodge a dragon.

Cronos's health dropped to fifteen percent, and she thrashed around. The change back into her dragon form was happening whether she wanted it to or not. They hit ten percent, then nine. This time the dragon didn't fly into the air but attacked them much more physically.

What big teeth you have.

Watching their tank's health fall like a rock gave him palpitations, but Tim kept on casting. He blew all his defensive cooldowns and let life devolve into a world that involved only two things, Healing Orb and Curse of Sacrifice.

At one percent, Cronos stopped taking damage.

Her dragon form fell away, and in its place was a beaten and broken woman. She looked up at Tim with a sad smile. "It seems even I can learn new lessons. It's too bad learning humility is such a kick in the teeth."

The last of her health started slowly ticking away. Then something amazing happened.

Eternia appeared floating down from the heavens. Cronos' health stopped dropping as the goddess extended her hand to help her to her feet. "Your time in this realm is at an end. Let me help you find peace in the next."

"You do me a great honor, Goddess, and it's not one I truly deserve." Cronos turned her eyes toward the adventurers. "Maybe there is one thing I can do for you before I go that will tip the scales of fate in my favor."

The goddess nodded in acceptance, and Cronos snapped her fingers. With that simple gesture complete, Eternia reached out, taking a firm grip of Cronos's arm, and they rose into the heavens together. When Tim turned his eyes back to the spot they'd been standing in, there was a beautiful golden chest.

It was loot time.

CHAPTER FORTY-SIX

"So what was all that about?" Cassie waved toward where Eternia and Cronos disappeared together. "It's not a lot of help to wave and fly off."

Tim looked up into the heavens. "Goddess things, and as to your second question, I guess we'll find out."

ShadowLily put an arm around his waist. "That's about as helpful as Cronos' last words."

It was true. His words were worth as much as dust in the wind. He didn't know what Eternia was up to and had even less idea what Cronos tried to reveal. The answer they were seeking could always be in the loot chest. It had been a while since they found items inside a chest, but it had happened. This situation might not be any different.

"Maybe it's in the loot," Tim ventured.

"In the loot, you say?" JaKobi ran forward.

The ember wizard made it about ten steps before Cassie's chain wrapped around his waist and yanked him back. "Not a chance, mister."

JaKobi bowed and moved out of the way. "It's only fair with

you saving my ass all the time."

"Don't you forget it." Cassie moved forward and laid her hand on the chest.

The tank pulled her hand back, leapt on top of the chest, and triumphantly hefted her bō staff in the air. "Necklace of the Dragon, it has magical resistances up the ass."

"Keeping it classy, as usual." Lorelei snickered as she moved to the chest.

The spirit archer turned toward them, taking a moment to process the piece of gear she received. "Mythical Wrist Guard of Tempted Fate. The item stores charges for every critical attack. When it reaches five charges, it's full, and the special effect activates. One of three things can happen when it does. Nothing, doubles my next attack's damage, or triples my next attack's damage but also takes fifteen percent of my health."

It was an amazing item but a risky one to use in key fights. The last thing they needed was for her special ability to trigger and kill her before he could get a heal off. On the other hand, he loved the idea of getting a supercharged attack, and there was a two out of three chance that nothing bad happened. Sure, it was risky, but it was the kind of risk that would pay off as long as he could keep up with the additional healing.

Hope my loot is as cool as hers.

"I think it's awesome," Tim blurted as everyone was thinking about the ramifications and the bonuses.

Lorelei grinned. "Damn straight it's awesome. The real question is how many times will it activate in a fight."

"Hope you brought your A-game because you're going to need it." ShadowLily nudged Tim as she moved toward the chest.

The mist slayer looked up a few moments later. "Not nearly as cool as Lorelei's, but I got a new pair of boots, and they boost all the right things in all the right places."

JaKobi glanced over his shoulder to make sure Tim wasn't in a big hurry and placed his hand on the chest. "Gloves of the Blazing

Sun. Boosts my newest spell and increases my stats. Nothing to complain about."

Tim knew the feeling well. It was nice to get an upgrade, but after seeing someone score a piece of epic loot, it was hard to get excited about a simple upgrade. Not that they didn't appreciate any upgrade, it was just some drops were more memorable than others. After his pants, he was due for a good roll.

Moving toward the chest, Tim tried to keep his hopes in check. "Hey, did anyone get anything besides loot?"

When four "no's" came back, Tim put his hand on the chest, thinking about when they'd find out what last surprise Cronos left for them.

Item Received: Dragon Hyde Jerkin

Dragons aren't easily killed in battle, and items made from their remains are even rarer. It might seem like a waste to use some of the most valuable material in the world to make a simple jerkin, but for Jalen the Clumsy, it was a simple matter of survival. He needed the extra protection and had the money to pay for the best. His legacy now lives on with you.

Hopefully, with a little less falling.

Increases all base stats by two and all secondary stats by one.

Tim held his breath as he looked over the description again. Sure, an additional plus one to his base stats wasn't all that big of a deal, but the increase to his secondary stats was amazing. This was the first time he'd ever received an item that increased those stats. It had been a while since he'd even thought of them at all. There were so many skills he had to increase that finding ways to up his secondary stats had fallen to the wayside.

With the update, Tim's Endurance hit thirty, and he received a small boost to damage reduction and a slight bump to his overall health. He wasn't as squishy as he used to be with the new armor pieces and increased endurance. Now he was turning into a healer who could stand in the thick of things without fear of dying to a single wayward hit.

"I got a new jerkin, with an increase to my secondary stats." Tim looked in the rest of his inventory to see if he received anything else and came up with bupkiss.

JaKobi looked incredulous. "Bro, nothing increases those stats. What an awesome drop."

Tim gave him a high five. "Thanks, man!"

"No information on the king?" Lorelei brought them all back to reality.

Tim shook his head. "Nope. Looks like we'll have to see if anything is waiting for us inside the castle."

"They better not force some random fight on us, like Cronos wasn't the real boss," Cassie grumbled as she led the way to the castle.

Smiling as he thought about what the fiery little tank said, Tim wouldn't have put a trick like that past the cruel developers that loved to taunt them with twists and turns in the story. This time the twist of another boss appearing didn't feel quite right. They defeated Cronos, and she'd promised them answers with the last words she spoke on this plane of existence. There had to be something they were missing.

"Let's get to the castle and find out." Tim reached out and stopped Cassie from taking off at a jog. "No running."

The rose garden faded away behind them as they worked their way back to the front of the castle. As they returned to the main path, the castle doors opened, and a woman walked out carrying a man in her arms like an infant.

Tim looked at ShadowLily, and she shrugged. His heart was racing. There was no way it could be who he thought it was, yet it wouldn't make any sense for it to be anyone but the king. If this was King Rasmus, who was with Prince Desmond at the castle?

"The Lady Cronos bid me return King Rasmus to you before sealing the castle grounds." The woman who must have magically enhanced strength walked forward and placed the king in Cassie's outstretched arms.

"With my duty done, let me show you to the borders of our land." Clapping her hands together, the woman created a portal and motioned for them to step inside.

Tim looked at Cassie carrying the vulnerable king in her arms. "I'll go first."

"Better let me." ShadowLily didn't have to say that she could survive a solo fight a lot longer than he could.

"I'm right behind you." Every fighter needed a good healer.

Tim followed her through the portal with Lorelei and JaKobi right behind him. Cassie brought up the rear with the king in her arms.

As he stepped out of the portal, Tim realized all his fears had been for nothing. The clearing they stood in was free of enemies and traps. The carriage was waiting for them, and Grant was already holding the door open. Cassie moved past the others with the sleeping King Rasmus held easily in her arms.

Tim cast Cleanse, but it didn't seem to have any effect on the king. If they wanted any real answers, they had to get the man back to Eternia and see if she could do more to heal him than he could. Once they revived the king, they could start planning the best way to help Prince Desmond get rid of the imposter.

Grant's eyes widened as the tank approached. "Is that who I think it is?"

Cassie grunted with effort as she lifted the king into the carriage. "Get us back to the inn as quickly as you can."

Tim turned to see the woman from the castle had followed them to the entrance. "Thank you for returning the king to us."

"Thank you for setting us free." The woman stepped back into the portal.

The shimmering border that marked the entrance to Cronos' land faded and left them looking at an empty forest as if the place had never existed. *Magic was so fucking cool.* Tim joined the others in the carriage.

"Let's get out of here." He tapped the top of the carriage, and it started to move.

"You weren't lying when you said this was the best food in the kingdom." Rasmus dipped his fork into some corned beef hash and ran it through some egg yolk before lifting it to his mouth.

Tim nodded at the comment as Joe and Roberto beamed with pride. "I'm telling you if my job were just to eat here twice a day, I'd be the happiest man in the world."

Eternia watched them all from her place by the fire. "It won't be long now before Desmond reaches out to us. You have to be ready."

ShadowLily lifted a glass of rumpleberry juice. "We're ready."

"The fight against the shapeshifter will be unlike anything you've ever faced. To come out victorious, you must be able to face your fears." Eternia smiled. "If you win, it will be a victory for the ages."

King Rasmus sipped his juice. "While you fight, I'll secure the stone for the goddess. So regardless of the outcome, before the fight is over, I'll have the stone safely into Eternia's hands."

Cassie ripped pieces off a giant cinnamon roll. "Just one more fight, and we finally get to take the battle back to Vitaria."

"This time, we'll be ready." Eternia stood. "Thank you, brave adventurers, for all that you've done. Let me bless you before you leave."

A wave of energy washed over the entire inn, and Tim felt refreshed as if he'd woken up from the best night's sleep he ever had. "Blue Dagger for life."

The cheer echoed across the room.

"Father, I have great news." Prince Desmond ran into the throne room. "The vile witch Cronos has been defeated."

The king stood and scowled with what Desmond could only describe as pure loathing. "Then we should honor the brave adventurers with medals and maybe something from the family vault."

He knew what the king was doing. Ever since the pretender had murdered his mother, he'd been searching for excuses to force Desmond into opening the vault. That was why he'd released Desmond from prison. So far, the prince had been able to politely refuse, knowing the imposter would never admit he couldn't open the vault himself.

The time for pretending was over.

"I think that would be a great idea," Prince Desmond replied smoothly. "Previously, I promised them the Stone of Immoratis. It seems like just the reward to honor their great victory."

The creature pretending to be Rasmus let out a low growl, and a bit of drool slipped down his chin before he was able to compose himself. "They deserve no less. Bring these adventurers before me and let us honor them as the heroes they are."

"It will be as you command, Father." Desmond swept from the room as if carrying out the creature's wish was his greatest desire.

Soon he would have his revenge for his mother's death. Desmond wouldn't rest until the thing that killed her was dead and burned to ash. As he walked from the castle back to the temple, and the only place he felt truly safe, the prince let out the first smile he'd had in days. The crisis was almost over, and they would soon be able to find their way back to a new version of normal.

"I'm going to miss you, Mom." Desmond whispered a prayer to the goddess, asking her to guide his mother's spirit toward the light and make sure she was as happy in the afterlife as she was with them.

CHAPTER FORTY-SEVEN

Prince Desmond met them outside the earl's gate. "Cherished adventurers, please allow me to join you as the captain of your honor guard and escort you safely to the castle."

Tim heard the words honor guard and thought prisoners was a better description for their trip than guests. "Thank you, Prince Desmond. We would be thrilled to have you join us." He held out his hand, giving the prince permission to enter their carriage.

When he sees who's inside, it's going to blow his mind.

"Grant, follow the king's men, no detours." He hoped the way he phrased it let the driver know the seriousness of their situation.

"Wouldn't dream of doing anything else." The carriage driver tipped his cap and closed the door.

Once the carriage was moving again, Tim turned his attention back to the prince. "You know all of us, but you haven't met our newest assistant."

"Assistant my ass." King Rasmus removed his hood. "I might owe you my life, but I'm still the fucking king."

Tim bowed his head in subservience. "Your Majesty."

"Dad." Prince Desmond reached out, unable to believe it. When his hand touched the king, he broke down in tears. "I have terrible news."

Rasmus moved swiftly, pulling his son into a fierce hug. "The Goddess Eternia told me everything. We will deal with the thing that killed your mother, and then we'll lay your mother to rest properly."

There was quiet determination in Rasmus' voice, but it was easy enough for all of them to see he was heartbroken. The burden of leadership didn't give the king the option of indulging in his grief until the kingdom was secure. Being sad didn't keep people fed or the forces of evil at bay.

It was heartbreaking to watch, yet the king earned Tim's deepest respect at that moment. A true leader would always put the needs of his subjects in front of their own. Tim was excited to see what the king would be like once he returned to his throne.

"I look forward to seeing her off properly." Prince Desmond's back straightened. "Now, tell me what the six of you have planned and how I can help."

Cassie slapped Prince Desmond on the shoulder. "You know, I was on the fence about you, but you're a pretty good guy."

Lorelei rolled her eyes. "What she meant to say is we're sorry for your loss."

"And happy to reunite the two of you," ShadowLily added smoothly.

The king chuckled as he watched his son's head move from person to person, trying to keep up. "I can see you've had your hands full dealing with these adventurers."

"I've been willing to indulge them because they don't only solve problems but generate sensational taxes for the kingdom." Desmond looked pointedly at Tim. "Yes, I know who Mr. Applebottom works for."

"Ah, I thought that inn looked familiar." The king slammed his fist into his leg. "The Blue Dagger. It sure looks different, and the food is so much better than anything else in the kingdom."

Turning back to the prince the king smiled widely. "I can't even explain to you the delights. We'll have to go together."

"Eat in the city? You're not going to have the chef come to the castle?" Desmond looked flabbergasted.

The king nodded. "I've been away from my people for too long. How can I ever hope to rule them if I can't understand them?"

"That carrot cake didn't hurt, right?" Cassie nudged Rasmus in the ribs, realized what she'd done, and scooted away. "Ah, sorry, Your Majesty."

The king waved dismissively. "Think nothing of it. It's been a long time since I've spoken with anyone who didn't constantly kiss my ass. It's quite refreshing in small doses." He raised an eyebrow as he waited to see if she got the point.

Cassie relaxed. "So what do you say we fill the prince in on the plan and get ready to rock and roll."

"Rock and roll?" Rasmus looked at them quizzically.

Tim grinned. "It's something we say where we're from when we're ready to kick some ass."

"That's something I can understand." The king leaned back in his seat and looked at his son. "Get ready. You're going to enjoy this."

Desmond looked at the assembled adventurers with excitement. "Of that, I have no doubt."

<hr>

The shapeshifter looked down on the assembled group of adventurers with a loathing smile.

Prince Desmond stood boldly before the throne. "Father, may I present to you the Blue Dagger Society. Slayers of Isadora and Cronos, saviors of our kingdom."

If the thing pretending to be the king was impressed, he gave no indication. "These are the ones that slew Cronos? I almost find it unbelievable."

The court gasped at his words. They thought they were coming to see a reward ceremony, and that clearly wasn't going to happen.

"Leave us!" The king roared from the throne. "I wish to attend to these slayers of witches myself."

As the courtesans and their guards filed out, the king looked at Desmond. "Shouldn't you be fetching their reward?"

"Originally, I hoped to see them honored, but you are right, Father. I will go and get the stone for them immediately." Desmond looked toward the doors of the throne room as they were sealed shut.

There's no getting out of this now.

Tim wasn't one to miss too many tricks. The pretender had locked them all inside the throne room together. If they'd ever questioned whether a fight was coming their way, they had their answer. How smart the both of them thought they were, each setting traps for the other when it had always been inevitable they would end up right here.

He bowed low and addressed the throne. "Your Majesty, before you see to our promised restitution, I wondered if I could beg one last boon from you."

"I grow tired of these endless demands upon my time." The imposter smiled, and his lips pulled wider, showing an extra row of teeth. "But speak your request, lest my son thinks me uncouth."

Tim bowed low again. "Thank you for your kindness. I have but a single request, and I hope you will honor it. If you could spare the good Prince Desmond for a few moments, I'd appreciate it if he could escort our servant to the temple? He's a huge fan of the architecture, and if I have to listen to him gripe about not seeing it the entire ride home, I'll lose my mind."

"Go." The king smiled. "I do enjoy a request that requires zero effort on my behalf. Open the doors," he roared. "But only Desmond and the servant leave."

Prince Desmond stopped in front of Tim and shook his hand. "Thank you for your service to the crown."

"I expect your father will fully compensate me for the risk." Tim smiled back, hoping he could wrangle a few more properties from the crown. "Please see that our servant is well-treated until we return."

"You have my word." The prince took the real king's arm and led him from the room.

They have work to do, but so do we.

The shapeshifter rose from the throne, shed his Rasmus-like skin, and stood to its full height. He was ten feet tall now, with hands and feet that looked more like claws for tearing into meat versus something to walk on. His mouth was wider than it should have been and lined with teeth so sharp it would've made Jaws jealous.

Now that his façade had lifted, the shapeshifter sighed. "I hate wearing that thing. It's so restricting."

Tim felt laughter roll up from his belly before he could stop it. The comment seemed so wrong for the moment, yet he loved it. It was like something from one of his favorite movies.

He grinned up into the devilish face of the shapeshifter and gave a little bow. "I'm happy to see your true face finally. I was getting tired of the Edgar suit."

"Mock me if you must, little human, but tonight I feast on the bones of adventurers, and tomorrow I take the stone to resurrect my mistress." The shifter smiled, knowing they had no way out of the throne room.

Cassie snorted. "You think we're scared to be in here with you? You should be scared to be in here with us."

Without another word, she charged into the battle.

"Oh shit, there goes the neighborhood." JaKobi fired his sunbeam with a grin.

Cassie and the shapeshifter clashed together. The creature used its claws and extra-long arms like spears as it tried to murder the tank. She took a few hits, and her health started to plummet. It didn't take long for Tim to figure out the boss had a stackable DOT titled Drain that was applied every time he hit the tank.

Cleanse worked to remove the stacks, but by the time he cast Curse of Giving, Curse of Sacrifice, and Hex of the Shattered Beast on the boss, the stacks were right back to where he had to be concerned. If they wanted to win this fight, the theme of the night would be casting Cleanse almost as often as his heals.

"Anyone not named Cassie who gets the DOT on them, call it out." Tim watched his Golden Retriever charge at the shapeshifter and burst from his back covered in red mist before disappearing.

The game was right, it was a little crazy for him to have the world's friendliest animal as his Hex Beast, but he couldn't help himself. Every time he used the spell, he loved watching the dog appear and return some of the damage done to Cassie back to the boss. There was something rewarding in working together with an animal, even if his pet was a spirit manifestation.

When ShadowLily entered the fray, Tim's need to cast Cleanse increased dramatically. The mist slayer wasn't taking as many hits as Cassie, but her damage reduction and health pool weren't nearly as big as the tank's. He kept his eyes flickering to her because there was no way she could call out every single hit. At least for the time being, Lorelei and JaKobi weren't taking any damage so things were going relatively well in the mana department.

At ninety percent, there was a random twitch of the boss's shoulder, and Tim cast his interrupt. It might have been a mistake to use it this early, but he didn't want to see what the boss' special attack was unless they had to. With the attack stopped, the boss was stunned for a second. Then he cast a buff on himself.

Incinerator: One hundred percent increase to fire damage.

Fire damage? He hasn't cast a spell yet.

As if on cue, the shapeshifter reached into the pouch at his waist and threw five golden coins into the room. As they flew from the creature's hand, they grew in size and landed on the floor. A pulsing red circle appeared around them.

The only thing Tim could think of as an explanation was the coins were landmines, but instead of popping in the air and releasing the ultimate destruction, these would release their inferno in a column of energy.

With the boss' fire attacks buffed, hitting one of those traps might as well have been a death sentence.

"Landmines!" he cried, hoping everyone had the good sense to stay away from the pulsing red circles on the ground.

Ten seconds later the mines went off, and gouts of blue flame launched into the air like erupting volcanoes. The flames faded away, but the scorch marks on the floor were still pulsing red, letting him know they would do damage if they stepped on those spots. Scorch marks weren't only for esthetics.

"Watch your feet," Tim called as he saw JaKobi's health plummet.

The ember wizard was busy putting out a fire on his robes. "You know, it feels a lot better when I'm the one doing the burning."

"I bet it does." Tim splashed him with a Healing Orb and cast a group Cleanse.

The group Cleanse was the right spell to use if something affected three or more of them. Otherwise, it was cheaper to cast the single-target version. In this instance, it saved him time from having to check the two women's stats as he turned his attention back to bolster their health.

Sometimes healing felt like running a cost-benefit analysis.

They cruised past eighty-five percent health, and Tim cast Behold My Power. It felt like the right time to drop his hardest-hitting spell. The shapeshifter already tried to initiate a special attack and buffed himself so it felt too early for a phase change. Stranger things had happened to Tim in fights, but that much coming at them all at once felt like overkill. The fights should get harder as they went on, not blast you out of the water before you had a chance to swim.

When the boss hit eighty percent, Tim watched intently to see if he saw the same twitch as before. "ShadowLily, interrupt!"

The mist slayer broke off her attack instantly and cast her interrupt. God, he loved playing with high throughput players. She didn't question his call, she did what he wanted instantly, and it worked perfectly.

Now it was Tim's turn to act. As soon as her interrupt hit, he cast Rectify and stopped the buff from going off. No one should be stepping in the fire anyway, but if they did, he wanted them to take as little damage as possible.

A grin spread across his face as he thought about their last few moves. Together they managed to stop an attack and the buff. Not only that, but the group did it without wasting an extra interrupt. Now they might have one available down the stretch when they really needed it.

Behold My Power activated as the shapeshifter threw out five more coins. Everyone in their group saw the attack the first time it went off so they were ready to avoid the perils of the fire swamp. Their real problem was the original five landmines, and the patches they left behind hadn't disappeared yet. A few more casts, and they were going to start having trouble moving around the room.

It's only ten spots. Ten isn't so bad.

Cassie rotated the boss a little so the next set of coins might cover an area they'd already hit. It was the right idea, but he didn't think they would see another coin attack until after the first phase change. Things were going well after stopping the special attack and the buff, but when things felt easy, it meant they were about to get hit with the whammy.

The boss hit seventy-five percent health, and all hell broke loose.

ShadowLily disappeared, and so did the shapeshifter. Tim had no idea what was going on, but it didn't make sense for them to stay spread out so they could be picked off one at a time.

"Group up." They rallied to him, backs together, watching for any sign of attack.

Tim thought they might get off lucky and that this part of the fight would come down to ShadowLily kicking the shapeshifter's ass mano-a-mano while they waited around. He wasn't worried for her. Tim knew she'd win. He was scared to find out what was coming for them.

The circles on the floor left behind from the landmines pulsed, and the surface started to shift. As it cracked, an insectile head worked its way free. Moments later, a wasp hovered in the air in front of them.

Lorelei was on it, using her bow to bring the creature down, but soon the other circles were disgorging hellish flying creatures. The group had to scramble to try and bring them down before they were overwhelmed.

Normally a few wasps wouldn't be that scary, but these ugly things had two-foot-long stingers dripping green poison. The drips left little *hisses* of steam when they hit the floor. Tim didn't want to know what it would feel like to have that vile stuff injected into him.

JaKobi took the lead, casting a few of his Flame Walls to herd the wasps into a kill zone, while Lorelei hit them with volley after volley of an AOE attack. Tim added Flame Burst to the mix as Cassie sat back and watched all the excitement.

The tank blew on her nails before buffing them on her leather vest. "What? I'm not getting close to those things."

"Might not have a choice, depending on how many there are in the next round." Tim turned, taking in the room as he waited for ShadowLily to return.

Ash fell to the floor as the wasps burned away to nothing. The game AI was right about lighting things on fire. It was kind of fun. Not that he'd start running around burning every innocent animal he saw for shits and gigs, but if something was trying to kill him, Tim had no problem burning it to death.

Everyone's health looked fine. With all the wasps defeated, this was the time to regenerate some of their mana. Tim had the feeling when ShadowLily reappeared, she would need a Cleanse and a lot of heals, so having the downtime to recharge was a pleasant surprise.

The middle of the room started flashing red, and everyone scattered out of the way. Flames shot up from the floor in a raging inferno of swirling heat.

That was an insta-kill mechanic!

When the flames winked out, ShadowLily knelt on the floor, bleeding from several wounds as the shapeshifter stood over her gasping for breath. Tim only had eyes for his girlfriend and started casting Cleanse to stop the damage so he could heal her properly. What he should have been doing was calling the attack because the boss was stunned, and this was their time to do as much damage as they could.

"Attack!" Cassie roared.

For the next five seconds, the boss took one hell of a beating. Tim would've loved to be a bigger part of the action, but his attention stayed focused on casting Healing Orb on his girlfriend before reapplying Curse of Giving to keep Cassie in the fight. With everyone's health back in a decent place, they fell into the rhythm of the fight.

The shapeshifter threw out his coins. They avoided the fire and the lingering spots it left as best they could. Cassie managed to interrupt the boss's special attack. That meant only the ranged DPS had their interrupts left, and they would need at least one more to survive, probably both.

"Your deaths are inevitable," the shapeshifter roared, using its magic to push them to the side of the room.

JaKobi snickered. "I thought my death would come because I

like eating cheeseburgers and washing them down with ice cream and brownies."

"Old age for me. I'm basically a saint," Lorelei added as she fired an arrow at the boss.

The arrow stopped a foot away from the shapeshifter and fell to the floor. Then he disappeared again. ShadowLily shouted something, some kind of instructions. Or maybe a warning? Tim couldn't make out the words. Everything around him was getting drowned out and muddy.

Holy shit, did he get sucked into one-on-one combat?

Sometimes the game seemed so unfair. It was hard enough being a healer. Having to face off against the boss solo was some next-level shit.

Thankfully his class centered around doing DPS. A more traditional healer might as well have cashed it in and hoped the next time they tried the fight, the RNG gods would be more forgiving and pick someone else. He didn't know how the rest of his group was faring without being up top, so Tim had to find a way to end this soon.

The one thing he didn't expect to see waiting for him as his vision cleared was a clone of himself.

The shapeshifter smiled and looked at its new skin. "Not much to look at, but powerful enough to end your life."

A blast of Divine Light launched from the shifter's hand. Tim threw himself to the side, hitting the deck hard. The first casts he made as he climbed back to his feet were Who Needs a Shield and Hex of the Shattered Beast. He didn't have a single doubt in his head that he'd be taking damage soon, and the more he could send back at the shifter, the better.

Plus, with his dog here, he didn't feel quite so alone.

Tim threw himself to the floor to avoid another attack and ate a blast of Divine Light as he returned fire. Cures of Giving and Curse of Sacrifice returned his health to one hundred percent, but the damage his first two spells did to the boss was like throwing raindrops in a river. To get out of this alive, he might have to get creative.

Rushing forward with his staff in hand, Tim swung the weapon at the shifter and felt gratified when it smashed into his side. He'd never used his staff as a direct weapon, and the creature wasn't expecting the attack at all. While the boss was distracted, Tim cast his highest single-target spell, Divine Light.

The shifter came at him with everything it had, and for the first time, Tim took damage in earnest. It was fucking weird casting spells and swinging his staff at himself. He'd wrestled with himself plenty in his life, normally over something trivial like going to a party on a school night instead of studying, but that was an internal battle.

This was something else entirely. It was like shadowboxing in the mirror. Only if he lost this fight, he'd be dead instead of merely tired.

Thinking of the people counting on him to man up was what drove Tim to push as hard as he could to win. He couldn't let them down. It simply wasn't going to happen. He'd screwed up fights before but not this time. This time he was going to come out on top.

Hex of the Shattered Beast activated, and an unexpected force threw Tim to the floor. A DOT started ticking, and his health plummeted like a rock thrown in the ocean.

He was stunned. Then the flames rose around him. Tim screamed, but the fire didn't burn his skin as he expected. This must be it, the transition back to his friends.

Like that, Tim was standing back in the center of the room. He wanted to rejoice at rejoining the group, but everyone's health looked as bad as his. How long had he been gone? Was there something worse than the wasps coming out of the fire spots this time? He'd have to get with the others and compare notes after the fight. For now, all Tim had time to do was heal.

The boss's health was at forty-five percent, but Tim's was lower.

Healing rain fell from the heavens, interrupted only for a moment when Tim stopped casting Healing Storm and cast Mass Cleanse to free himself from the DOT and anyone else it might be affecting. As soon as everyone's health hit fifty percent, he turned off the waterworks and sent out three Healing Orb to cover the group in Hydrate. With the heavy lifting out of the way, Tim focused on Cassie as she battled the boss toe-to-toe.

"Lorelei, watch for the shoulder shake, and interrupt." Tim knew it was risky leaving JaKobi's interrupt until last.

The ember wizard had a way of getting lost in his rotation and not reacting to the calls as quickly as the others. Tim was putting a lot of faith in his friend and knew it would reward him when the right time came.

"I'm on it." The spirit archer growled as she dodged a burst of fire from the floor and sent a wave of arrows at the boss in response.

With the fight back in full swing, they were all waiting for the new wrinkle to show itself. It didn't take long for them to see the first thing that changed. Intermittent pillars of flame burst from random floor sections, and now the shifter threw out ten coins at a time. With the extra fire, additional coins, and the DOT on the tank, his healing was depleting his mana at a rapid rate.

Tim did his best work when things got dicey. Everything else fell away, and his casts came so rapidly his fingers hurt. They'd been able to handle ten wasps with ease, but twenty or more was asking a lot. Tim was pretty sure they could handle the flying invasion, but he hoped they didn't have to take the chance when they were this close to victory.

All they needed to do was stick with the plan.

At thirty percent health, a beam of light at ankle height swept across the room. They'd seen this trick before and knew how to beat it. If the developers added a second beam they had to duck under like last time, the fight would turn into a total shit show. They all handled the movement well, but it always made things more interesting. All it took was one little slip, and it was time to see Barbara.

Whatever happened to a good old-fashioned tank and spank or the ever-present loot pinata?

When the shapeshifter hit twenty-five percent health, Tim expected one of his friends to disappear into the void to face one more battle. Instead, the mechanic swept them to the edge of the throne room. Flames covered the far wall and started moving slowly forward. Tim watched the fire frantically, thinking it was fucked up that they would die because he must've missed some mechanic.

Then Tim saw a gap in the flames.

"Come on." He ran toward the gap. Then he noticed the next wave of flames coming toward them.

He sprinted now. "Hurry!"

Cassie didn't hesitate for a second. She picked up JaKobi and sprinted. The group made it through the first gap and ran for the next one. They zig-zagged their way across the throne room until they reached the boss. The shifter's shoulders started to shake as Cassie tossed JaKobi off her shoulder with a grunt.

"Make him hurt!" Cassie ran toward the shapeshifter.

Tim cringed, waiting for the boss's mega attack to go off. If he didn't die, he'd pick up the pieces as best he could, but if JaKobi didn't get his interrupt off, the fight was probably over. They were so close to ending this thing it would be a shame to die now.

A few seconds ticked past, and Tim opened his eyes. He wasn't in Barbara's waiting room so they must not have died. If they weren't dead, he had fucking work to do. JaKobi was lucky they were still in the middle of the fight, or he might have punched the mad bastard for cutting it so close. He was going to have to give him a new nickname after this.

Maybe the Heart Attack Kid.

The shapeshifter hit fifteen percent health and blasted all of them with an uncleansable DOT. This was it, the final race to the finish. Could Tim keep them alive long enough to win? He didn't hesitate for a second to start casting Healing Orb on the group.

When things got real, Tim slipped into a totally different mindset. This was his time to shine—the moment he lived for. There was no way he'd let them down.

The battle took a turn against them as the uncleansable DOT stacked with the shapeshifter's normal attack. With both getting pounded by double damage, it was all he could do to stem the tide. Even when he used Cleanse to set the two melee fighters back to even footing, it lasted only a few seconds. The damage was piling up. Maybe he'd been a little too cocky.

If things didn't improve quickly, Tim would have to change stances and hope Cassie could handle losing his defensive protection.

The boss hit ten percent. The entire group's health was reeling.

Tim pulled the plug on his Way of the Boulder stance and flipped into Way of the River. He cast Hex of the Shattered Beast on Cassie and got back to doing as much damage as possible, now that his heals were going out to the entire group. The healing they received was less than it would have been if he flipped Way of the Boulder to each person as he healed, but now he was healing everyone at once without having to cast Healing Storm. It was cost-effective as long as Cassie didn't die.

By the time the boss hit five percent health Tim was casting Curse of Sacrifice on repeat. Every blast returned a small portion of his health because of his stance, so it eased the burden of the curse on his health pool. At this point, he didn't care if he ended the fight at one hit point. He wanted it to be over and for them to be victorious.

Small pulses of energy flashed from the shapeshifter. It was all unavoidable damage, and Tim cast Who Needs a Shield to try and buffer as much of it as he could. Instead of breaking down and casting Healing Storm like he normally would, Tim continued to focus on casting Curse of Sacrifice and Divine Light.

The extra damage was nice, but in his current stance, the damage he was doing was the only thing keeping them alive. The only time he stopped damaging was when something forced him to cast a Cleanse.

The party's health was falling fast, but the shapeshifter's was falling faster.

With one final scream, the Shifter spun out of control. Its body turned into a version of Tim, then ShadowLily, then the king, before finally exploding in a burst of golden motes.

They did it. The fight was over.

CHAPTER FORTY-EIGHT

"I really, from the bottom of my heart, love getting new fucking loot." Cassie watched as the motes rose into the heavens and the golden chest appeared.

JaKobi pulled her into a hug and kissed her. "Doesn't feel too bad saving the kingdom. I kinda like being a hero."

"He's not even bragging." Lorelei had a smile on her face that would have lit up the sky brighter than a full moon. "I really thought we were toast there for a second."

ShadowLily wrapped an arm around Tim's waist. "That's my man, coming through in the clutch."

Tim brushed some imaginary dust from his shoulder and moved toward the chest. "Biggest heroes get first dibs."

"And he's so modest." ShadowLily gave him a look that said he wouldn't be going first if he valued having sex any time soon.

Tim gave a nervous laugh. "You know, on second thought, maybe someone else should go first."

He didn't think his girlfriend would ever use sex as a weapon like that, but why take the risk? He knew he'd get a piece of loot regardless of what order he touched the chest. As awesome as getting his next piece of loot sounded, the real question was whether the king and Prince Desmond secured the stone. At this very moment, the Stone of Immoratis could be sitting in Eternia's hands.

It was one hell of a plan for them to sneak out and power up the goddess while the Blue Dagger Society fought against the shapeshifter. Thankfully they stalled the boss permanently, but if they hadn't succeeded, as long as they battled the creature long enough, good would have carried the day. Tim would have loved to have seen the shapeshifter's face when the king strode back into the throne room at the head of an army. Thankfully for the guards and their families, that particular scenario never played out.

"So who's going first?" Tim looked around the group, his eyes settling on ShadowLily's last.

She laughed. "You are. I just didn't want you to be so damn smug about it."

"Smug isn't something I'm known for. Maybe you meant to highlight one of my other wonderful qualities? Perhaps my loyalty to my friends, or that thing I do with the hot sauce that you like so much."

The mist slayer let out a little giggle. "Well, there is always that." She pushed him forward. "Show us how it's done."

If there was one thing Tim knew how to do, it was when to accept a gift. "Don't mind if I do."

It felt like it had been a while since he was first up, but it probably hadn't been that long. He didn't know why, but he felt nervous, like his piece of gear would set the tone for everyone else. Yep, that was it. He was altruistic by hoping he got awesome loot to inspire others.

What a load of shit. He just wanted something cool.

Reaching out and hoping for the best, Tim laid his hand on the chest.

Item Received: Arlen's Boots of Chaotic Intent

Arlen was a man of many passions. That tended to come out

in the magical items he enchanted. With so many of them being unpredictable, his business fell to the wayside, but several of Arlen's magical items are still floating around the kingdom to this day. Equip any two or more pieces of Arlen's gear to receive additional bonuses.

+3 Endurance +4 Intelligence +6 Wisdom

The stats were nice, but he was giving up two dexterity in the switch, and his boots increased mana regeneration. While the additional protection and stats made the switch a no-brainer, Tim hated to see his dexterity go down at all. If he ever needed to use his daggers again, that skill was priceless. Not to mention it helped him dodge attacks. Something he was rather good at despite the game's insistence that he tossed his body around like a rag doll.

Maybe those flops and flails were cool parkour moves to the untrained eye. Oh man, he better not even think stuff like that or he'd pay for it later. The game had a way of keeping him grounded when he got too big for his britches, and normally it was death.

You're a good AI, a great AI, and clearly, I toss myself around as you say, Tim thought as he moved down to read the item's special ability.

Special Ability: Chaotic Intent

While Arlen's many skills ended up being a detriment as much as they were a boon, he sometimes made incredible enchants the world had never seen the likes of. Arlen often claimed all of the credit for his fantastic items, but what it really came down to was his lucky boots. Every skill used while wearing these boots will be subject to Chaotic Intent. The special ability will reduce or increase the effectiveness of each cast by between one and ten percent.

Tim knew everyone was watching him, but he was still trying to wrap his head around the item. The special ability made it risky. A negative ten percent roll at the wrong time might kill them, but a plus ten and he could be the group's savior when they should be dead. It was a risk. He'd have to watch his numbers and see how the item felt. If the boots trended more positive, they were a keeper. If the item kept his stats even, he might wait and see if he could track down another of Arlen's items of a larger benefit before replacing them outright.

Turning around to face the group, Tim let a smile crack his features so they knew the item was good. "I got a set-piece, but it's got a wonky special ability."

"How wonky?" JaKobi asked as he made his way forward.

Tim almost laughed out loud. For some reason, he saw himself inside Willy Wonka's chocolate factory. Finding Arlen's items was like when Charlie received the factory at the end of the movie. As long as it wasn't the Tim Burton version, the next item he found in the set would make the boots even more powerful.

"Plus or minus one to ten percent effectiveness on every skill used." It sounded weird saying it out loud, but Tim had the feeling that with a few more pieces of Arlen's gear, the odds of those numbers being on the plus side would be in his favor.

JaKobi patted him on the back. "That's pretty cool, man. Set items are the best stuff in the game."

Lorelei moved past them to put her hand on the chest. "But not until you get more than one."

Turning away from the chest to face the group, Lorelei wore a smile as well. "Necklace of Deadly Precision."

Tim leaned in closer to get a better look. "Are those dice?"

"Yep, but mine only increases my skills effectiveness," Lorelei smugly replied as she stuck out her tongue and blew him a raspberry.

That seemed a bit unfair unless the increases were lower. Tim put the thought out of his head. He didn't care who had the best items in the group, only that each item helped them win. Lorelei was an amazing DPS, and any extra damage she did would help all of them. So instead of feeling cheated about his item, he basked in the awesomeness that was their group.

"Don't go ruining my tough-guy vibe, but I'm happy for you." Tim hugged her.

ShadowLily laughed. "You've never had a tough-guy vibe. Trust me, that's part of what I love about you."

She moved away from Tim, reached out, and put her hand on the chest. She turned a moment later, looking like a college kid who received a free pizza sent to their dorm room. "Ring of the Silent Predator. Boosts my stealth and damage out of stealth."

"And the stats." The mist slayer put a hand to her forehead and pretended to swoon. "Are fucking unbelievable."

"Damn girl, save some for the rest of us." Cassie made her way to the chest, then stopped. "Hey, babe, why don't you go first."

JaKobi looked at her like it was a trap, but then he went for it.

Right before he reached the chest, she laid her hand on it instead. "I'll make it up to you later."

"Seems like a good deal for me." The ember wizard waited to see what his girlfriend pulled from the chest with a twinkle in his eyes.

Cassie turned back to the group. "Bracers of Strength, not the greatest title, but they do exactly what you think. Also, special ability to swap my strength with any other stat for five seconds."

"Whoa, so you could switch strength and dexterity for the ability to dodge more, or strength and willpower to recover more mana? That's a pretty handy talent." Tim thought about all the potential ways an item like that could be useful and was a little jealous.

Wisdom to Dexterity and activate Quick Feet, he'd run a mile before anyone else even took a step.

Cassie was beaming with pride. "I really do love it." She turned to JaKobi. "Time for you to put our gear to shame."

"If I don't get something epic, I get to do the thing with the butterscotch?" When Cassie nodded, he added, "Then I don't even care."

He slammed his hand down on the chest. "Come on, big

whammy, give me the whammy!"

Tim laughed. He'd never seen someone try and get worse loot so they could have kinky sex.

JaKobi looked crestfallen as he turned. "Sun Staff of the True Believer, and it's fucking awesome."

"It's okay. I already placed the order for butterscotch." Cassie winked at him. "You know it's one of my favorite games too."

JaKobi gave a wild fist pump and pointed at Tim. "Are you ready to go? I have plans."

"Damn straight I am, but first, we have something to show them." Tim lined up next to his friend as the chest disappeared, and they got down with their new dance.

The ladies cringed as they watched, but the boys were having more fun than Kid 'n Play. They only stopped and looked up when someone at the back of the room cleared their throat. The real King Rasmus was standing before them with an amused expression.

"That was something you don't see every day," the king commented offhandedly to the prince.

Desmond was trying to keep a straight face but couldn't quite manage the task. "It certainly was."

King Rasmus moved toward the group, pulled a wooden box from his inventory, and presented it to them. "We didn't have time to make it out of the castle, but as promised, the Stone of Immoratis."

The king handed Tim the box, and he passed it to Cassie for safekeeping. "Thank you, King Rasmus, for living up to your word." He turned slightly. "You as well, Prince Desmond."

Desmond waved dismissively. "You did all of the hard work. It is we who find ourselves in your debt yet again."

"Along those lines, we should hold a great celebration to honor the brave adventurers." Rasmus looked thrilled by the idea. "The entire kingdom would celebrate."

Tim looked at the group for confirmation, and he felt confident enough with what he saw there to proceed. "As much as we'd love a big party, our quest for the goddess continues."

Bowing his head as if in mourning, Tim continued, "We've heard about the queen and think it would be much more fitting to honor her sacrifice. Without her steadfast will in the face of certain death, we wouldn't have the stone now, and Vitaria would have won."

The king looked sad as he thought about his wife. It must have been a real blow to be released from Cronos' grasp only to find out his wife was dead. Tim saw ShadowLily die once, and even knowing she could come back, it almost broke him.

"I can see the wisdom in your words." King Rasmus extended his hand. "You have my thanks, and each of you can pick an item from my treasury for your service to the crown."

Extra loot was always a great bonus.

Tim shook the king's hand and Desmond's. "If you ever need us, Liz at the Blue Dagger Inn can always get in touch with us."

Cassie tapped her wrist. "We have a goddess waiting. Let's get moving."

The king bowed to them. "When you finish with your quest in the desert, come and see me again. For adventurers with your talents, there is always work available."

"Then you will see us again shortly." ShadowLily returned the bow. "How do we get out of here with all the doors locked?"

"I'll handle that." Rasmus winked at her. "Guards!"

The doors flew open so quickly it was like a tornado had burst into the room.

The king addressed the head of his guard. "See these adventurers returned to their carriage and safely back to Blue Dagger Inn."

"Yes, Your Majesty." The man saluted and motioned for them to follow him out of the throne room.

Tim couldn't believe it. After all their work, they finally had the stone and good news for Eternia.

CHAPTER FORTY-NINE

Eternia was waiting for them by the fireplace in her room.

It was funny how Tim could imagine their great victory so differently than from how it happened. There was no ceremony like at the end of *Star Wars*. No one was going to pin a medal on his chest. Instead, he knelt on one knee with the rest of his group right behind him.

While this moment didn't have the fanfare and the fluff, it was much more intimate. He saw the appreciation in the goddess' eyes, and it meant the world to him. This was a special moment. The tide of fortune was turning slowly in their favor. Soon the goddess would be back to full strength, and they could take the fight back to Vitaria.

Eternia had a way of looking at a person and knowing them as intimately as if they had been friends their entire lives. As he knelt in front of her, Tim hoped she could feel his gratitude. The quest she had sent them on was daunting, but it had also been rewarding.

The grin he was wearing as he met Eternia's eyes threatened to split his mouth at the corners. "We have retrieved the Stone of Immoratis and present it to you now."

Cassie stood, pulling the wooden box from her inventory. She moved forward with purpose and placed the box into Eternia's waiting hands. "I think you'll find this is what you've been looking for."

Eternia took the box and opened it slightly. A smile spread across her lips. "I can already feel my power returning. In a few days, I'll be strong enough to reactivate the portal network. A few days after that I'll be back to full strength, and our battle in the desert will continue."

Tim rose to his feet and felt the warm glow of a job well done spreading through him. This quest had taken everything they had, they even died, but in the end, they came out on top and delivered the stone. It felt great, and they still had rewards to claim. He could tell Eternia wanted some privacy so she could do whatever she needed to activate the stone away from their prying eyes.

"Will you be here in the morning to go over our next steps?" Tim knew she wouldn't miss the hint that he was trying to leave.

Eternia set the box down on the table next to her chair before standing and pulling Tim into a warm embrace. When the goddess released him, she moved to Cassie and the rest of the group.

When she finished showing her affection, Eternia returned to her seat. "I would think the five of you would be looking forward to a little downtime. Enjoy this moment, for soon all of Promethia will need your services again."

The goddess looked thoughtful. "As my power returns, I can already spot several locations and adventures where you could make a difference, but our first duty must be stopping Vitaria."

Ushering them from her room with her gaze, the goddess smiled warmly. "So go and indulge yourselves in life. For the next three days, your only duty is to do nothing but think of yourself, to recharge your energy for the fight that lies ahead."

"Wait, we're getting a vacation?" JaKobi clapped. "I can finally go to the library."

Cassie hooked her thumb at him. "This guy gets his first vacation in the game, and he doesn't think *beach party*. He thinks of going to the library."

"Is it wrong I was thinking about the forge?" Tim looked at ShadowLily for confirmation.

The mist slayer kissed him. "Of course not, as long as you start tomorrow. Tonight you're all mine."

"Sounds like I win twice on that deal." Tim couldn't believe his luck.

ShadowLily tugged his arm, pulling him from the room. "I'm also hoping to win twice."

"Oh snap! "JaKobi catcalled as they made their way toward the door.

They were about to leave when Tim jerked them to a stop. It didn't feel right that they could all celebrate, but Lorelei couldn't see Neema.

"Eternia, I know it's not my place to ask, but…" His voice trailed off as the goddess nodded.

Eternia stood from her chair once again and took Lorelei's hand in hers. "The portals will be active in three days. Enjoy your time with her."

It dawned on the spirit archer what Tim had asked for. She ran toward him and pulled him into a hug. "Thank you."

"Just looking out for one of my friends." Tim returned the hug and laughed as the goddess touched Lorelei, and she disappeared.

ShadowLily tugged Tim's arm. "That was some sexy stuff, mister."

"I do have my moments." He let himself be dragged out the door and into their private suite.

"Babe, I'm heading down to Joe's to get something to eat," Shadow-Lily announced right before the door closed.

Normally he would've been worried about missing a delicious meal, but he knew she wouldn't come back without something for him. He deserved this shower. He'd earned it in the throes of passion. Sometimes a good roll in the hay was better than a week's worth of cardio—okay, it was better than cardio all the time.

While he was in the shower was also the perfect time to hand in the last of his pending quests. The last thing he wanted to do was leave a big pile of quest clean-up for tomorrow. Tim had the feeling despite their need for a vacation, they wouldn't be on one as long as they thought. Adventures had a way of finding them.

Tomorrow, Tim would spend the day at the forge. He'd been away from Ironbeard's shop for way too long.

Part of him wondered if swinging the hammer would be easier now that he didn't have the strength of a six-year-old.

He pulled up his user interface and went straight to his quest updates. Despite the fact he earned this shower, if he were MIA for more than an hour, he would be in a lot of trouble.

Quest Complete: Veil of Madness

You've already received the only reward promised for this quest, the Stone of Immoratis. In his generosity, the king has offered you the choice of an additional item to show his appreciation for all you've done. Select your reward to complete the quest.

Tim pulled up the list of items the king offered them. It didn't take him long to zero in on something he wanted. With a single mental *click*, he selected the item, and it appeared in his inventory.

Item Received: Arlen's Bracelet of Balance

Now and then, the stars aligned when Arlen made an item, and it came out perfect. Or in this case, downright spectacular. This bracelet increases the chance of obtaining a positive roll of Chaotic Intent by a small amount. It also looks pretty cool and comes with additional stats. +2 Endurance +4 Dexterity.

After all the mental wrestling he'd done about changing his boots out because of the loss of dexterity, Tim managed to secure an item that not only replaced the loss but increased the stat a little bit. It didn't do much for his main stats, but the special ability and the extra bonus to secondary stats he cared about made it an irreplaceable upgrade.

The king outdid himself.

The experience from the quest was something he'd almost forgotten about, but it moved his meter so close to the next level that turning in Eternia's quest should earn it for him. Was there a better feeling in the world than when a person worked hard to achieve something and got it? He didn't think so. The work and sacrifices behind the outcome were what made winning so special.

Working hard always paid off in the long run.

Quest Complete: Stone of Immoratis

You've retrieved the Stone of Immoratis, and the goddess is powering up. Don't worry. She didn't count your request for Lorelei against the favor she owes you. I'd think carefully about what you want before asking because you might never have this opportunity again.

This quest will remain marked as incomplete until you cash in on the favor. Until then, enjoy the gold and experience that you so rightfully deserve.

System Message: You have received twenty gold

System Message: You have gained a level.

"Ba-da-boom, ba-da-bing!" Tim cheered to himself in the shower.

Not only did he have a favor to call in from the goddess when she was back to full strength, but he had one more stat point to put in place before his vacation started for real. Tim turned off the shower and dried off. Without a thought, he dumped it in strength. Every stat point was one closer to his goal of twenty.

Once dry, he equipped his armor and headed for the door. ShadowLily wasn't back yet, and he didn't have broken legs so he went to join her at the restaurant downstairs. If nothing else, he could help her carry the food back to their room.

It was a good thing Tim didn't wait because when he made it downstairs, there was a huge spread of food and everyone was celebrating together. Even King Rasmus and Desmond were there. It was the perfect ending to an epic quest.

"Long live the Blue Dagger Society!" Tim called, and they all cheered and *clinked* their glasses together before returning the toast.

LIST OF TIM'S CURRENT STATS AND SKILLS

"Tim" level twenty-two Hex Witch

Primary Stats

Strength: 17

Endurance: 34

Dexterity: 30

Intelligence: 62

Wisdom: 74

Perception: 7

Vitality: 5

Revitalization: 5

Luck: 8

Notable Gear

Weapons

Simple Dagger of Dexterity, +1 (X2)

Greater Staff of Yin, +3 Endurance, +7 Intelligence, +7 Wisdom

Orb of Concentration, +5 Intelligence +4 Wisdom

Armor

Circlet of Divine Wisdom, +1 Endurance +3 Intelligence +5 Wisdom

Shoulder Guards of the Spotless Mind, +1 Intelligence +2 Wisdom +1 to Perception, Vitality, Revitalization, and Luck

Hex Witch's Armament, +2 Endurance +2 Dexterity +6 Intelligence +8 Wisdom

Dragon Hyde Jerkin, +2 to all base stats, +1 to all secondary stats

Bearhide Wrist Guards of the Faithful, +1 Endurance +1 Wisdom, Special ability: Bear Necessities

Paul's Gloves of Mending, +7 Intelligence +4 Wisdom

Belt of Divine Inspiration, +1 Endurance +2 Intelligence +4 Wisdom

No That's Not a Brown Spot Leather Pants, +3 Endurance +2 Dexterity +4 Intelligence +3 Wisdom, Special Ability: Flee

Arlen's Boots of Chaotic Intent, +3 Endurance +4 Intelligence +6 Wisdom, Special Ability: Chaotic Intent any skills effectiveness will be increased or decreased by one to ten percent

Jewelry and Accessories

Arlen's Bracelet of Balance, +2 Endurance +4 Dexterity, Special ability to influence the outcome of Chaotic Intent

Wristband of the Faithful. +1 Endurance, ten seconds of double mana regeneration

Ring of Luminosity, +1 Endurance +2 Intelligence +3 Wisdom

Necklace of Hydration, +1 Endurance +2 Intelligence +5 Wisdom

Trinket of the Smiling Monkey, +1 to random stat

Skills

Hex of the Shattered Beast: Novice rank three

Appeal to the Goddess: Novice rank five

Curse of Sacrifice: Novice rank six

Night Vision: Apprentice rank one

Backstab: Apprentice rank four
Rectify: Apprentice rank four
Throwing Knives: Apprentice rank four
Sneak: Apprentice ran six
Disturbance: Apprentice rank five
Quick Feet: Apprentice rank five
Shadow Master: Apprentice rank six
Small Blades: Journeyman rank one
Snare: Journeyman rank one
Dodge: Journeyman rank six
Flame Burst: Journeyman rank six
Behold My Power: Journeyman rank seven
Who Needs a Shield: Journeyman rank seven
Divine Light: Journeyman rank eight
Healing Storm: Journeyman rank eight
Curse of Giving: Master rank one
Cleanse: Master rank one
Healing Orb: Master rank three

Stances
Way of the River
Way of the Boulder

Buffs
Weaken Undead: Journeyman rank two
Armor of Eternia: Journeyman rank seven
Attacks of the Faithful: Journeyman rank seven

Open Quests
The Stone of Immoratis

Hey guys Bradford here. I hope all of you are safe and healthy. If nothing else, Covid has taught us to cherish the time we have with the people we care about. I know for certain it made me think about my parents and how I need to spend as much time as possible with them because they won't always be around.

But enough of that talk, let's talk about something happy. As I'm writing this note, I am already halfway through the next book. After struggling a bit with everything going, I finally feel like I'm back in a groove. It's also my birthday at the end of August, so I'm always looking forward to that. We'll just say I'm going to be thirty nine third time :-)

I've also been blessed this year to meet some cool folks in the cannabis industry. Special shout out to Matt from Grow Sciences. He's a busy guy but always makes time to answer a few questions —nothing like getting a chance to learn from the best. As I've taken up cultivation as a hobby, it's been fun to see and learn from some really great growers. Oddly enough, cannabis cultivation sparked my interest in growing all kinds of things. I have now successfully grown bell peppers, thyme, basil, cilantro, jalapenos, halbenaros, strawberries, and tomatoes.

And one outdoor succulent that I couldn't kill if I tried.

If you've been looking for the website, we had a virus and lost everything. It happens, and now I'll make backups so that it won't happen again. I built the thing myself (not tech-savvy), and I have to work on it in between projects, so it may take a minute, but it's not going away, I promise.

Anyways it's been an exciting twenty twenty-one. I'm looking forward to the end of the year and starting some new adventures. Stay safe, stay healthy, and tell someone in your life how much they mean to you today. Kindness is never the wrong choice.

Oh, and Justin Fields!!!!!!! GO BEARS!

~Bradford

Thank you for not only reading this book, but this entire series and these author notes as well.

I find it interesting that Bradford is cultivating cannabis. (Nice alliteration, by the way.)

BWAHAHAHA…. My auto-correct just tried to fix the phrase (that I had misspelled) 'cultivating cannabis to 'cultivating cannibals'. Boy, that would have changed the meaning in a horrible and yet grossly captivating way.

Auto-correct shenanigans aside, I often fantasize about growing plants. I say fantasize because I just don't see myself doing this any time in the near (or far) future. I know my grandfather loved to grow his plants I have an issue with patience.

An issue I'm not really that hard-pressed to fix. My father has followed his roots and has grown plants (tomatoes and other items) for decades. My generation (three brothers and one sister) and I'm not sure any of us truly grow plants.

Well, more than my older brother Darryl who grows house plants. While that is close, it doesn't truly check the box off in my mind. In order to pass, we need to do what Bradford is doing and grow all sorts of plants that someone can eat.

And that might be why I'm not into it so much. You see, I'm not a vegetable eater. I don't eat salads, and I'm not much of a fan of fruits and vegetables in their raw state. Give me a good ketchup and I'm golden, but not sliced and put on the same hamburger.

Blended, cooked, spiced, and put in a bottle, and that tomato tastes pretty good.

So, I am in my fifties with a couple of years to go before I hit the downward side of this decade. I'm wondering if I will finally find the Anderle' GreenThumb' bug by age 60.

Stick around. I'm sure we will both be a little surprised by the answer.

Anyway, stay safe and sane out there, and I look forward to talking to you in the next book!

Ad Aeternitatem,

Michael Anderle

Ascendancy Legacy

The Arena

Jar of Souls

Guardian of the Grove

Demon Stone

The Rising Darkness

Redemption

Ascendancy Origins

Rise of the Fallen

Butcher of the Bay

Night of the Demon

The Bozley Green Chronicles

Possessed

The Galactic Outlaws

Forced Compliance

Genetic Purge

Smuggler's Legacy

Fortune Hunters

Star Talon

Lost Signal

A Galactic Outlaws Story

The Marchenko Incident

Smuggler for Hire

Origin Ice

<u>The Fairy of Salem</u>

Witching Hour

The Wild Hunt

<u>Standalone Titles</u>

Crimson Stars

CONNECT WITH THE AUTHORS

Connect with Bradford Bates

Facebook:
https://www.facebook.com/bradfordbatesauthor/

Twitter:
https://twitter.com/Freetheblizz

Website:
http://www.bradfordbates.com/

Connect with Michael Anderle

Website: http://lmbpn.com

Email List: http://lmbpn.com/email/

https://www.facebook.com/LMBPNPublishing

https://twitter.com/MichaelAnderle

https://www.instagram.com/lmbpn_publishing/

https://www.bookbub.com/authors/michael-anderle

ABOUT BRADFORD BATES

Bradford Bates is a full-time author, husband to an incredible wife, and father to four furry rescue dogs. He lives in sunny Phoenix, Arizona, trying to not melt in the oppressive heat of the summer. When he isn't busy writing the next book, you can find him playing video games and watching scary movies.